A PAIR OF SHARP EYES

KAT ARMSTRONG

Hookline Books

A Pair of Sharp Eyes

Kat Armstrong/Hookline Books, Bookline & Thinker Ltd
www.hooklinebooks.com

Book Layout ©2019 BookDesignTemplates.com
Cover design by More Visual Ltd

A Pair of Sharp Eyes/Kat Armstrong -- 1st ed.
ISBN 978-1916410336

To Bill, Eleanor and Tom

A Pair of Sharp Eyes

Chapter One

Wiltshire
Tuesday 23rd October, 1703

At dusk the wind rises, and rain beats against the leaking stagecoach windows. I give thanks to God that the driver let me sit inside. Yet the air is fuggy from so many cramped and sweating passengers, and I am in the most uncomfortable place of any, a quarrelsome gentleman on each side of me, and the floor so full of cloak-bags and bundles of clothing there is scarcely room to squeeze my feet.

Two raw country misses whisper opposite and do not meet my eye. At midday their father delivered them to the turnpike in Chippenham, determined his daughters should ride inside, though I heard him grumble to the coachman about the cost of their fares, and he never stopped for his girls to kiss him good-bye, but returned to his waggon without a word. My own father would not have been so lacking in tenderness to his children. In the corner next to these maids is a slight, bearded man I would put at one-and-twenty. He scribbles calculations in his notebook and takes no part in the chit-chat around him, nor is offered any.

A stout gentleman in a blue velvet frock-coat and tight white breeches continues to speak.

'As you would see if you were to visit my plantations in Spanish Town, Mr Cheatley, negroes are not worth your concern.' He has been wrangling with the other gentleman since I took my place at Calne. 'You would never wring your hands over the plight of an ass or a carthorse. A working animal is just that.'

Mr Cheatley, as pale-faced and meagre as the other is swarthy and fat, shifts irritably and chews his lip before indignation spurs him into speech.

'Mr Osmund, I could not enjoy my wealth if I knew it derived from the subjugation of my fellow man. My business is manufacture, and for the sake of my conscience and my eternal soul, every one of those I employ are true-born Englishmen, and fairly paid for their labours.'

I am forced to swallow back a 'Bravo, Sir.' Neither would welcome an interruption from a girl of fourteen.

'Ah ha.' Mr Osmund smiles pleasantly. 'Remind me, what do you manufacture, Mr Cheatley? Brass, is it?'

'I own an iron-works. Our foundries produce sundry goods. Nails, beads, chains.'

'Chains, you say. For what purpose?'

'Chiefly aboard ship.' Mr Cheatley shakes out his handkerchief as if to dismiss his interrogator, and makes a small performance of blowing his nose.

'And the beads?' A crafty look comes over Mr Osmund's jowly face. His stubble is so black it looks like ingrained dirt. 'What be their destination?'

'Africa's West Coast. The tribesmen prize our pipe beads very high.' Mr Cheatley coughs. 'I have just been up to town, at the invitation of a business associate. You may have heard of him: Master Ralph Fowler, Renter Warden of the Worshipful Company of Ironmongers.'

'Indeed. But let me see … your profits are bound up with the negro trade just as mine, d'you not concede? For how do the African princelings pay for their barrels of beads and nails?'

Mr Cheatley frowns and blinks, and if a certain friend had not told me how a ship is fitted out for carrying human cargo, I might pity him his probing by Mr Osmund.

'I cannot be held to account for the destination of my goods. I sell to the highest bidder,' he says plaintively. 'If others export my manufactures to purchase captive labour, why, I lament but cannot prevent it.' The curls of his grey wig quiver, and he fixes his gaze on the other as if to implore his assent.

The burly gentleman considers the point, an amused gleam in his eye, before slapping his broad thigh and pronouncing: 'No cause for self-examination, Mr Cheatley, as I have said already. The Africa trade is a lawful and moral one which, if it does anything, lifts the negro out of darkness into the light of rational Christian understanding.' He grins and throws up his hands. 'We are to be congratulated for the enlightenment we propagate. Excuse me, ladies.'

By this address he refers to me and the other maids. One is about my age, fourteen or so, the other a year or two older. Both peep from beneath their bonnets and blush. Mr Osmund pulls out a flask and draws from it greedily before smacking his lips and replacing the stopper. Then he bethinks himself and offers the flask to Mr Cheatley, who shakes his head with a twitch of the nose and says, 'Thank you, Sir, I am replete.'

'As you wish.' Mr Osmund lifts an eyebrow and tucks the flask away.

'How long since you arrived from Jamaica, Sir?' Mr Cheatley asks.

'Three months. I sail back to Spanish Town a week today, after I've met with my fellow shareholders in Bristol. We own a substantial company under-writing ships and enterprises relating to the export-import trade. I was detained in London longer than expected.' Mr Osmund shifts complacently in his seat, his belly overspilling his lap. 'By a lady who was kind enough to accept my hand.'

Mr Cheatley inclines his head. 'Congratulations, Sir. May I enquire where is the lady?'

'Ordering her wedding clothes. Her dressmaker in St James is working night and day to prepare her trousseau. We're to be married in St Mary's Redcliffe on Tuesday next.' Examining his fingernails, he smiles at the thought.

'Redcliffe? Forgive me, Sir, the name is inauspicious. You have heard the latest news from Bristol? Perhaps not? The coachman told it to me when we last changed horses.'

'Not another loss at sea? Damn it, we should have crossed to Spanish Town before the winter storms. Eliza is fearful already; a wreck will hardly calm her nerves.'

'I hear no tell of shipwrecks. This is closer to home. A murder—a series of murders round Bristol and Somerset, the latest in Redcliffe. All were youngsters asleep in hay-lofts, stables and other outdoor places. Bristol folk are up in arms, hunting a pedlar named Red John. He left two brothers for dead in an old quarry. It's said they'd been horribly abused.'

The country girls' eyes are as round as buttons, and the younger steals her hand into her sister's.

Mr Osmund shakes his head. 'The children of the idle poor have always been preyed on and always will. I daresay the parish won't miss them.'

His words recall the day we were 'consoled' with a similar suggestion when my brother's fatal injuries left my mother and father with one less mouth to feed. My heart pounds and I cannot let such a cruel remark pass. 'The boys' families will miss them, Sir, don't you think?'

Mr Osmund's eyes widen with surprise. 'Well, well.' His lips twitch as he decides to take my question in good humour. 'A tender-hearted young person we have before us, Mr Cheatley. Your compassion does you credit, Miss. Ah ha, you blush now. Most becoming.' He winks at the sisters opposite.

The memory of Tom gives me strength. 'Please don't mistake me, Sir. I lost my brother lately. It taught me the truth of Scripture when it tells us God is no respecter of persons. My brother was much loved and is much grieved for.'

I speak steadily, and no one would guess there are tears trapped in my throat. The coachman who killed our Tom hoped to salve his conscience by giving me my seat today for nothing, but as my mother told him, a place in the Bristol stagecoach is scant recompense for a life. Mr Osmund seems at a loss. He folds his handkerchief and takes another long drink from his flask before subsiding in his seat, wordless.

The coach clatters on, lurching and bucking along the miry road. The sisters close their eyes as daylight fades. Soothed by his brandy, and wrapped in a travelling-cloak, Mr Osmund begins to snore. Next Mr Cheatley joins him, a fact I much regret since his nodding head finds its way to my shoulder, requiring me to shake him off at intervals.

A Pair of Sharp Eyes

I can't help being aware of the only passenger still alert, the quiet, foreign-looking man in the corner opposite, who wears his own hair in dark locks that reach beyond his chin. When portly Mr Osmund hiccups in his sleep the foreigner catches my eye, and thereafter, when one or other of our companions produces an extravagant snore or mutters a word or two of nonsense, he sends me a look as if to say, 'These people are not like you and me.'

At last, when the rain becomes so heavy it rattles the shutters, the young man rises, pulls down the blinds, and makes this an excuse to begin a murmured conversation.

'I know you alighted at Calne, Mistress. Have you come far?'

'I took the carrier's cart from Erlestoke, Sir. My sister is wed to a farmer there.'

'Erlestoke?' He hesitates over the word; pronounces it with a faint hiss. 'A village?'

'Near Westbury.'

He nods, though I do not think he has heard of either place.

'And you are travelling to a situation in Bristol, Miss—?' Again, there is something particular in his way of speaking. It has a rhythm I have not heard before.

'Amesbury. Miss Coronation Amesbury.'

'Honoured to make your acquaintance, Miss Amesbury. Mr Aaron Espinosa.' Since he is seated, he makes a show of bowing from the waist. 'You must be sorry we're obliged to break our journey in Bath tonight. The roads this winter ...' He shakes his head.

'I'd hoped to reach my sister's house without the trouble of a night in Bath.'

Mr Espinosa's expression is as sympathetic, his tone as delicate, as Mr Osmund's was coarse and careless. 'The West-gate Inn is very comfortable, Miss Amesbury. And the fees not excessive.'

I wish my blushes did not give me away quite so readily. After a pause he says hesitantly: 'Your mother and father will miss you now you have left to make your way in the world. Or are they deceased, begging your pardon?'

What a strange, stiff way of speaking he has. From his sallowness I hazard he must be an alien—Spanish or Portuguese, though in honesty I do not know what either race is like. I try to quell the feelings produced by his question but I know my cheeks redden.

'My dear father died last year,' I say quietly. 'My mother lives in Salisbury, as I did for a time. Our cousin lives there, her late husband was a clergyman.' I could add that I gained what little learning and worldly knowledge I have in my own village, not Salisbury, but no one will draw me on that subject.

He clears his throat.

'My condolences, Miss Amesbury. The loss of a parent is hard to bear.'

I detect he has known sorrow himself from the way he plays with his thumbs. This may be why I run on and say more than I intend.

'We was dealt another blow, Mother and I. A month ago our cottage was burned down and all our belongings were lost.' I nearly add, 'Even the little nightgown we kept when my brother died, and the wooden ship and sailor Father carved and painted for him', but my mouth is too dry to let out the words.

Mr Espinosa clears his throat. 'A fire is a great misfortune,' he says. 'One of the most terrifying ordeals a person might endure.'

He seems to speak with particular feeling.

'Have you experienced a fire yourself, Sir?'

He nods reluctantly. 'Yes, Miss. When I lodged in Whitechapel.'

'Was it the same as happened with us? A chimney blaze?'

He rearranges his jacket collar. 'It is painful to admit that some malevolent person thrust a lighted paper under the door when I and a fellow lodger, also a Jew, were abed. Only the good offices of a neighbour saved us.'

'Someone sought to burn you alive?' My skin prickles at the thought. 'Because you are a Jew?' Having only a hazy idea of what a Jew is, I want to ask, *Because you wear your hair a certain way?*

Mr Espinosa's eyes are fathomless. Eventually he says: 'People mistrust those different from themselves, Miss Amesbury. It can make them desperate.'

Wicked, I want to say. 'I never heard of anything so barbarous. Did they catch them?'

He drops his gaze and his silence says all. In my mind I see the event unfold: the two young men fast asleep, unsuspecting, while down in the street a hooded creature creeps forwards with a burning roll of paper, only to melt back into the darkness as the fire takes hold.

'Mr Espinosa, your story makes me question the wisdom of going to Bristol in hopes of a new life. They are sure to consider me foreign, coming from thirty miles away.'

'No, no. Do not perturb yourself, Miss Amesbury. Bristol teems with young people seeking their fortune. They come in from every place within a hundred miles.'

'Is that what you did, Sir? Went to Bristol to seek your fortune?'

He looks startled. 'After a fashion. I came with my master, Mr Sampson the banker, when he moved to Bristol to establish a business. There are many opportunities for those with enterprise and means. I've just returned from London on his behalf and ...' He stands up and re-draws the blind in an attempt to staunch the flow of rain-water into the carriage from the ill-fitting leather. '... I shall be glad to find myself back in Bristol and only wish it weren't necessary to stay in Bath tonight. For all its popularity I confess I've never relished Bath and its crowds of visitors.'

Just then my stomach lets out a betraying growl; it is more than sixteen hours since I ate breakfast with my Wiltshire sister and her husband.

'We'll be there soon,' Mr Espinosa says. 'In the meantime, won't you take one of these?' He takes out a handkerchief which he unrolls to reveal a couple of hard, flat cakes the colour of oatmeal. 'Not exactly delicious, but sustaining, and a good repast for one bound for Bristol. Ship's biscuits, sailors swear by them.' He taps one with a knuckle to demonstrate its toughness.

However light-headed, I am not foolish enough to indebt myself to a man I do not know.

'Thank you, Mr Espinosa, but I'm not in the least hungry.'

He tilts his head, accepting the rebuff, and I try to shut my ears as he munches.

In a short while the coach descends a steep hill, the road twisting this way and that, and not long after the mud and potholes beneath the wheels give way to gravelled road, and at last the postillion sounds his horn, the coachman hauls on the reins, and we come to a creaking, rattling halt, horses stamping with eagerness for their oats, the outside passengers clambering down with thumps and exclamations of relief. Up fly the window blinds, released with a tug by tun-bellied Mr Osmund, and I peer out to glimpse lamps on either side of an inn door, a flurry of grooms running out for the horses, and the landlord standing in a canvas apron with a tally in his hand.

We inside are last to leave the coach, and I am thankful on alighting to find my box still lying in the basket behind the wheels. It looks small among many four times its size. The inn master's wife, a tall, stooping woman in a yellow gown, listens to a soldier who cares nothing for the number of folk kept waiting while he harries her for coach times to Exeter in the morning. I am standing patiently in line when Mr Osmund seizes my hand.

'Excuse me, Madam,' he says to the landlady. 'This young person would like to dine in my rooms if you would be good enough to send up supper.'

I try to break free, but his grip is strong. 'Please, Sir, let me go,' I say, and at that moment Mr Espinosa steps from the shadows.

'The young lady is a close friend of my late mother's, Ma'am, and I am her chaperon until she reaches her sister's house. Forgive me, Sir.' He bows to Mr Osmund. 'I fancy you must be mistaken as to the young lady's identity. It's dark, and we've been half-asleep this past hour.' Taking my other hand, he indicates the sisters, who stare but lack the wit to voice surprise. 'Miss Amesbury wishes to share accommodation with these ladies.'

He looks directly at Mr Osmund, who purses his lips before letting go of me. My relief is tempered by his growling 'damned little Israel' in a voice the rest of us hear clearly. I feel a prickle of shame that anyone, most of all a gentleman, could speak so, and stiffen in case Mr Espinosa is stung to retaliate and the two should stoop to blows.

But Mr Espinosa turns aside with a shrug, and as we move inside I cannot help thinking that his dignified silence is more of a rebuke.

Even so, I should insult him myself, were I a man.

Chapter Two

Bath

The landlady smooths over the awkwardness of Mr Osmund's defeat.

'Dear me, we're full to the rafters,' she says, looking over the tally and ushering us inside. 'You three maids will have to share. Your names, if you please, ladies, and where you're from?'

'Miss Amesbury. From Erlestoke, near Westbury.'

The elder sister draws herself up as tall as she can, which is not very. 'Miss Bridget Lamborne, and my sister Miss Jane Lamborne,' she announces. 'Both of Manor Farm, Chippenham.'

'Chippenham, eh? We don't have many from there as a rule.'

Miss Lamborne looks a trifle put out, and when the landlady exclaims that she knows Erlestoke well, and has a brother living close to it whom she is mighty fond of, Miss Bridget shoots me a sour glance and pulls Miss Jane's fingers out of her mouth as if to say it may be late but this is not yet bedtime. In the light of the hallway I note that both have hair the colour of rust, and ghost-white skin to go with it, but Miss Bridget is plainer and heavier than the other, and her face is marred by angry spots.

'The lad will carry up your boxes. Meanwhile you can take yourselves into dinner.' The landlady turns to greet another guest.

The rich, fatty smell of roast meat hangs in the air and I recall how long I have been hungry.

'You must take the floor tonight,' Miss Bridget informs me, as we hand our boxes to the boy. 'My sister and I will share the bed, naturally.'

'Don't trouble yourself, Miss,' says the lad. 'There's three paillasses laid out in the garret you be in.'

'Then I'll go next the window,' I say, before Miss Bridget can claim the one furthest from the door. 'Some grumble about draughts,' I add cheerfully, 'not I.' The elder sister bites her lip but can think of no rejoinder.

'Still here, ladies? Dinner's that way,' the landlady says, indicating, and Miss Bridget forgets her needling at last and follows me to the dining-room. I open the door to find a dozen or more guests seated round the table, while a huge log glows in the hearth and a side of pork burnishes on the turn-spit, along with a shoulder of beef and three or four plump chickens.

A table runs the length of the room, and a small, round-shouldered woman waits upon the company, her face shining from the heat of the fire as she scurries to serve the noisy diners. Adding to the hubbub of voices and clanking tankards are the strains of a fiddle played in a corner by a musician who grimaces, eyes screwed shut, as he saws with his bow, and a piper whose piercing tune has some of the diners tapping their feet and one or two wincing when he hits a high note.

I am curious to see what kind of people call at a coaching-inn, and glad to find I am by no means the humblest customer at the famous West-gate. Seated at the table is a mix of travellers, some well-dressed; one or two in working-clothes; and a family who may be poorer even than me, for the woman nurses a baby while her husband feeds a tribe of little boys with morsels cut from his own plain supper of bread and cheese.

I gaze at the pork with its bronzed and savoury crackling, and my mouth waters.

'I believe I could eat a whole leg of pork by myself,' Miss Jane says, as we clamber into our places on the bench. 'Though I hope supper ain't too dear,' she adds, turning her watery blue eyes on her sister in case the harmless remark provokes her.

Fortunately, Miss Bridget is absorbed in looking over the bill of fare, and from her frown and moving lips I suspect she may not be such an able reader as she pretends.

More guests enter, and to my dismay I see Mr Osmund choose a place a short distance from us on the other side of the table where Mr Espinosa is seated.

'What a difference twenty-four hours can make,' Miss Bridget says suddenly, putting down the bill with a loud, affected sigh. 'To think this time tomorrow Jane and I will be dining in the servants' hall at No. 3, Queen-square, Bristol. I doubt you've heard of Queen-square, Miss Amesbury. It is a very fine address—best in all of Bristol. Our master and mistress have a great household with more than two dozen domestics, and a coach and horses besides. I am to be chamber-maid, Jane kitchen-maid. And you, where are you expecting to be this time tomorrow, if I may ask?'

'I have no situation quite yet,' I say. 'I shall be looking for work when I arrive.'

'Ha, good luck with that.' She says it as if work is nigh impossible to find. 'I daresay you know about the hiring-man?'

'Of course,' I say airily, though Miss Bridget seems to see through my pretence and continues.

'He charges a high fee, naturally. But if you are unlucky and have no friend to help you find a good position, it is what you must pay.'

'Did you have a friend then, Miss Lamborne?'

'Yes, indeed. My aunt, Mrs Gibbons, put in a word for each of us, and when her mistress heard of all our qualities she said, "Mrs Gibbons, my dear, please send for those nieces of yours before any other lady in Bristol snaps them up."' At the finish of this speech Miss Bridget gives a little peal of laughter, and God forgive me I should like to snap her up and spit her out too, the stuck-up baggage.

Just then the serving-woman comes to take our orders, and while Miss Bridget makes a lordly show of querying the price of every item Miss Jane asks me in a whisper: 'Will dinner be more than a shilling each, do you suppose?'

'I think I will just ask for one slice of meat and a dish of bread and butter.' I reach under my skirts to feel my purse, reassured by finding it still half-full.

The serving-woman reaches us at last, and when I give my order Miss Bridget nods and says: 'The same will do for my sister and I, if you please,' her tone as proud as if her customary fare is venison and sweet sack.

A Pair of Sharp Eyes

We wait a weary time to be served, but when the woman finally plants down the serving-dishes in front of us, Miss Jane brightens.

'Shall I say Grace?' she asks her sister, who glances at the throng and says drily: 'I believe we could do without Grace this once.'

Unbidden, I hear my little brother Tom lisping: *By God's hand we must be fed, Give us Lord, our daily bread, Amen*, but with an effort I push the thought away, and reach for the first victuals I have taken since dawn, saving a cup of beer at dinnertime in Devizes.

None of us wants to chat until our bellies are filled, and I cannot help but be conscious of Mr Osmund, who presently rolls his glass in his hand and fixes his gaze on me.

'Pay no heed, my dear,' says the landlady, who has just come into the dining-room and sits down smiling as warmly as if I am her long-lost cousin. She has noticed my discomfort. 'A gentleman is sure to admire a pretty girl. Do you three ladies mind my joining you?'

'No, certainly,' Miss Bridget says, shuffling up quickly as she takes in the landlady's appearance.

She has changed into a low-cut, pink silk gown with contrasting sleeves of a dull red like faded rose petals, and a cap of crimson satin with lace frills and white ribbons trailing down the back. Her hair is black and done in long, shining curls, and her complexion has not the least brownness but is creamy pale as though she never stood uncovered out of doors.

'So, ladies, she smiles, 'you must be vexed to have to break your journey, and yet we in Bath are happy to extend hospitality to those who would otherwise lose the chance to visit our fair city.'

Miss Bridget cuts across me to introduce herself and explain that I have no situation to go to in Bristol. 'Whereas my sister, Miss Jane Lamborne, and I were lucky enough to be appointed chamber-maid and kitchen-maid to a wealthy merchant in Queen-square. I daresay you have heard of the houses new-built in Queen-square, Ma'am? It was arranged by letter—our aunt who is housekeeper there spoke to her mistress, listing our merits and willingness to work, and it was fixed in no time. Queen-square is the best address in all of Bristol, and our master and mistress have a coach and horses and a country mansion besides.'

I think Miss Bridget fancies herself lady of the house instead of the wench who will be emptying the piss-pots, but I hide this thought under lowered eyelashes. The pink-gowned lady gives my arm a kindly pat, and I notice her hands are smooth and ivory-pale as her face, with well-shaped nails and a gemstone on the middle finger of each: a brilliant for the left, on the right a garnet. And her ears are decked too, with pearl drop earrings, a cluster of tiny garnets set above the pearls.

'Don't you fret, Miss—?'

'Amesbury.'

'How d'ye do, Miss Amesbury. Mrs Buckley, Ma Buckley to my friends.' The landlord glides over, bowing low and winking as he sets a dish in front of her. 'Thank you, Jack.' She spreads her napkin on her lap and contemplates her dinner with satisfaction before picking up her knife. Popping a morsel in her mouth she continues. 'Miss Amesbury, be reassured. Bristol is thriving; every week young people travel in from the countryside, and few go home unless for a holiday once in a while. Act obliging, smile nicely when spoken to; in no time you will be on your way to earning three or four pounds *per annum*. Many a kind mistress gives her maids petticoats and stockings, and you will be all found, two meals a day and a weekly allowance of tea and sugar if your master trades with the Indies.' She leans towards Miss Bridget. 'Are those your terms?'

Miss Bridget blinks. 'Thereabouts.'

'See?' Mrs Buckley turns and looks at me confidingly, one be-ringed finger stroking the side of her nose. I catch a scent of rose-water, and a less welcome hint of gravy on her breath. 'Now then, ladies. I daresay you won't have heard of the amazing bath-house that lies a stone's throw from where we sit?'

'I've heard of the bath, ma'am,' I say eagerly, 'my mother's cousin spoke of it when I lived with her in Salisbury last year. I believe it's very fine.'

A Pair of Sharp Eyes

I also believe it to be a place where ladies bathe and men go to ogle, but my companion looks too respectable to speak of a place where lewdness is order of the day, and my answer pleases her for she beams and beckons the tapster to refill our mugs with beer, pressing a crown into his hand before any of us can protest. I remind myself to make sure she does not insist on treating us to dinner when the time comes for the reckoning.

'The bath is splendid,' Mrs Buckley declares. 'It offers many benefits both for bathers and those who prefer to drink the waters. It's highly efficacious for those with pimples and other blemishes: you, Miss Lamborne, with your prodigious *freckles* would find the waters astonishing useful.' Miss Bridget flushes, and Mrs Buckley sweeps on. 'Patients suffering from gout and dropsy have been known to leave Bath with their health restored. As for the poor creatures undergoing the mercury treatment ...' The Lamborne sisters are wide-eyed, and Mrs Buckley shakes her head. 'Enough of such talk. Bristol may be a famous port, but Bath outdoes it for elegant amenities. The Roman Emperor Augustus was the first to extol Bath in his writings, you know. He brought Queen Cleopatra here to cure her of the green-sickness. And our own noble Queen Anne visited this year, and was treated to a musical extravagance finer than any London might provide. Since her highness, more and more persons of wealth and importance flock to the waters. Look around you.'

She glances down the table where more diners have arrived. A lady in a blue embroidered gown sits next to Mr Osmund, hanging on his word. Just as I look across, he leans over and makes some remark to Mr Espinosa that causes the lady in blue to rock with laughter and deliver a feigning blow to Mr Osmund's sleeve.

Unhappiness and indignation are written on Mr Espinosa's face, but the table is crowded and he is unable to escape his persecutor. Instead he turns to face the other way, folding and unfolding his napkin by way of distraction. I am conscious I am the original cause of bad feeling between these gentlemen, though when Mr Espinosa catches my eye he gives a nod as if to say he bears me no ill will.

'Your friend from the stagecoach, Miss Amesbury,' Miss Bridget says slyly, 'you must be sorry to have him seated so far away.'

I ignore this sally, and help myself to more bread and butter. A moment later the serving-maid brings out a large steaming platter of roast pork and places it in front of Mr Osmund and his pretty companion. The meat is neatly carved and appetising, and I am surprised to see Mr Espinosa veer away in disgust as Mr Osmund seizes the dish and thrusts it in front of him with a yelp of laughter. Mr Espinosa's face turns scarlet while with a roar the fat fellow heaps his own plate with meat, and proceeds to tuck in.

'Did you see that?' I ask Mrs Buckley. 'What's the joke?'

'Bless you, you innocent.' She pinches my cheek. 'Jews do not eat pork. They consider it unclean, you know.'

Looking at Mr Espinosa I see she is right, for though he has turned to look the other way he holds a handkerchief over his mouth.

'Do they eat beef, Jews?'

'Of course. I expect the maid will bring him supper presently.'

But some time later Mr Espinosa is still waiting, and from the careless way the maid splashes his jacket with gravy as she serves another guest, I see she is content to let him go hungry while the rest of us eat. I know I may be noticed by my fellow diners, but after helping Miss Lamborne and Miss Jane to another slice of bread and butter I rise and carry the dish to the other side of the table and, wordless, present what is left to Mr Espinosa. The startled faces around me are easy to ignore, and the gentleman smiles gratefully and helps himself to bread.

'You're most considerate, Miss Amesbury.'

'Not in the least, Sir. Short commons if one diner waits while the rest are nearly done.' Overhearing my remark, the serving-maid tosses her head, but I care not. I have eaten my fill, and though this is said to be the best inn in Bath, I did not find the pork as tasty as it looked, nor the butter as fresh as it should be. The serving-maid may think herself better than I, but on my return to my place I see Mr Osmund pinch her backside as she takes his empty plate, and she forces a smile when she would plainly like to spit in his drink.

A Pair of Sharp Eyes

Mrs Buckley has been nodding and smiling as Miss Bridget runs on, talking of fourteen bedrooms and marble floors. She will enjoy scrubbing those floors on bended knees, and scraping out fourteen grates each winter's morning.

'Yes, granted you will find Bristol very prosperous,' Mrs Buckley says, tapping her fingers to the melody from the corner of the room. 'Sugar, they say, is sweeter than gold. Yet you know, my dears, Bath trumps all for pleasure: titled folk and gentry come here to enjoy every manner of entertainments. Opportunities for advancement spring up each week—why, if I were a young lady intent on service, I might choose Bath over Bristol, you know.'

While she speaks, Mr Osmund kisses and fondles the hand of the lady in blue, and I wish I could drag my eyes away from them.

'Why don't she chide him? He's so ugly,' I whisper.

Mrs Buckley nudges me with her elbow. 'Beauty is in the eye of the beholder, dear. But perhaps you would rather escape such sights now dinner is over? Don't be shy, I'm known for taking young visitors under my wing. I make it my business to provide every ease and comfort during their stay. What if I were to chaperone you three ladies to see the famous baths when I have paid our good host?'

Miss Bridget shifts uneasily. 'We promised Father we'd be abed by nine o'clock.'

'Well now, I expect your good father is a little out-dated in his understanding of town hours. In Bath we have scarcely begun by nine. Don't deny me the pleasure of treating three such mannerly young people.' She pats the purse hanging from her waist. 'As for the baths, you'll relish telling friends at home that you have seen with your own eyes the place that makes our city famous far and wide. I should be honoured to pay the small admission fee on your behalf. Nothing delights Ma Buckley quite so much as seeing the excitement on a young girl's face as she makes her first entrance to our grand attraction.'

Mrs Buckley is hard on herself, for no one would consider her old. I thought we were about to set off but the tapster hurries to her, beckoning once more, and she has him fill our mugs to the brim a third time, with the remark, 'My treat, dears. Chance to be merry before you take up your employ tomorrow. Your good health.'

She takes only a sip of her own drink before setting it down, perhaps regarding herself as too 'old' to risk a sore head come morning. But Miss Bridget lifts her mug and downs the contents in a couple of swallows, and there is a wobble in her step when she stands up. The lady waves us back while she pays the landlord, and none of us has courage to protest. How could we, when she is so kind and cheerful, even picking up a napkin and dabbing the corners of Miss Jane's mouth?

'There now,' she says, surveying her charge. 'Can't have you seen outside with grease stains on your chin.'

Miss Lamborne is prompted to say: 'My sister always was a careless eater.'

'But a very pretty one,' the lady responds gallantly, and Miss Jane simpers, not in the least offended.

Chapter Three

A stagecoach arrives as we leave the inn, its passengers disembarking with gasps and groans as they straighten their limbs, and I am grateful I did not have to journey as they did, by the uncertain light of a lantern, wearied by the lurching and jolting of the carriage and listening out with dread for highwaymen.

The roads may be dark, but the rain has passed and in town all is gay and bright despite the late hour, the shops lit up and hawkers and stallholders crying their wares.

'I suppose 'tis market-day,' Miss Bridget Lamborne says, surprised as I am by the crowded scene.

'Gracious, Miss Lamborne, this is not Chippenham, you know.' Mrs Buckley chuckles. 'Bath is a resort for gentlefolk, we do not depend on Master Barley-seed and Mistress Butter-churn to provide our shopkeepers with customers. Come, ladies, let us cross over the street to admire those window-counters, for I daresay you never saw their like in Wiltshire.'

Mrs Buckley leads the way, pausing to let us dawdle at a draper's shop, where the counter is laden with bolts of patterned cloth and baskets of silk ribbons. Miss Jane is in raptures.

'Look, Bridget,' she cries. 'See this red check? Would it not look handsome with my best green gown?' She sucks in her breath. 'And taffeta, beautiful taffeta. How it catches the candlelight.' Miss Jane holds up the cloth, heedless of the draper who shifts and frowns behind the counter to see her making free with his goods. 'See, Miss Amesbury? One way crimson, the other gold.'

The man clears his throat warningly, and I look to Mrs Buckley, expecting her to remind him who she is, but when he meets her eyes his expression is unfriendlier still.

'Why does he scowl?' I ask in an undertone. 'Does he not welcome customers?'

'Some shopkeepers in Bath are ridiculous high and mighty,' she says. 'Pay no heed to the ill-natured fellow. I expect he took me for some duchess who failed to pay her bill last season. Now then, ladies, we're almost there, you know. The West-gate is marvellous convenient for the baths. A mere hop and a step divides the two.' As Miss Jane trips on a loose cobble, Mrs Buckley grasps her elbow and guides us into a square overlooked by a large building made of soft yellow stone, the entrance flanked by torches. 'Prepare to be astonished,' declares our hostess. 'We're about to enter the bathhouse. Do you sense the heat?'

The evening is chilly, but my nostrils fill with something like rotten eggs, strong enough to make me wonder at those who drink the water if it tastes as foul as it smells. Miss Bridget covers her nose, then remembers her manners and takes her hand away.

'See?' Mrs Buckley says, nudging the girl's arm. 'They say those who need the waters find them pungent.' She runs a finger down Miss Bridget's inflamed cheek. 'What did I say about those freckles? Such a shame you ladies cannot sample the hot bath, it being so late. I expect you would be shy at the prospect, would you not? And yet here it is usual and proper for all and sundry to bathe in scanty dress, and some little fellows and their sisters frolic in the suits God was pleased to have them wear on their birthdays, and why not? The benefits to health outweigh considerations of propriety and custom. Contact with the water on as great an area of the body as may be achieved is the thing.' She throws back her head and I cannot help noticing that her neck resembles nothing so much as an old turkey-hen's, and I wonder if Mrs Buckley can be quite the buxom young matron I took her for. Then she adjusts her neckerchief as if conscious of my judging eye, and I am ashamed at my unkindness.

At her invitation we join a line of visitors waiting to buy tickets in the entrance to the bath-house. Few are the invalids I expected to see; most are well-dressed, and from their lively chatter appear in rude good health. A lady in a low-cut satin gown and bright pink petticoat fans herself as a gentleman offers a stream of compliments. When he turns I am shocked to recognise Mr Cheatley, whose nose is redder than it was this afternoon. He even staggers a little as though the worse for drink.

'Are all these people here for the waters, Mrs Buckley?' I hear the doubt in my voice. Indeed, one or two of the ladies have so much flesh exposed I wonder to see them among people of quality. 'Surely they aren't invalids?'

'To take the waters, yes, and also to spectate, and saunter, and be amused. Some of the fair sex will be dressing after their immersion, and readying themselves for supper. You will soon see how popular the place is.' As proof of her words Mrs Buckley curtseys to three young men in velvet coats who turn at the sound of her voice and salute her familiarly, one kissing her hand before letting go with lingering regret and following his friends inside.

'Admirers of mine, though I see you smile, Miss Amesbury. You think me vain.'

'No indeed, Madam.' I want to say that she is handsome for a woman her age, and that her gown is as fine as any I can see, but we have reached the ticket-master at last and before I have time to deliver my compliment she unties her purse.

'Good evening to you. Yes indeed, four tickets to spectate. I thank you, Sir.' She transfers the monies without my seeing coins change hands, and the official gives her four printed slips which she folds and tucks into her purse in a few swift movements. 'There now, ladies, a treat awaits you. The Romans would be astonished at the enlargement of the pools since their time. There's room in the greatest for five dozen bathers, you know.'

'I can't believe there will be much to see at this time of night,' I murmur to Miss Bridget as we move through. And yet the hubbub of voices implies the opposite.

'I suppose Mrs Buckley knows the customs here a little better than you do, Miss Amesbury. There are plenty of folk about at least.'

We arrive on a long, low balcony or covered terrace surrounding a sunken bathing-place. No one is in the water but people of all ages throng the balcony: women of fashion, ladies in bathing-dresses and frilled caps, as well as one or two scantily clad children with deformities such as bandy legs and sway-backs; but by far and away the largest group is that of young men in laced frock-coats and curled wigs, and most bow to Mrs Buckley and eye us girls with cheerful curiosity. I am not very comfortable under such scrutiny, and wish our hostess would let them know we gain no pleasure from the men's smiles and lifted eyebrows. But when one tall gentleman with a monocle has the impudence to turn that device upon us, Mrs Buckley merely smiles and pokes my rib as if to say she shares our triumph over the male sex.

'I wish I could jump in this minute,' Miss Jane says, leaning so far over the balustrade she risks the granting of her wish. 'I love a swim.'

'Oh, so do I,' I tell her, suddenly remembering Well-Head Pond at home, and the long summer days we spent before and after harvest-time when we were children. 'My sisters, Meg and Liz, and I often used to swim.'

'Indeed, Miss Amesbury.' Miss Bridget is scathing. 'In our village swimming was left to the lads.'

'In Erlestoke girls swam as much as the boys. My father used to say he was glad of it, having seen a man fall in the River Frome and drown in a yard of water. We slipped down to the pool early, before the lads were about. None saw us.'

'Or so you thought,' Miss Bridget sniggers.

'Remember when you fell in the horse-pond, sister?' Miss Jane asks, pink-faced. She laughs. 'What a whipping Father gave you for the state of your clothes.'

'I'm surprised you remember, Jane, since you weren't above three years old at the time. Sure you're not confusing it with the day our Lenny pushed you in the dung-hill? There was no fuss about spoiled clothes that day—you weren't hardly wearing any.'

'Ladies, ladies. You are not on the farm now.' Mrs Buckley waggles her finger in mock-reproof. 'See that personage over there, a little to the left? Is she not a great beauty? That gentleman there in the dark red coat, he is wildly in love with her, you know, even though the lady is betrothed already to the gentleman in the hat with the ostrich feather. Do you see him? He is very handsome and rich, and yet all believe the lady would elope with the other if she could. Her father prevents it; he is a viscount, you know. She dares not thwart him.'

I wonder at Mrs Buckley's knowledge of these people; she seems acquainted with all of Bath. To think she is familiar with such quality at first hand, those with titles as well as money, is astonishing. The sisters Lamborne have descended to sly pinches, carrying on their quarrel by covert means, while Mrs Buckley rests her elbows on the balustrade as if content to pass another hour in contemplation of the bath and its visitors.

'It is very busy here, Madam,' I say, beginning a speech in which I plan to argue for an early return to our lodgings; but Mrs Buckley is distracted by the arrival of a group of gentlemen in showy coats and breeches, and seems not to hear me. She waves at one of the party, who has the sauce to blow us a kiss.

Miss Bridget, too entranced by the bath to notice, leans over the balustrade and gazes at the water.

'Is it deep?' she asks.

'Amazing so,' Mrs Buckley says, attentive to her guests again. She points at a smaller pool on the far side. 'The Queen's bath behind the Great Pump is preferred by the ladies. That may explain the numbers of gentlemen idling at its edges,' she adds archly. To my dismay she makes another signal, urging the new arrivals to join us.

'I wish they wouldn't stare,' I say, as one of the approaching gallants lifts his wide-brimmed hat and peers at me.

Mrs Buckley straightens up. 'Goodness, you are nice for a girl come from the country.' She shoves my shoulder as if she hardly credits my shyness. 'Did you not have sweethearts among your hedge-cutters and plough-men? These are elegant men about town who clearly consider the three of you very pretty. And why should they not? Come, ladies, walk this way. It is why people come here of an evening, you know—to see and be seen. Give me your cloaks, they are not needed while we are under cover. Let these gentlemen admire your smooth, young shoulders. Good evening to you, Sirs.'

'Good evening,' they chorus, bowing.

'Thank you, ma'am, I had rather keep mine on.' I clutch my collar as if I expect Mrs Buckley to undress me forthwith, but Miss Jane has no such fears. She undoes her ribbons and, stripped of her cloak, holds herself tall, preening as the gentlemen form a kind of loose circle around us and bite their lips at the sight of her plump figure.

'Why, Miss Jane, how elegant you are,' Mrs Buckley says, and glances round to gauge her audience's agreement. I am surely mistaken when I think one man gives her a nod, and when I check a moment later he is looking the other way quite innocently, so I think I imagined a connection between him and Mrs Buckley which does not exist. Nonetheless I am uneasy, all the more so when Miss Jane begins to rearrange her muslin neckerchief the better to display her bosom.

'Should we not return to the West-gate now?' I ask Miss Bridget under my breath. 'I don't care for being paraded like a beast at auction.'

She huffs. 'Gracious, Miss Amesbury. Like Mrs Buckley said, you are a stuck-in-the-mud, ain't you? For those of us beginning work tomorrow, a little fun tonight don't come amiss.' One gentleman, who sports a dark green riding-coat faced with scarlet, lifts his hat, and Miss Bridget juts out her chest and pouts as if she would let him kiss her if he dared.

Another gentleman grins and tries to take my hand, but I whip it away.

'Mrs Buckley,' I say loudly.

She looks at me in bland surprise. 'Don't tell me you'll hold out against an evening of pleasure, Miss Amesbury. There is always one prude, is there not?' She addresses this question to another pair of gentlemen who loll close by, and who fall to sighing and tutting to indicate they share her regret at my aloofness. The elder of the two, a greybeard with deep-set cunning eyes, steps forward to offer me his arm.

'I beg your pardon, Miss,' he says to Miss Bridget. 'But you'll admit your friend is an uncommon beauty. As are you all, of course. May I ask you to walk with me a little, Madam?'

'No, Sir, thank you, Sir.' When he continues to hold out his arm I add forcefully: 'I am tired.'

The gentleman pulls down his mouth into a show of disappointment before holding his arm out to Miss Bridget. She shakes her head, but by her fluttering eyelashes lets him know she is by no means averse to the offer.

I decide to appeal to Mrs Buckley's mercy.

'Please, ma'am, I would like so much to return to the inn now.' I lower my voice. 'These gentlemen are playing with us, I don't like it.'

For the briefest moment I glimpse a flash of what might be anger in her eyes before her manner changes.

'Miss Amesbury, forgive me. I thought to divert you and your friends for an hour or two while you were in Bath. It was foolish of me to think you would enjoy yourselves in a place esteemed by people older and so much worldlier than you are. The three of you are good, sweet country girls, and I am sure you are ready for your beds. Excuse us, gentlemen. These ladies long to retire. They thank you for your compliments and I assure you, Sirs, they will all be in bed within the hour.' Her careless reference to bed raises a snigger from her listeners, though to my great relief the men withdraw, casting back only one or two regretful glances as we move off.

Mrs Buckley leads us further down the covered walk.

'Is the exit not the same way we came in?' I say. The candles are few here, and there are scarcely any walkers. In an alcove a lady and gentleman are locked in an embrace, too engrossed to look up as we pass.

'Oh no, dear. The exit is quite other than the entrance where we bought our tickets. Now then, I have a very good proposal for you all, by way of rounding off the evening. Before we return to the West-gate we shall call on my dear old friend Mrs Charlton. She is quite elderly and frail, alas, but she is uncommonly fond of young people and would be more pleased than I can express if we was to visit her now, just for a short while, you know.'

I remember my sister Meg's insistence that I should on no account accept an invitation from any person on my journey, however friendly-seeming they might be, and feel a shiver in my insides when I consider I have already accepted hospitality from Mrs Buckley, even if, thankfully, it has been without evil consequences.

'You are very kind, Mrs Buckley,' I tell her firmly, 'but I had better say goodnight.'

'I would like to meet your friend, Mrs Buckley,' Miss Bridget says. 'Even if others can think only of their beds.'

Her spite, though I am used to it by now, is stinging, and to insist on returning to the West-gate does, I confess, seem ungracious when the sisters are so agreeable.

'Very well,' I say. 'As long as the visit is quick. I am weary, you see, having started out so early this morning.'

'You are a sapling, Miss Amesbury, with all the freshness and vigour of your tender years. See how much stronger you are than you imagine. It is almost yester morning since you left home. The abbey clock struck eleven a moment ago—did you not hear?'

My heart thumps. 'I did not. In that case ...'

'No, no, I brook no objections. Half an hour to meet my oldest friend is all I ask.' Mrs Buckley hands over the sisters' garments. 'Put on your cloaks again, dears, just for the moment's walk to Mrs Charlton's house.' She rearranges her own shawl and looks expectantly from face to face. 'I said this was the way out, did I not?'

We come to a side-gate that I cannot think is used by many visitors to the baths, being low and damp underfoot, and the passageway beyond it poorly lit, but Mrs Buckley unfastens the latch as if she uses it every day of her life.

'Mrs Charlton lives just around this corner. Take care, Miss Jane, the way is slippery.'

Looming over us is a great, dark church with soaring pinnacles.

'But this isn't West-gate street where we came in,' I say, bewildered. 'Mrs Buckley, where are we?'

'No, indeed. This is Abbey-street. And this the abbey, which used to be full of monks and nuns and now is a church where the rich and titled come to worship. Such a shame you cannot be here on Sunday to see them parading through the square in their finery. But come along, ladies. Mrs Charlton will be enchanted to meet you.'

I am glad to be away from the baths and their gawping gentlemen, but I do not like the look of the dingy street ahead.

'Mrs Buckley, we don't know Mrs Charlton. Past eleven o'clock is late to call on a lady we have never met.'

'Mrs Charlton is my friend. She will not be happy, I assure you, until she has offered a glass of her delicious elderberry cordial to my new young acquaintances.'

'Elderberry cordial?' Miss Jane cries eagerly. 'We only have that once a year. Mother makes it for Christmas, don't she, Bridie?'

'Ah, your dear mother. Such a clever housekeeper. And how proud she must be of her beautiful daughters.'

'Beautiful? I should say so! I never saw such lovelies.'

We spin round to find a gentleman striding towards us. His brocade waistcoat gleams in the light from the abbey porch, and I am nearly certain he is the older gentleman with the hard, deep-set eyes who tried to give me his arm when we were in the bath-house.

'Sir Roger,' exclaims Mrs Buckley. 'You are all chivalry, indeed you are. To escort us to my friend's house, too kind, Sir.'

He bows. 'Your servant, Madam. As ever. And yours, dear ladies.' This time he eyes Miss Jane with particular interest, and she bobs a curtsey and lets out a nervous giggle.

'Well, what do we wait for? Proceed,' the gentleman says, waving us towards a narrow lane and following close behind 'til Mrs Buckley stops.

'Here is Mrs Charlton's house,' she says. 'Just as I knew, the lights are on. She's expecting us.'

'The other fellows will be here directly, Madam,' the gentleman says. He has unfastened his coat already, as if he assumes he is invited in. 'They merely wished to pay a brief call at a tavern, you understand.'

'Ah! Like all young bucks, they seek to enjoy themselves to the utmost. You see, dear ladies, they know that Mrs Charlton abjures strong spirits, and they do not wish to embarrass her by asking for refreshments she has not the wherewithal to provide.'

The building before us is smaller and shabbier than most cottages in Erlestoke; its sole glazed window is cracked and dirty. I try to tell myself that perhaps this is usual in Bath, where the houses are crammed together and the passage of people and vehicles must throw up mud.

'I wish we were about to climb up to our garret at the West-gate,' I whisper to Miss Bridget.

'Heavens, Miss Amesbury.' She gives a sour little laugh. 'An old lady invalid cannot be a danger to us. Speaking for myself, I shall be glad to take the weight off my feet while we take our cordial.'

So eager is she indeed that she sweeps past me to join Mrs Buckley on the doorstep, whereupon Miss Jane clutches at my arm.

'I never thought I would find friends so quick when I left home today, did you, Miss Amesbury?' She points back at the way we came and together we gaze up at the abbey, shadowy and vast. Miss Jane thrusts her face at mine, gasping a little at her clumsiness as she loses her footing once again. 'Those beautiful shops, those gentlemen so handsome and admiring. I believe I shall never forget my night in Bath, shall you?' She hiccups. 'And it ain't over yet, that's the best of it.'

A Pair of Sharp Eyes

Chapter Four

A shutter swings open, spilling candlelight across the cobbles. I hear drunken laughter and catch a waft of tobacco smoke. Mrs Buckley produces a key, alarming me with the thought she is no mere visitor to the house; but before she fits it in the lock the door flies open and a party of gentlemen bursts forth, shouting and bearing aloft one of their number. Their victim shouts and wriggles frantically.

When I glimpse his bloated face and recognise Mr Osmund I shrink back.

'Don't struggle,' one of the bucks commands, 'take your punishment like a gentleman.'

'Put me down, damn you,' Mr Osmund cries. He must be twice the weight of any of them, and jerks so violently they have a job to hold him. Yet they are determined, and as we watch his breeches are seized and they strip him to the ankles.

'Bastards! Let me go! Give me my clothes.'

'Not likely. Ladies, give this scoundrel a kicking. He's acquired a taste for black flesh out in Spanish Town, for he is on the eve of his wedding and yet he passed over the charms of one of his own countrywomen for a negro girl. Didn't you, Mr Planter? Let these native beauties show their displeasure. Come now, don't be shy, Sir.' They thrust his naked haunches at us; Miss Bridget makes a show of kicking him, though she only grazes his flabby hide, but Miss Jane titters and scuttles behind her sister, while I cannot resist landing a blow that causes the gentleman to bellow and squirm to the great amusement of the rest.

'Well done, Mistress. You felt that, didn't you?'

I hold my tongue, lest Mr Osmund know me by my voice. The river is close by, and the gentlemen drag him, roaring and writhing, to the banks. Cheering, they swing him aloft and, on the count of three, heave him in.

He shrieks, staggers to his feet, falls, thrashes helplessly and begins to blubber. The bloods watch with glee; they clap and jeer and send up a chorus of 'huzzahs' as Mr Osmund slips again and emerges with weed dripping down his face. One tormentor orders the others to be quiet, and steps forward. 'I hope you shall remember this, Sir, next time you resolve to bed a whore. It will be the town sewer for you and no mistake.'

The spectacle of Mr Osmund soaked and hollering distracts us from Mrs Buckley, who calls in vain for us to go inside. Suddenly a slight young woman hurtles from the house, clutching a lace shawl to her bosom and scrambling to put on her shoes. I catch a good view of her face for a moment, and it is dark as polished wood, and very pretty, her features finely sculptured and her eyes pretty too if she were not so frightened.

If this lady has been forced to endure Mr Osmund's attentions and the brutish behaviour of his companions, I am sorry for her.

'Come back here, you whore,' Mrs Buckley screeches. But the girl is at the far end of the street and has more sense than to stop. 'I'll fetch you back if it kills me,' Mrs Buckley adds. 'Get inside,' she says furiously, turning to the three of us.

The sisters goggle, too scared to move, but I see my chance. 'Farewell, Madam,' I blurt out, then I take my petticoat in my hands and pelt towards the abbey, across the empty square and past the bath-house. The hubbub continues within, but the streets are dark and deserted, and the wind is rising. I hurry quick as I can until I reach the turning onto West-gate and halt for a moment to catch my breath.

Am I pursued? Bath is small but I strain my ears and hear nothing but the swaying trees and a faint sound of quarrelling from a nearby tavern. The street is empty. Mrs Buckley has given up hope of snaring me.

Then an owl alights with an outraged shriek in a nearby tree and my heart jolts so hard I nearly faint. I am alone, in a strange, cold city where no one cares what may become of me.

A footstep rings out; I spin round and a black-clad figure almost sends me flying. I have never screamed so loud. 'Mr Espinosa!'

A Pair of Sharp Eyes

'Miss Amesbury! Forgive me, you moved so fast. Something alarmed you. I mean before this.'

We are caught between terror and laughter. Recovering a little, I am eager to explain myself, in case he thinks I was wandering the town of my own free will.

'The woman who sat next to me at dinner, Sir—she coaxed me and the others to go with her.' I point, hoping he guesses my meaning. 'To—to a house we ought not to have entered.'

'Out after curfew? Did you carry lanterns? You're lucky the constables didn't take you up. Where are the others?'

I am mortified to admit the truth. 'I left them, Sir. If I hadn't Mrs Buckley would have dragged me in. They wouldn't listen, at least the eldest wouldn't. They are silly girls—ignorant. Though the younger has no malice in her.' Shame floods me. 'Poor Miss Jane, I should have made her come away with me.'

'At least you are safe.' From his tone I wonder if Mr Espinosa was defying the curfew himself to search for me.

'Will you go back with me, Sir? Mrs Buckley cannot entrap me with you as witness. We may be in time to bring the sisters away unharmed.'

He is so kind and good; his response is instant. 'Of course. Here, hold hands.' His fingers again, thin, warm; his grip surprisingly firm. 'Show me the way.'

Together we hurry back past the baths and the abbey, the moon, as it was, masked partly by clouds. At the end of Abbey-street I stop to take my bearings.

'This way, I think. Past that broken shop-sign. It's not a respectable street—I knew it wasn't. There's the house, do you hear?'

Raised voices carry through the sour, damp air: raucous laughter, someone's protest, then, unless I imagine it, a woman crying out in fear.

'Mrs Buckley won't let them go, I know she won't.' I wring my hands. 'She was purveying us like stolen rabbits round the bath-house. I should have left her then.'

Mr Espinosa eyes the house, lips pursed. 'Such women are practised tricksters, Miss Amesbury. Be thankful she didn't have you carried off by bullies.'

Something in his voice makes me wonder if he has had dealings with Mrs Buckley in the past, but before I can ask another high-pitched sound comes from the house and Mr Espinosa clenches his fists.

'Stay here.' He strides across and hammers on the door-panel. The house seems to hold its breath, then footsteps thunder down the stairs and the door flies open. A man glares out, hair tousled, shirt open to the waist, yet his stockings are white and his shirt is laced and ruffled. I am sure he is the hard-faced gentleman who wanted to take my arm.

'What is this?' He leans forward, squinting through the shadows. 'Damn you, a Jew! How dare you disturb the house of honest Christians? Mrs Charlton is abed.'

Was I wrong to distrust Mrs Buckley's story of her invalid friend? But a moment later my former hostess appears behind him and nudges his shoulder. 'Sir Roger. Pay no heed.'

He shakes her off, none too gently. 'Call the others, Madam. We'll deal with this hook-nosed fellow. Fetch George and Thompson. Between us we'll kick him from here to Israel.'

'A moment, Sir.' Mr Espinosa's tone is steady. 'Two young ladies visited this house tonight, and I am come to see them to their lodgings.'

'God damn you, they are none of your business.' Sir Roger strikes Mr Espinosa in his chest, attempting to dislodge him from the threshold. Mrs Buckley makes another attempt to intervene, but when Mr Espinosa stands his ground Sir Roger plants a blow on his jaw and two more gentlemen pound downstairs.

'Ha! He's all yours George,' Sir Roger steps aside to let the tallest past. George is twice the size of Mr Espinosa, and when I see his sword gleaming my blood curdles.

'Murder! Help!' I leap from the shadows. The men had not seen me and they cry out in alarm, but before I have time to shield Mr Espinosa, Sir Roger jerks me out of the way.

'Who are you?' he bellows. 'His whore?'

'I am no whore. I met this gentleman today, and if you injure him I will report you to the justices, so help me God.'

'Impudent little bitch.'

He holds me so tight my wrist is burning, but I remember a wrestling trick my father taught me, and twisting my hand suddenly down and outwards, force him to release his grip. He shrieks.

'Christ, my thumb, she's broken it.'

A heap of hats and boots and walking-canes lies behind the door, and I lunge for the nearest article, a metal-topped cane the width of a hazel-pole. Before Sir Roger can stop me, I bring it down on George's back. He yelps and tries to kick out, but he is clumsy and I dodge him.

'Bold slut. Keep hold of her, Thompson, a whipping will teach her manners.'

Thompson makes a feint for me, but I still have the cane and he cannot reach past it.

'God's blood, are we to be bested by a girl and a Jew?' His intoxication is George's undoing. He trips on the doorstep and lands heavily on his backside, dropping his sword which Mr Espinosa kicks into the gutter.

'Damn me, I can't move. Help me up, for pity's sake.'

Sir Roger and Thompson do their best, but George is heavier—and drunker—than either, and slumps back with a thud.

Sir Roger follows my example and looks down for a weapon. Nearest to him is a riding-boot with a high heel, and he hurls it at Mr Espinosa, evidently forgetting that a boot is neither rigid nor intended as a missile. It travels just far enough to strike George's head, causing that gentleman to set up a roaring which carries halfway to the river, judging by the windows that burst open and the cries of 'Peace, for God's sake' that echo down the street.

Between that and George's protests the commotion is akin to a pitched battle. A night-watchman looms out of the darkness.

'Peace! Quiet, or I'll have the lot of you in the roundhouse.' To underscore the point he smites the ground with his cudgel, and though he is whiskery his threat is enough to frighten the gentlemen into submission. Wincing, George hauls himself to his feet and joins the others in scrabbling to find his boots.

'We'll be on our way, man, give us a moment.' Sir Roger pulls a coin from his pocket and stuffs it in the watchman's hand. 'Here's for your discretion. I give you goodnight, Sirrah.' Having donned their boots all three seize their belongings, and flee before the watchman stops them.

'Sir Roger, George, Mr Thompson, wait,' cries Mrs Buckley. She stamps her foot. 'Come back, you rogues. None of you've paid me a penny yet.' But the night has swallowed them up, and there is no reply.

The watchman shakes his cudgel in her face. 'That's the least of your worries, you old bawd. I'm reporting you for keeping a disorderly house.' His face speaks his disgust. 'It's not six months since you were last before the bench. As for you two, come with me.'

'A moment, Sir,' says Mr Espinosa. He holds a handkerchief to his face and his voice is muffled. 'We were staying in Bath overnight, and left our lodgings to find two young gentlewomen brought to this house under false pretences. We have still to find them.'

'Then I shall search the house on your behalf and take all four of you to meet the constable.'

Mrs Buckley gives a coarse laugh. 'Gentlewomen? That's not what I'd call them. You'll find no gentlewomen in my house, I assure you.'

I still have my cane; I brandish it at her. 'What have you done with Miss Bridget and Miss Jane?'

She faces up to me for a moment, then bethinks herself and calls upstairs, her voice as rough as it was formerly sweet. 'Come down, you two, your friends are 'ere.'

Timid sounds of a chair being scraped back, and then a door is opened and two cautious sets of feet cross the landing. The sisters appear at the head of the stairs, the elder defiant, the younger on the brink of tears.

'Get out,' Mrs Buckley says. 'I want you gone. Quick, and don't darken my door again, you jades. Helping yourself to my wine and dainties, teasing my gentlemen then calling for your mother. Good riddance.' She rattles the door until the maids scuttle past, Miss Jane still trying to fasten her cloak as the old vixen yells, 'Off with you!' and bangs the door in their faces.

'You see how it is,' Mr Espinosa says to the watchman. 'Am I at liberty to see them to their lodgings?' The watchman searches his face as if for clues, then gives a brisk nod.

'Count yourselves lucky I don't charge you. Show's over,' he says contemptuously, his attention turning to the faces in the windows opposite. 'Back to your beds. Go on.' There are a couple of groans of disappointment which the watchman answers with a glare before the shutters close one by one.

'I'll bid you good night and allow you ten minutes to be off the streets.' To underline his authority the watchman holds up his lantern to watch us pick our way back towards the abbey.

Just as well I never expected thanks from Miss Bridget, for she gives none. Silent, she stalks ahead, chin lifted high. Miss Jane, however, collapses in my arms as we turn the corner, stumbling and clutching her belly while Mr Espinosa keeps at a polite, short distance behind us.

'You're safe now, Miss,' I tell her. 'We'll soon be at the inn. I'll wash your face and help you to bed; before you know it, you'll be sound asleep.'

She gives a sob. 'I been such a fool, Miss Amesbury. I let one of them talk me into going with him to another room. It was small and dark and smelled of something awful. He—hurt me very much.' She cries as if her heart will break. 'Father will kill me if he ever knows what I done. He sold our mother's silver teapot that we might travel respectable to Bristol. We was never meant to leave the Westgate Inn, and I don't know why we did.'

I look her over. As far as I can tell in the moon's weak light her dress is undamaged and her person bears no marks of ill-usage. I suppose the brute fondled her roughly and made her kiss him, but I think she is still a maid, at least I pray she is.

'It's over now, Miss Jane. None will ever know of it. Mr Espinosa won't gossip, will you, Sir?' I look back at the gentleman. 'That's right, isn't it, Sir? You'll not tell anyone what you've seen?'

His face is grave. 'You have my word. Wait a moment.' He takes off his jacket and stepping forward, drapes it over the shivering girl. As soon as we begin to walk again Miss Jane whispers.

'He's a Jew, ain't he? His word means nothing.'

My face and neck flush hot with indignation. 'Miss Jane, if you say such things, I won't be your friend. He is a good man, his actions show it. Those gentlemen back there would claim they were Christians. I never remember Christ saying it was right to hurt innocent girls, do you?'

She hangs her head, mumbling. 'My father used to say a Jew would fleece you soon as look at you.'

'Mr Espinosa risked himself for us, Miss Jane. What would have happened if he had not?'

A fresh sob is her answer.

We reach the inn to find it closed for the night, the front in darkness save for a small, dim lamp above the door.

'Now what do we do?' Miss Jane quavers.

'Go through the back,' Mr Espinosa advises. 'Someone in the kitchen will let you in. Go on.' The sisters obey and scuttle through the coach-arch; but I stay where I am, determined to give thanks.

'If it wasn't for you, Sir,' I begin. A pale light falls on Mr Espinosa's face and I see that what I took for a shadow is a wound below his cheek. 'Oh, but you're hurt.' Blood has soaked his neckerchief; his fingers are wet with it.

'It's nothing,' he says, though he presses the cloth to the cut again. 'Sir Roger caught me with his signet ring, that's all.'

I try to examine the injury but he shies away. 'It looks worse than it is. Better see to your little friend. Good night to you, Miss Amesbury.' He bows, and before I can ask if he has a room at the Westgate too, he walks away into the dark.

Chapter Five

Bath
Wednesday, 24ᵗʰ October, 1703

'Poor Miss Amesbury,' says a familiar voice. 'Sighing for your un-common-looking gentleman-friend, are you?'

Miss Bridget and her sister join me outside the inn, where the morning coach to Bristol is due to leave at any moment. The rain has cleared and the sky is bright above the shining rooftops. The morning would be pleasant except I hoped to share my journey with Mr Espinosa and confess I thought to find him here. However, I suppose he has travelled with the post in order to arrive early at his master's, and I resent Miss Bridget's hint my heart is taken. I shan't be cowed this morning by her snubs and eternal references to Queen-square.

'What a relief to see you here, Miss Bridget,' I reply. 'How pite-ous you were first thing today, groaning and hugging your pillow. I thought you might faint over your breakfast porridge.' I give a droll laugh.

'We're both well, thank you very much,' she retorts. 'We've de-cided to ride outside today, in case you wondered.'

Miss Jane looks fearfully at the coach's sloping roof. 'Have we, Sister?'

'Yes, Jane. The weather's fine and we save ourselves four shil-ling.'

Mr Cheatley and Mr Osborne emerge from the inn and the latter rakes me over with his eyes.

'I believe I will ride outside too,' I say. 'Come on, Miss Jane.' I make an effort at gallantry. 'The fresh air will blow away your head-ache.'

'How bold and cheerful you are, Miss Amesbury,' puts in the el-der sister, 'considering you have no idea what will become of you today.'

'Oh, I shall strive and thrive in Bristol, make no mistake,' I say, though my heart flutters at the thought of searching for my sister's house all by myself.

'Let's hope you're right, for Bristol is a by-word for cut-and-thrust in every walk of life, our aunt said so in her letter, and we are very glad we have good places arranged.' Miss Bridget sighs with satisfaction, not knowing how tempted I am to 'accidentally' tread on her toe, though her feet being so big and clumsy in her wooden pattens she would fail to notice, having all the feeling of the great lumbering carthorse that brought her into Chippenham.

'What if the coach overturns, Sister?' Miss Jane asks, as the ostler checks the traces. 'Three folk were killed on the turnpike near Chippenham a few weeks back.' She flinches on the boy's behalf as a horse whinnies and nips his hand.

'It won't overturn, hen-brain,' says Miss Bridget, thrusting her box at the postillion busy loading at the back of the conveyance. The younger girl's eyes are moist, and I take pity on her.

'Come on, Miss Jane, you go first. Hold tight.' I clamber up to join her. The top is more awkward than I thought, there being no seats nor any rails to keep a hold of. 'Sit between us, and if anything should happen, which it won't, you'll be safe. I like to ride up high, I can see further.' To annoy Miss Bridget I hum and tap my fingers while the last passengers settle in their places. Then the coachman flicks his whip, Miss Jane grabs my arm, and off we go.

By and by Miss Jane looks less fearful as we trundle out of Bath, being glad, perhaps, to put the town behind her. Meanwhile our fellow travellers are a less troublesome lot than yesterday's. Two lads on their way to positions as footmen; another who says he begins an apprenticeship with a master-weaver in Redcliffe. A woman in a brown checked shawl has a fretful baby in her arms and must be sorry to sit opposite Miss Bridget, who scowls and tuts whenever the child cries, though in a little while it sleeps, and the mother's own eyes glaze over, while the three young fellows fall to boasting and jesting between themselves and leave me to my thoughts, Miss

Bridget being too travel-sick to chit-chat, and Miss Jane too frightened.

I would have neither know it, but I almost wish the distance were further now we draw close to Bristol. Two days ago I waved away my Wiltshire sister's quibbles, assuring her I would find a place as soon as I set foot here, but now I wonder why I claimed such a thing. The country we pass through is nothing like Erlestoke; the hills are steep, the roads rougher than at home, and even the houses look different, being built of coloured stone instead of flint.

'What a mansion,' Miss Jane breathes, as we pass a front with twenty mullioned windows. 'Imagine being housemaid there.'

'The manor house at Erlestoke is finer,' I say loudly, and Miss Bridget can hardly contradict, though she pulls her red cloak around herself and feigns deafness.

Little by little the houses increase in number, many with imposing chimneys and tidy plots where rows of trees and gravel walks are visible behind walls of pink and grey stone that match the houses. A mile or so later my heart flutters as we round a bend and glimpse the city walls, high and turreted.

'Temple-gate, ain't it?' one of the lads asks, setting off a noisy discussion of the routes in and out of Bristol, but when the coach slows, all are silent, and I can't help remembering the ancient gatehouse in Salisbury, lived in by a retired churchwarden whose only business was to weed the cobbles and dole out comfits to passing children. Bristol's Temple-gate is guarded by two porters, and every cart must stop to pay a toll and have its load examined.

'What are they searching for?' Miss Jane wonders. A farmhand huddles on a crate while an officer counts the sacks in his waggon.

The apprentice-weaver smirks. 'It's forbidden to sell in Bristol unless you belong to the city. That fellow wishes he had not set off today.'

'Will they put him in gaol?' she asks fearfully.

'Fine him. He won't smuggle again, don't you worry. Ah! Here's our turn.' His words are drowned out by the postillion's horn as we pass through, and conscious of Miss Bridget's sly eyes I look about as brightly as if I had come to Bristol for a street-fair.

A dozen market stalls line the street, and the way is thronged with folk who stroll carelessly along as if the place were not crammed with carts but spacious as a garth. Rabbles of boys, car-men hauling great laden sledges, hurrying housewives, and here and there a fine gentleman in a laced frock-coat, and stranger-looking folk such as a black man on a street corner selling chap-books from a tray, and a wizened man huddled in a doorway, one arm made of wood and a grey raised scar running from his forehead to his chin.

The coach slams to a halt at the sign of the Red Lion, and an ostler runs out to the horses as we climb down and wait to claim our boxes. By the time I have mine the sisters are being greeted by their aunt, a gaunt-faced woman in a red serge petticoat and apron of dark green calico. While they curtsey and recite messages from home, she looks them over sourly and bids them dust down their clothes. Chastened, Miss Bridget straightens her hat and neckerchief, and checks she still has her purse, and I am glad this is not my own first venture from home, notwithstanding that was to the safety of our cousin's house in Salisbury. Miss Bridget should tuck her store of coins in her clothes as I do, and set aside the vanity of displaying a fine purse.

I hurry over as they turn to leave.

'Farewell, Miss Jane, Miss Bridget. I hope all goes well with you.' Miss Jane replies with a shy smile and presses my hand, and I cannot help thinking she is sorry to see the last of me. I am sorry too, though to forestall my tears I tell myself I shan't miss Sister Bridget's carping ways.

A chart is nailed up at the inn door, displaying the roads in and out of Bristol and the departing times of waggons and coaches. There is no map I might use to help me find my sister's house, only notices and bills of sale. One is an advertisement for a *Blackamoor named Joseph, 26 years old, healthy, 5 feet 10 inches, to be offered at auction on October 31st.* I picture an upstanding fellow proud of his chance to serve his master in a Christian land, and envy Joseph the roof he shall have over his head after he is sold.

My heart gives a jump as my eyes alight on a nearby notice. *Information sought concerning the whereabouts of a man wanted for the horrid and bloody murders of six youngsters in Bristol and Redcliffe since November last. The man suspected of these abominable deeds is said to have red hair, and to be six feet tall. He speaks with a foreign accent; is thought to be burnt in the hand and missing his right ear. Intelligence to be supplied to Frederick Grainger Esq. at the Sign of the Anchor, Corn-exchange.*

I shudder at the picture the words conjure in my mind, and turn away before I lose heart altogether for life in Bristol.

'Which way to All-Saint's-yard?' I ask a woman in a queer, old-fashioned fustian gown and petticoat. I am surprised that more folk in Bristol are not clad in silk; many are quite plain. She looks at me askance.

'Where be you from? I can hardly make you out.'

'Wiltshire, Ma'am.'

Her black-toothed husband grins. 'Fresh from the country, eh?'

She jabs his ribs. 'You want Corne-street, Missy, then ask for the tannery.' She speaks as if I am slow-witted. 'Over the bridge, my lover, can't miss it. Keep on 'til you find the High-cross. Like this one here we call Temple-cross but twice the size. You'll see the tower of All-Saints on this side.' She points. 'Then best ask the way again.'

It is as well the woman keeps her directions simple, for I am too dazzled to take in lefts and rights or ups and downs. It's further to the bridge than I thought, and breakfast at the West-gate seems a long time past, and when I smell a pie-seller my mouth waters and I tell myself sternly my task is to find Liz, not waste my money. The woman was right, the bridge is easy to pick out, though the sides are packed so tight with shops and houses that once upon it you cannot see the water. I know it is there by the masts and prows sticking up, and the smell, which is like a privy in summer, and I join the people streaming over to the city, marvelling that nothing I have seen is more wondrous than this, buildings stood crosswise on a bridge spanning a river wider than a village green.

Once upon a time a cruel, contemptuous old gentleman asked why I dreamed to rise above my station. I think back to my reply, lest I am tempted to bolt to the Red Lion and buy a coach ticket to take me back to Erlestoke and my life with Meg and her dozy husband, John. 'I am good enough for any man,' I said then, and I say it under my breath now. The houses here may be tall and some with gables like pastry-crusts and a dozen windows, but I have equal right to be here as anyone.

I pass one great church, glimpse the spires and towers of others, then beyond the bridge I find the High-cross just as the woman said. To one side lies yet another church, which I take to be All-Saints. They are godly folk, it seems, these citizens of Bristol, despite their love of money.

'Watch it!' a voice cries, and I leap back before a cart knocks me off my feet. The vehicle goes full trot despite the crowds. I am in danger of having my neck broken, and I wish I could walk backwards except then I would miss the carts coming the other way.

'Is that All-Saints-yard?' I ask a sailor. I know him by his blue jacket and canvas trousers, though I remember Meg saying to have nothing to do with seamen, who are known for drinking and whoring, and would rob as soon as look at you.

Meg was wrong, because this fellow never answers, but continues his rolling way along the street. But a milkmaid overhears my question.

'That's right, sweetheart. Through that little alleyway, that's All-Saints.' She is all dimples and smiles, and her apron spotlessly clean and her sleeves likewise, and I think most foolishly as it turns out, that All-Saints will be clean and welcoming as she is, so that when I come out at the end of the alleyway, which is dark and smells no better than a pig-sty, my spirits sink. This is not a yard but a row of higgledy houses with barefoot children on every doorstep, and the roofs patched and falling in, and the walls streaked with damp, and the ground a quagmire.

I crush the memory of Miss Bridget crowing over the 'well-appointed chamber in an upper storey but overlooking the square, you know' that she and her sister were told was theirs. I may be equally fortunate, and find a place in no time, and as likely in Queen-square as any lesser quarter of the city, though this thought produces a second recollection, which is of Meg failing to persuade me that I missed the last day for hiring, and would be better waiting now 'til Christmas-time.

A round-shouldered old woman in a faded apron sits spinning on her doorstep. She pauses warily at the sight of me, though in truth there can be little to rob in such mean dwellings.

'Good day, Mistress. I'm looking for my sister's house—Mrs Elizabeth Eardley.'

'Are you now?' She looks me over, trying to find a resemblance between me and Liz. The old woman must be satisfied, for she says, 'Your sister's at work, she don't get home 'til after six.'

'She said her husband would let me in.'

The woman shakes her head. 'He's at work too, or more likely drinking down the harbour. Your sister has a hard row to hoe in more ways than one. Still, you can help her now you're here. You look likely enough.'

'Oh, but I'm not stopping long. I've come to find a place.'

She wipes her mouth on her hand. 'High and mighty. "A place," eh?' Her face softens. 'Take no notice, my lover, I'm pulling your leg. There are places aplenty in Bristol for those who'll work. Trouble is, young folk these days are idle, most of them. Show us your hands.'

Hiding a smile at her forthrightness, I obey.

'That's more like it.' She grins approvingly. 'You've worked for your living. What are you? Weeding-woman like your sister?'

'No, Mistress. I used to help my father with his plot, and I can sew, and cook, and mind babies, and run errands, and I lived in Salisbury for six months and nursed my mother's cousin.' I want to add 'And I was the friend of the squire's son in Erlestoke, until the old man cast him off for yearning after marrying me,' but I vowed to put that behind me when I came to Bristol, and I shall, though it pains me not to boast that I can read and write, and play a hymn or two on the old squire's spinet. I long to tell the old woman that by sewing I don't only mean I can mend a handkerchief but I can cross-stitch because the squire's daughter showed me how, and her brother taught me *Carpy deum* and *Veeny veedy veechy* in order that I could out-quote any snot-nosed Salisbury curate who tried to slap me down.

The old woman struggles to her feet, groaning at the effort. 'You'd better come in along of me 'til your sister's home. Don't look frightened, foolish maid, I told her I'd take you in if you was early. My name is Mistress Jervis. If you carry in those sticks I'll boil the kettle and we'll have ourselves a bite of dinner. You can put those nimble fingers to good use after, carding wool. That's their house, see?' She points to a house even lower than her own, the eaves hung about with pelts and furs.

'Tell me those aren't polecats dangling down.'

She laughs, and the laughter turns into a cough that bends her double. 'And foxes' brushes and mouldiwarps and a few rats for good measure. He's one of the lazy sort I told you about, though he's not so young neither. They fined him and still he's too idle to clean up after hisself, and throws the guts in the yard. It's a filthy trade, vermin-catching, but as you're sure to hear him say, some poor devil must do it.' More rasping laughter.

Her words chime with what I know of my brother-in-law, yet my spirits rise when the old spinster shows me her dwelling, for it is not the hovel I expected but a comfortable room, small to be sure, and the floor beaten earth, but that floor has been swept this morning and the kettle shines brightly, and I am bid sit on a stool by the fire while Mrs Jervis picks over a handful of cracked wheat and talks to her finch that hops about in a cage above the door, and when I have been shown how to card wool her way, she boils the wheat and puts in milk. She stirs it awhile and then we sup our frumenty and she sets to yarning, telling me she is old enough to remember the day King Charles had his head cut off, and that her great-grandmother came to Bristol near a century ago, after her cottage was swept away by a flood that razed a thousand homes along the coast of Somerset and drowned ten thousand sinners.

By and by she falls silent, her eyelids flutter, and she begins to nod. I take up my carding combs and set to work, except my own eyes are tired, and between the late hour I kept last night, and my comfortable place by the fire, which glows and makes the little room snug, I slide into a dream where figures pass across my inward eye in a jumble of all I have met since leaving Erlestoke. Mr Espinosa with his strange and earnest way of speaking, Bridget Lamborne airily declaiming the beauties of Queen-square, Mrs Buckley thrusting her powdery face at mine and telling me I am ripe fruit for the plucking.

When an ear-splitting screech jars me awake the room is dark and I cry out.

'Oh God, what is it?'

Mrs Jervis cannot answer until she has cleared her chest. 'Mr Bill Eardley is what it is. He has a habit of strangling the creatures he catches, if his snares don't do the job for him. It's sport in his view.'

Her fit of coughing over, she cocks an ear. 'Coney.' Another scream rends the air, more human-seeming than animal. 'Two conies,' she concludes. 'Don't be sorry, least ways you'll eat well tonight and perhaps tomorrow.'

Reluctant though I am to greet my brother-in-law, I cannot trade on the spinster's hospitality any longer, so I get up and put the little wool I cleaned back in the basket on the hearth, along with the combs that clattered to the ground when I woke suddenly.

'I thank you for my dinner, Mrs Jervis, and for the stories you told me, and I must be on my way.'

She rises and takes my hand between her wrinkled thumb and fingers. 'A word to the wise. Stand up for yourself with Mr Bill Eardley. Your sister won't and it has made a tyrant of him. Don't breathe a word to either, but I told the constable about the dead rats he left lying in the yard. Magistrates fined him a shilling, and serve him right. Though your poor sister paid a different price, Lord love her, for he has an evil temper.' An idea strikes her, and her face lights up. 'If he ever lifts a hand to you remember old King Charles. Tyrants come to bad ends.' She mimes the action of the executioner's axe, pretending the blade slices through her neck, and follows this with a merry burst of laughter, as if she is wont to go about Bristol chopping off the heads of those who vex her.

I am tempted to offer a warning in exchange, which is to remind her that old women who get across their neighbours are liable to wish they had not. I have lived long enough to know folks detest a woman who sets herself at odds with any man.

Chapter Six

Bristol
Wednesday, 24ᵗʰ October, 1703

One thought is in my head as I knock on Liz's worm-eaten splintery door: I cannot stop here long.

Bill rests his great hairy paw on the door-frame to block my way. 'Uh. Another Amesbury expecting to be kept.'

When Bill came courting—the only man willing to overlook how scrawny Liz was after the smallpox—he wore breeches stitched from moleskins, and he wears those greasy breeches now, along with a torn coat of some thicker pelt, and a black cap stuck about with rabbit-tails and eagle claws. His squat dwelling stinks as he does. A mix of graveyard mould and rancid butcher's block.

'Will you let me in, Brother?'

He thinks about it, sly-eyed; steps aside; jerks his head. Carrying my box, holding myself proud, I walk inside, only to trip and nearly fall on the hollow dirt floor, the light being so dim I cannot see my way. One rank-smelling room, the rafters low and smudged with smoke. Sole sign of Liz's presence is a pair of wooden head-combs lying on the bed. I set down my box on the rough plank that serves as a table.

'When's my sister home, Bill?'

'When Elliott lets her go,' he grunts. 'The old devil finds every way he can to keep her toiling for him. Don't touch that jar, thinking you're clever to help yourself to a drop of tea without asking. 'Tisn't tea, 'tis poison for the rats.' He puts a black hand to his throat and makes a choking sound, laughing at my look of disgust. 'I'll be back when I've sold what I catched today,' he adds, and swinging open his coat to show me half-a-dozen rabbits tied to his belt, he slouches out, leaving a trail of bloody drops behind him.

When his thumping footsteps fade I sit myself on a stool and vow I will not cry. I am weary is all, and footsore, and did not imagine

A Pair of Sharp Eyes

Bill Eardley's greeting would be quite so harsh. Nor did I expect to find the place as mean. One wooden candlestick is the only homely touch. A heap of wire snares lies in one corner, and above them, on a great black hook, a pair of long, curved butcher's knives I suppose are for skinning the pitiful creatures Bill catches in his traps.

I was never close to either of my sisters, but when, long after twilight, Liz returns, I jump up and hug her tight. She is even sparer than I remember, and does not return my hug. Her smile is fleeting.

'So, little sister, you found us. Did Mrs Jervis take you in?'

'From noon 'til Bill came back.'

'Gossip about us, did she?' Liz sits to pull off her boots, and her feet are just as I remember them, with knuckly toes, and pale and bony ankles like our mother's. 'Still, old Jervis is kind enough. Did you keep away from the quays on your way from Temple-gate?'

'Yes, Liz.'

'Don't cast up your eyes, girl. Who has lived in Bristol twelve months? And who just rolled into town with grass-seeds stuck to her hem?'

'You. Me.'

'There then.' She edges a piece of kindling into the fire. 'We live plain, as you see. The landlord bleeds us dry.' Her thin brown face is defiant. 'I warned you the place was small.'

'It's well enough.' Yet I am sure Bill Eardley misled my sister when he made his offer. He averred he owned his dwelling-place outright; he did not confess it was made of cob and mouldy thatch, or that he merely rents it.

'You have it neat,' I tell her. The room is so bare it could hardly be otherwise.

'Neat? I can sweep the floor one-handed while the other does the grate.' She casts a bitter glance at the bed. ''Til I came here I thought everyone but tinkers slept apart from where they ate.'

'Liz. I slept in the box bed by the hearth 'til I was six.'

'Grown folks I mean. You know what I mean.' She speaks in a rush, as though she longs to unburden herself. 'One room, no chimney save a hole in the wall that lets the rain in, a few inches of stony ground for a garden, a cracked jar for a cooking-pot. Even old Jervis owns a kettle. I expected to better myself when I came to Bristol.'

'Believe me, you were better here once Father fell sick.'

If Liz picks out a hidden thread in my meaning—who was left to care for Father after she and Meg left home?—she gives no sign. 'I thought to make my fortune,' she says bitterly. 'I never stopped to consider I'd nothing to sell.'

'Furs, maybe?'

'Bah! Not the kind he fetches.'

'You've found work, though, Liz. Steady, and close by.'

She shuts her eyes, and the lids are blue like the circles round them, and above them her hair is dull and threaded with grey, and her lips so thin I can scarcely make them out. Then she blinks and fixes me with a stare. 'You were a fool, Corrie. You should have pleaded with Cousin Mary to let you stay in Salisbury. You might have found a husband there.'

'Among the dried-up clergy in Cathedral Close? Liz, I burn to tell you something. It was my fault Father died.'

'Don't be foolish. He died of hunger and hard work, like every other Amesbury.'

'Yes, because Squire Lloyd let him go. And he only did because of me. When I came back from Salisbury, Robert Lloyd asked me to marry him. He said he'd loved me since we were children. Remember how we roamed the woods and fields, the two of us, before he went to Oxford? Salisbury had turned me into a beautiful young lady, Robert said, and he was determined to wed me.'

Liz is looking at me in mocking disbelief, tinged with envy. 'Then why didn't he?'

'The Squire heard of it, and banished Robert to Jamaica.' I have kept my secret all these months; tears run down my cheeks. 'I shall never see my love again, and if I did he wouldn't thwart his father's wishes.'

Liz tilts her head, considering. 'You may not like it,' she says at last, 'but you were lucky. How would you have fared, married into gentry? His friends would have disowned the pair of you. His father would have cut off his inheritance. His mother? She'd have hated you.'

Liz is dripping hot wax into my wounds.

'I swore I'd never say his name again. Please, Liz, let's talk of other things.' I wipe my eyes, and inch my stool back from the fire. 'I did wonder if there'd be room for me here with you and Bill.'

I am hoping she will tell me why, after three years' marriage, there is no baby, but she ignores the bait. 'I split two fingernails today,' she says. 'See? Damned weeding, one day I'll break my back.' She pushes her fist into her spine, grimacing.

'You shouldn't over-work, Liz. The granmers used to say a young wife shouldn't be too thin.'

She thumps the table. 'You think I'm addle-witted. I know what you're saying, nosy so-and-so.'

'I only wondered.'

'Don't pry. I'm regular as church bells, and don't tell me I'm skinny, you little besom.' She chucks back her head. 'If you want to know whose fault it is, why don't you look at Bill? He's pickled his bollocks with rum like the rest of him. And good thing too.'

'Oh Liz.'

'Why? Would you want a child if you had to bring 'em up here, dressed in skins like a savage, and sleeping in a borrowed garden trug?'

I can't help laughing. 'Liz. It wouldn't be that bad. He'd buy the baby a christening gown.'

We both laugh heartily.

'Oh aye, and a lace cap and a silver rattle.' Her face grows sober. 'Most probably he'd wait 'til I was out and drop it in a well.' Her eyes fill with tears.

'He wouldn't, Liz.' I reach out, though she pulls her hand away. 'When Mother said Tom was on the way, Father slammed the door and spent the evening wandering Salisbury Plain. Soon as Tom was born Father was overjoyed to have a son. He died broken-hearted for his boy.'

Liz is bound up with her own sorrows, but she knows how I nursed Tom and never slept or ate for a month after we buried him. She stands up, rummages beneath the mattress, and pulls out a paper parcel and sets it down before us. Then she reaches for the small basket she brought home from Elliott's, and hands me a small, hard pear.

'Sugar?' I say, peering at the paper. 'How's that then?'

'Bristol's where sugar's at, remember. I hide it from Bill or he'd put it in his rum.'

We sit companionable by the little smoking fire and take turns to dip the sour green fruit in the sticky grains.

'God, but I'll have cramps from eating unripe fruit.' Liz wrinkles her nose and picks a shred that has stuck between her teeth. 'Mr Elliott tried to give me better today, but I take only the ones too poor to sell.'

'I relish it with this sugar, though. I wish I could have fetched you a pot of honey, Liz. All I brought was a lump of cheese. Here.' I open my box and hand her the cheese, tied up in a piece of muslin. 'Don't let Bill have it.'

'Good Wiltshire honey, eh,' she says, stowing the cheese under the mattress. 'I wonder where Father's bees flew to.'

'They didn't fly, dunder.' The longer Liz and I are sat together, the more Wiltshire I sound. 'Father's friend Silas put 'em with his own skeps.'

'Even now I can't believe the cottage is gone, and Father dead, and Mother moved to Salisbury,' Liz says. 'I think of them as they was.'

'I don't,' I say sadly. 'If you'd picked your way over the ashes of the house-fire you wouldn't neither.'

'I suppose.' She leans back in her chair, and rests her chin on her hand. Then she looks up.

'Corrie? There must have been something saved from the fire besides a few spoons. What about *Pilgrim's Progress*? And *Robinson Crusoe*? I loved old Crusoe and his Friday.'

'It all went up, Liz. Everything. If not gone, plastered in soot. I took what I stood up in.'

I don't add that Mother gave me eighteen pence to give me a little security when I arrived in Bristol. Liz was ever prone to jealousy, especially when it comes to Mother.

Luckily she has lost interest in the story, or lost heart.

'God, I be tired. Remember how Father used to say his joints ached?' She runs her hands over her knees, then rests her head on the chair back and shuts her eyes.

***

I waken to find the room cold and the fire turned to ash. Liz startles as soon as I shift and I wonder if she's fearful. She must be, married to that lump.

'Run to the pastry-shop, will you, Corrie?' She stands up and feels in a crack above the door lintel, and counts the pennies in her palm, frowning.

I think of Bill's resentment when he greeted me.

'I'll fetch for you, Liz, but I cannot have you buy my victuals.'

She tosses her head. 'I daresay I can provide your first night in Bristol. Fetch us three slices and quick as you like. Go on, don't argue. The pie-seller with the orange stockings and black waistcoat is cheapest; he's on the corner with the High-street. I'd come with you if my feet weren't like red-hot coals.'

'Well, perhaps this once.' I rise and wrap myself in my cloak, though a thought strikes me, and I cannot step out into the night until I have spoken it.

'Liz, when I was on my journey people were talking of a string of boys murdered in Bristol in the last few months. Is it true?'

She busies herself putting coins back above the lintel, and does not answer.

'It is then.' I cannot hide my shock. 'And one just this last week?'

'Monday. Near the rope-walk on St-Augustine's-back. There's been half-a-dozen in the last two years. Every one a boy, so you don't need to fear. Two hundred turned out for the last one's funeral.'

'I heard they were stable-lads or beggars, sleeping in lofts or under hedgerows.'

'Aye, killed where they were sleeping. Folk reckon there's a pedlar called Red John preying on young lads.' She picks up the poker and jabs the embers in the grate. Her face glows reddish-black.

'Why don't they hunt for him?'

'He fled up country, they say. Vanished in the autumn mist. Though I think he's hid on board a ship. Who'd pick him out among a crew of sailors when half are thieves and pirates? Like I keep telling you, stay away from the rough lot round the quays. You have no understanding of a place like Bristol. Ships sailing in from every corner of the world, folk who speak no tongue you understand, men who fight and whore, and women no better than they should be.'

'Liz, I came to find a place in a respectable household and that is what I shall do.' I push a stray lock of hair beneath my bonnet and look at her straight. Then I can't resist asking, 'Liz, how does he kill them?'

'Cuts their throats. And leaves no trail of blood behind to trace him by. The magistrates come asking all the washerwomen if they've been given any laundry with bloody stains on.' She flushes. 'I take in washing now and then, I ain't ashamed of it.'

'Of course you ain't. Did any washerwomen say they had seen aught wrong?'

'We all did. We washes sheets and shirts and petticoats with every kind of stain on them. I never found any linen steeped in blood, and if I did, I shouldn't tell the magistrates.'

'But Liz, what of the poor lads with their throats cut?'

'If I told tales about my customers I should never earn a penny. Besides, I've no tales to tell. I promise you, Corrie, if I did, I'd tell you all.'

'Then promise to tell me about the city and the quays when I come back. Bill knows a few pilots, doesn't he? I saw so many masts when I came over the river. I did hurry past, I promise you.'

'Pilots? They're a reckless savage lot. "Sharks" they call them up the river. Go on. I'll tell you the little I know when you bring back that pie. I'm famished. Lord, but I'm tired too.' She rubs her face, and seeing her sickly complexion and sunken cheeks I feel a pang for my sister. Marriage has aged her twenty years in two. 'Listen, Corrie,' she mumbles, rising to unlatch the door. 'I'm pleased to offer you a bed for a week or two, but no longer. We'll be out of here ourselves soon, looking for a cheaper room.'

'Cheaper?'

'We owe rent, or Bill does. We shall have to share with another family. I'm sorry, Sister.'

I go to kiss her to show I bear no ill feelings, but she flinches from my touch and up close there are bruises on her throat which are plain despite the meagre light and the neckerchief she wears to hide them. Whatever she claims about Bill's debts I guess why she wants me gone.

Liz would never let her husband degrade her own sister I tell myself, as I step into the yard, altering my certainty to 'I hope she has the means to prevent it,' for it is many a year since I lived with Liz, and I know her less than I once did, while all I know of Brother Bill is that he cares for no one but himself.

***

An hour after we have fallen asleep, I by the hearth, Liz on her bed of straw, Bill blunders in and kicks the door shut, promptly tripping over a stool and swearing fit to wake the dead. He reeks as he always does, of rum and dung and slaughter, and not satisfied with what he has drunk he throws off his hat and coat and fumbles in the dark until he finds the ale jug. I lie as still as may be while he gulps and then devours the slice of pie Liz left out for him. Either he forgets I am there or cares nothing for it, for next he thumps the jug down on the table then draws back the blanket, climbs on my sister and does his grunting work on her for all the world like a boar that serves a sow. He rolls off, still in his filthy boots, and moments later sets to snoring. My poor sister is evidently used to such treatment, for she makes no sound or movement, and by and by joins her softer snores to his.

It is fortunate Liz banked up the fire, for besides my cloak I have only the straw she lent me to lie on. The draught from the door is sharp, and as I saw when I arrived, the floor is green with damp. Even so, being worn out I sleep until at last the watchman calls four o'clock, wakening me from a dream in which a black figure shuffles towards me and I cannot move.

Someone drops to his knees with a grunt of pain. A split-moment later I am pinned by a hand on my chest and another at my throat.

'Saints alive, Bill!'

He plants his filthy palm over my mouth; I gag at the smell of rabbit guts and his foul breath in my face.

'What you hiding in that shift of yours? Come on, Miss Coronation Amesbury, I said you couldn't stay rent-free. Give me what you owe.' He pulls at my clothes with greasy fingers.

Now I see why Liz stows her few pennies in the wall. 'Leave me be, you rogue.' I try to keep my voice between scolding and jesting.

'You must have money for how'd you get here in the first place?' He shoves his hand under my shift and gives my leg a painful squeeze, whereupon my temper flares.

'If I have money it is not for buying rum for you.' I twist out of his hands and give one of them a nip.

He squawks and kicks out at me as I struggle free.

'You bit my thumb, you bitch.'

'Shush, brother. Liz'll hear.'

He shoves me but I return the compliment threefold, enough to push him back towards the bed. Straight off Liz wakens.

'Not again,' she groans. 'Leave a body in peace, won't you?'

'I got up to fetch a swig of ale. Shut your mouth.' Bill knows I will not rouse Liz further by nay-saying him. 'Here, give me some blanket, lazy mare.'

'I'm fairly starved with cold,' she grumbles, and while I wait for my heart to slow, I listen to them bicker over who has most of the paltry coverings, and whose turn it is to hunt for firewood tomorrow.

I wait for Bill to say, 'Your good-for-nothing sister Corrie can find some,' but perhaps he is fearful of Liz guessing what he was at when he jolted her awake, for he makes no mention of me. I lie until dawn, fretting over the time I may take to find another place, wishing that once I have done so it will be in my power to save my sister from a man as unlike the ideal husband as I can possibly imagine.

Despite everything, the thought brings a smile to my lips as I lie on my musty pile of straw waiting for dawn and wishing my feet were warmer. Did I not swear a month or two ago that the ideal husband does not exist within these shores?

Chapter Seven

Thursday, 25th October, 1703

We rise before dawn and say our prayers in darkness. Bill Eardley never troubled to light a fire before leaving so breakfast is cold water—Bill has drunk the beer—then Liz and I set off for work, Liz saying she is certain her master will hire me for the day.

I came to Bristol to better myself, not to weed for tuppence, but I would like to earn something, so long as it is only 'til I find a place in service.

We take a narrow, muddy lane that leads behind a street of handsome shops, then make our way past a row of orchards. The sky is streaked with light by the time we spy the high stone walls enclosing Mr Elliott's plot.

'They screen the wind and help to keep out thieves,' Liz says. 'You'd be amazed how brazen folk are, stealing crops, or trampling them for sport. Mr Elliott has his boy stay up all night to guard the strawberry beds in summer. She pauses, frowning. A dozen men and women huddle round the gate.

'What's this? Who are all these people?'

'They're waiting to be hired,' I say. 'We should have got here earlier.' But I do not really mean it. I should be glad if Mr Elliott turns me down.

'I've never seen so many hoping to be hired this close to winter.' Liz walks fast, but she hesitates as we grow near. The crowd is silent, their faces grim, and some of the women are weeping. Liz mutters. 'I hope nothing's befallen Mr Elliott. He was feverish on Monday, he said it was just a head-cold.'

I am conscious of all eyes upon us as we file through to the gate. A round-eyed woman catches eagerly at Liz's arm. 'You haven't heard. A boy's been murdered in Mr Elliott's garden.'

'No.' Liz steps back; her knees give way for a moment until she recovers herself. 'What boy?'

'Tom Roxall's son. Bled to death—butchered where he lay. Go on, Mistress, get you in. Mr Elliott will tell you everything.'

Liz's face is sickly grey. She waves me through and bangs the gate. 'I don't believe it,' she says, hurrying me to a shed to our left. 'I spoke to Davy Roxall yesterday.' Her fingers fly to her mouth. 'I boxed his ears for letting rabbits eat the winter-salet.'

'Mistress Eardley.' An elderly man in a canvas coat totters towards us with red-rimmed eyes. 'You won't believe what's happened.' He fumbles for a pocket handkerchief. 'I stepped out last night for supper, leaving Davy to mind the garden as he always does. On my return I went to bed. Then, when I walked across to waken him at first light, I found him lying with his throat cut. Poor Mr Roxall. He's gone to fetch a trestle to carry the lad away.' The old man gives a sob.

Liz shakes her head as Mr Elliott begins to protest. 'Show me. I've a strong stomach, Sir. So does my sister here. We are country girls.' She looks at me and I stifle a plea to spare me such a dreadful sight. As I do whenever I am fearful, I think of my father, his trust in me and his belief I could rise to any difficulty in my way.

'Yes indeed, Sir,' I say earnestly. 'By no means should you deal with such a thing alone.'

Mr Elliott bites his lip, but seems too distressed to argue. Instead he nods, and on trembling legs leads us across the plot. Liz lifts her skirts and walks purposefully in his wake. I wonder at her cool-headedness, though I recall how she was always sober when the rest of us were in pandemonium.

To the end of my days I shall not forget what lies behind the bothy door.

'Don't look, Mistress,' Mr Elliott begs, but in vain; Liz at once stoops next to the little body and draws back the blanket covering it.

A child with a mop of dark and tangled hair, and a face as innocent as I ever saw, the eyes blue and wide open, and the lips parted in surprise, almost as if the boy had looked up from his slumbers to see a face he knew.

Yet the throat has been cut so savagely the head is half-severed from the trunk, and the bed is soaked with blood.

Liz turns to Mr Elliott. 'This is Red John's work and no mistake. Look away, Corrie.' She leans over the corpse, blocking my view so I cannot see if further injuries were inflicted.

Liz cannot hide the pale, small limbs altogether; it is plain the child is naked.

'He may have taken the clothes to sell them,' Mr Elliott says pleadingly, but Liz makes a sound of disbelief.

'What's this?' Her eyes alight on an object lying in the corner of the bothy. She picks it up. A long, wide-bladed knife such as butchers use, the blade dark with clotted blood.

'Good Lord preserve us.' Mr Elliott's voice shakes. 'It wasn't dawn when I found the boy, and it was still half-dark when his father arrived. We didn't see a knife. I never thought to look for one.'

Liz looks on the shelf for a rag and, holding the blade away, wraps the knife securely. 'I'll take it home for scouring. The magistrates might want to see it. If not, I'll give it to my husband. He's ever in need of knives and suchlike.'

'He's a vermin-killer, isn't he? You must tell him to apply here if he wants work, Mistress. I mean when I re-open.'

'Thank you, Mr Elliott. I have told him of your kind offers before now.' I can see from Liz's face she will never let Bill Eardley near the place. 'This is my sister, Sir. I hope you'll pardon the liberty. She's staying with me. Our mother's house burned down a few weeks back.'

Despite his distress the old man looks me over. 'You could have helped with the autumn sowing, Mistress. I should have been glad of someone to plant the beans.' He draws a shuddering breath. 'But I can't hire you now, I promised Thomas Roxall I would close today from respect.' He turns to Liz. 'Be glad, Mistress Eardley, you weren't here when I had to break the news to Thomas.' Another tear rolls down the old man's cheek. 'But I should be obliged if you would stay today. The murderer stole nearly all my tools and helped himself to half the crops. I want to set the place to rights as best I can. I won't ask you to deal with the bothy, I'll do that. Poor child.'

Hesitating in case she takes too great a liberty, Liz puts an arm around his shoulders.

'Let's tell ourselves Davy was sound asleep and never knew what happened. Come, Mr Elliott, you'll feel better once we set to. Coronation here will help, she won't expect paying. I don't wish to leave you, and I can't allow her to walk home alone.'

Mr Elliott nods, and far from resenting her familiarity, rests his head on her shoulder and draws breath, gathering his strength. He may be aged, but I wish Liz had met a kind widower like him instead of Bill.

Between them she and Mr Elliott rake the floor, lifting the spoiled straw and stained rushes, then Liz carries out Davy Roxall's flock bed and between us we remove the truckle he slept on. Mr Elliott says it is old and worm-eaten and he cannot bear to look at it again.

I am given an axe and told to heap the pieces in a pile for burning, along with the spoiled straw and a blood-stained nightshirt we find bundled in a corner of the bothy, along with a quality blue-and-white striped neckerchief the murderer failed to see when he stripped the child. While the bonfire smoulders in the icy air Mr Elliott writes an inventory of the tools he has lost, and Liz digs over the plot where the thief pulled up the cabbages and roots and gouged deep footprints in the soil.

'How will Mr Elliott recover from his losses?' I ask quietly, when the old man has gone back to his cottage. I have the only remaining tool, a rusting shovel, and Liz and I are labouring in the cabbage bed. The earth is claggy and hard to work, and I am conscious I have not eaten since last night.

'Master pays into a mutual society. They'll compensate him. The shock's worse than the losses for a man his age. Poor Mr Elliott, he's bewildered.'

'So must you be, Liz. To think you spoke to the boy only yesterday. How many lads have died in Bristol now?'

She points down the garden, ignoring my question. 'Look, Mr Elliott's lit the kitchen fire. He'll give us a good breakfast even if he doesn't pay you. After Father he's the kindest man I know.'

'I heard half-a-dozen have been killed so far. They were talking of it on my way to Bristol. And now it's seven.'

Liz lifts a clod of earth and flips it over. 'Who knows exactly?' Her voice is defiant. 'It could be less. Two of them drowned in a quarry one hot day in August. People blamed Red John, but the rest could have died by accident.'

'You say that, Liz, and yet it could be more were murdered. What if a boy was on the streets, and someone cut his throat and threw him in the river? No one would know.'

'Don't say such things.'

'I'm curious is all. Who'd be desperate enough to kill a child for a sack of carrots and a few old spades and pitch-forks? Is it the same who killed the other boys? The murderer could be a local man, not a pedlar. He could be someone well known—even someone well-to-do.'

'You always were a morbid creature, Corrie Amesbury. Haven't we seen enough today to give us nightmares? Come on, let's find our breakfast. If Mr Elliott thinks you've worked hard, he may pay you after all. So when we have eaten, more digging, less talking.'

'Yes, Liz. I won't say anything untoward in front of him, I promise.' I clamp my lips shut to show I mean it. Yet as we put down our tools and go to the water butt to rinse our hands I wonder at my sister. By her own estimation she is a 'country girl'. I never knew her dodge an ugly truth before.

But then Liz, as I reflected earlier, is always level in a crisis. For weeks I wished the Lord would take me too after Tommy died, and Liz kept telling me it was sinful to despair.

I must not think of Tommy now, not when that other poor young boy lies soaked in blood. It would unseat me, whereas if I take a leaf from Liz's book and restrain my grief I might find out something bearing on the crime. After all, Liz knew Davy Roxall. She may know more about his murder than she thinks she does. I will bide my time 'til I can sound her out.

Chapter Eight

Friday, 26ᵗʰ October, 1703

Next day I call at two dozen houses between All-Saints and St-Nicholas. Each smirking footman and ill-favoured housemaid informs me that their mistress refuses to speak to unknown callers and has no need for a servant in any case. Not one glances at my letter from Cousin Mary, in which she lists the qualities of honesty and diligence required in a domestic, assuring whomsoever it concerns that I possess such qualities and more besides, such as cleanliness, punctuality and sobriety.

Cousin Mary does make me sound like a shining example, and I hope no one who reads her letter notices what she does not say. My mother having told her of the business with the squire's son, Cousin Mary refused to add discretion to my virtues.

Saint-Nicholas is at the foot of the hill that rises to the north of Bristol, and once past the churchyard I am almost at the river. I smell the quays before I see them: a briny fish-stink in the wind that catches my skirts as I round the end of Frog-lane. And hear them: cries of labouring men, shrieks and screams of gulls, creak of timbers and great hollow thuds as crates and barrels are heaved and rolled from deck to quay and up the wharves to the warehouses that line the great, wide harbour.

Liz was wrong to be anxious; I am invisible to the swarms of people here. The risk is being crushed under the wheels of a cart or knocked off my feet by a swinging jib, not losing my honour to some brutish sailor.

I hurry between rows of these warehouses, smelling spices from one, tobacco from another, and from the last, molasses and something sweet and cloying I fancy might be vanilla. I ought to leave and resume my search for work, yet the harbour draws me on, notwithstanding buffets of icy wind that make me clutch the sides of my bonnet and give thanks for my warm cloak.

A Pair of Sharp Eyes

I am eager to see the river itself, and press forward, dodging a pair of men with a sea-chest so heavy they are obliged to drag it over the rough cobbles, swearing and grunting as they go. The way is claggy with seagull droppings and some black oily dirt peculiar to the place, and I keep my eyes down to avoid tripping on the stout ropes anchoring each ship to the quayside. The oozy mud that lines the river banks reeks worse than any ditch. I hear water slapping the hulls and jetties, but cannot see it, the river being thick with vessels, foreign-looking ones with fancy flags, skiffs with a single pair of oars, and schooners dwarfed by the great triple-mast slave ships of which I count three by the time I near the end of St-Augustine's-back.

No sailor seizes me or offers me rude words; I might as well be nobody in my straw bonnet and homespun gown. A warm gust from a factory chimney brings a scent of burned molasses with it, and a memory of nibbling gingerbreads at the fair in Devizes at Whitsuntide; and the strangeness of the scene begins to weigh on me. The ships' masts are indeed as tall as steeples, and yet this is not Salisbury with its beautiful cathedral and chattering choristers and sober clergymen, but a vast place devoted to business and foreign trade, and every nook and cranny of it teems with folk I do not know.

I am about to turn and retrace my steps when I notice a rowing-boat being tied up at the quayside. Its passengers, mainly negroes, are busy clambering ashore, while the man in charge of them, a hawk-nosed, grizzled, wiry fellow in a moss-green coat, chivvies them up the wharf with rough cries of 'Faster!' and 'Quit crying'.

I am used to passing black faces on the streets of Bristol, but these people are weighed down with fetters and chained together by their necks and ankles, and I fancy from their drawn expressions and stained clothes they have been many months at sea, and come from some sailing-ship at anchor on the river. Their first steps on English soil draw half-a-dozen bystanders, and unable to resist I weave through the little crowd for a better view.

'Your head's in my way,' grumbles a dame with a basket on her arm of foodstuffs bought at market, but she winks when I beg her pardon, and offers me a cobnut from a paper cone. From her cheerfulness and those of others about me it is almost as though we assemble to watch the Punch and Judy man, though the scene we witness is plainly one of misery.

While half-a-dozen of the negroes are roughly herded by a couple of sailors towards the city, where I suppose they shall be offered for sale, a tall young man is rudely separated from the rest by the man in the green coat, who unlocks the padlock chaining him to his fellows, fixing him instead to a leather leading-rein tied to his own wrist.

The enslaved man trembles and calls out to his companions, but the overseer orders him to be silent, following this with a slap that leaves an angry welt on the negro's face. Powerless to respond, his eyes express his outrage.

The man then picks out the next in line, a slim, dark-skinned woman about my age, handing her to a carrier in a brown smock and frayed straw hat whose waggon waits above the wharf.

As well as wearing collars, both negroes are shackled at the ankles so that even when no longer linked to the rest they walk with short and painful steps. Collars and shackles alike inflict red running sores which are dreadful to see, but their distress, expressed in sobs and groans, seems to arise less from bodily suffering than from the prospect of parting from one another. The man in green tugs at the negro to go with him along St-Augustine's-back, while the carrier points impatiently for the weeping girl to climb aboard his waggon.

No carrier could afford a black servant; I suppose he is sent to fetch her by some lord from Somerset or Gloucestershire. The pair shed piteous tears, clutching each other's hands despite their keeper's rough commands. The young man seeks to comfort his loved one with a torrent of words, their meaning alien to our ears but his agony plain enough.

How the man in charge of this fellow, who is as handsome and upstanding as the other is wizened and ill-favoured, can be so callous as to bellow at the prisoner and tear him from his grieving lady is more than I can fathom. Harsher still is the rude-looking carrier, for when the negress falls to her knees, pleading to be allowed to stay, he yanks her to her feet, livid with indignation, and kicks her towards his vehicle.

The lady cries out, clutching her belly with both hands. She is so thin that her condition has not been evident until now, but I judge her a few weeks before her time, and wonder how she endured a sea-voyage. Enraged, her lover lunges towards her, intent on protecting her, only to find himself the victim of the overseer's rage, who punches him to the ground and follows this with a savage blow to the negro's head with a pistol butt.

One or two spectators gasp at the gouts of blood that follow and the farmer gives up trying to bully the young woman, seizing and bundling her into the waggon. At this her lover emits a howl of such anguish that one or two of the onlookers around me murmur, and a joiner shakes his mallet and cries, 'For shame!'

Deaf to all protestors, the farmer jumps onto the driver's seat and lashes his horse so viciously the cart leaps forward. The overseer, meanwhile, busy yelling at us to mind our own business, fails to notice the negro hastening as fast as his fetters will allow in the wake of the moving cart. When the laughter of the audience at the sight of his hobbling progress alerts the attendant, he shrieks with rage and chases after the fellow, bringing him down with a blow that leaves him lifeless.

I should scarcely be surprised if the man in green did not proceed to shoot the negro, and perhaps he might have done if the sight of a gentleman dismounting from his horse did not interrupt his fit of rage.

The startled driver almost drops his weapon. 'Mr Tuffnell, Sir!'

'What is this, Roach? I trust you haven't lost one of my slaves already?' The mildness, even good humour, of the question, is in stark contrast with what I witnessed.

Roach hastens to explain himself. 'Forgive me, Sir, but yonder fellow has been the worst trouble of any blackamoor I ever brought ashore. Two hours in the long-boat while he writhed and cried and struggled and protested, then he threw an oar into the water, God knows how he contrived to do it, and near as dragged me overboard when we was in the middle of the river. I hope I haven't injured him to your detriment, Sir, but I say you ought to be glad he is quelled, at least for now.'

Mr Tuffnell is bright-eyed, cheerful, and attired in a smart black suit and neat silk shoes. It does not occur to him to question Roach's version of events. He simply bends to inspect the prone figure, and straightens up when the young man's eyelids flutter.

'Here.' Mr Tuffnell takes out a leather flask and lets a few drops splash the negro's face, nodding briskly as the man emits a groan. Satisfied, Mr Tuffnell gestures to Roach, who hastily steps forward and drags the moaning victim to his feet.

'Tell Mr Wharton to lock him in the warehouse. The sale can be postponed 'til he has cooled his heels. Hear that, fellow?' Mr Tuffnell speaks slowly and loudly to the negro. Then he winks at Roach, checks the fine gold timepiece at his waist, and whistles for his groom to bring his horse.

'Mr Tuffnell, Sir!' God help me, but before I have time to think the gentleman is looking at me in surprise. I believe he mistakes me for a beggar, for he pauses, sighs and fishes for his purse.

I point at the negro. 'Your charity should be kept for this unlucky man, Sir. Your servant beat him cruelly.'

Amusement ripples through the onlookers. I go on. 'He half-killed him, Sir. All because the man sorrowed at parting from his wife. The negro should see a surgeon, and this man should pay the fee.'

Mr Tuffnell stares at me for a moment, then barks with laughter. The little crowd has swelled now, and from the back comes a call: 'Out of the mouth of babes and sucklings.' Other onlookers murmur 'Aye', 'Well said', and someone advises, 'Fetch a surgeon.'

Mr Tuffnell decides to face down these critics, dismissing them with 'Be off with you all.' However, he offers the negro his flask again, and even hands him a handkerchief to staunch his wound.

Painfully, slowly, the negro responds, holding the handkerchief to his bleeding head and seeming to nod to Mr Tuffnell's brisk enquiry that he does well enough. Shortly afterwards the black man manages to take a shuffling step or two, and Mr Tuffnell mounts his horse, leaving Mr Roach to follow after him, holding the suffering slave by the leather strap he fixed to his collar when he picked him from the line.

The other slaves having long since departed, and the farmer's cart having left likewise, the crowd, realising that the show is over, begins to drift away. I am about to do likewise when a low whistle alerts me to a figure peering from the corner of a nearby building.

'Mr Espinosa!' There can be no mistaking the young clerk's long locks, black eyes, and air of earnest watchfulness. 'I am surprised to see you, Sir. I'd have thought you'd be hard at work in your counting-house.'

He does not answer, beckoning me with his finger on his lips. Puzzled, I follow him to a small courtyard behind the building, which must be a shop, though its doors and windows are boarded, and the yard itself has a gloomy air.

'What is it, Sir? I think I had better be on my way.' The place is dirty and confined, and I shiver to think what Liz would say if she could see me here in the company of a man I barely know.

His face is grave. 'Forgive me, but I must warn you, Miss Amesbury. That fellow who beat the negro is Mr Tuffnell's right-hand man. He's feared across Bristol for his ill temper, and I enjoin you to be wary of him.'

'Wary? What can he do to me?'

Mr Espinosa speaks with greater urgency. 'Miss Amesbury, you held Mr Roach to account, and he is likely to bear you a grudge for it. Believe me when I say that he would tie a boulder to your feet and toss you in the harbour if he could do it unobserved.'

'I don't believe you.' I jut my chin to show defiance, though my heart beats fast.

Mr Espinosa bites his inside lip. 'When I advised you to beware of Mrs Buckley I was right. Was I not?'

I feel my cheeks redden. 'Well, I thank you for your trouble, Sir. I will watch my back.' A thought strikes me. 'Mr Espinosa, it was your voice I heard just now, quoting from the *Book of Psalms*. Why do you advise me to take care when you yourself are reckless?'

He snorts faintly. 'Mr Roach didn't know it was I who spoke. When you have lived a little longer in this city you will learn that subtlety is the best, indeed the only way, to defend one's principles. Provoking a figure such as Mr Roach is unlikely to serve the interests of those subordinate to him.'

'Sir? You do talk very long-windedly.'

'I mean that openly attacking Mr Tuffnell's man is likely to cause more suffering to the negro. Told they are unfair, people will go to any lengths to prove it.'

'I think I understand. All the same, I don't regret doing what I did.'

For the first time during our encounter the young clerk smiles. 'You are brave and kind, Miss Amesbury. Only you must strive to temper those qualities with judiciousness.' He sees me hesitate, and amends his words good-humouredly. 'In a word, be *careful*.' Then the clerk replaces his hat, and checking in each direction to ensure no one observes him, walks away, leaving me to make my exit from the yard.

The rowing-boat is at its mooring, but all are gone when I emerge. I am glad to find the place deserted, and I tell myself sternly that I must not come here again, however long and dull my search for work may prove.

A Pair of Sharp Eyes

Chapter Nine

Saturday, 27th October, 1703

Later I changed tack, as sailors say, and called at back doors instead of street ones. Then, over supper, I was made to listen yet again as Liz and Bill agreed it was a crying pity our cottage burned down when it did. Better the disaster had been before a quarter day, as I should have been certain to find work if I had come to Bristol at Michaelmas. Or Christmas. Or Lady-day.

My plan to sift Liz over Davy Roxall's death is hopeless. The weather grows foul so we are rarely without Bill, and I doubt Liz would confide in me in any case. When I asked her in a whisper what she had done with the knife used to kill the lad she bade me be quiet, and said she had given it to Mr Elliott, out of reluctance to call upon the magistrates herself, and doubted the knife could throw light on the matter, being the kind used for flaying by housewives as well as butchers, skinners, tanners and so forth, and having no mark upon it that could help the magistrates find the man who left it in the bothy.

Sorry though I am to give up my wish to track down the murderer, it does not seem a likely prospect, now a day or two has passed. Indeed, when I look at the matter with cold reason I would be putting myself in mortal danger to follow such a course. There needs no proof that whoever did the deed will stop at nothing.

And yet I wish I could bring the guilty man to justice somehow. It may be the memory of my dead brother, but it grieves me to think that the slaughterer of those boys goes unpunished when other men hang for far less bloody crimes.

Running out of doors to call at, and wishing these notions were not jangling in my head, I do not turn my nose up at conversation with a ragged girl who falls into step with me on Corne-street. Her feet are bare, her face is smudged with ash, and she has a long, thin loaf of bread wedged under her arm.

'You're new,' she tells me.

'From Wiltshire.' I nod eastwards.

'Is that same as London?'

'Nearly.'

'You hungry?' She must be simple, for she brings forth the loaf and tears it into two. 'Go on, I got it for nothing. I cleaned out the ovens for the baker.'

The bread is dry and stale but the flavour good, and it is filling. Liz did not feed me this morning; the fire was out and she was late for Mr Elliott.

'I don't know when I last ate white bread. Thank you, young Miss.'

She tears off a bite. 'He puts chalk in his flour,' she tells me cheerfully.

'They will fine him then.'

'Not he.' The girl crosses bony fingers. 'He's like this with the aldermen. Bum-mates with 'em. Where you working?'

'Nowhere particular.'

Her sharp little face is shrewd. 'Get yourself to the quays. They're always looking for folk to fetch and carry. There's work for maids now. Mothers won't let their lads out of their sight. You've heard about the murders, have you? Seven boys in one year with their throats cut.' Her eyes gleam. 'Most of the sailors come into port were pirates once upon a time. Any hole is good enough for them.'

'I heard it was a pedlar doing it.'

'Truth is, no one knows who's doing it. Meanwhile, I earned three pence from errands yesterday.' The maid is certainly not right in the head, for she rummages in her bosom and shows me the coins with no thought I might rob her.

'I don't know Bristol yet. Perhaps they wouldn't trust me with their letters. You had better keep your money safe, young Miss.'

'Pah! They will.' She stuffs the coins back inside her dress. 'Here's a tip for you. Ask for Mr Wharton. Tell him you know Jane.' She taps her pointy nose. Then, as quickly as she sidled up to me, she is off, darting through the crowds around the market stalls.

A Pair of Sharp Eyes

I doubt if much good can come of advice from such a queer little creature. But the bread she shared becomes a fading memory as the day wears on, and by midday I reason that running errands is just what I should like to do, by way of learning the lanes and paths around the city, and earning money while I knock on doors.

Hardly have I gone a dozen yards along the waterfront when I spy a gentleman in a black coat and stove-hat, his mouth pursed in annoyance. His chin is clean-shaven, and he holds a paper which he flicks against his coat-skirts.

I curtsey to him, and the brown and white pointer in the doorway of his warehouse springs up as I approach.

'Can I carry that letter for you, Sir?'

'You might, except I don't know you. Do I?'

'No, Sir.' I make my voice higher than usual, hoping he takes me for younger than I am. 'My name is Coronation Amesbury, Sir. Late of Erlestoke Parish in Wiltshire, now of All-Saints, Bristol.'

'Well, Mistress Coronation.' He speaks with a half-smile, soothing the dog's head to quieten it. 'My errand-boy is sick and I have this letter for my wife who lives at the Hot-wells. Could you bring me back a receipt to prove you didn't lose my letter the minute my back was turned?'

'How much will you pay me?'

'A penny on your return,' says the factor drily. 'There may be other letters need carrying later, so don't set your price too high.' He frowns. 'Oh, very well, be off with you. I can find another willing soon enough.'

Just then a street-seller threads his way past with a tray of warm yeast buns, and my mouth waters.

'No, Sir. Thank you, Sir. I am glad of the work.' I put out my hand and the gentleman gives me the letter, a tightly folded sheet of yellow paper with the scarlet seal new and bright upon it.

The address is in a clear hand, but he assumes I cannot read.

'To Mrs E. Wharton, Crossways House, the Hot-wells,' he says, pronouncing carefully. 'Go west towards the River Avon, the house is a quarter of a mile beyond the city gates. Next to a green bordered by old beech trees.' He narrows his eyes, sceptical. 'You don't have the least notion where I mean.'

I straighten up, offended. 'I'm quick, Sir, I shall find it.'

He smiles despite himself. 'Be sure you do.' And he turns to a waiting carter and begins an earnest discussion over a delivery of hogsheads expected over an hour ago. I leave the carter blaming the cooper for the delay, and Mr Wharton cutting in to say he wants none of his excuses.

The road west out of the city is quieter than the one I came in by, and I hope the Hot-wells cannot be far when, half a mile or so after the quays, a sign points to another watering-place. 'Jacob's-wells' brings to mind Mr Espinosa, and I wonder whether there may be other 'Sons of Israel' as Mr Osmund styled them, living here in Bristol. I have seen none, so perhaps Mr Espinosa fled ill-treatment in London only to find himself friendless again, excepting his master Mr Sampson.

I conjure a picture of Mr Sampson. A brooding, heavy-built gentleman with a crusty manner and a soft spot in his stern old heart for Mr Espinosa. Or perhaps he bullies Mr Espinosa and owes him two years' wages, and sends him to London in all weathers and especially when the roads are bad.

I am spinning stories as fast as Mrs Jervis spins her wool. Most likely Jacob's-wells is a quarter Jews have made their own, just as in Wiltshire charcoal-burners have their cluster of dwellings at Lane-ends, and the bargees make settlements along the River Avon. In which case Mr Espinosa may be affianced to a pretty Jewess with eyes as dark as night and the two of them are soon to set up in Jacob's-wells in a neat house with glass windows and a brand-new feather bed.

I avow I would be very happy it were so, though I hope the lady is deserving of so pleasant and kind a gentleman.

Puzzling this out puts in the time until I leave the city walls behind and reach a stretch of green bordered by neat orchards, some apple trees but mostly pears. A trio of old men sit beneath a beech tree, puffing pipes and holding their feet out to the sun, and a straggle of children play under the eye of a bigger girl, a baby on her knee rolled so tightly in a shawl that nothing shows of it but a tuft of fierce black hair. I feel a pang of homesickness, it being much like Erlestoke on a quiet morning and most unlike the city just behind me, and the baby bringing to mind my brother as a babe-in-arms.

'Do you know which is Mrs Wharton's house?' I ask the girl. A number of four-square houses face the river, and one or two are new-built in a grander style, with great windows and tall flights of steps. She points to a cottage of red stone, ivy and woodbine clinging round its porch, the chimney pouring smoke. Not a simple cottage but not a gentleman's residence either, as is proved when the lady herself answers my knock.

She is young and slight, with dark hair showing under a white cap, and wears sprigged calico, yellow and green, with a green petticoat and a light green neckerchief and checked green and yellow shawl. A baby crows somewhere within the house and an older child sings a ballad out of tune. The walls of the passage are freshly painted and the flags covered with thick clean rushes; after dingy All-Saints'-yard I am quite dazzled.

'From Mr Wharton, Madam,' I say. She takes the letter eagerly, tears it open, and although it cannot be many hours since she saw her husband, her eyes fill with tears as she scans the message. Then she folds the paper and keeps it in her hand.

'Will there be an answer, Madam? I am bid bring a receipt.'

'No answer.' She tears the corner from the letter and marks it with a pencil hanging at her waist. 'This will do as proof you found me.' She glances once more at the contents of the letter before sighing and tucking it in her bosom. Her face takes on a wry cast. 'Don't say you are waiting for me to read my message aloud, child?'

I turn pink as I remember Liz's accusation yesterday. 'Excuse me, Madam, I hope you don't think I wish to pry. I only wondered what the "E" is for.'

She ignores this. 'There is nothing in my letter I need to hide, it is perfectly dull to anyone save myself. Mr Wharton kindly writes to reassure me that a dear friend of mine is safe and well. She left for London some weeks ago.'

After this pointed frankness I am hardly able to meet her eye.

'Mother! Mother, hurry!' A high-pitched cry rings through the house, as if the child who warbled so cheerfully has met with an accident.

'Heavens.' Mrs Wharton grabs her skirts and races down the passage, and after a moment's doubt I follow on her heels. The screams grow louder; I fully expect to discover her little son smothered in flames from the kitchen fire, or standing in a pool of blood.

We burst in to find a boy of five years or so struggling to release his baby sister from a wooden feeding-chair, her head trapped between the hoop that holds her in and the seat itself. Her face is grey.

'Darling!' In a single movement Mrs Wharton moves her son aside and seizes the child, contriving to pull her gently out, though her little arm is entangled as well as her head and shoulder. Her body is lifeless and her mother wracked with fear, though she is calm enough to shake the child and tap her cheek and begin blowing on her face in a desperate effort to rouse her. The boy sobs lustily, and perhaps the sound is what brings the baby back to life, for she gives a sudden piercing cry, throws out her arms, and in the next moment the kitchen fills with the clamour of two howling children, added to which Mrs Wharton bursts into happy tears and I find myself gabbling words of comfort, taking it upon myself to fetch a chair for Mrs Wharton then lifting the boy into my arms, where he falls on my shoulder and weeps as naturally as if he has known me many a year.

When at last the baby is quiet and her brother lets me dry his tears, Mrs Wharton, still trembling, bids me sit.

'How lucky you were here to help us,' she says, dabbing her own face and laughing a little at her confusion. 'Won't you stop a little longer, Mistress, and let us recover?' She draws a few deep breaths and kisses the baby on the crown of her lace-capped head, trying despite her shaking hands to calm herself. 'Master Harry and Baby Emma were about to take their morning milk. I'll write my husband a note, so he knows why you were delayed. Does that answer your fear of being thought a laggard?'

She tries to sound light-hearted but her face is clammy, and I do not like to leave her so soon after her fright, so I thank her and watch while she goes to the cupboard and brings out a jug and three wooden bowls, and divides the milk between them, taking care to fill each equally. Then she fetches a china feeding-cup and pours the contents of one bowl into it, all the while gazed upon by her little daughter, who seems to have suffered no lasting effects from her mishap, and gulps her milk as soon as the cup is in her grasp.

It is my first chance to look about, and I note that the kitchen fire is fallen into an ashy orange glow as though lit hours ago. Apart from a strange-shaped candlestick on the window-ledge there is nothing that does not remind me of home, though the house is bigger than our cottage. The little garments airing by the fire are embroidered with the same designs my brother wore, flowers and suns and moons and stars picked out in red; and the well-stocked shelves glimpsed in the pantry are those of any housewife. For a moment, though Bristol is where I wish to be, I would give much to be back in Erlestoke for an hour, aged five years old and waited on by my mother in her own neat kitchen.

Mrs Wharton places down the bowls, and her son follows his sister's example and sets to swallowing greedily, contemplating me with grave grey eyes over the rim of his vessel. The milk is fresh and thick and sweet, and I empty my own bowl quicker than I intended.

'So,' Mrs Wharton says, plying her jug again and shaking her head to dismiss my refusal of another helping. 'I was asking if you were from Gloucester. I suppose I should first have asked your name.'

It is plain to me that Mrs Wharton is lonely, or why would she be so well disposed towards an errand-girl?

'Coronation Amesbury, Madam. I took a long journey of my own a day or two ago. I joined the London stagecoach at Calne.'

'And my friend was on the London stagecoach in September, going the other way.'

'Forgive me, Madam. It is hard to say farewell to those we love.'

She stares, as if deciding whether or not she can speak openly to one of my station.

'I am a Jewess,' she says finally, picking up her son's empty bowl and gazing into it. 'My friend Hannah was Jewish too, and we were happy in each other's company. There are few of our tribe in this part of the kingdom—indeed more blackamoors live in Bristol than Jews do.'

'Tribe, Madam?'

'It is a word Gentiles use when speaking of Jews.' She sounds a little bitter.

'I know nothing about Jews; I never met any where I grew up.' I am about to say that I have met a Jew since leaving Erlestoke, but the baby begins to hiccup, and Mrs Wharton, still nervous, turns her attention to the child. Mopping the baby's milky hands and chin with the hem of her bib she says tonelessly:

'You may wonder why we live so far from the city. It's safer for us here. Our simple neighbours are less inclined to call names after my children or leave unsigned notes beneath the door suggesting I go elsewhere. My husband is not a Jew, you see, and this is what some dislike, his being married to a woman who doesn't share his faith.'

'They should mind their own business. Bristol folk are a mix of Welsh and Spanish and all sorts, so why do they heap insult on you? From ignorance.'

She laughs. 'You speak as I would have done when I was young. How old are you, may I ask?'

'Fourteen.'

'And I am twenty-three, and must seem old to you.'

I begin to feel uncomfortable with this lady's frank way of speaking. Her loneliness must be deep indeed.

'No indeed, Madam. I have a sister of twenty-four in Wiltshire, and my Bristol sister is twenty-two. They are not old and nor are you.'

'Well, thank you.'

Master Harry, having finished his milk and made a thorough job of transferring his milk moustache to his smock, decides to have his share of the conversation.

'Do you know my father?' he asks, resting his head on the table so that I am obliged to bend my neck sideways to meet his gaze.

'I have met him. Briefly, that is.'

Next Harry, having slid the length of the table at the risk of grazing his ear, tumbles to the floor.

'My father is important, is he not?' He stands up and turns a circle, arms outstretched. 'He is a shipping agent, the best in the whole of Bristol.' The thought makes him spin again, and once again he lands in a heap. I wait for Mrs Wharton to chide him for risking his clothes, but she merely sighs as if to say boys will be boys.

'I'm sure your father is an excellent agent,' I say, remembering Mr Wharton's authority in speaking to the luckless carter.

'My father works for Mr Tuffnell, one of Bristol's richest gentlemen. Do you know him?'

My heart jolts, but I glance down at my calico petticoat with its mud-stained hems, and laugh. 'If Mr Tuffnell is rich I am hardly likely to know him.'

'You might have carried a letter to him before the one you brought Mother. Ha!' the little fellow exclaims, triumphantly snatching up the paper where Mrs Wharton dropped it in her agitation.

'Harry.' She sends him a reproving look and, chastened, her son hands the letter back.

'Time you went outside and helped yourself to fresh air, young man.'

I take the hint, and rise to my feet.

'Mr Tuffnell is a famous merchant with a great house in Wine-street,' Harry says, rushing his words before his mother can stop him, 'and last year he wed a beautiful lady with hair down to her waist. It is a great sadness they have no children,' he concludes solemnly, reminding me of the way my brother liked to repeat his elders' gossip even when he scarcely understood it.

It is Mrs Wharton's turn to blush. 'Enough. Out in the yard now, find your hobby-horse. Leave the door open so I can see you.' When he is out of hearing she turns to me. 'I should be grateful if you forget Harry's thoughtless words, Mistress. Bristol is small and it doesn't become us to tittle-tattle about those we depend on for our livelihoods.'

'Of course, Madam. Thank you kindly for the milk.'

'My husband is always in need of young people willing to carry letters and messages, so we may see you again.'

'Yes. Though I hope in time to find a place.'

'I'm sure you shall. There are plenty of openings in Bristol. One thing ...' She stops.

'What, Ma'am?'

'Be cautious. Don't feel obliged to take the first place offered to you.'

'Oh?'

'Not all masters and mistresses treat their servants well. In Bristol especially, where profit is king and some servants are worked almost as hard as slaves in Jamaica and Barbados. Try to judge the household before you join it.'

'Thank you, Madam, I will.'

Out in the yard Mrs Wharton watches from the doorway as I rumple Harry's curls and offer his hobby-horse a make-believe apple and tell him what a clever brother he is.

'Your father will be proud, Harry, when he learns how you raised the alarm and tried to free Baby Emma. You helped to save her life.'

'Will you tell him so?'

'You will want to tell the story yourself, when he returns this evening.'

'Sometimes Mr Tuffnell keeps Father on business far into the night, and then he is only home when I am fast asleep, and gone again next morning. I do not like Mr Tuffnell, even if he is the richest merchant in all of Bristol. Indeed, I hate him.'

'Ssh, Master Harry, your mother will not want to hear you say such things.'

'Why? She hates him too, though she pretends to like him.'

'I'm sure she does not. Hatred is a wicked thing, and your mother is a good lady.'

'Ha! You are wrong,' says the boy, and I leave him whipping his hobby-horse instead of whipping Mr Tuffnell.

I think over our exchange as I make my way towards the city gates. Mrs Wharton looked uncomfortable when she offered her advice. I wonder which households she has in mind, and how she comes by her information, living far from the city and unlikely, I would say, to have friends among its servants.

As for young Harry's judgment of Mr Tuffnell, I cannot think that gentleman as severe an employer as the boy says, else surely Mr Wharton would seek employment elsewhere. Of Mrs Tuffnell all I know is that she is comely and has amazing long hair and wishes to bear a child, none of which suggests a lady who ill-uses those who work for her, though I suppose if she is unhappy she might be bad-tempered and her moods hard to fathom.

I smile to myself for running on this way. When I have done inventing Mrs Tuffnell, beautiful, barren and forlorn, I shall put her in league with Mr Sampson, who has not paid his clerk for twice twelve months, and feeds him on nought but ships' biscuits bought at cost from Mr Tuffnell's hard-nosed agent Mr Wharton.

Now I pick up speed, for Mr Wharton will be questioning what has taken me so long. I hope he is less tight-fisted than I fancy him to be, and pays me promptly, and in full.

Chapter Ten

Mr Wharton is busy with another delivery when I return. The sweet fragrance of sugar hangs in the air. I can taste it as I breathe and wonder how Mr Wharton resists sampling the contents of a hogshead once it is open for inspection.

I curtsey. 'Here is your receipt Sir, from Mrs Wharton.' *From your wife who is kinder than I thought she'd be, having met you, Sir.*

'Thank you.' He examines the paper and returns to his work.

I cough as discreetly as I can. 'We agreed a penny, Sir.'

He pauses, chisel in hand, then reaches slowly into his pocket and passes me a coin. 'Come back quicker next time.'

My spirits leap. 'Next time?'

'I'll have another letter to despatch by three o'clock.'

'Certainly, Sir.' And I speed away before he thinks of some reason why he will not need me after all.

When I have eaten my fill of warm wheaten bread while sitting on a garden wall near Baldwin-street, shooing off the sparrows who would like to share my feast, I walk back to Mr Wharton's warehouse and find the agent where I left him, stooped over his desk with his pointer sleeping on his feet. He folds his letter and raises a finger to bid me wait. Then he holds a length of sealing-wax above the flame of his rush-light, and drips wax upon the paper before impressing it with the brass seal hanging at his waist.

Once I watched a person dear to me seal a letter with red wax. The memory causes a pain within me, and my hand steals to my heart. Fortunately, Mr Wharton is too business-like to notice.

'This way,' he says, marching me to the wharf. His dog, displaced from its warm resting-place, slinks between two hogsheads to escape the bitter wind. Mr Wharton points across the river. 'Over that bridge, then follow the quays to the Sign of the Hope and Anchor. That brick and timber house next those cranes, d'you see? Ask for Mr Cheatley's man, Harry Dunmore. Tell Mr Dunmore you'll wait until he has been to his master and brought back the papers we require Mr Cheatley to sign.'

So close to the river the Hope and Anchor cannot be respectable. 'I am willing, Sir, except I don't care to set foot in a harbour alehouse.' His face darkens and I add quickly, 'But perhaps someone can ask Mr Dunmore to step outside on my behalf?'

'How you go about it does not concern me. I pay for the result.' His tone is somewhat kinder than his words, and he softens the blow when he shows me two pennies. 'These will be your reward. Only if he gives you the documents of course.'

'Of course. Thank you, Sir.'

'John! Good day to you!'

A figure salutes Mr Wharton as he hurries down the quays. A slight young man with long dark locks of hair beneath his hat, and a notebook in his hand. A moment later Mr Espinosa's face mirrors the astonishment writ on mine.

Recovering himself, Mr Espinosa removes his hat. 'Miss Amesbury!' In contrast to his manner at our last encounter, his voice is warm and open. Mr Wharton looks amazed between us.

'Good day, Mr Espinosa,' I say.

Mr Espinosa laughs at Mr Wharton's puzzlement. 'Henry, this young lady was a fellow passenger when I came down from London.' He points at the letter in my hand. 'I see you've found employment, Miss Amesbury, if not the domestic situation you were hoping for?'

It is my heart-felt wish that Mr Espinosa had not discovered me about to scurry off on the orders of his friend.

'A stop-gap measure, Sir. I have tried a great many households to no avail.'

Mr Espinosa's reply is as kind as ever. 'It may be difficult to obtain a place between quarter-days.'

Mr Wharton nods as earnestly if the question relates not to some rag-tag errand-girl, but to a mutual acquaintance.

'Indeed … I would add that at this time of year some vacancies are in households where conditions for the servants are worse than they ought to be.'

He and Mr Espinosa seem to avoid each other's eye. I begin to wonder what monsters there are in Bristol if servants are treated so unfairly.

Then Mr Wharton recollects himself, gesturing at my letter. 'Forgive me, Aaron, Miss Amesbury was about to take a message for me.'

'And I came to ask if Esther had any message for my sister.'

Esther! I had guessed Elizabeth or Eleanor.

'Only that she is thankful for your sister's letter, and will write to her before the week is out.'

Mr Espinosa nods and settles his hat on his head as if to leave, and Mr Wharton turns to me, though I see him trying to contain his impatience for Mr Espinosa's sake.

'Shall I take the letter for you now, Sir?'

'Miss Amesbury. Your servant.' He bows as gravely as if I am a lady, not a ragamuffin errand-girl.

I had thought Mr Espinosa about to depart, but I reach the bridge and glance back to find the gentlemen's heads bowed in discussion.

My mother often used to say *The world doesn't only spin round you, Corrie.* For all I know, Mr Wharton and Mr Espinosa are not agreeing over Miss Amesbury's failure to find respectable work but forgot me before my back was turned. Indeed, the more times I look back to see the gentlemen still conversing, the more I believe Mr Espinosa's query about his sister was a ruse, and that he and Mr Wharton have some business matter to debate.

***

Picturing a tavern crammed with roistering sailors, I wonder what Liz would think if she could see me. But to my good fortune I find a man seated on a bench outside the Hope and Anchor, and when I say I am seeking Mr Dunmore he pulls his pipe from his mouth and says deliberately: 'Then you'll be pleased to hear you've found him.'

I explain my commission and Mr Dunmore, a stocky, short-necked man whose wig is too small for his great, shining crown, listens with a mocking look, then takes a long draught from his tankard and wipes his mouth. 'Return to your master and tell him Mr Cheatley has no intention of signing, it having been a gentleman's agreement between himself and Mr Tuffnell, and signing therefore sup-er-flu-ous to the business.'

'But why won't he sign?' The thought of the tuppence I stand to lose spurs me on to embroider what the agent said. 'Mr Wharton wishes me to remind you, Sir, that it is usual practice.'

'Like I said, it's superfluous. Which is as much as to say, Mr Cheatley don't need to, he don't wish to and he won't.'

His stubbornness is most provoking. 'Excuse me, Sir, have you asked Mr Cheatley?'

Mr Dunmore holds his pipe at arm's length and lifts his eyebrows so high I think that paltry wig of his might tumble off his head.

'You brought me a message, girl; I have a message you may give to Mr Wharton, namely next time he has a request he should step across here and deliver it in person. Mr Cheatley deals with the master, not his whelp.'

I shan't let a low, crooked, ill-looking fellow such as this speak as if I were no better than the jackdaw that listens to our conversation from the chimney pot.

'Mr Wharton will be very disappointed, Sir.' Hoping that Mr Tuffnell's name will carry more weight than his agent's, I add boldly, 'and so will Mr Tuffnell, for Mr Tuffnell takes a particular interest in this matter.'

'Do he? And what say we to that? We're not surprised.' Mr Dunmore bellows with laughter and knocks back the last of his ale, setting down the tankard on the ground and folding his arms. Then he draws a deep breath and closes his eyes as if to take a nap.

I wish I could think of some rejoinder to quash Mr Dunmore, but none presents itself, so I turn and begin my journey back. I have no idea what I might say to Mr Wharton. I rehearse several fine phrases, such as 'Mr Dunmore is a very rude, obstinate fellow, Sir,' and 'I much regret to say that Mr Dunmore is the kind of man who brings disgrace upon his master with the manner in which he conducts his business.' I settle on, 'Mr Dunmore refuses to do business with us Sir, and I am sorry but I tried my best.' It is more civil than declaring that Mr Dunmore is a scoundrel, and his master Mr Cheatley as dishonest as his name implies.

The warehouse, however, is locked on my return, and Mr Wharton nowhere to be seen. The tears I was too proud to shed when Mr Dunmore mocked me threaten to overspill when I reflect I have missed my chance of earning more this afternoon; and with that thought I make my tired way back to All-Saints'-yard, readying myself for Liz's disappointment at my paltry wage, and the insults I am likely to endure on the subject from Brother Bill.

A Pair of Sharp Eyes

Chapter Eleven

Monday, 29ᵗʰ October, 1703

'Is the mistress of the house in need of any servant?'

The plain-faced maid at the yard door twists her mouth into a sneer. I should have thought twice before trying for a place in Queen-square, but I dreamt last night of Miss Bridget Lamborne, and woke to the thought that I am good as she. I am certainly better than this buck-toothed baggage, who only shifted to answer the door when I had knocked three times.

'If my lady were in need of a servant she wouldn't wait for 'em to come calling like a tinker. I'm forbid to speak to any who take the liberty of importuning, so if you'll excuse me, I have work to do.' She tosses the dirty contents of a bucket into the street, narrowly missing my skirts, and bangs the door in my face.

Telling myself that Queen-square is sure to harbour more than its share of the exacting unkind masters and mistresses I have heard so much about, I walk back to the harbour. I do not have far to go before I encounter Mr Wharton striding down the quay.

I hasten to explain myself.

'I came to find you after speaking with Mr Dunmore, Sir, but you was gone. Mr Dunmore refused to speak to his master. He took your letter but said plainly that Mr Cheatley would never sign any agreement. I did try to alter Mr Dunmore's opinion, Sir, but he forbore to listen.'

Mr Wharton shakes his head impatiently. 'Why are you late this morning? You must take a message to the master of the *Prudence* immediately. The ship is due to sail tomorrow at first light.' He hurries me along the quay. 'See the Guineaman?' Mr Wharton points at the mouth of the river where among half-a-dozen smaller sailing vessels lies a three-mast cargo ship, its sails neatly furled. 'That's the *Prudence*. Follow the bank until you reach her long-boat—the skipper is a Mr Gip. You'll know him by his linen waistcoat and long brown coat. He's on lookout today for final messages and supplies. Tell him I sent you and he'll row you to the ship. There, ask for the master himself, Captain Stiles.'

'But Sir, I can't go on board a ship.' For the first time it strikes me how reckless I have been, undertaking work no respectable person would consider.

Mr Wharton gestures at the quays. The only people in sight are labouring men and carters. 'A fortune hangs in the balance—the whole purpose of the voyage is in peril. I'd go myself if I weren't due to meet with Mr Tuffnell. Great heavens, girl, Aaron told me you had enterprise and spirit. You will be there and back in two hours.'

My pride is piqued. 'Thank you, Sir, I have crossed the Avon by ferry-boat without ill effect.' Then I falter. 'Though ferry-boats don't serve as home to a crew of sailors who know they won't see land for weeks. Why can't Mr Gip deliver the letter?'

'Because Mr Gip is a law unto himself and I don't trust him.' Seeing my face, Mr Wharton regrets his candour. 'I mean of course that he is a very sound long-boat captain with an unsurpassed knowledge of the river, but he is not the kind of man I wish to place in charge of a document vital to the successful prosecution of a year-long voyage. My apologies, I confuse you. I mean that Mr Gip is like many seamen, fond of his rum, and might not scruple to throw my letter to the winds.'

'And what of me, Sir? What if he decides to throw me to the winds? Or leaves me aboard and rows away before the ship sets sail?'

Mr Wharton grinds his teeth. 'Very well, here's sixpence—a whole sixpence, mind—which I will give you now, if you do as I ask. Another thing I will say, if you are still reluctant. Mr Espinosa stands to lose if this affair is not resolved. I know you respect Mr Espinosa, and he helped you in your hour of need. I'm sure you would be pleased to repay the debt and help him in your turn.'

I cannot really hold out any longer under this barrage of ready coin and urgent persuasion, and besides, I have yearned to be on the water ever since I came to Bristol. Although Mr Wharton is blunt and short-tempered, I do not really imagine he would put me in danger, especially when Mr Espinosa would hear of any evil that befalls me.

'Very well. I do owe a debt to Mr Espinosa.'

'And you would like to earn a sixpence.'

'And I would like to earn a sixpence.'

He drops it in my palm then hands me his precious letter, biting his lip as if he is no more sure of my success than I am. Out here in the pinching wind he looks younger and less certain of himself than he generally does as master of Mr Tuffnell's affairs.

'Have confidence, Sir. I will put your letter in Captain Stiles's hand myself, and Providence will go with me and bring me safely back again.'

I perceive a faint embarrassment in his features, but he is plainly relieved to hear me sound so confident. 'When Providence has done so, be sure to come and find me. I'll return to the warehouse after my appointment.'

***

By a wooden jetty on the opposite bank of the river stands a lean man in a dark brown coat that reaches to his ankles. He surveys the river broodingly, arms folded, eyes narrowed. He reminds me of a cormorant watching for its prey, or a hunched night-heron with a dagger beak: his nose is long and bony, and he wears his collar turned up against the cold.

Nearby a lad stacks crates ready for lading. I keep my voice low. 'Is that Mr Gip?'

He nods. 'Watch it, Miss, he has a temper.' The lad sets down the crate he was carrying on his shoulder, and heads back for the next.

I pick my way down the jetty, wishing I had thought to wear my pattens. The mud sucks and clogs my feet with every step. 'Sir?' I try to sound at ease. 'I was bid by Mr Wharton to take this to the *Prudence*.'

Mr Gip checks the seal of the letter, then looks me sourly up and down. His face is so gaunt I am conscious of his skull-bones. I wait for him to refuse to take me, but after a moment he pushes the letter back into my hand and nods at a row-boat tied at the foot of the jetty. A quantity of brackish water lies in the bottom, along with two bottles of liquor jammed in a wicker basket, a cask of wine, another basket full of dirty potatoes, and three items that alarm me though I pretend I do not see them. A cutlass and a pair of pistols.

'Well?' he asks.

Below us the boat bumps and thumps against the timbers. The gap with the jetty is wider than I would like. I hold up my skirts and try to look as if I climb into a long-boat every day.

'I would be obliged if you could keep the rope taut, Sir.'

'You mean the painter.' He continues to hold the rope slack in his hand as if intent on vexing me. My descent is cumbersome; the ladder fixed to the jetty is wet and crusted with barnacles and I step with the utmost caution, being determined not to lose my shoes.

'So. Another saved from drowning,' he says drily, as I attain the boat and sink onto a bench. 'You'll have to use a rope-ladder to reach the ship. I hope you can do it in those clothes.' He implies the absurdity of wearing a dress to go to sea.

Before I have time to answer Mr Gip leaps into the bows, making no use of the ladder nor taking any heed of my yelp as the boat lurches under his weight, then seizes the oars and begins to row with great energy, and in a moment we are free of the other long-boats crowding the riverbank and out in the harbour, the wind behind us and droplets of water flying in our faces from the motion of the oars and the slicing of the prow through the waves. The river is thick with vessels through which Mr Gip weaves skilfully, paddling first with one oar then the other to avoid the obstacles to our progress, until we reach a stretch of water free from shipping. On each side the city rises directly from the river, a jumble of low houses to the south, and to the north the view is crowded with church spires and market crosses and, towering over all, the pinnacles of the cathedral. There is so much to see I forget to be alarmed until a sudden wave rocks us sideways and I wonder how it would be if Mr Gip took it in his head to push me overboard, or a gust of wind capsized the craft. But I need not worry because Mr Gip shows not the smallest interest in me, and after a brief interval the *Prudence* looms up, and for the first time I feel sick not from the motion of the boat, or imaginary dangers, but at the real hazard I am about to face in scaling such a vessel.

Mr Gip stands the oars upright in the locks, and both of us contemplate the ladder dangling from the deck. It is made entirely of fraying rope.

'I love to climb a tree,' I reply, determined to deny Mr Gip the entertainment of seeing me afraid. Though a tree does not flap and twist like this ladder does. The first time I lunge for it the wind whips it out of reach.

'Best tuck your skirts into your stockings,' says Mr Gip with a leer. Reluctantly I follow this advice and gather my courage to catch hold of the rope. Providence arrives in the shape of a mariner who, noticing the long-boat, leans out from an upper deck and calls down through cupped hands.

'Wait, Miss. We'll fetch the steps.' His head disappears, and no time he and a fellow crew member lower a stout wooden ladder over the side of the deck.

'There, Miss. Keep a tight hold, and don't look down.'

I tell myself I can climb a wooden ladder even if I must do it under the malicious eye of Mr Gip. Taking hold of the rungs and placing my feet on the lowest I focus on gaining the top as fast as possible. By dint of keeping my eyes on the step directly above I manage to quell the dizziness which would be fatal if it overcame me.

My palms are moist and my face must be pale, and truthfully, I could kneel and kiss the boards beneath my feet when I reach the deck, but the sailor kindly makes no remark on my trembling appearance as, very gentleman-like, he helps me down.

'Welcome aboard, Miss. Bravely done.'

I wipe the sweat from my face and try in vain to smooth my hair which the breeze has tugged from under my cap. The ship's timbers creak and the horizon shifts slowly as the vessel rides the swell. From the rigging a sailor watches me grip the balustrade as I try to find my balance. Such a man is braver and more agile than a steeplejack, and it makes me queasy to see him shin up even higher until he swings a leg over a cross-piece and begins rapidly to stitch some tear in the furled sail invisible to those below.

Dragging my eyes from the man perched high above our heads, I fumble for my letter. 'I bring a message from Mr Wharton for your captain.'

'Mr Wharton's lucky to catch him, we set sail tomorrow. Captain Stiles is with his lieutenant below the quarter deck, if you care to come this way.' The friendly mariner sets off towards the stern with the wide-legged gait I have observed among seamen, but he is nimble, being more accustomed to navigating the clutter of ropes and cleats than I am, and before I catch him up an old man with skin like greased leather staggers towards us, clutches my arm, and says, his breath hot and pungent:

'You remind me of my little sweetheart what I never saw since I left Portsmouth in '83. She was a dainty blossom like you.'

My rescuer doubles back and yanks his hand away. 'Let go of her, Mick—if the master sees you he'll sentence you for being drunk on duty. Make yourself scarce until you're sober, man. Excuse him, Miss, he's not a bad fellow, only he likes his can of flip. Don't mind all the noise, the shrouds are being readied and the bosun's overseeing a last repair of the rigging.' He gestures to the back of the ship, where tiered decks give way at last to one that is open, and overshadowed by a mast thick as my waist. 'That's the mizzenmast, Miss, what we call aft. Mind out, Miss.' A length of massy timber swings across our path.

I have just recovered from the near-blow when two men barge past dragging a huge water cask, and another lumbers up with a hencoop on his back.

'Is it always as busy as this?' I ask my companion.

'The day before sailing it is. How do?' He salutes one of his fellows, a slight, beardless man in a black cap and breeches stiff with pitch.

'Where are you sailing to, Sir?' I ask, while my eyes are drawn to the rigging as the man with the cap swarms upwards like a squirrel.

'Calabar, Miss. West coast of Africa. Did you note how low we sit? The hold is full of metal.'

'Metal?' I wonder how such a small, graceful ship contrives to stay afloat.

'Your African prince is a great lover of things metal, Miss. Pewter bowls, pipe beads and bugle beads, copper and iron bars. And muskets and fuzees and blunderbusses, for use in their infernal wars. Six hundred tons we carried when we made the journey last year. And brought back three hundred hogsheads of sugar and two hundred of tobacco from the West Indies. She's one of the tidiest vessels in Bristol, the *Prudence*, for her length.'

'Whose ship is she, Sir?'

The question surprises him.

'Mr James Tuffnell's, of course. There are others in the consortium, but he's the principal. You'll know his name.'

'I've heard it, Sir. Did another vessel bring his slaves ashore this week?'

'Mr Tuffnell has shares in all sorts of business. I daresay he likes to import a few slaves now and then, when one of his ships sails from the Indies. He's among Bristol's most successful merchants, Mr Tuffnell. And his captain Mr Stiles is a shrewd master, as you'll see when you meet him.'

'I'm glad I met you first, Sir.'

He taps his nose good-humouredly. 'Talk to old Wilks, Miss, for a sound education in all things concerning Bristol shipping. You're from Salisbury, ain't you?'

'How can you tell?'

'Can't, Miss. I had you down as a Highland lass.' His face is poker-straight. 'I grew up near Chippenham, that's how.'

'I met some girls from Chippenham on my way to Bristol,' I say, following him up a short flight of steps. The ship is finely carved, many of the decorations gaudily painted and some gilded. Everywhere smells powerfully of the sea, that rotten, salty tang I know from the quays; yet the ship itself is clean, her decks scrubbed and the glass in the cabin windows polished to a shine. 'Miss Lamborne and her sister Jane—perhaps you know them?' But Mr Wilks is intent on bringing me to his master, and without replying, he unfastens a studded door and shows me into a room panelled and furnished much as if we were on dry land, well-sized, with homely comforts and only the lowness of the ceiling hinting at our situation. A smell of brandy hangs in the air, along with beeswax and a whiff of mildew.

Two gentlemen are sitting at a table and barely glance up as we enter. A pair of heavy tomes lie open between them, and the walls are covered in sea charts. From his braided cap and epaulettes and serious air I take the elder man to be Captain Stiles, and it seems the other writes in one of the great volumes at his dictation. After a few minutes' respectful listening to latitudes and leagues and forecasts, both of us standing with hands clasped, Mr Wilks clears his throat, prompting Captain Stiles to look up.

'What?' he barks.

'Young lady from Mr Wharton, Sir,' says Mr Wilks, 'thank you, Sir,' whereupon he retreats, drawing the door smartly shut behind him.

'Well?' Mr Stiles's face indicates that he is far from impressed to find a female on board his vessel.

'Letter for you, Sir.' I present the item.

Captain Stiles pushes out his bottom lip. 'It's fortunate for you I'm not superstitious,' he says, reaching for a pen-knife. 'Ah well, I daresay Mr Wharton knows me to be a rational man.'

Humming genially, he prises up the seal and spreads the letter out. His breathing, silent at first, becomes faster as he scans the lines. Then he rubs his forehead and leans back in his red plush chair.

'Sir?' asks the lieutenant, whereupon the captain jerks upright.

'That bastard Cheatley!' he bursts out. 'He's altered the prices of his iron and pewter after lading. Blasted hypocrite! Son-of-a-bitch! To treat Mr Tuffnell with such contempt after all these years. Not to mention the rest of us.' The enraged captain brings his fist down on the table, and the brandy glasses nearly topple with the force.

'What reason does he give, Sir?' asks the lieutenant. Judging by his smooth, pale chin he is young, though his wig and uniform lend authority to his appearance. The captain picks up the letter, his fingers trembling with rage.

'"Fresh connections in London,"' he recites. 'Offering better terms, presumably, than Mr Tuffnell could six months ago when the deal was made. Damn the man, how are we to trade with the coast-tribes knowing we cannot make a profit?'

'We could turn away some of the crew, Sir. One or two would be no loss.'

'Mick, you mean? The rest are good men, and we need them on the Middle Passage. We can't exercise the negroes without sufficient hands to sluice the decks and prevent them from rebellion. Blast Cheatley, I never trusted him. Here, girl.' He scratches a hasty message on the reverse of the paper and folds it over. 'Take this to Mr Tuffnell, and tell him he cannot be more enraged than I am.' Before I have time to think of a reason why I would really rather not deliver a letter to Mr Tuffnell, the captain nods to the lieutenant to show me out.

Bless Mr Wilks, for he has stood nearby the captain's cabin, chewing on a plug of tobacco and waiting to escort me to the ship's side.

'Thought I'd better cool my heels 'til you was done, Miss. I'll see you down the ladder, don't doubt it. We won't let you plummet off and drown in Bristol mud. Now where's this meant for now?' He peers at my letter.

'Wine-street.' I make sure to sound casual, though my heart patters at the thought of meeting Mr Tuffnell. He is sure to remember my outburst over his right-hand man.

'Mr Tuffnell! You are a lucky maid. He's thought a handsome fellow, though you are too late, you know. He was married a year ago or more.'

'So I hear.'

'To a beautiful young lady with pots of gold to add to his own. One of the richest couples in Bristol.' The seaman chuckles, and I wonder what he would say if he knew the contents of Mr Wharton's letter.

'Can I ask, Mr Wilks, are the Tuffnells decent folk as well as rich?'

He stops, surprised, and the shadow of a seabird overhead crosses his face as he considers.

'Christians, you mean? Well now, it's said Mr Tuffnell ordered a new coach last month, reason being to carry him and his lady to church on dirty winter mornings.'

'But I meant is he a good man? Is he kind?'

'Too kind, some would say. He gave his wife a negro page-boy on her wedding day. Mr Tuffnell is famed for his devotion to his wife, you never saw such a liberal husband, folk say.'

I see I will get nowhere with Mr Wilks when it comes to an impartial judgment of Mr Tuffnell's character.

'Ah, I know how it is,' he says, seeing my pursed lips. 'You're after a place in Bristol, and hope to work for rich folk.'

'I don't seek luxury, Mr Wilks. I only want to earn an honest living.' And a little more besides, I add silently.

'And where better to find it than Bristol? But as for Mr Tuffnell, don't raise your hopes. Most of Bristol would like to work for him.'

'Really?'

'Yes, indeed they would.'

Just as I feared, climbing down requires more care than climbing up, but I am growing used to ladders, and a few minutes finds me safely in the boat along with my resentful pilot Mr Gip, who points for me to sit behind him this time, no doubt to stop me talking. I am content to sit quiet, and with his back towards me am able to read the words scrawled by Captain Stiles on the outside of Mr

A Pair of Sharp Eyes

Wharton's letter. The ink is faint but I have no difficulty making out the inscription, though its meaning eludes me: *Given our readiness for sailing, I enjoin you to say we will meet Mr C's revised terms. Tight-packing will make up the shortfall.*

I pull my cloak around me, cold after the fug of the captain's cabin and my descent to the long-boat, and as we travel down the harbour and the city draws close, I ponder the captain's words. *Tight-packing.* Surely with the *Prudence* ready to sail no cargo may added now. Yet what else can the captain mean? The mystery is beyond me to solve and I put it out of mind, concluding that I have no understanding or experience of sea-faring, and must assume these men know what they are about.

Back in harbour Mr Gip sits, his oars in the rowlocks, and watches me scale the jetty without offering his hand. His lip curls when I ask the way to Wine-street.

'Wine-street? Your chance to find out if Mr Tuffnell is as handsome and charming as so many claim. You should have asked me; I'd tell you otherwise. But then.' He gives a rasping cough and hawks into the water. 'I have a low opinion of those who profit from the Atlantic trade without risking their lily-white skins. The merchants say it is they built Bristol. They forget whose labour they depend on.' With a tar-blackened finger he prods his chest. 'The likes of me. Off you go with your letter, you won't see me again. Twelve months 'til we return to port, and I'll be dead by then. Blown up by pirates or struck down with bilious fever. Blasted bloody Mr Tuffnell. He knows no more about the sea than you do.'

Mr Gip unplugs his bottle and drinks a long draught of liquor, and I leave him muttering and cursing as I make my way to the city in search of Wine-street.

Needless to say I am glad to escape the malevolent skipper and relieved to find myself on dry land. And yet a part of me would thrill to be onboard a ship tonight, waiting to set sail. Not for Calabar, though—the West Indies.

Yet I shall never own enough to pay my passage to Jamaica, and it is useless—and painful—to dream of such a thing.

Chapter Twelve

Nearly hollow-bellied with hunger I stop at a cook-shop and use part of Mr Wharton's sixpence to buy a helping of pease pudding and a slice of barley bread. Spying a row of steps encircling a market cross, I sit down to eat.

Captain Stiles did not trouble to re-seal Mr Wharton's letter, being out of temper and in too much hurry to rid me from his ship. I cannot say precisely how it comes to pass, but as I take my first mouthful of pudding the letter falls open. Although I consider for a moment folding it again, I tell myself that reading it does no one any harm, and besides, the liberty is never likely to be discovered.

To Captain W. Stiles
St. Augustine's-back, 29th October, 1703
Sir,
It falls upon your humble servant to inform you of a matter whose import I much regret since it is certain to grieve and disappoint you.

Rather than hold you in suspense, Sir, I will spell the matter out forthwith. Mr Tuffnell's associate Mr Josiah Cheatley has this day confirmed that he will not accept the terms agreed when the present voyage to Guinea was arranged in March, having forged fresh connections in London whose terms would be more advantageous than ours were he to avail himself of them. In short, rather than six hundred and eighty-two pounds five shillings, he insists upon seven hundred and fifty-two pounds, seven shillings, and sixpence sterling in exchange for the iron manufactures due for export in the Prudence. *Mr Cheatley begs us to understand that if we fail to meet his revised terms of an additional ten per cent he will no longer agree to a part in any future consortium of which we are a member.*

It does not require stating that payment to Mr Cheatley for his manufactures was promised on the safe and satisfactory conclusion of the voyage, and is thus due many months hence; but whenever the date should fall, in availing himself of so much greater a proportion of the profit, Mr Cheatley renders the voyage vastly less advantageous to ourselves.

In addition to this matter is one that shall be divulged to Mr Tuffnell in person, Sir, later today. I trust this secondary news, which reached me via a friend whose master has links with men of business in Jamaica, including a certain owner of a large estate in Kingston, is of little significance; and that Mr Tuffnell has no reason besides the above to consider his circumstances less secure, and his prospects less satisfactory, than he has been accustomed to regard them since the first of his profitable ventures to Guinea and the West Indies. However, on arriving in Jamaica it may be wise of you not to represent yourself as better connected via your master than is justified by intelligence at the present time.

I am, Sir, your humble and obedient servant, and, I hope, your trusted and respected friend,
Henry Wharton.

Well, my curiosity is roundly punished, for I am scarcely likely to discover the 'secondary' matter Mr Wharton refers to, or the identity of the mysterious planter in St John's, unless I change into a fly and buzz in through a window when he visits Wine-street. As for the information in the first part of his letter, it is shocking to think a ship may be laden and ready to set sail and its chief investor subject to sharp practice, and yet I am not really surprised to learn it, for on reflection Mr Wharton's tone is more exasperated than outraged, as though Mr Cheatley's conduct is much as he expected.

I tuck the letter away and rise to my feet, whereupon a builder in a dusty leather apron takes my place under the cross and sets to champing on a pastry.

'Can you tell me where to find Mr Tuffnell's house, Sir?'

Swallowing noisily, he shows off a set of long and crooked teeth. 'Past the Market House, below the walls, overlooking the tower of St Peter's. You're in chucking distance.' He waves his crust in the direction of a covered market-place, and resting it on his grimy knee, gulps from a leather bottle.

'That's me done for my dinner,' he says, and gets to his feet; for a moment I think he is ready to show me to Mr Tuffnell's, but without a farewell he turns and strides back to his place of work, a half-built house across the way. In truth no one in Bristol has time or inclination to spare me a glance. Which might be lonely, but is a kind of giddy freedom after Erlestoke where we all knew one another's business.

Wine-street is busy with people on foot, and riders picking their way through the traffic, and most of all with car-men hauling sledges, for though it is wide and prosperous compared with All-Saints' yard, many of the houses boast cellars where merchants, wishing to save the cost of running a warehouse on the quays, or perhaps unable to afford such conveniences, keep goods at home where they are less likely to be stolen. At intervals along the street, therefore, hatches are propped open and pairs of delivery-men are lifting crates, bales and barrels through them and onto sledges, or else lowering such items to be stored or divided up for sale. A short way past the Market House I reach a door whose lintel is painted with the word *Barbuda*, and look up to find an imposing building four storeys high, with wide, glazed windows, a steep roof and, from what I can see, a stable at the rear as well as a handsome garden and perhaps an orchard, judging by a pair of apple trees visible through a paling.

A youngster is hard at work sweeping the front. He has been occupied some time judging by the muck waiting to be wheeled away, and he stops as I approach, playfully balancing his chin on the handle of his shovel as if glad of an excuse to rest.

'Where can I find Mr Tuffnell, young man?'

'At the Tolzey Walk?' His tone implies I ought to know where he means. 'Or you could speak to Mrs Tuffnell if you go through the yard. Suke Cross the scullery maid will let you in.' He grimaces. 'Don't look for kind words from her.'

'Is she bad-tempered?'

He rubs his ear. 'Very.'

A Pair of Sharp Eyes

On cue a sulky girl in a dirty linen apron barges through a side-gate and grabs the shovel.

'Yammering when you should be working, George Goodfellow.' She thrusts the shovel into his hand. 'Get on with it, before I tell Mr Roach what a lazy devil you are.'

'Mr Roach?' I repeat, sounding as innocent as I can. 'Who's he?'

She glares. 'What business is it of yours? He is Mr Tuffnell's groom, and the master of this idle lad.' Dodging her raised fist, George sets to with the shovel (though I glimpse him grimacing at Miss Pot-Scrub when her back is turned), and leaving him to his task, I show Suke Cross my letter.

'Pardon me, Miss. I was asking where I could find your master.'

'He's at the Tolzey. He'll be home soon,' she snaps. 'Give your letter here. George! Move! I want the whole street spotless or you'll miss your dinner.' And to ram the point home she grabs the waiting barrow by its handles and bangs it down.

I do not intend to trust my letter to a shrieking scullery maid, but before I can say as much the street door opens and a lady appears, no doubt curious to see the cause of the commotion.

Mrs Tuffnell is young, no older than my sister Liz, smooth-complexioned and with large black eyes, her mouth a vivid pink and her hair arranged in tousled shining curls beneath a cap of lace. Her sleeves are finished with ruffles, as is the neckerchief half-covering her bosom, while her petticoat is cherry-red taffeta and her gown red velvet in a darker shade; but more eye-catching than the lady is the child on her arm, the handsomest little black fellow you can imagine, dressed head-to-toe in the most expensive suit I have seen on a child, twilight blue satin trimmed with red and gold braid, gold rosettes on his knee breeches and gold buckles on his blue stuff slippers. Yet his face is blank, his eyes are dull, and I remember my mother saying she always knew if a child was frightened or unhappy.

I curtsey to his mistress.

'Begging your pardon, Madam, a letter for Mr Tuffnell.'

She puts out a hand. Her fingers are soft, the nails well-shaped. She smells of something sweetly fragrant, geranium oil or rose-water, perhaps.

I keep a firm hold of the letter, though I hardly know why. 'Shall I run to the Tolzey Walk, Madam?'

'Oh no, indeed no.' She inclines her head. 'Poor James, belea-guered night and day. He won't thank you for interrupting his busi-ness-dealing. Let me have the letter. Don't fret, girl. I'll give it to him as soon as he comes home.'

I cannot think of an excuse to say no, and so with reluctance I hand it over, adding, 'I was told to ask for a receipt, if you please, Madam,' though in truth neither Mr Wharton nor Captain Stiles mentioned one.

'Very well,' she says with passable good humour, though her ir-ritation is clear as day. 'Come into the house and I will write you your receipt. No need to stand and stare, Susan Cross, I heard Mrs Hucker just now tell you to scrub those pots, and yet I find you standing in the street, ear-wigging your betters.' If looks could kill, George and I would be dead alongside Mrs Tuffnell; Miss Pot-Scrub turns a furious shade of scarlet.

'Step in,' Mrs Tuffnell says, indicating to me, and as soon as I obey she shuts the door firmly behind us, leaving Pot-Scrub to go in through the back.

The hallway of the house is panelled in dark oak, and the furniture finely carved, and I am led into a room that was once perhaps a shop but is now a room for business, indicated by the large table in the middle of the floor, and a writing desk in the window with books and ledgers on it and several pens and a silver ink-well.

'Now then,' Mrs Tuffnell says, absently stroking the cheek of her page-boy, 'let us see if your Bristol papa has a scrap of paper I may borrow.' She riffles through the desk. 'Shall we tell the errand-girl what we mean?' Without waiting for the boy to speak, she contin-ues, 'Pug here was born in Jamaica and brought to Bristol last year on my husband's orders, and it is my fancy that we are his Bristol parents since he bid farewell to his negro mother and father when he left the Caribbean for his new life.'

Pug? Why do you call by him a dog's name, I want to ask?

'Pug' leans over his 'Bristol mamma' as she writes, and when she finishes he picks up the slip of paper and puts it on a pewter salver before presenting it to me with a bow.

Mrs Tuffnell watches with an eager smile.

'Is he not the cleverest black boy you ever saw? So quick and obliging. Thank you, Pug,' she says, and swoops on him, gathering him in her arms and raining kisses on his head. Most lads his age would baulk at such treatment, but this boy is either content or else afraid to offend, for he submits to Mrs Tuffnell's caresses without resistance, though I notice he does not kiss her in return.

'Now then.' She pats his hand. 'You must let Mamma read her letter.' I inwardly protest, 'But it isn't yours,' as, without a trace of embarrassment, she rips the paper open, pulls out a chair and sits at the table to digest the contents.

I would like very much to see her face as she reads, but she waves me towards the door. Then, as I have my hand on the knob, hoping a servant will arrive to show me out, she calls me back.

'On second thoughts, you may take a note to Mr Tuffnell, since you were on your way to the Tolzey in any case. Hand me a pen, dearest Pug, so I may write your Bristol papa a few words.'

I suppose the lady is in love, for she sighs and blushes as she writes, and looks at me coyly when she is done. Then she adds her seal to the letter, pressing her signet ring into the melted wax, and regarding the results with smiling satisfaction.

'No need to mention the letter you brought, girl, I have wrote Mr Tuffnell all about it.' Saying this she picks up Mr Wharton's letter again, crumples it in her fist, and tosses it into the fireplace. 'There!' she says, as the paper catches alight, flares and turns to ash.

'May I show her the way to the Tolzey, Mamma?' asks the boy. His voice is plaintive, and I wonder how much fresh air he gets, waiting on a lady whose plump figure and snowy hands hint that she is fonder of the tea-table than of setting foot outdoors.

'Pug,' she reproves. 'You are too precious to send with someone I don't know.'

His face falls, and she thinks again. 'To the corner, then, and no further. Run and change your shoes. Stuff slippers are not for crossing muddy streets.'

When the boy has sped away she lowers her voice: 'Is he not the prettiest child you ever saw? I shall never forget the day my husband presented Pug to me. He was ashen-faced after his voyage, mere skin and bones. We burned his clothes and fattened him on cakes and cream, and had the tailor make him two new suits. People stare so when we walk out. He carries my prayer-book on Sundays, you know. I call him my Afric son, other times my little Moor.'

Having exchanged his slippers for leather shoes, her page returns and listens to the end of this gushing speech with lowered head. Mrs Tuffnell plants a dozen kisses on his neck, telling him she loves him, but his manner changes the moment we leave her company. He scuffs his way down the passage in silence, and when I put my hand on his shoulder, ready to enquire if he would rather let me find my own way to the Tolzey, he shrugs me off.

'Or I can ask the stable boy to show me the way. George Goodfellow, is it? What is your name, besides "Pug"?'

'You can call me Abraham.' He eyes me sullenly. 'I want to show you the way. She said I could.' But he speaks as though he is used to being granted his wishes only to have them thwarted.

'Then of course you must,' I say, as Abraham lifts the latch of the street door and leads me out. His fingers are warm and his small palm soft, and he clutches my hand tightly when a passing waggon splashes us with mud.

'Poor George,' I say as we pick our way along the muddy pavement. 'All his good work undone. He will have to hope Suke doesn't blame him for it.'

'I wish Mrs Tuffnell would dismiss Suke Cross,' is the reply. 'She shouts at everyone but Mr Roach. She deserves to lose her place.'

'Does she?' If so, there would be a vacancy at Barbuda House for which I might apply, though I admit I would prefer a position elsewhere than the scullery. 'Mr Roach is the groom?' I ask lightly.

'And Suke's particular friend.' Abraham picks up a stone and flings it to the ground. 'A worse bully than she is. I saw him hold a knife to someone's throat one night.' I see a flash of panic in the boy's eyes as he realises he has said too much.

'Well, Bristol is a rough-and-ready place, I daresay. As long as he didn't draw blood from the man he threatened.'

'It wasn't a man.'

'Who was it then?' But Abraham will not answer, and kicks his stone along the ground so he need not meet my eyes.

'Abraham? Who else works for your master and mistress?'

He looks up, his face brightening slightly at the change of subject. 'Mrs Hucker the cook. Nell Grey the housemaid and Jonty the footman.'

'And are they kinder than the others?'

'A little,' he admits,' adding sadly, 'sometimes.'

'Is it far to the Tolzey?' It seems wise to distract him from the subject of his fellow servants.

'Not at all.' He stops, pointing to a set of arches I noticed on my way to Barbuda House. 'That's the Tolzey. Mr Tuffnell goes there every day but Sunday.'

'Your Bristol papa is one of the richest men in the city, isn't he?'

Abraham looks at the Tolzey with contempt. 'Mr Tuffnell is not my "papa." My father ran away, no one knows where, and my mother is dead.'

'I thought Mrs Tuffnell said you had left your real parents behind in the West Indies.'

Abraham hunches his shoulders and speaks tonelessly. 'My mother was tied to a post and whipped until she fainted, and she died the day after. Mrs Tuffnell tells falsehoods even though she goes to church on Sundays.'

'Mrs Tuffnell may not know what befell your mother, Abraham. Jamaica is a great way off. Or she may be afraid to distress you.

Who whipped your mother? Why did they do such a thing?' But I remember what I was told about some plantation owners and their treatment of their slaves, and I do not really doubt the boy.

'She scolds me every day and sometimes beats me and locks me in the cellar.'

'If you are naughty she must correct you.' I speak half-heartedly, for my mother and father never beat us and would not have locked us in a dark place however wilful our behaviour.

'She does it to be cruel. She is not my "mamma" and I am not her son.' Despite his efforts, tears roll down his cheeks and threaten to bring forth tears of my own on his behalf.

I reach into my pocket and pass him my handkerchief. 'You must be careful what you say, Abraham—what you repeat to strangers. Mrs Tuffnell may have her moments of temper but she is fond of you, I am sure.'

He shakes his head. 'She was fond of Philo before he died. She forgot him in a day. She used to sit him on her knee and now she does the same with me. And I am eight years old.' Another shower of angry tears.

'Eight?' I say, feigning astonishment. 'You're so well-grown I thought you nine at least. Was Philo your mistress's dog?'

'Mine, not hers. I found him starving in the yard. I taught him tricks. And now he's dead.'

'That is sad, but you know dogs do perish. They eat all manner of noxious things, or catch the distemper.'

'Philo never would have died if it hadn't been for Mr Roach.'

'Poor Philo. Perhaps you may find another stray soon.' As I say this I am afraid I must sound much as the fine lady did who advised us to forget my brother Tom. 'I think you'd better run indoors before your mistress sends someone to find you,' I say, shaking his hand gently. 'I hope to see you again one day, Master Abraham. Perhaps you may be more cheerful then, indeed I'm sure you shall.'

'I shan't. I am unhappy every day. Unhappier still since I lost my dearest friend.'

'I'm sorry if a dog was your dearest friend.'

A Pair of Sharp Eyes

'Hannah was my friend. Mrs Tuffnell's maid.' Abraham has forgotten my handkerchief, and sniffs and wipes his nose with the heel of his hand. 'She was good to me—to everyone. One day she left without a farewell, and I am forbid to mention her. I wish I could wear a leather jerkin and sleep in the stable loft with George Goodfellow, but instead I am tricked out and made to pour my mistress's tea and wind her wool, and even comb out her hair because she has no lady's maid since Hannah went.'

He pushes my hand away at the end of this outburst and darts back to Barbuda House, leaving me in no doubt that Hannah must be the same who is Mr Espinosa's sister, and the great friend of Esther Wharton, and whose time in service is the cause of the warnings I was given about certain Bristol households. Yet I must wonder whether folk such as Mrs Wharton and even Mr Espinosa can truly understand how for some a servant's place with a well-off family—even where the mistress is ill-tempered—might be preferable to seeking labour every day and finding none.

***

The Tolzey is a narrow walk behind a set of arches, notable for a row of round bronze trading 'nails' or counters, each of which is in use by a huddle of merchants when I arrive. Among them are a number of prosperous-looking widows, as well as one or two planters whose broad bellies and liverish complexions remind me of Mr Osmund, though most are well-dressed citizens of Bristol whose clerks wait while their masters pore over papers and rub their chins as if to say the terms proposed are not quite as they need to be.

Standing at the bronze nail nearest the entrance is Mr Tuffnell, dressed in a fine, black woollen suit and listening with ill-concealed impatience to a short, squat alderman with a heavy gold chain of office round his neck. Mr Tuffnell exclaims with ill-disguised relief at the arrival of a gentleman in fashionable grey silk who, bowing low to the alderman, succeeds with one or two polished phrases in dislodging him from their company.

As soon as the old fellow stumps off, the two embark on a spirited but low-voiced discussion of the alderman's failing brickworks due to 'lack of clay, lack of fuel, and lack of wit'.

A clerk stands at a respectful distance with an armful of papers and a pair of quill pens.

'I've brought this for Mr Tuffnell,' I tell him.

The clerk lifts a finger to bid me wait. 'He won't welcome an interruption now, Miss. Let him finish his meeting. The other is a lord, you see.'

I take his advice, and from our station a few yards away it is easy to overhear the conversation between the two.

'Of course, we hoped the *Prudence* would set sail some weeks ago. The captain needed a neap tide and a strong north-easterly,' Mr Tuffnell says. 'So large a vessel requires both to clear the Channel. She'll soon make up for lost time.'

The lord asks something about the terms agreed with Mr Tuffnell's partner. His languid manner is quite at odds with Mr Tuffnell's lively air.

'Oh, very good terms, my lord,' Mr Tuffnell says. 'Mr Cheatley has many deep concerns, as they say. His manufactory in Bristol is long-established, and I have every confidence in him. He's my chief partner in the *Prudence*, though lesser men have smaller shares—why, even my agent Mr Henry Wharton invested a percentage. Small by my standards, but a significant outlay for him.'

The lord says something in an undertone. Mr Tuffnell appears to brush the remark aside. 'I admit the last year has been challenging,' he says. 'Two voyages incurring losses ... a claim lodged with our underwriters, which no man of business is pleased to find himself obliged to make. But the *Prudence* is a bigger vessel than those others, Captain Stiles is a sound fellow, and we shall hardly fail with the coastal traders when we can offer them munitions on the scale made possible by our partnership with Mr Cheatley.'

The lord nods sagely. Then he leans forward, smiling. 'And are rumours correct that you may be expanding your interests in Jamaica very soon?'

A Pair of Sharp Eyes

Mr Tuffnell throws up his hands. 'You have my measure, Sir. No chance of keeping enterprises secret here in Bristol. It's true, I've recently made connections of a personal kind in Jamaica.' He smiles a little bashfully. 'Since my marriage. In time I hope they'll strengthen my hand in selling my negroes, and my sugar, at a higher margin than is possible when I rely on the offices of strangers. In a year or two, when the *Prudence* comes in, I may even look to buying an estate myself—contracting sugar production to an experienced man, of course.' He slaps the lord's shoulder. 'Exactly as your ancestors left the running of your Somerset estates to stewards and yeomen farmers these seven hundred years.' Both men laugh, the lord nodding sheepishly at the comparison.

Their conversation having reached a pause, the clerk clears his throat. 'You may give in the letter now, Miss.'

Mr Tuffnell may be rich and important but he is not above looking me over as thoroughly as he would a negro slave. If we were not at the Tolzey I daresay he would try to kiss my hand or worse. Fortunately, he does not seem to recognise me from the quays.

'From your wife, Sir,' I say boldly. Without a blush at this reminder of his married state he takes the letter and scans the contents, all the while watched over with frank curiosity by the lord.

Mr Tuffnell looks up smiling. 'My wife is an angel, Lord Fitzhaven. She received just today a small dividend from her property in Jamaica. The land and the operations on it are in her name, and yet she seeks my approval to make a modest donation to a charity case—a distant relative of hers fallen on hard times. Such openness and trust in a wife can't be valued too highly, my lord. To incur liabilities through an extravagant spouse would be a pitiable state of affairs, and yet some unlucky gentlemen are in that position exactly. No such risk with my dear Maria.'

'You are fortunate,' agrees the lord, though from his uncomfortable expression I wonder if he has personal knowledge of the evil Mr Tuffnell describes.

'She is the most generous of benefactresses, and yet she never calls on me to fund her acts of charity,' Mr Tuffnell repeats.

The alderman has waddled back, and interposes himself between the gentlemen. 'Eh?' he asks. 'What's this you say? Talking of some milk-sop philanthropist? Not you, boy, I hope?' He digs Mr Tuffnell in the ribs.

'No, no. My wife. An improvident relative duns her for a few shillings, and she seeks my consent even to this trifling act of kindness.'

'Does she now?' The alderman narrows his small dark eyes. 'A few shillings mount up by and by. A relative is harder to shake off than your common or garden sponger.' He taps his fleshy nose with a fat finger. 'Be on your guard, Sir. It will be pounds, not shillings, next.'

I see Mr Tuffnell is vexed by this advice though he succeeds in not rising to it. The old man totters off, and the other two begin an earnest discussion in which the lord seems eager to know how he might obtain a loan from Mr Tuffnell, and Mr Tuffnell seems equally eager to avoid offending the lord with a refusal.

Neither remembers me, and I turn to leave when the clerk gives a sudden sneeze and drops a quill. It rolls towards Mr Tuffnell and I stoop unthinkingly to pick it up, determined to prise the quill from the crack into which it fell. I hear the lord snort and Mr Tuffnell mutter something the meaning of which I easily guess, and I rise with as much dignity as I can and hand the clerk his pen, reflecting that these great men are no better than the louts who go to sea on their behalf. Indeed, Mr Wilks who helped me on the *Prudence* was more gentlemanly than Mr Tuffnell or his hard-up lordly friend.

As I leave the Tolzey, and glance back at Wine-street where the fine brick chimneys of Barbuda House stand high above all others, I realise I have another cause to be indignant, for Mrs Tuffnell told me I was going to the Tolzey, and yet I only did so at her bidding, and she paid me nothing.

So aside from my sixpence my day in Bristol has gained me little beyond a cautiousness toward Mr Tuffnell and his wife that would satisfy even Mrs Esther Wharton—though doubtless Abraham would say I still have much to learn.

A Pair of Sharp Eyes

Chapter Thirteen

Tuesday, 30ᵗʰ October, 1703

When the wind began to rise last night, Liz, Bill and I were forced to pull our stools so close up to the fire our shins were scorched. Then we lay shivering through the night as the house walls creaked, and trees were stripped of twigs and even branches. This morning the sky is mottled grey, leaves spin on the street corners, and down at the river the *Prudence* has vanished from her mooring. Mr Wharton looks up from his papers as if he has forgotten who I am.

'Any messages today, Sir?'

'No, nor any day this week. The ship has sailed, my work is done.' He takes a breath, releases it, then sees my disappointment and adds, not unkindly, 'The cook-shop on the High-street may want a pot-washer. It's busy for them, the day of sailing.' He bends over his accounts once more, and I see now that he was only civil to me in the presence of Mr Espinosa, and gave me work because he needed a swift pair of heels, and that my dreams of becoming Mrs Wharton's friend and confidante and Mrs Tuffnell's lady's maid were the silliest dreams I ever had, for to Mr Wharton and his friends I am nobody, of no account or interest.

Accordingly, I trudge back to the city, and since I cannot return to All-Saints'-yard before nightfall, and have no notion how to fill the time, I take Mr Wharton's advice and try the cook-shop. It stands on the corner where the High-street meets the Shambles, and is more than an ordinary shop of its kind, being a meeting-place for folk arriving in Bristol or waiting for their ship to sail, and crowded and noisy and filling the air for yards around with the smell of broth and frying bacon. It serves as an office for the passing on of news by word of mouth, and many posters are nailed to the sides of the shop, some advertising rewards for the return of runaway apprentices and negroes, others asking for information about thieves and highwaymen. This morning my attention is caught by a large new poster referring to the *horrid and unnatural murders of several young boys between March 1702 and October 1703, believed to be the cruel and wicked work of a hawker known as Red John.*

I had noticed this cook-shop on previous mornings, for among the printed notices are small hand-written ones, in which out-of-work servants state their availability for hire, and I had wondered if I should post a notice there except Liz warned I should pay sixpence for the privilege. The street door, normally propped open, is shut against the weather, and as I open it a blast of hot air greets me and I breathe the scent of boiling meat and vegetables. Women in travelling cloaks talk at the tops of their voices while children cling to their petticoats. A good fire burns in the hearth and a serving-woman hands out dishes of stew, and parcels of cooked food that customers seated at the back of the shop wait to carry home.

I take my place in line, jostled by the sailors' wives, until the serving-woman asks me what I want.

'I was told you might need a pot-washer. Mr Tuffnell's man of business said to try here.'

She looks me up and down; her eyes are shrewd.

'I've worked for Mr Wharton now and then,' I tell her. 'I believe he'd vouch for me.'

A customer behind me screeches. 'Get a move on. Some of us haven't eaten since last night.'

The woman nods to me. 'Go on then. Through to the back-room.'

There I find a low stone sink, a jar of sand, and a bucket of cold water. Dirty pots wait on a shelf, and before I can make a start a boy runs in and dumps down a stack of pewter plates and a tray of wooden trenchers thick with grease and gravy.

I have just dealt with them when the serving-woman brings in a pair of brass pots, the insides black with burned-on fat. 'You picked a good day to ask for work,' she says. Out in the kitchen the women's voices grow louder and more shrill.

'Are most of those wives of sailors on the *Prudence*?'

'And other ships. They've all been waiting for the wind to change.'

A Pair of Sharp Eyes

I scrub and rub until my hand is sore, and at midday I am let stop for a few minutes, and given bread and dripping. When the sailors' wives have had their fill a dozen butchers crowd in and order ale and beefsteak, and after that a procession of hungry tradesmen come in for bacon and boiled cabbage; but finally the light begins to dim and the woman locks up and ladles me a bowlful of soup. 'Martha Downey,' she says, indicating the bench next to the counter, and sticking out a hand as damp and swollen as my own.

She plants herself down next to me. Sweat darkens her sleeves under her arms, and her hair sticks to her forehead. 'So who are you?' she asks, blowing on her soup.

'Corrie.'

'*Coral?* What possessed your father and mother to call you that?'

'Corrie. Short for "Coronation." My father was a supporter of King William and wished to remember when he took the throne.'

'I'd be quiet about that if I was you. "Coral" would serve you better. You're not from Bristol, are you? Most Bristol men would sink a knife into any Dutchman they met on a dark night. Bloody Dutch, bloody pirates. My Ned hates every man Jack of them.'

'Is Ned a sailor?'

'Sail-maker. Off to Africa this morning on the *Prudence*, not due home for twelve long months or more. Let's hope he brings us back a few gold coins. If he does, I promised to forgive his endless sea-wanderings and not ask about the whores who've shared his hammock.' A throaty laugh before she takes a spoonful and I drink a little of my own soup.

'I was on the *Prudence* yesterday.' I cannot resist an audience for my story. 'I carried a letter to the captain. The long-boat skipper rowed me out and I scaled the ladder by myself.'

'So that's what they're calling it, is it?' She bursts out laughing. 'If you could see your face! Prim little country girl. What d'you think of the *Prudence*? Fine ship, isn't she?'

'She looked so tiny from the shore, then when we were waiting to climb aboard ... even the water casks on deck were this big.'

'You should see the main hold. My old man says it's solid cargo, hammocks slung in every leftover corner they can find. But wait 'til they trade that cloth and metal for slaves. They fit her out all over again with chains and bunks, and then it's a floating goal, wind screaming in the sails and the negroes crying and wailing below like the damned in the mouth of hell.'

I shudder, remembering how my beloved Robert spoke of slave ships when we lived in Erlestoke, but Mrs Downey seems unconcerned by the picture her words have painted, and rises to her feet. 'Right Corrie-Coral, whatever-your-name-is, rinse these last dishes and you can get off home.'

At that same moment a shrunken old fellow in a fustian coat and patched breeches lets himself in through the back of the shop, wheezing and sighing and sinking onto a chair without a bye-your-leave. I wait for Mrs Downey to throw him out, but she fetches a bowl of stew and places it in front of him. 'There you are, O'Malley. Mop up that rum before they drag you to the roundhouse.'

And with her face full of satire, she stands over him as he eats. 'Come on, O'Malley, what is it? You look miserable as sin.'

The steam from the soup makes his nose run, and he wipes it on his sleeve. 'I'll tell you, shall I? Only don't lay the blame on me if you can't sleep tonight. Bristol is heading for Judgment Day is all.'

She throws up her hands. 'And what was it last time you had a dream? A plague of locusts? I caught a cricket on the hearth in May if that's a plague.'

'Ha, ha. This time it isn't any dream, Missus, I wish it was. I blew in from Barbados late last night, and I never knew such a crossing as we endured. If the storms out west follow us here, we'll have the worst winter for a century. Winds to pull down steeples and smash every ship in the Bristol Channel to smithereens.' He bangs his bowl on the table. 'Dig yourself a cellar is my advice, and make it on high ground.'

'You mad old prophet you,' she says fondly, fetching a cup of beer and slapping his shoulder as she sets it down. 'I be glad to see you, you know, for all your bad tidings. There's none like you, O'Malley, even if you love to scare us from our wits.'

'I'm telling you gospel truth,' he protests, 'what weather they have in the Indies is like to be here a week after,' and as if to prove his point the back door slams shut.

Mrs Downey winks. 'Best get yourself gone then, before the roofs blow off. Come on, O'Malley, the rest of us have homes to go to if you don't.' She turns to me. 'You can have this, condition on bringing it back washed tomorrow.' She pours the dregs from the pot into an earthen jar. 'And take the parings to the pig, will you? Out the back, mind you latch the gate.'

'So you'll be wanting me tomorrow?'

'I can't promise. You can ask.'

In the yard the pig trots over and while he guzzles I look past his sty to the plot with its tidy rows of leeks and cabbages and wonder how Mrs Downey came to buy her shop, and whether she was a servant first, and for how long. How many years, I wonder, before I can hope to own a shop like this one, or is such a possibility as far off as my being maid to Mrs Tuffnell?

I set off for All-Saints. When Mr Gip spoke of the voyage ahead of him, he claimed he might never return to England, instead dying on board in battle or from fever. Listening to O'Malley's talk of tempests, who is to say that the dear friend I knew in Erlestoke survived his passage west? Though whether he did or didn't makes no difference, since I shall never see him in this life.

The rain has begun in earnest and the wind is almost a gale as I make my way up St-Nicholas-street with my small pot of soup and my lonely aching heart.

Kat Armstrong

Chapter Fourteen

Wednesday, 31ˢᵗ October, 1703

After working two days at Mrs Downey's shop, and tired of pot-washing, I toy with returning to Mr Wharton's warehouse, but more than likely Mr Wharton has awarded himself a holiday now the *Prudence* has set sail, and is breakfasting this very moment with his wife and children, comfortably seated in his parlour in the Hot-wells with a dish of tea and Baby Emma on his knee.

Liz tells me the hiring-man may be found at the New Inn, so I make my way to the High-street, resigned to giving up half a shilling to register my name.

Just before the bridge a sight has drawn a crowd to gather by the roadside. The master of a coach-making concern has thrown open his gates, and a glittering new coach is being wheeled out of the workshop for approval by a lady in a blue gown and silk-trimmed blue headdress. Her face is hidden from view, but her page is clearly visible as he holds her skirts out of the mud. His hair is black and densely curled, and I do not need a second look to know that this is Abraham and Mrs Tuffnell.

The new coach is a splendid object, sleek and gleaming, as light and elegant as any I ever saw. The limner has finished the carriage in gloss blue, with red-and-white linings and a gilded coat of arms adorning the centre of the glazed and curving door. The wheels are high and as narrow as whipcord, and the fittings shine like gold.

Mrs Tuffnell claps and laughs and salutes the maker in a voice which carries across the street, assuring him that her dear husband will be along presently to look the equipage over for defects, and that meanwhile she is determined to take it for its first outing, up to the market cross and back again, when her groom is finished putting her two bays in the traces. Mr Roach stands balefully to one side during this discussion, and I suppose he has been made to walk the horses through the crowded streets while Mrs Tuffnell tripped ahead of him with her 'Afric son'.

Abraham hops from foot to foot, quieter than his 'mamma' but radiant at the prospect of trying out the new conveyance. Mrs Tuffnell has him tricked out in a miniature coachman's cape to match the livery of the vehicle: red-and-white braid on blue broad-cloth, and bright gold buttons at the neck.

Having no particular place to go, and eager to postpone my interview at the inn as long as possible, I stand at a distance to watch the maiden journey, an awning on the side of a shoe-maker's shop enabling me to stand unseen by Mrs Tuffnell, who has eyes only for her coach. She strokes the paintwork, opens and closes the door, exclaims at the artfulness of the design, and at last climbs in and waves to the onlookers, whose expressions are a mix of envy and admiration. The crowd grows, and the groom is puffed up with his own importance as he chases off a barefoot lad who runs up and touches the back of the coach for a dare to please his friends. An old fellow in a tattered military tunic stumps across and seems to ask questions about the manufacture of the undercarriage, while a street artist sets up his easel a few yards away, intent on making a hasty sketch of the scene. It is like a show at a fair, everyone amazed and excited and Mrs Tuffnell most of all, until I notice that the horses, fidgeting at the noise, are reluctant to enter the traces, and are only persuaded to do so after repeated efforts by the groom. He might better use soft words and bits of apple to coax them in, but instead he shouts and elbows their flanks, causing them to whinny and show their teeth, and in my opinion it serves him right if he is bitten.

The horses' skittishness makes Mrs Tuffnell less eager to try her new possession. She confers with the coach-maker, who seems to propose that they delay the outing until the beasts are docile. But another idea occurs to her, and next thing she leads her page-boy forward, shaking her head and smiling reprovingly at his unhappy protests, and despite the child's frightened looks, insists that he climb up to the driver's seat and take the reins, so she can stand back and admire the spectacle of her two extraordinary gifts placed together.

The boy looks exceedingly unhappy, the horses flicking their tails and stamping to convey their discontent, his seat so many feet above the ground, and the reins, no doubt, a muddle in his hands.

The groom says something to Mrs Tuffnell, the coach-maker looks doubtful, whereupon the groom prods him lightly to dismiss his fears and goes across and kicks away the blocks.

The bays, twitching, sense the lack of hindrance and break into a gallop, causing the boy to scream as the coach leaps forward. Being light and newly oiled it speeds quicker than any vehicle I have seen in Bristol, the onlookers gasping with astonishment as it gains the end of the street before most have taken in its departure. The boy's fear causes him to clutch the reins tighter instead of letting go; he is, though, pulled from his seat and very shortly onto his toes, as he strains every sinew to try and hold the horses back.

I break into a run instinctively, but have no hope of catching up. The coach hurtles towards the busiest quarter of the city as the terrified horses make for home. I glimpse them narrowly avoiding a line of market stalls, forced to slow when a timber cart crosses their path, and these obstacles give me enough time to reflect it may be possible to prevent the destruction of coach and driver. A memory of my father running to the aid of a runaway waggon flashes into my mind. Pushing back my bonnet I race past the outraged stallholders, and Providence is by my side, for just before the Market House is a slope, not long but steep, and I take a deep breath and bawl above the sound of the wheels.

'Pull left, boy.'

Abraham shows no sign of hearing, and I repeat the words, screaming, and then, finally, God love him, he obeys, and the horses veer towards the rise, which, though it cannot stop them dead, slows them into a sweating, shaking trot. Next I gather my gown in my two hands like the country hoyden I used to be, and heedless of the mud and slippery footpath, sprint 'til I am almost level with the horses and can smell the heat and foam of their heaving flanks, and then I make a drumming sound with my tongue, the same mysterious drumming that would startle Snowy and bring her up short when I was let to ride her by the person I do not think of any more, except when I cannot help it.

The horses' ears prick, their eyes widen; they halt despite themselves. The groom, who has caught us up, lunges for the nearside bridle. It is over; the coach is at a stop.

'Are you all right?' The terrified child has fallen in a faint. 'Abraham!' I forget my dignity and hurl myself at the steps below the box, cursing my skirts for hampering me.

The boy might have slid sideways onto the stony road or forwards into the traces where the horses would have crushed him, but luckily he went backwards in his fit, and lies against the seat rest. When I reach him he mumbles and his eyelids open briefly. After a moment's confusion he seems to know me, but his lips are blue and when I touch his hand it is deathly cold.

'Poor mite. Let me help you down.' I take him in my arms; he is alarmingly thin beneath his cape, and I wonder what his doting 'mamma' feeds him on. Dainty morsels better suited to ladies than to growing children. Though he is eight years old or more I manage him easily, and when we are stood on the road he huddles against me like a puppy and does not let me go.

Mrs Tuffnell arrives at the scene at last, her cheeks blotched with crimson.

'Careless, foolish wretch. You could have wrecked my brand-new coach and broken the horses' necks.' Her hand flies out and she slaps his cheek. I am shocked to see that rather than provoke his mamma's wrath anew by crying, the child's face closes, and he neither speaks nor makes a sound though tears stand in his eyes. I hear my mother warning me to hold my tongue, but my temper is up at the sight of such injustice.

'Madam, no child could hold back bolting horses. He's lucky to be alive.'

She stares at me. 'I know you. You brought that—trifling letter from Mr Wharton.'

'I did, Madam. Miss Amesbury, Madam. Won't you take pity on your page? He's had such a fright.'

Mrs Tuffnell pinches her lips, turns pale, seems to vie with herself as to what to say.

'He tried his best to stop the horses, Madam. I daresay you couldn't see from where you stood, but I could see.'

When she speaks her anger is in retreat.

'You are right, I suppose. I waited so long to see the coach completed, impatience got the better of me.' She affects not to notice Abraham stiffening at her touch, but wraps him in her arms and covers his head with kisses. 'Poor child, was Mamma thoughtless? Forgive her, won't you? Here, kiss me and tell me you are better now, and this was a foolish interlude best forgot. Mr Roach?' She turns to the groom. 'Walk the coach and horses back to the workshop. My husband will be there in a quarter-hour, and I daresay he need not know about this mishap. Abraham, you have no cause to weep.' She presses on him a handkerchief. 'You are a brave boy. When Papa arrives you mustn't tell him you were so bold as to drive the new coach by yourself. You will sit inside with me and Papa, and let Mr Roach drive us home. Do you understand?'

I expect Abraham to agree without demur, but he must be afraid still, for he shakes his head and tears drip down his cheeks.

'Please. Mamma,' he adds, before she can remind him of the title she prefers. 'May I walk home? I'll ride in the coach tomorrow, I promise. Don't make me now, please.'

'Nonsense. The way to go on after a fright is to face the cause of it. You will ride home with us; I shan't hear another word.'

Abraham falls to the ground and writhes weeping at her feet. I can tell when there is no use reasoning with a child, and break in again.

'Madam, should I not take the boy back to Wine-street? It would be a pity to mar Mr Tuffnell's pleasure in seeing the new coach.'

Mrs Tuffnell frowns; she taps her foot. 'I suppose there is something in what you say. Very well, take him back and wait in the yard for my return. Here,' she fumbles in her purse and brings out a coin.

'As you say, it would be a pity if Mr Tuffnell were to imagine Pug had come near to injuring the coach. Let us make sure he hears no word of it.'

I crouch at the boy's side, and help him to his feet. 'You gave yourself a fright, Master,' I say, squeezing his shoulder gently. I might have rather said, *Your vain and foolish mistress nearly brought about your death.* 'Shall we go home to Barbuda House? Come, you and I will walk together and I will tell you about a little boy I knew who you would have liked very much if you had met him.'

By the time I have finished this speech the boy has dried his eyes and Mrs Tuffnell is watching with a smile—not so much admiring my success as glad she need not explain the drama to her husband.

'We will wait at the coach-makers for Mr Tuffnell, Mr Roach and I.' She glances back to the cross-roads where the High-street meets the Corn. 'Very well, girl, take him home.'

Chapter Fifteen

In the yard at Barbuda House Abraham tugs my hand.

'Will you come in, Miss? Just for a little while.'

'I can't. Not without an invitation from the lady of the house.'

'Oh, please,' he wheedles. Away from Mrs Tuffnell his recovery is swift. 'I've something that will amaze you, truly. The servants are on their half-holiday, none will know. Wait here for me.' He indicates a small tiled passageway leading to the offices. Then he darts inside and I can hear his footsteps clatter up the stairs.

When he reappears my heart leaps into my mouth. He bears a silver collar, engraved with 'Abraham' in large capitals.

The boy unclasps the fastening. 'Won't you try it on?'

'I had rather not,' I say, laughing, but to please him I stoop and he carefully places the collar about my neck.

The silver is cold and heavy and exceedingly uncomfortable.

'I can't see my feet,' I say, as my jaw catches on the rim. The collar is four inches wide, and not generously made; it pinches my throat.

'Last time she tried to make me wear it I struggled until she gave up and had me whipped.'

'Take it off, please, Abraham. It will look very bad if Mrs Tuffnell suddenly returns.'

'Ha! She has the key.' He sees my face and looks ashamed. 'I have a spare, Mistress, here it is. Keep still.' He stands on tiptoe, unlocks the catch with a tiny silver key, and removes the device, taking care not to snag my hair as he does so.

'Come while I put it back. Don't be afraid, no one will see us. Mr Tuffnell has a pair of elephants carved in ivory that you would like very much, and a book of tinted pictures of all kinds of animals found in Africa.'

It seems so long since I saw a book, never mind one with pictures in it, that I cannot resist.

'Very well, only we must be quick.'

He leads me up to a small parlour furnished with two carved chairs, a small round tea-table, a green plush sofa, and a shelf of books, among them the Bible and Foxe's *Martyrs*, but also a volume as handsomely bound and gilded as any I have seen. Abraham takes it down as casually as if it were his plaything.

'Be careful, Master. I hope your hands are clean.'

He casts up his eyes, props the book on the table, and with his tongue between his teeth turns the pages until he finds what he is looking for.

'Look at these,' he says, stroking the paper. 'Parrots are found everywhere in Africa. When I was very young my father told me about the parrot he owned before the English captured him. It was tame, and could say its name and count to twenty.' Abraham squawks. 'Koro, Koro.'

'I should love to see a parrot. What beautiful creatures.' The picture is of a flock of birds perching in a bare-branched tree, their plumage vivid green and softest grey.

Abraham seizes the book and leafs through it. 'This is a giraffe. And this one here a crocodile.'

Together we pore over a dozen pictures, each more vivid than the last. Encouraged by my interest, Abraham roars like a lion, lumbers like a hippopotamus, and finally leaps around the tea-table in imitation of a gazelle, before closing the book and returning it to the shelf.

'Abraham, I must go, indeed I've stayed too long. We'll be in trouble if I'm found.'

'You can't leave until I have shown you Mr Tuffnell's ivory elephants.' He crosses to a small oak press I had not noticed, and proceeds to draw back the doors. They are stiff and heavy, and I am about to insist he lets them alone when the door to the parlour flies open.

Chapter Sixteen

'Don't move an inch, girl, or I will strike.' Mrs Tuffnell holds an iron poker in her hand. 'Abraham, run for help.'

I fall to my knees. 'I'm no thief, Madam, I swear. Please, Madam, I told the child I shouldn't come inside the house, but he begged me so. I was about to go, I promise you I was. The boy wanted to show me the book and the elephants, Mrs Tuffnell, I shouldn't have agreed to it, I am very sorry.'

She brings down the poker on my shoulder, and the pain is so searing I cry out. 'Artful girl!' she exclaims. 'To take advantage of a child. I suppose you pricked the horses' withers to make them bolt, purely to impress me with your quickness. I am no fool; you will be sorry you tried to deceive me!' She delivers another blow that sends me reeling, though fortunately she uses her fist this time, or she would surely render me unconscious.

She is armed, and heavier than me, and her temper is up. My only hope is to throw myself on her mercy. 'Madam, I ought not to have come in, I know I shouldn't. I took pity on your boy, he seemed lonely and the mishap with the coach had unsettled him. I was just about to go, as soon as he'd showed me his master's book of marvels.'

Mrs Tuffnell nods at Abraham. 'Is this true? If so, I shall whip you for bringing a stranger to the house.'

God bless the child, for it must be sorely tempting to cast the blame on me, but Abraham speaks calmly, his large brown eyes fixed on Mrs Tuffnell. 'I begged her to come in though she said she should not. I wanted to show her the book and my silver collar. It was my fault, Madam, don't punish her.'

Perhaps his docile reference to the collar helps my case, but whatever the reason Mrs Tuffnell's anger fades as quickly as it rose, and still eyeing me with some suspicion she slowly puts down the poker on the hearth. 'You are lucky, Mistress, I choose to believe him. As for you, Pug, you may look forward to a beating when your guest has gone.'

There is none of the rebelliousness I saw from Abraham earlier. He takes himself unbidden to a corner and stands with his face turned to the wall, hands clasped behind his back.

'I was wrong and foolish, Mrs Tuffnell,' I say, trying my best to sound truly contrite. 'I pray you, don't treat the lad too harshly, he only hoped to entertain me.'

'Time you were on your way.' Mrs Tuffnell unties her hat strings and begins to unfasten her gloves. Then she stops and looks at Abraham's bowed head.

'You have a useful effect upon my black boy, I must say. I tire of whipping him to make him quiet. I never saw him so meek.'

'He's been very civil with me, indeed he's a credit to you, Madam.'

Mrs Tuffnell addresses Abraham's back. 'Then you'd better continue to be civil when your friend has gone. Oh, come here, child. Don't cry.' For two large tears splash the floor at the boy's feet, and once more Mrs Tuffnell repents of her severity. She steps across and takes his chin in her palm. 'Dry your eyes. If you leave me in peace awhile I may forget my anger. Stand quietly and we will see if you still require a whipping in another hour.'

I dip a curtsey. 'I should be on my way, Madam.'

'Yes, though I would be obliged if you would help me with these wretched buttons.' Her gloves are fastened with tiny pearls, and she struggles to undo them. 'And my boots. Would you unlace them, Miss Amesbury?' Once I have done so, she stretches out her toes. 'That's right, gloves on the side-table, if you please—boots by the door. If you could hang my coat on that peg, Mistress, and pass my shawl. There.' She yawns extravagantly. 'I miss a maid to help me with small things. Abraham is all very well, but he can't attend me as Hannah did.'

I make sure to give no sign I have heard the name before. 'Hannah, Madam?'

'A rude, disagreeable girl who I was forced to turn away. She was impertinent, and encouraged him to be so.' Mrs Tuffnell jerks her head in Abraham's direction. 'However, I will allow that Hannah knew her way around a lady's wardrobe.'

It is extraordinary to hear myself, not two minutes after Mrs Tuffnell threatened me, saying, 'I believe I can claim the same, Madam. I nursed my Cousin Mary, a gentlewoman, and she owned seven gowns, six petticoats, and I had charge of everything.'

She narrows her eyes. 'Lord, you're a child. I doubt you can launder and press linen. Or starch lace. Let alone darn hose.'

'I can do all those and more, Madam. My father was a husbandman, and Mother taught us to make butter, and cheese, raise chickens, sew and brew and bake and clean and do all the work a housewife does.'

Mrs Tuffnell contemplates me kindly. 'You are an honest, hardworking farm-girl, but hardly have the higher skills I require. I run a manufactory in my still-room. Notwithstanding her many vices Hannah was an excellent servant when it came to assisting me. You can't claim knowledge of producing the aids to beauty that are my stock in trade.'

My confidence deserts me. 'I can't, Madam, no.'

Mrs Tuffnell nods, but then, without warning, her frown vanishes and her mood alters to a kind of restless enthusiasm. She turns to Abraham, addressing him archly as if she forgets she has ordered him to stand still. 'But what are we doing, Pug, omitting to show Miss Amesbury our still-room? Newly arrived from the country she would find it vastly interesting. We must take her at once.' She holds up a key hanging from her waist. 'Come, Mistress.'

As Mrs Tuffnell goes towards the door her back is turned, and I risk a glance at Abraham. His face remains expressionless. So why do I detect something I am sure is amusement in his eyes?

Outside the chamber a housemaid polishes the banisters. As we troop downstairs I decide that this young woman, in contrast to the scullery maid, is amiable, for her eyes are grey and mild, and she does not look askance at my plain attire but smiles pleasantly and steps aside to let us pass.

'You may leave my chamber for today, Grey,' Mrs Tuffnell tells her. 'Make sure you sweep your garret, mind, and turn both beds, not just your own. We don't know when I'll find a replacement for Hannah. I may at any time.'

'Yes, Ma'am.'

Nothing could contrast more sharply with our reception from Miss Pot-Scrub as we enter the kitchen. She thumps down a heavy dish so hard she makes the table shake.

'Scrub!' Mrs Tuffnell is outraged. 'It shall come out of your wages if your master's pewter goes to the workshop to have the dents removed. And if you mark the table you will have the pleasure of sanding it 'til the marks are gone.'

Mrs Tuffnell's reprimand does nothing to improve the sour expression on Pot-Scrub's face. If she could do so without her mistress seeing, she would poke out her tongue at all of us.

Unawares, or caring nothing for the scullery maid's opinion, Mrs Tuffnell hums with pleasure as she unlocks a small door in a corner of the kitchen.

'Come on, don't be shy.' She gestures for me to enter.

Mrs Tuffnell spoke the truth upstairs. Her still-room would interest any visitor. The deep, wide shelves, the wood scrubbed and scoured as clean as if it were a dairy, are filled with dozens, perhaps hundreds, of jars and pots, some larger ones earthenware but most of fine white porcelain, as well as several glass vessels of various shapes and sizes. There is a marble pestle and mortar, a grinding stone of polished granite, a pair of scales and a set of tiny brass weights such as druggists use, and most curious of all, a cabinet whose wooden drawers are labelled with mysterious legends. *Tinct. Pl. Tinct. Pl. Alb. Traganth. Gum Arab.*

'Are these herbs, Madam?'

Mrs Tuffnell gives a droll laugh. 'This isn't a shop for turning out common remedies or drying blackcurrant leaves for cottage tea. My preparations are for the use of gentlewomen.' She unlocks a drawer and reveals a tray filled with a white, chalk-like substance, the larger pieces neatly wrapped in paper. Mrs Tuffnell tips a small quantity onto a saucer, then sets it aside and unlocks each drawer in turn, scanning my face as she does so.

Every drawer contains some coloured mineral or preserved ingredient which, from the strong, musky aromas rising from them, include civet, perfumed bark and something she calls orris. 'Made by grinding the root of a particular flowering plant,' she says. 'Irises— you did not have those in your father's garden.' We had irises aplenty, but I shake my head in agreement. Sliding shut the drawer, Mrs Tuffnell reaches for a small stone jar, touching her fingertips to a dusty-looking lump of reddish clay, and rubbing the resulting powder on her hand. It produces a smear of deep crimson. She looks at me in triumph. 'Can you guess? No? It is rouge, Mistress, such as ladies wear on grand occasions.'

'I saw ladies wearing rouge in Bath,' I exclaim, then wish I had not brought Mrs Buckley to mind.

She nods. 'Indeed. It is also worn on less grand occasions. That is, when the ladies can afford it.' She takes down a small, shallow pot from the shelf above her head and lifts the lid carefully to reveal the contents. 'Go on. It is rose of attar. One of my trade secrets, you must not tell anybody that I add it to my rouge. Put some on your cheek there. What we term your "apples."' She offers me a looking-glass. It is heavy, the handle made of chased metal, and bright as silver.

I blink at my reflection. I look like someone other than myself. Older; wealthy.

'Tip your head back.' She uncorks a tiny vial, and before I can protest, drops something cold and wet into my eye. 'Keep still. Let me do the other.' My sight is blurred; I put my hand out for the counter. Again, she flourishes the looking-glass.

'Do you see what has happened? Look how huge and beautiful your eyes are. To gentlemen, they are irresistible. Don't be afraid, girl. It does no harm or half the ladies in this town would be blind.' She dabs a fine limner's brush in the saucer, and using the looking-glass to guide her, applies the powder to her own face. Then she looks up expectantly. 'Say you have worked too hard, helping your father with the harvest, and your face is brown and weathered. My white lead restores your complexion in an instant.'

Her face is as snowy as her page-boy's shirt collar. It looks like a mask made of paper for a mummer's play.

'I don't suppose a farm-girl could afford white lead. But you look ... lovely, Madam. Very pretty. I never saw fairer.'

She preens. 'This is only the beginning. One must also use rouge, mixed with a little almond oil, and paint a red paste to the lips, and before that, pluck away the eyebrows and replace them with ones made from soot and wax, or shreds of mouse-skin. And I like to add a patch or two, it is the way in high society, you know. Hannah, for all her faults, had the nimblest fingers when it came to cutting patches.' She shows me a small box filled with miniscule black circles, hearts and half-moons. 'I wear them here,' she says, placing a finger on her cheek. 'Mr Tuffnell likes me to wear one here.' She selects a tiny black silk heart and holds it to her bosom.

She sees my eyes slide to her page-boy. 'Oh, do not trouble about Pug. He knows all the secrets of a lady's dressing-room. I caught him playing with my plumpers the other day.' A wag of the finger. 'Plumpers are placed inside the cheeks, to improve the profile.'

'It is all most interesting, Madam. I expect you have a great many customers.'

'I do. Now you've been initiated into my Temple of Beauty you needn't be fooled when you go about Bristol and see some fat grand-mamma with a face as delicate as a virgin's. She's one of my ladies, for certain. It's done discreetly, of course. I wouldn't dream of tittle-tattling about those who buy my preparations.'

She begins to put her pots and jars and packages away, lost in thought. Then she stops. 'Though I'm in some difficulty at the present time. Grinding powders and distilling are time-consuming, exacting tasks, and I lack a maid to help me, as I explained.'

'My mother used to say she didn't know how she'd run the house without me, Madam. I did all the work of salting cheese, sieving meal and grinding spices.' In truth our fare at home was plain, but Mrs Tuffnell is not to know. However, she remains doubtful.

'Yes, yes. These aren't the accomplishments I require. Could you weigh a drachma? Use an alimbec? Describe a tincture?'

'I'm a quick learner, Madam. I used to mix Cousin Mary's draughts. I made her poultices and salves, and purges, and the physician said he never saw a cleaner sick-chamber.'

'Purges,' Abraham giggles. His smile vanishes at Mrs Tuffnell's hard stare.

'Pug thinks it a joke,' she says, cuffing him so hard tears spring to his eyes. 'You might think he'd take a lesson from Hannah's dismissal.' To my dismay she grips the boy's collar and pulls him close, speaking softly. 'You and Hannah chose to help yourselves to my still-room, and daub your faces, and Hannah paid the price for your insolence.' She releases him none too gently, and turns to me. 'He's a child, and I told him I'd forgive him. Hannah should have known better. I whipped her and turned her out of doors.'

This story, if I had not spent the last interval delivering letters in the wind, assuring Liz between-times that I could do better than join her as a weeding-woman, might prompt me to remind Mrs Tuffnell politely of the time, and depart Barbuda House vowing never to set foot there again. But I can manage Mrs Tuffnell and her moods, and her little page will be a sort of companion. I do like her still-room, with its scents and secrets. If I stay here awhile I may learn enough to make face-paints of my own to sell, or at the least, find work in an apothecary's shop.

'Please, Madam, consider me. I should like to work for you.'

She runs her tongue over her teeth, scrutinising me as if some falsehood may lurk behind my words. Then she straightens her shoulders. 'Good. Very well, you may begin as my maid forthwith, with special duties in the still-room.'

My heart patters now there can be no gainsaying the deed. 'I hope I shall please you, Madam. I do work hard. I'm quick.'

'I know,' she says, her eyes darting to Abraham, in a reference to the mishap with the coach. 'Therefore, can you go quickly to wherever you're lodging, pack your things, and return by five o'clock? My husband and I have an engagement this evening. It suits me very well if you were here to dress me.'

I laugh a little out of nervousness. Then I catch sight again of the shelves with their enticing pots and potions, and a smile breaks out across my face as warm as the sun that peeps in at the still-house window. 'It suits me too, Madam. I'll be here directly. Thank you, Mrs Tuffnell. Thank you very much indeed.'

Chapter Seventeen

Intent on walking through the kitchen with my head held high, I am caught unawares by Abraham, who slips into the yard ahead of me.

'Good-bye, my friend,' I say. 'I'll see you when I bring my box. Will you greet me? Or will you be abed?'

'Not I. When Mrs Tuffnell dines out Nell Grey lets me sit up late.'

'I hope you take yourself off before Mrs Tuffnell comes back, then. She's a strict mistress, is she not?'

'She's a liar,' he says calmly. I glance upwards; the air is still and I pray the lady cannot overhear us.

'Don't swear, Abraham, or I shan't talk to you.'

'It's true. Hannah was sent away not for stealing, but because Mr Tuffnell tried to kiss her on the stairs.'

'Abraham, if Mrs Tuffnell were to hear she'd do worse than cuff you.'

'I don't need telling what she'd do.' He turns and lifts his shirt. From his shoulders to his waist, his narrow back is covered in small welts.

I draw a wincing breath. 'I see I must be obedient and civil when I am Mrs Tuffnell's maid.'

Abraham shrugs, and tucks in his shirt. 'We did sneak into the still-room that afternoon, Hannah and I. We thought she was out visiting. We were only play-acting.'

'Go on.'

'Hannah made herself over as an old duchess with purple cheeks and bright red lips. I plastered my face with white lead. People here put on blackface. Why should I not do something alike?'

'A good question. Though it was not your white lead.'

He pouts. 'She has enough to paint the privy outhouse if she wanted. She only found out because Suke Cross told her where to find us.'

'Be comforted, master. I'm here now, and that makes two of us to wreak revenge on Suke Cross.' But the lad does not smile or otherwise acknowledge the joke, and I leave him sulkily kicking a tennis-ball about the yard.

***

The wind is cruel and the sky darkening as I walk back to All-Saints'-yard. Today is the last day of October and I feel blessed to have found a place by wintertime. Barbuda House will be a great deal warmer than Bill Eardley's draughty makeshift hut.

That shiftless hulk of a brother-in-law is hunched on a stool by the house door when I turn into the yard.

'Good day, Brother. I'm only come to fetch my box. If you could be kind enough to tell my sister I'll be back to see her on my first half day?'

'Oh ho, ho.' He chuckles nastily. 'Been offered the post of lady's maid to the mayor's wife, have you? Thought not. What is it? Pot-washer in a hot-meat shop, with a pile of straw to sleep on?'

It is a moment of sweet triumph. 'You were closer to the truth the first time. Maid to Mrs Tuffnell of Barbuda House, Wine-street.'

Bill's mouth opens. His thoughts seem to rearrange themselves. Then he slaps his thigh. 'Well done, girl.' He apes a gentlewoman's fluting tones. '"Barbuda House, Wine-street."' Another chortle. 'You're made, girl. Get your feet under the table, save your wages a year or two, the three of us will set up shop together.' He sticks out a hand.

I tuck my own behind my back. I shall not shake on any deal, and Bill can think twice if he expects to gain from my good fortune.

'Thank you for your kind wishes, Brother. I must fetch my box.'

'No, no. I wouldn't dream of it. I shall fetch it for you, Miss Amesbury of Wine-street.' He sets down the trap he was oiling, and goes inside.

Bill had success last night, for there are three traps laid out on the ground for cleaning and re-setting, as well as a heap of the knives he uses to skin his catches. Some are thin-bladed, others broad and heavy. One in particular with a polished handle looks familiar.

'Here you are.' Bill reappears with my travelling-box under one arm. 'I expect you'll want to leave Liz a little something for her hospitality.'

It is hard not to give in when he speaks so insolently and cheerfully, but he would never pass on any money supposing I were fool enough to trust him.

I smile. 'I have a gift, yes. Perhaps you would be kind enough to give it to her for me, with my love.' I take my box and lift the lid. A small card lies on top with three pair of new silk buttons stitched to it. 'Cousin Mary gave me these when I left Salisbury. I know Liz is fond of blue.'

He scowls. 'She's fonder still of ready money.'

'I offered her money and she refused. She's proud, my sister. She knows how little I have.'

Even Bill looks ashamed. He picks up a knife, peers at it, and looks about for his whetstone. Then he sets to sharpening the blade, frowning and examining it as if the business is an important one and I am forgotten.

I could depart at once, but there is a question I must ask.

'Bill? That knife there, the big one with the handle made of horn. It's not the knife Liz found in the bothy? Liz said she had given it back to Mr Elliott, in case the magistrates came for it.'

He pauses, knife in one hand, whetstone in the other. His thick, hairy fingers are black with grit and dirty water. 'Do you accuse us of thieving from Mr Elliott? That's my knife, girl. They're all my knives. Liz never spoke of any knife to me, and if she had I would have said to give it back.'

There are but ourselves in the yard. The neighbours are at work, and Mrs Jervis's door is shut. Even the barefoot children have been driven inside by the biting wind.

'Of course you would, Bill. I thought it a little like the one we found, but when I look closer it has a different handle altogether. And the blade is longer.'

He nods. 'Good.' A pause, and he resumes work.

'Well. Remember me to Liz, won't you?'

Bill grunts. It is plain he is glad to see the back of me. And I him; I would not ask to lodge beneath his roof again if no other house were standing.

However, I must try to call on Liz as soon as possible to remind her to return the knife to Mr Elliott. I am certain it is the one we saw, and I would be sorry indeed if Mr Elliott or the magistrates accused my poor sister of stealing it. Or of something even worse.

***

I was right when I judged the Tuffnells' maid good-natured. She appears in the kitchen as soon as I return, and I am sure she has been listening out for me.

'Miss Helen Grey,' she says, offering her hand. 'Nell Grey will do.'

'Pleased to meet you, Nell Grey.' It feels very sober to introduce ourselves like grown-up folks. 'Miss Coronation Amesbury. Friends call me Corrie.'

'Follow me.'

We climb two pair of stairs, and Nell Grey throws open the door of an attic room with a narrow window, a set of hooks, a wooden chest, and two bed-steads, on each of which there is a tolerably thick feather bed, a wool blanket, a small pillow, and a counterpane. 'That one's yours,' she says. 'You'll need your own pair of sheets.' A charcoal drawing of a dimpled, round-faced woman in a mob cap looks down on the wall above her own bed.

'We're allowed a fire on the coldest days so long as we gather and carry in the wood ourselves,' Nell Grey continues. 'Only when it snows, mind. The shutters fit tight, see?' She closes them, and although the room is dim, the rush-light she brought with us casts a warm and friendly glow. 'It's dark, to be sure, but then it's nearly sundown.'

'Does Abraham sleep here?'

'Not he. He has a little room off Mrs Tuffnell's bedchamber.'

'And is he there now? He told me he intended to stay up tonight. I'm surprised Mistress allows it.'

Nell Grey's face falls. 'He's usually sent to bed at six. But tonight Mr Roach locked him in the cellar.'

'Why?'

'For throwing stones at Mr Tuffnell's horses.'

'And did he?'

'Not on purpose. You know what boys are like. I think Mr Roach was angry with Pug for another reason. Pug claimed Suke Cross and Mr Roach were kissing. We servants are forbid to court one another, as you may suppose.' She flushes.

'Does Mrs Tuffnell not object to Mr Roach punishing her darling?'

'Her darling? She is somewhat ... changeable, is that the word? She loves Pug but she was busy deciding what to wear.'

My hand flies to my mouth. 'She bid me help her dress. I'd better find her straight away.'

Nell Grey grimaces. 'Rather you than me. All Hallows is the most important feast of the year for the Society of Merchant Venturers. Watch out she doesn't thrash you with her hairbrush if her dress fits ill. The handle is made of ebony, and very hard it is.' Lowering her voice, she leads me back downstairs and turns left. 'Here's our mistress's chamber. Good luck.' Wishing Nell Grey had not left me so abruptly, I knock softly and announce myself.

'Enter,' comes the command. And when my fingers struggle to release the door catch, a rather less lofty, 'Hurry up, girl.'

I am determined Mrs Tuffnell shall not find me the bumpkin she took me for. I obey her every order as fast as I am able, and little by little as her stays are laced and her petticoats arranged and her bed-gown put on over the rest her mood lightens and she ceases to snap. By the time her attire is complete the sweat runs down my back, but she is too entranced to notice.

I allow she looks very well. Her waist is narrow yet her figure full, and any blemishes in her complexion are hidden by a careful application of white lead. She covers this with a dusting of red ochre, finely ground, then allows me to paint a cupid's bow on her lips, and advise her where best she should place the patches on her neck and shoulders.

Bearing in mind Mr Tuffnell's fancy, I am so bold as to suggest her left breast.

She stands and slowly turns before her pier-glass. Her shoes are dainty, with neat turned heels, and white silk ribbons to fasten them, and her stockings are white silk likewise, and her gown rose-pink, her sleeves the same, and her petticoats are red-and-white striped, and her hair dressed with long, curled crimson ribbons, while her bed-gown, close-fitting gold brocade, is adorned with flowers and leaves embroidered with seed pearls, gold sequins and gold thread. She is perfectly turned out, from her glossy tresses to the lace gloves she bids me pull on for her, wearing plain mittens on my own hands lest I damage the patterning of tiny pearls.

'Fetch my husband, Amesbury.' Her eyes dance. 'Go on, hurry.'

In the next chamber Mr Tuffnell has just completed his own toilette. I enter to find the footman putting away the cone and box of powder for dressing his master's wig. The merchant stands before his own glass in a fine black frock-coat faced with yellow silk, a deep pink waistcoat edged with wide gold braid, a dazzling white stock and white silk stockings, and narrow black shoes tricked out with gilt buckles.

I take care neither to remark on Mr Tuffnell's appearance nor let my eyes rest on his elegant calves and smooth complexion. Even the prospect of his wife in her finery does not deter him from ogling my bosom as I speak.

'Mrs Tuffnell's ready to step out, Sir.'

Humorously, he consults the timepiece hanging at his waist. 'Only two hours. Very good. For our wedding she was in her dressing-room for four.' The manservant smiles but wisely says nothing.

But when Mr Tuffnell catches sight of his wife he forgets to be merry. His mouth falls open.

Flushed and bashful, Mrs Tuffnell smiles. 'It's the petticoat I wore for our wedding, James. Only the bed-gown is different, at least the sleeves and lace are new. Oh, and you haven't seen this gauze shawl before.' Shyly, she turns one way then the other.

He shakes his head. 'You're as beautiful as Queen Anne herself, dear Maria—the Queen in her first flush of youth. Your waist so slender, the whole shapely beyond words. Your hair ... I never saw it arranged better. Turn round again, my angel. These sleeves show off the whiteness, the delicacy of your arms.' He beams. 'The other men will be wild with jealousy. I'll have to be on hand lest some palsied old alderman tries to steal a kiss from these rosebud lips.' He plants a lingering kiss of his own, careless of my presence until his wife gives a cough. Then Mr Tuffnell stands back to admire her once again.

He gives a start. 'But where's your page? He ought to walk behind you. His dark looks will throw your radiance into even sharper relief.'

Mrs Tuffnell's white lead is applied so thickly she must be careful not to crack it, but she allows the smallest frown to pleat her brow. 'I fear the hour is far too late to keep Pug up, James.'

'Nonsense. He's not an infant. You are too careful of his comfort, Maria, he must learn to do as he is bid. Amesbury, fetch Pug right away. The scamp had better have washed his face and changed his linen.'

I am about to explain that Abraham is in the cellar and very likely grimy by now, but Mrs Tuffnell frowns pettishly.

'Really, James, I'd rather Pug stayed home. He looked uncommon sulky last time we took him out to supper. Then he complained the next day of stomach pains after eating candied figs. Jonathan can walk us to the Merchants' Hall, we don't need Pug this time.'

Mr Tuffnell's indulgent smile shows he cannot deny his wife anything tonight. 'Very well, if you insist. But remind me to show Master Pug the rod if he looks sulky another time, little devil.' Wistful at missing the chance to show off his wife and her black boy, he adds, 'Are you sure we shan't take him? I may have to send you home before me, if one of my partners insists on talking business late into the night.'

A Pair of Sharp Eyes

'Then I would feel safer with Jonathan, dear heart. This time of year the streets are dark.'

'They are, it is true. Very well then. Here, let me rearrange this shawl once more. You do look beautiful, Maria—did I say so?'

From his avid gaze you would think Mr Tuffnell had eyes for no one but his wife. Yet when I hand him his silver-topped cane he contrives to squeeze my fingers—for the briefest moment, you understand—so that far from wishing I were not dressed in plain calico and brown wool, and about to spend my evening supping gruel in the kitchen, I feel sorry for Mrs Tuffnell. She doesn't know her beloved James one jot, and if she did, she would think him the least faithful gentleman in Bristol.

'Shall I wait up for you, Madam? You'll need me when you undress.'

'Not tonight, Amesbury. I'll be kind and say that after your long day you'll be glad to retire betimes.'

'Pardon me, but will Mr Tuffnell help you unlace, Madam?'

'What? Oh, yes, Mr Tuffnell can help if assistance is needed. You must be with me at first light, however. I'll want you to brush my clothes and repair them and put them away and launder my linen. That will do for now, girl.' Dismissing me with a wave, she takes her husband's arm and off they saunter, leaving a fragrant blend of civet, rouge and lavender-water in the air behind them.

There is a flurry downstairs as Mr Tuffnell shouts for Jonathan the footman, and Jonathan dashes to find Mr Tuffnell his umbrella, and Mrs Tuffnell refuses to cover her raiments with a plain grey cloak, and all agree it cannot rain, then at last the street door shuts and Nell Grey and I hide at the chamber window and watch the threesome walk the length of Wine-street, Mrs Tuffnell stepping daintily over puddles with the help of her husband, the footman walking at a respectful distance behind his master holding the umbrella.

'I'll introduce you to Jonty properly tomorrow,' Nell Grey says. For some reason her nose is pink. 'He looks handsome in his new grey livery, I think.'

'Though Mr Tuffnell is the handsomer. Isn't he tall?'

'Yes, but dark. I like fair better.'

'Why don't they use their carriage?'

'That's the joke of it. The streets are too narrow. I heard Mr Roach complaining they will scarcely have any use for it. She don't mind. It's only for show. There.' Nell Grey watches with satisfaction as the threesome turn the street corner. 'Now we can have our supper.'

'Shall we not rescue Abraham? He must be cold.'

She looks askance. 'I dursn't risk Mr Roach's wrath. Don't fret, he will let him out by and by. He won't want Mrs Tuffnell to come home and find her pet missing. Come, let's see if Cook won't leave out a bit of bread and dripping for poor Pug. Gracious, I am hungry myself, ain't you?'

And though I take my chance when Nell Grey is out at the necessary, and speak through the cellar door to ask if Abraham can hear me, there is no reply. I tell myself he is most likely fast asleep.

Chapter Eighteen

Thursday 1ˢᵗ November, 1703

The following morning Mrs Hucker has just shown me to the sink where I am to wash Mrs Tuffnell's linen when Mr Roach charges in.

'Abe's lying out there in the yard.'

George is just behind the coachman. 'He's dead!'

Jonathan, seated at the kitchen table with a cup of small beer, leaps to his feet as the rest of us—Mrs Hucker, Suke Cross and I—rush outside. I glimpse a bundled figure in the corner nearest the stable before Mr Roach tears off his coat and throws it over the corpse, too late to conceal the bloody neck and the ghastly sightless eyes. Suke Cross screams and throws herself into Mr Roach's arms; he pats her shoulder awkwardly before taking a step back.

Nell Grey, who had been sweeping grates, comes running to see the cause of the commotion. Her eyes alight on a small brown hand just visible beneath the coat and she begins to cry.

Mrs Hucker raises her face to the window that overlooks the yard and fills her lungs. 'Mr Tuffnell! Mr Tuffnell!'

Jonathan joins us, deathly pale. 'The master's coming. Be quiet, all of you.'

Mr Tuffnell takes in everything at a glance, though he is too late to prevent his wife, who has followed him outside, from collapsing in a faint as she realises who lies beneath the coachman's coat.

'My dear Maria!' Mr Tuffnell bears up his wife, whose form is as limp and lifeless as her page-boy's. 'Amesbury, help.' Somehow we scramble back into the house, Mr Tuffnell lowering his wife into the chair nearest the kitchen hearth, Nell Grey and I running to fetch water and a napkin to moisten our mistress's forehead.

I am dimly aware of Mr Roach and Jonathan carrying the body into the scullery and shutting the door so the rest of us are spared the sight of the child laid out on the stone sink where I was due to wash my mistress's linen. We struggle to revive Mrs Tuffnell as the men call for George Goodfellow to fetch the constable, and Mrs Hucker and Suke Cross vie with each other to grieve loudest for a boy neither regarded when he was alive. Mrs Hucker shrieks and wails, hysterical, and Suke Cross blubbers like a baby, every now and then gasping out, 'Poor lad, poor little lad,' as if Abraham was her own brother instead of the object of her senseless jealousy.

Finally, Mrs Tuffnell gives a feeble moan.

'Thank the Lord.' Mrs Hucker sinks onto the bench and fans her face with her apron. 'I thought her dead too.'

The sun is not yet risen, and the kitchen remains chilly despite the fire. I unpin my shawl. 'Sir, put this around her.' Mr Tuffnell drapes the shawl tenderly around his wife's shoulders, examining her face as if afraid she may succumb to another faint.

By and by he supports her through to her usual chair in the parlour, while Nell Grey, with more patience than Suke Cross deserves, offers the scullery maid her arm and brings her in their wake. Meanwhile I run to the kitchen for a taper to light the candles above the fireplace.

When our mistress is settled and Mr Tuffnell has gone out to the scullery, Mrs Hucker permits herself to sit. She twists and worries the corner of her neckerchief. 'How could someone do such a thing? To Mrs Tuffnell's precious boy?'

Mrs Tuffnell's own voice is childlike. 'What has befallen Pug? Did I faint? Oh, my head hurts so.'

'Calm yourself, Madam. Mr Tuffnell has the matter in hand. Don't distress yourself. It will be put to rights soon.' I am afraid to repeat the awful tidings, and with soothing nonsense I distract my mistress as best I can, though everything is said above the grim sound of Mr Roach's tread in the scullery. I catch Nell Grey's eye. Suddenly I cannot bear to stay in the room another moment. 'Excuse me, Madam, I'll fetch you a warmer shawl.' I scuttle into the passage, and as I hoped, Nell Grey comes after me.

'It must be Mr Roach did it.'

Her eyes widen in alarm. 'Ssh. Don't speak so loud.'

'Who else could it be? He's a bully, and he took against Abraham.'

'Corrie, it isn't for us to name names.'

Just then Mr Roach steps out of the kitchen. His face is blotched, and he grabs Nell Grey by the hand. 'Come with me. And you,' he says to me, 'you can tell the master what you know.' He drags us to the kitchen where Mr Tuffnell has shut the scullery door and stands by the fireplace wiping his face.

'This pair can vouch for me,' Mr Roach says. He is out of breath. 'Tell Master the truth. I put the lad in the cellar yesterday for his own good. It was the last time I set eyes on him.' It is unfortunate that Mr Roach makes reference to his eyes, given that they flash dangerously as he speaks.

'Well?' Mr Tuffnell demands. 'Can you maids confirm it?'

I believe Nell Grey is on the brink of tears, though I am not sure why unless it is the thought of what lies in the room behind us.

'Mr Roach did put the child in the cellar last night, Sir,' I say. 'As far as I know, he left him there.'

'I said it!' Mr Roach is triumphant. 'For that matter, this girl here could have killed the lad. Forgive me, Sir, but she is the only stranger in the house.'

Nell Grey gives a little jump.

'Sir, Corrie Amesbury and I were in our beds by eight o'clock. I can vouch we were together all night long.'

Mr Tuffnell looks inquiringly at Mr Roach.

'Mr Tuffnell,' the coachman says heavily, 'I allow I should not have been so severe with the lad, but you would not have had him lame your horse. Many a man would have taken a whip to him.'

'Of course you were right to chasten him for throwing stones at Caesar. There is no reason to suspect you of involvement in his death. No hint of that is in my mind.'

'Well, Sir. I thank you.'

'However, you must explain how you were able to enter the cellar. I have the only key, and it was with me at the Tolzey yesterday.'

Mr Roach's face is a study in injured amazement. 'The cellar wasn't locked, Sir. You must have forgotten to lock it last time you went in there. I didn't lock the child in. I told him, "Stay put 'til I say otherwise, or risk a hiding." And give him credit, Sir, he did. At least at first. I wish he had done so all night long. If he had, instead of venturing out when we was all asleep, he might be alive now.'

'Indeed. Well, you did a wrong thing, Roach, by entering my cellar without permission. However, I am prepared to overlook it. It would seem petty to rebuke you when so grave a matter is in hand.'

'Thank you, Sir.'

I am not a little astonished by this easy way of passing over what is surely a breach of trust between man and master, but a knock at the door announces Jonathan's return with the constable.

Mr Tuffnell beckons them down the passage. 'Come in, Constable. I expect my footman informed you what has happened. My house is under attack from some person unknown who has robbed me of a valuable servant. My wife is distraught.'

'I understand. If I could see the body, Sir, and you could show me where it was found?'

'Certainly. You girls, get yourselves back to your mistress.' We obey, though not before I hear Mr Tuffnell adding, 'The boy's throat was cut, though fortunately less blood was shed than one might expect. Nevertheless, it is no fit sight for women.'

In the passageway Nell Grey and I embrace for a moment.

'I am unconvinced,' I whisper. 'Mr Roach was the last to see him alive.' I think back to Mr Roach's cruelty towards the negroes on the quays. 'What if he killed Abraham in a fit of rage?'

Nell Grey shakes her head. 'He's acting strange because he helped himself to rum from Mr Tuffnell's cellar. He's frightened the master will find out.'

'How do you know?'

She pauses, her hand resting on the parlour door handle. 'Because Mr Roach nearly fell down in the yard last night. He couldn't walk, never mind cut anybody's throat. Come on. You must attend Mrs

Tuffnell, and neither of us needs Mr Roach to think we are talking about him in dark corners.'

I do as she says, and Mrs Tuffnell is glad to see me, and has me busy rearranging cushions at her back and fetching the promised shawl. Nell Grey is ordered to light the fire, and Mrs Hucker pours our mistress a glass of sherry wine. She keeps up a patter of cheerful nothings, but the parlour walls being thin, I can hear Mr Tuffnell telling the constable who Abraham was, when he joined the household, his age, Mr Roach every now and then adding, 'That's right, Sir. That's it.' At one point Mrs Tuffnell's eyes meet mine and there is no doubt she knows very well what has happened even if she is not yet able to speak of it.

By and by the constable comes in saying that this is another instance of the pedlar striking at a defenceless child, and in the meanwhile we must lock our doors and pray for the culprit's swift discovery. Mr Tuffnell declares he will not sleep 'til the murderer is found, though I catch him looking at the mantel clock while the constable is speaking, and I fancy he hankers after work as usual.

When they are gone I take Mrs Tuffnell back to her room, keep her company while she cries and eventually lapses into a fitful sleep, and at last I begin to put away her finery from the night before.

As I go about my tasks, I wonder why I feel so much mistrust towards my fellow servants. Mr Roach is too loud and indignant; I am surprised Mr Tuffnell is so ready to accept his innocence. Jonty is weak; I cannot picture him harming anyone. And yet the constable let out that the footman insists on keeping vigil over the corpse, and washing and dressing it with his own hands, despite Mrs Hucker protesting it is the work of laying-out women, and I wonder why Jonty feels such sorrow. As for Mr Tuffnell, he must know he was remiss in failing to bolt the cellar yesterday, and that he does not reprimand Mr Roach as severely as he should.

Even Nell Grey may know something she does not tell me. If she is afraid of Mr Roach I can scarcely blame her for shielding him. And yet I am sorry she shirks the truth if privately she thinks him responsible for the murder.

I have a suspicion of my own. I believe these people would like the world to forget Mrs Tuffnell's page, for he was only a slave, and a negro, loved for his presence rather than himself; and when all is said and done Mr Tuffnell can buy another 'Pug'.

Yet I shall not forget Abraham, who liked and confided in me in the short time I knew him. I can listen at doors, and spy on everyone, for thanks to my mistress I am continually running back and forth to kitchen, scullery, parlour and bedchamber. If there is any wrong-doing I shall find it out. And take it to my master, and ask what he intends to do.

A Pair of Sharp Eyes

Chapter Nineteen

Friday, 2nd November, 1703

Mrs Tuffnell has a dark grey shawl about her shoulders when I carry in her breakfast. Her face is more woeful than Nell Grey gives her credit for.

She being in need of kindness, I take particular care when setting out the toast and tea things. 'Perhaps you'll be easier in your mind when the funeral is over, Madam,' I say gently.

She frowns, and I think I have overstepped the mark. Then she reaches for a letter lying ready on the table. 'Be discreet, Amesbury. Take this to the other end of Wine-street, and ask the attendant to show you to Mr Ayres's apartment.'

Stealthily I feel the letter: it contains a quantity of coins.

'Mrs Hucker wants me to buy the fish, Madam. I can take this on my way.'

'Then you need not explain yourself to Cook or any other.'

'No, Madam.' I dearly wish you would explain yourself, I long to say. What 'attendant' does she mean? Does she send me to a Bedlam? She glances at the window.

'Ah well, sun's up,' she says, as contentedly as if she has forgotten Abraham's death entirely. 'I've an order for a dozen perfumed washballs to make for a customer in Castle-street. And you have your letter to deliver, so let's not dawdle, girl.'

I suppose I should not condemn her for welcoming a distraction from the grief weighing on the house, but Mrs Tuffnell's moods are so changeable I begin to wonder if she is not affected in some evil way by the ingredients of her still-room.

As she hurries off, forgetting me in her eagerness, my eye falls on her desk, which is in its usual muddle. Among the mess of documents, receipts and druggist's bills is a letter in her own hand, but the signature at the bottom is one I never saw before. *Maria Buckingham.*

I step back and upbraid myself with the thought of what would become of me if Mrs Tuffnell ran upstairs unexpectedly and found me prying into her papers. If my mistress chooses to use an alias it is no business of mine.

And yet, I reflect as I go downstairs, knowledge once gained cannot be forgotten. The proof that Mrs Tuffnell is not all she seems may have more in it than meets the eye, and should remind me to be on my guard against trusting her too readily.

These ideas make me nervous, and as luck would have it, just as I am leaving Barbuda House I run into Mr Tuffnell in the passage.

'Heavens, Sir, you startled me.'

'We are all shaken today,' he sighs. Yet he loves to rest his hand on my upper arm, and his thumb wanders to my bosom. 'Poor girl, you must wonder where you've landed up.'

'Hopefully the murderer will be found and brought to justice, Sir.' I try to prise free, but he clamps my hand.

'And where are you off to this morning, if I may ask?'

'To market as usual, Sir. For mackerel.'

Mr Tuffnell lolls against the wall and adopts a knowing tone.

'Indeed? What's this, Amesbury? Taking messages to your sweetheart?' Before I can prevent him his hand is inside my neckerchief and pulling out my mistress's letter. His expression softens instantly.

'My wife indulging her benevolent nature. Dear creature, she is a model of charitable generosity. Here.' He produces a silver coin from his pocket. 'Add a half-crown to her dole.'

He saunters off to tease Nell Grey into bringing him a pot of tea in the midst of Mrs Hucker making dinner for the household, and I make my exit before he invents a reason to call me back.

What neither Mrs Tuffnell nor her spouse is pleased to tell me is that Mr Ayres lives in what is known in plain speech as a debtors' prison. I daresay they consider me a simple country girl; but I know a turnkey when I see one, even if a spunging-house is not a place I ever set eyes on, nor do I know of any person forced through debt to stay in one.

A Pair of Sharp Eyes

This grim building, which lies at the dingy, neglected, half-aban-doned end of Wine-street rather than the bright and spacious portion where Barbuda House is to be found, stands cheek-by-jowl with Bristol Newgate. The windows are secured with iron bars, and an air of extreme want hangs over the place, the ground around it being dank and weedy, the roof missing many tiles, the buildings them-selves in poor repair. A wall-eyed fellow in torn stockings guards the entrance, and he shuffles from his sentry-box to bar my way.

I flourish Mrs Tuffnell's letter.

'I'll take that for you.' He reaches out a greedy hand.

'Thank you, Sir, but I was told to give it to none but Mr Ayres.'

He snorts. 'As you like.'

I follow him across a scabby patch of grass where barefoot chil-dren play at Fives, and a skinny kitten is forced to chase a rag tied to her tail. The place is divided into a dozen tenements, each door bearing the inmate's efforts to mark it with such items as sprigs of heather, knots of coloured ribbon and withered flowers. The turnkey knocks on a door that has a trio of pheasant's feathers nailed to it, and without waiting for a summons, kicks it open and retreats to his sentry-box, leaving me to introduce myself.

Mr Ayres sits next to the fire, if a single smoking branch can be called a fire. His cell is tiny and bare, and the smoke is not enough to mask the smell of damp, cold stone. I suppose Mr Ayres would be worse off if he had to share his cell with another prisoner, but he might be warmer if he did.

'I come from Mrs Tuffnell, Sir. With this.'

He takes the letter carelessly, but I notice him feeling for its con-tents and quickly tucking it in his sleeve. 'Oh,' says Mr Ayres, his tone injured as he sees me turn to leave. 'Are we not to pass the time of day? Very well.'

'If you would like me to stay awhile, Sir, I shall, of course.'

He looks about himself as if the meagre furnishings strike him for the first time. 'I can offer you that packing case by way of a chair, or if it be too primitive, this four-legged stool. Though recently re-duced to three legs it is serviceable if you treat it with respect.'

'It will do very well, Sir.' I lower myself gingerly onto the stool, wishing it stood a little nearer to the hearth.

'I must apologise for the absence of refreshments.' Mr Ayres shakes his head, surprised. 'It is my time-hallowed custom to offer wayfarers a beverage, and victuals into the bargain. But alas my provisions are quite run down. Take it that I would have set in front of you a feast of dainties, snippets of fried bread, lightly poached eggs, herrings in oatmeal, perfectly fresh cheese.' He sighs. 'You must wonder how I come to be in such a place.'

'I suppose any one may run up bills and find himself without means to pay them,' I say.

Mr Ayres jerks upright, indignant. 'I daresay I have, as you put it, run up bills, and yet who in this fallen world proceeds through life without incurring debt? When one's station requires a certain splendour in one's attire?' He gestures at his waistcoat, on which may be glimpsed remnants of gold thread, frayed and faded. 'The obligations of friendship cannot be subordinated to considerations of sobriety or economy. Largesse is the thing that distinguishes us from the lower animals. To load the board with luxurious foodstuffs, fragrant pineapples from the isles of the Caribbean, peaches from England's finest glasshouses, fricassées, ragouts, jellies and junkets. Once upon a time my house was the resort of the highest ranks in the kingdom. Do you advise I should have stinted my guests? Given dry bread and green bacon to a duchess, asked my lord to slake his thirst on home-brewed beer instead of filling his cup to overflowing with the grapes of Burgundy and Champagne?'

Mr Ayres speaks with passion, and yet his eyes sparkle and I suspect that a very little would be enough to tempt him into laughing at himself.

'I suppose it might have been prudent to water his wine down a little. Not to give the duchess rotten meat, but boiled ham can be very pleasant with a few green peas, Sir, and is cheaper than roast beef.'

'Alas, you have the small soul of one who never dreams of rising above her station. Tell me, where are you from? Wiltshire, is it? Ha!

I was a close friend of the Bishop of Salisbury once upon a time. Good old Bishop Burnet forgets me now, I fear.'

'I hope you are mistaken about my dreams, Sir. I do certainly hope never to fall below my station.'

I regret my jibe, for his face loses all its cheerfulness. Instantly he is no longer a once fine gentleman possessed of dignity, but a gaunt old man in a threadbare coat.

'Would you like me to pass on any message to Mrs Tuffnell, Sir?' I say, ashamed of my sharp tongue. 'Or my master?'

'Tell Mrs Tuffnell I am obliged. Inform her I was distressed beyond measure to hear of her loss.' He eyes me. 'You are surprised. But even here, in this half-forgotten house of penance, we are not bereft of news. I knew of the murder the day it happened.'

'Mrs Tuffnell will be glad of your condolences, Sir. He was a fine child and greatly loved.'

'And Mrs Tuffnell is laid low with grief.' He pronounces this as if to test the words.

'She has been distressed, Sir, naturally. I happened to be present when she learned the news.'

'I imagine consoling her was not an easy task, the circumstances of the death being what they were.'

'It is a dreadful trial for everyone in the household, Sir.'

'Mrs Tuffnell can be trying herself when she is out of temper.' His voice grows light as he speaks his thoughts aloud. 'I wonder if she is a kind mistress.'

I hardly know if I should answer. There is a pause, and I say: 'She was kind enough to offer me a place, Sir, and gives me no cause for complaint.'

'Good, good,' he says, voice vague. His eyes widen. 'Whereas the dead boy said otherwise. He found her harsh.'

I choose my words with care. 'Abraham missed his home and his family, Sir. He chafed a little when his mistress sought to correct him.' Behind my back I cross my fingers and pray that if Abraham is listening, he forgives me.

Drily, Mr Ayres regards the vaulted ceiling of his cell. 'I see you are not to be tempted into saying anything Mrs Tuffnell would not wish to hear. A loyal servant. Yet is that quite what she deserves? As a near relative I may be frank where others hesitate to judge. I would describe her as … capricious.'

I resent his persistence in trying to trip me up, and nearly retort that my father never failed to speak kind words of me. I am certainly not to be tempted into speaking ill of Mrs Tuffnell if she is his relation.

'She is a fair employer, and as you see yourself, Sir, she is generous. Her husband, Sir, asked me to give you this. I am sorry, it slipped my mind 'til now.' I wait for Mr Ayres to accuse me, but instead he jumps up, snatches the half-crown, tosses it, nods at the ringing sound it makes, then kicks aside a loose brick in the floor and drops the silver into the hole before replacing the brick. The contrast between his sly way of speaking about Mrs Tuffnell and his expression of artful satisfaction makes me smile despite myself.

'You are right, Mistress,' Mr Ayres says. 'Mrs Tuffnell is generous to all. The epitome of generosity no less. In making her acts of charity regular and well-judged she is also wise.' He sees my surprise, but offers no explanation for this puzzling remark. A smile overspreads his thin lined face. 'Thanks to her I will have veal for dinner today, and a glass of ratafia. Though it might be politic to report that I intend to eke out her funds by eating porridge for a fortnight. I leave it for you to judge.'

I take this as my cue to leave, and rise. 'I will be sure Mrs Tuffnell and her husband know of your gratitude, Sir.'

Mr Ayres's lips pucker, and I see he considers he has met a kindred spirit, one who knows the gulf between what is said and what is thought and felt. 'I am sure that you will make a pretty speech on my behalf, Mistress. Do, pray, call on me again.'

'I am honoured, Sir.'

'And I.' He bows from the waist, as if I am the spirit of his friend the duchess, though his eye gleams satirically as if to say, 'You and I both know you are a servant.'

A Pair of Sharp Eyes

As I leave the spunging-house for the fish market I reflect that I am puzzled by Mr Ayres. Pink-complexioned, with hair that is greying but once was fair, he looks as English as I am with my ruddy cheeks and round blue eyes. Whereas Mrs Tuffnell, whose hair is thick and dark and eyes are black and darting, is the copy of the Spanish and Portuguese sailors on Bristol's quays. In certain lights, without her blessed white lead, she is almost as dark-skinned as Abraham.

Family likenesses are not to be relied on, for which I have cause to be thankful. I would not like to share looks with my Wiltshire sister Meg, for all she prides herself on her milkmaid's plump smooth hands; and poor Liz was never pretty even before she was stricken by the pox. I do carry the marks of my late father, however, so well that I myself can see it.

I am in danger of feeling not a small degree of pride at my talent for noticing the lack of semblance between my employer and Mr Ayres. Then I reflect as I make my way back to Wine-street that I may be as foolish as Mrs Tuffnell thought me when she sent me to the spunging-house. It never crossed my mind 'til now to wonder why her loving husband has not paid off Mr Ayres's creditors and given the old gentleman back his liberty.

Chapter Twenty

Tuesday, 6ᵗʰ November, 1703

Last night Mr Tuffnell insisted his family stay at home, fearing the many bonfires lit for Gunpowder Plot Day would lead to riots and assaults. This morning Mr Roach speaks to a neighbour's groom, who says a party of revellers ran across two papists in the early hours, beat them with staves and left them for dead. Though one was carried to a hospital, the other died upon a stretcher before he reached it.

Young George Goodfellow is due to go home to Keynsham for a holiday, and the intention had been for him to travel on foot, but after this news Mr Roach volunteers to take him on horseback and Mrs Tuffnell says she is content to have him use her own brown mare, adding she would not risk the life of another child, and can manage without her horse a day or two.

On our way home from the market Nell Grey and I witness a negro woman weeping as her child is taken from her, the boy having been sold to a wealthy man who stands idly chatting to the seller, a sea-captain, while the mother grieves and the child, clutching the pommel of his new master's saddle, cries despairingly.

We walk back through streets where all I see is brutishness: children struck by their fathers; women cursed at by their husbands; horses thin and covered in untreated sores. Not for the first time I wonder if I have left Erlestoke for a city where the sole aim is to make money, heedless of the cost in misery and pain.

Yet rather than run back to Wiltshire I see a lesson to be learned. I think of Abraham's agony as he lay dying from his wounds, and though I cannot prevent the buying and selling of other children, I am more determined than ever to find out what happened to my young friend, and why.

During the quiet of household prayers I reflect again on this, and decide to ask Mr Espinosa for his opinion of the matter. He is sure to join the funeral procession in the morning and I shall catch him then.

***

Wednesday, 7ᵗʰ November, 1703

At ten o'clock the undertaker and his men shoulder the little coffin, and the bells toll as we begin our walk to church. Mrs Tuffnell leans on her husband and trembles so violently that my master signs for me to take her other arm. The other servants bring up the procession, and the street is lined with onlookers. I notice a dozen negroes in the crowds; one or two may be free men, or sailors, but others must have been granted a holiday, or else they come without permission from their owners, intent on paying their respects to a youngster of their race.

The bells fall silent, and those spectating cross themselves before turning to leave as we file into church. Some benches are filled already by friends of Mr and Mrs Tuffnell; I recognise the ladies who call on my mistress in the afternoons, and wonder which among them Abraham most disliked for their teasing attentions.

At first I do not notice Mr Espinosa, who stands apart with an uneasy air, as if he fears he is not welcome. He takes a seat on a bench at the back of the nave, and I am pleased to see Mr Wharton nod to him, though Mr Wharton himself sits near the front, close to his master.

St Werburgh is not a beautiful church. The walls are drab, and the parson afflicted with a brown wart on his chin, and he cannot say his 'r's,' so that we are enjoined to remember Abwaham, and I wish the parson would not harp on about the God's love in his sermon, when the world feels empty of that virtue, and I wish the coffin was not so small, and that Mrs Tuffnell and her friends would not weep so loud. I weep too, not only for Abraham but for my brother Tom, and by the time we leave the church I am crying for myself, for the losses I have endured and those to come.

'Corrie?' Nell Grey indicates for me to go with the rest. A baked ham waits at Barbuda House, with two dressed chickens and a handsome salmon, and Mrs Hucker set a third fowl aside for the servants since in the flurry of the morning none of us took breakfast.

'I will come in a moment, Nell Grey. Let me stay awhile, please.'

She takes in my over-wrought state. 'Very well, but don't linger, else you will displease *her*.'

The church falling quiet, I kneel and say a prayer for my father and brother. I had forgotten Mr Espinosa until that gentleman quietly clears his throat and I look up to find him watching me. Excepting the two of us, only an aged stooping verger remains in the chancel, snuffing the candles one by one and no doubt waiting for us to go.

'Miss Amesbury.' Again, the familiar catch as he pronounces my name, but whereas the parson's speech was comic and misplaced, Mr Espinosa's distinctive way of speaking is pleasant to my ears. I stand and curtsey.

'Sir.'

'I'm walking back to Mr Sampson's. Shall I take you to Winestreet on my way?'

My tears rise afresh. 'Thank you, Sir. I am ill today. I don't know why, I only knew the boy a day or two.'

'The death so brutal ...' He leaves the sentence tactfully unfinished, and offers me his arm.

The church door slams behind us, and our eyes meet. No need to spell out the verger's resentment at a Jew who dares to enter a house of Christian worship. We pass an old seaman sitting cross-legged at the lychgate, and Mr Espinosa finds a ha'penny and drops it in the man's lap. The seaman mumbles thanks, and I note inwardly that Mr Espinosa's faith is no barrier to Christians accepting his charity.

'There is still no word of the murderer, Sir.'

'Or murderers,' he corrects gently. 'Mr Wharton says the same. None of the reported sightings came to anything.'

'Everyone blames Red John.'

He tips his head: of course they do.

'Did Mr Wharton tell you the house was locked during the attack?'

'I took it as a false rumour.'

'I know myself that the windows were fastened tight, Sir, and Mr Tuffnell locks the doors each night before he goes to bed. Mr Roach says someone must have gained entry beforehand, and hid within the house.'

'Barbuda is not large. Where could they hide?'

'The puzzle keeps me awake. The other maidservant and I, we can't help fearing someone in the family is the culprit.'

A moment's silence.

'If you believe it, Mistress, you should seek a place elsewhere.'

'I do not really believe it. The boy was loved.' My throat narrows and I cannot speak. Mr Espinosa pauses, and when he speaks his voice is low.

'I am glad to hear you say so, Miss Amesbury. I had the opposite impression when I saw him.'

'Abraham was a child not nine years old, and a slave. Of course he complained at times.'

'You misunderstand. I merely saw him out with Mr Tuffnell's footman. There seemed to be a disagreement, and the footman boxed his ears.' Mr Espinosa coughs. 'Boxed his ears is perhaps misleading. The footman struck him hard—knocked him to the ground. The boy lay as if unconscious for several moments.'

A trickle creeps down my spine.

'The footman walked off. I watched, and eventually the child got to his feet, dazed, and a bystander gave him a rag. The boy's mouth was bloody where he struck the pavement.'

'Are you certain it was Jonathan Berwick?' I want to say: could it truly have been Jonty, who was white and speechless when he saw the body? 'They went for walks together. I'm told he gave Abraham sugar from his own store when the servants took their tea. The housemaid assured me of it.'

'I am certain, yes. Berwick is his name, now you remind me of it. He worked for Mr Cheatley, the iron manufacturer, 'til last Lady-day.'

'I thought him a fixture at Barbuda House.'

'He is good-looking and charming, is he not?' Mr Espinosa sees me redden, and hurries on. 'He is a footman, it is his role to be smooth and civil. I shall make enquiries as to why he left his last employment. Perhaps you can make some of your own, Miss Ames-bury—establish if he was ever seen by others to beat the boy. Here, you had better go in, had you not, else they will suspect you of con-sorting with a wicked usurer.' He lifts his hat, watching me until I have unlatched the side-gate and he disappears from view.

***

In common with other merchants Mr Tuffnell keeps a share of im-ported goods not at his warehouse where they are at risk of theft, but in the cellars of his home, to which he holds the only key. Now and then Mrs Hucker needs a box of tapers or a cask of wine from the pantry, but once she has fetched what is wanted she returns the key to Mr Tuffnell, and I never saw any other venture into the cellars at Barbuda House, unless it were Mr Roach or some carter under my master's direct orders.

After noon, the funeral behind us and the guests departed, our everyday routines resume, and Mr Tuffnell leaves for the quays and returns an hour later accompanied by a dozen barrels. They are too heavy to be taken through the house, so Mr Tuffnell unlocks the kitchen cellar door and goes below to unfasten the hatch at street level, where the carter unloads the sledges.

I happen to be in the kitchen smoothing a pile of Mrs Tuffnell's linen, and the range where the irons lie to heat is close by the cellar door, so that each time I pick up or return one to the fire I have a clear view down the stairs and catch glimpses of Mr Tuffnell in his shirt-sleeves as he rolls the barrels across to rest them with their fel-lows.

The steps are not timber like the ones upstairs, but built of stone, and the walls cut into the rock, so the cellars are more like caves than an extension to the house, and judging by the dead-smelling air escaping from them, as dark and damp as any cave. I wonder at Mr Tuffnell undertaking the work himself, instead of calling for Mr Roach.

'Horrid, ain't it?' Nell Grey says when she comes into the kitchen. 'I know it's full of slugs and other crawling things.'

There is no risk of Mr Tuffnell overhearing, because the hogsheads rumble like thunder, and he is shouting to the carter.

'Wait 'til the *Prudence* comes in next summer,' Nell Grey warns me. 'There'll be so much sugar in store we'll have wasps and bees all through the house.'

I point at the whitewashed wall beyond the door. 'Does Mrs Hucker ever hang game or joints of beef down there?'

'What is it?'

'Blood, big splashes of it, see? On the steps, and there, on the wall.'

Nell Grey frowns, but there can be no mistake, for the staircase nearest the top is freshly painted like the kitchen, and the red-brown stains are plain as day.

'Abraham died in the yard,' Nell Grey says. Her eyes are wide. 'He didn't know what befel him, Jonty swore he didn't.'

I have broken out in goose-pimples. 'How did Jonty know?'

'He said the boy's eyes were open in surprise.'

'Nell Grey, did Jonty ever harm Abraham, do you know?'

'Jonty? He whipped him for stealing cake the other week, but we all did that one time or another. Abraham was forever stealing. He was a boy.'

The blood looks recent, and there is plenty of it. The more I stare, the more I see. 'Nell Grey, tell nobody of this. If the blood is Abraham's the killer will be desperate in case the matter is found out.'

She squeaks with fear, for Mr Tuffnell appears at the top of the steps as I finish this speech, and neither of us can be sure how much he heard.

'Sir. You look warm, Sir. Shall I fetch you a cup of something?'

'Thank you, Amesbury.' He shuts the cellar door, and carefully locks it, and if he notices the bloodstains he gives no sign, whistling and eyeing me as I bring across the ale jug.

'Take some to the carter, Nell Grey.' As soon as she has left the kitchen he grabs my arm.

'What were you saying when I came up?'

'Beg pardon, Sir, I don't remember.'

'Beg pardon, Sir, you do remember.'

I lower my eyes and pretend to blush.

'Come on.' He shakes me a little. 'I heard the word "killer." What were you saying?'

'Forgive me, Sir. I was telling Nell Grey I had a killing pain. I am sorry, Sir, but I beg you to excuse me.' I set down the jug and clutch my stomach. 'Like I told Nell Grey, I have my terms today.' Before he says a word I run out to the garden, where I seek the privy and remain there long enough I can be sure he will have gone away.

For the rest of the day I long to find Mr Espinosa and tell him of my discovery. Not until the following afternoon does my chance come, Mrs Tuffnell taking to her bed with a headache after dinner, and Mrs Hucker ordering us maids out, saying she will have herself a nap like Mistress.

The weather is wet, but it is rare enough we have a holiday, so Nell Grey, Suke Cross and I put on our bonnets and cloaks and set out for Broad-street, Suke relishing the chance to regale us with stories of her many ailments, Nell Grey and I jumping puddles and dodging dripping eaves while I try to steer the chat away from boils and earaches. I earn myself a gentle nudge from peacemaker Nell Grey, and as we reach the walk Suke rounds on me.

'I must say, Miss, we were all a good deal more content in the kitchen before you came to Barbuda House, with your carping tongue and your sideways smiles. You think yourself so much better than the rest of us, and yet you are only a country miss who came to Bristol before your landlord threw you on the parish. Don't look surprised, I met another Wiltshire girl and she told me who you really are, for all your stuck-up ways.'

It takes me but a moment to guess who she means.

'I shouldn't be quite so gullible if I was you, Suke Cross. Miss Bridget Lamborne was never told anything about me or my family, and yet I know about hers. She has a father who cares nothing for her, and she was sent here to be Pot-Scrub to a family of parvenus. Upstarts, to the likes of you. Lamborne? Born liar, more like.'

We turn onto the street where Mr Sampson keeps his shop. The door and shutters are locked for early closing.

'Ha!' Suke Cross says. 'You're disappointed, aren't you, Miss? You was hoping to pass the time of day with your dark-eyed Jewfriend, wasn't you?'

'Leave off, do,' Nell Grey says. But before we have time to stop her, Suke Cross sprints to Mr Sampson's door and hammers with all her strength. From a distance Nell Grey and I watch as an elderly gentleman cautiously emerges. Suke says something, he replies and retreats, and she comes dancing back to us, bright-eyed.

'Be prepared for shocking news, Coronation Amesbury. Your favourite is in a "dangerous condition".' She smiles mockingly, savouring her power, until Nell Grey says, 'Come on, Suke, tell us the matter. I hope you're not taking pleasure in another's misfortune.'

'I'm curious is all, same as you two. Mr Espinosa left work late last night. Mr Sampson had a long list of accounts for him to copy, and it took 'til nearly nine o'clock before he finished. He set off for his lodgings, whereupon some bully, a footpad or robber, set on him, beat him black and blue, stole his coat, and threw him in a ditch. If his friend Mr Wharton had not gone looking for him the Jew would have died from loss of blood. The surgeon dressed his wounds and forbid him leave his bed for a week. Mr Sampson himself is nursing him. Oh, Coronation Amesbury, you look done in. I am so sorry to be the bearer of bad tidings.'

Nell Grey, God love her, takes my arm. 'Never mind, Corrie. Mr Espinosa has a good nurse, I'm sure he'll recover.'

'Though he is certain to be badly scarred,' Suke says, with relish. 'It was his own fault, from what his master says. It was pitch black last night, no moon. He should have known better than to walk the streets alone. Did you ever see such an out-and-out Jew as Mr Espinosa, with his yellow face and hooked nose and sly black eyes?'

'And did you, Nell Grey, ever see such a good-for-nothing bedraggled little scrubber as Miss Suke here, with her face like dirty paper and her eyes goggly as a frog's, and her nose so big I can't help myself.' God save me I shall have such a beating from Mrs Hucker, but I seize that misshaped snotty nose and pull it 'til Suke screams. Nell Grey has to push between us to prevent an outright fight, Scrub having dragged me down to her level at last, which I swore she would never do.

'I knew she was sweet on him, the brazen,' Suke screeches.

'I'm not sweet on him, you toad. I'm sorry he's hurt, that's all. Your crowing over it makes me seethe.'

'All right, Suke, you come home with me and tell Mrs Hucker you had one of your nose-bleeds, and need a poultice, and Corrie, you must stay out another hour 'til tempers cool. What a pair, one full of silly spite, the other a hot head who'll be lucky to keep her place if Mrs Hucker hears of this.'

'Which she will,' Suke spits.

'She'd better not. Mr Espinosa is a friend of Mr Wharton, and Mr Wharton is Mr Tuffnell's agent.'

Suke makes a feint at me, but Nell traps her hand firmly beneath her arm and drags her away while I, overtaken by giddy shakes, sit down on a stone and forbid myself to cry.

***

Mrs Hucker is standing in the scullery door when I return.

'Baggage,' she snaps. 'Fighting in the street like a Redcliffe washer-woman. Bringing your master's house into disrepute. You're lucky you didn't break Suke Cross's nose and find yourself on a charge of common assault. Lady's maid! I'll whip your arse with my lady's riding crop if there is ever a repeat of what you did today.'

I clamp my tongue between my teeth so I cannot answer back.

'Stay out, girl, 'til Mr Tuffnell locks the house, and serves you right if you get cold and wet. Tomorrow you'll be wetter still, scouring the floors while Mrs Tuffnell makes her visits. Suke can have my mistress's fireside for the afternoon.'

Mrs Hucker would love to see my shoulders quiver as I cross the yard but I shall not give her that pleasure, and when I see the gargoyle at the corner of our neighbour's house, the one of a woman's head with two fat chins, I stick out my tongue and say, 'There, you are nearly as ill-favoured as Ma Hucker, and you talk more sense than she does too.'

Then there is nothing to be done save trudge to Liz and Bill's for shelter from the rising rain, and pass off the occasion as a half-holiday granted by Mrs Tuffnell as a perquisite.

The days being short and dark, both Bill and Liz are home when I arrive. Bill answers the door, grinning unpleasantly when he sees who calls.

'Ho! I told Liz you'd be back within the week. Mind, I don't blame you.'

Liz appears, wiping her hands on her apron. 'We heard what happened. Come in, Corrie.'

'You needn't worry, Brother, I'm not stopping. My mistress sent me to town, and I thought I'd call on my way back.' I sit on the stool Liz pulls up to the hearth, and watch her pour a cup of small beer.

'Go on then.' She passes me the cup. 'Tell us everything. Bill knows a fellow who works for Mr Tuffnell, don't you, Bill? He reckons the house was broken into overnight.'

I had hoped for news of the death at Mr Elliott's; I had reckoned without news of Abraham's death spreading so fast. 'It looks that way.'

'Roach says he's sure of it,' Bill says. 'The black boy was in the house when the rest went to bed.'

I might have known Mr Roach would be a friend of Bill's. 'So we believe.'

'I should watch out if I was you, Corrie,' Bill says. 'Could be you next.'

'Thank you, Brother. I sleep in the garret with the housemaid.'

Liz casts a nervous glance at Bill. 'All the victims have been young boys. I would be frightened to go back to Mr Elliott's otherwise.'

'In Wine-street all the servants blame Red John,' I tell her. 'None can explain how he broke in, but he's the only culprit.'

Liz sends Bill another anxious look. 'Some say Red John is John Hench. Bill knows John Hench, don't you, Bill? Not that I'm saying I agree with them.'

'John Hench,' Bill begins, his voice thick and slow as though he corrects a half-wit, 'is a pedlar and a one-time sea-faring man who has lived through five attacks by pirates. For every wagging female tongue that names him as the murderer, ten strong men would knock those women down for slander. So shut your mouth.' To my relief Bill uses his disgust as an excuse to get up and leave.

The scrape of his boots has barely faded when Liz grips my arm. 'Bill can say all he likes, but John Hench is wicked, Corrie. He walked into the Sailor's Rest on Marsh Street the night Mr Tuffnell's page-boy died, and his hands were red with blood.'

My heart thuds. 'Bill told you that?'

'Only he said John had been fighting and come off worse. Bill woke me up to make a poultice to take to Hench. Mr Elliott lets me pick some of his comfrey to make knitbone.'

'Why does Bill help such a man?'

'He owes him money. They gamble, and Bill loses. And I think John Hench blackmails him. Bill sells some of the conies he kills, and the farmers would take him up for poaching if they knew. He brags in his cups, and John threatens to turn him in.'

I begin to see why a man like Bill Eardley bullies his wife, if he is bullied by other men.

Liz rises. 'I wish I could offer you a better supper.' She looks ruefully at the pot, which smells as if it holds the usual thin brew of greens.

'I would love to eat with you, Liz, but I must go home. Can I ask you something? What happened to the knife found in the bothy?'

Instantly, her face closes. 'I threw it in the river.'

'Why?'

'In case anyone started saying it was Bill's. It looked like one of his. It wasn't, but it looked as if it was.'

'Hasn't Mr Elliott asked for it?'

'No. He said he never wanted to see it again. Poor man.'

I want to say that Bill is more likely to be suspected if the knife cannot be accounted for. 'Liz, can I ask a last question before I go? Will you tell me any future gossip you hear about John Hench?'

'You always was a nosy beak, Corrie Amesbury. Remember when you found out the old squire was seeing a woman down in Westbury?' She chuckles.

It is pleasant to part on good terms, but I am not ready to talk on that subject.

'It was not very difficult to find out. Horrid old hypocrite.'

'But no one knew until you spotted him creeping home on Backlane, and put two and two together. Yes, I will tell you anything I hear, but only if Bill's out.'

Liz being so proud of her quick-witted sister, I baulk at lowering myself in her eyes by telling her what happened when I met the old squire that day. Thankfully she does not know the tale of the maid he despised yet tried to ruin.

Chapter Twenty-One

Tuesday, 13ᵗʰ November, 1703

In the week or two following the funeral I begin to see how trying life must have been for poor Abraham. Mrs Tuffnell, considering me both servant and companion, calls me at all hours of the day, sometimes to listen to her chatter, sometimes to help her dress for a call, most of which are dull affairs and leave her ill-at-ease. Nell Grey is envious that I am a lady's maid, but I find it vexing to be up to my elbows in suds and a voice comes from upstairs: 'Amesbury? Come here, I am bored to death.' Or Nell Grey and I have just sat down to our dish of tea, and I have to leave mine in the grate where Suke is likely to drop a bluebottle in it, and go running to the apothecary's shop for the Hungary-water Mrs Tuffnell wants, or to buy the jujubes she sucks to make her breath sweet for her 'angel' when he comes home.

Today, however, Mrs Tuffnell orders me to come in and shut the chamber door, and in a low voice explains I must go to a shop I have not visited before.

'If you mention it to anyone, Amesbury, you shall be turned away without a character, do you understand?'

She produces a wooden casket and takes from it a diamond ring which she parcels up, securing the paper with thread and sealing-wax.

'Carry this to Mr Sampson's shop in Jewry-lane. I show great faith in you, Amesbury. Not every mistress would trust so new a servant.'

I turn my eyes on her, surprised. 'You may trust me, Madam, you have my word on it.' Then I add, as innocently as I can: 'May I ask, is Mr Sampson a money-lender?'

She pauses, sealing-wax in hand. 'Off you go at once, Amesbury. And come straight back.'

A Pair of Sharp Eyes

***

Mr Sampson answers my knock directly: a small, slight man with peppery black hair, a brass eye-glass, and an old-fashioned frock-coat neatly mended at the cuffs and elbows.

'I am sent by Mrs Tuffnell, Sir.'

'Good day to you, Mistress.' He ushers me inside his small shop, where, as I expected, poor Mr Espinosa is nowhere to be seen. 'Every day it rains,' Mr Sampson laments, 'and we are foretold gales and storms all winter. Ah well, I should be grateful for these sound stone walls. So, Mistress, what does Mrs Tuffnell send me now?'

Mr Sampson places the package on the shop-counter and carefully breaks the seal, examining the ring while my own eyes are drawn to the crowded shelves behind him.

It seems Mr Sampson deals not only in jewellery but in rolls of linen and moreen, parcels of Moroccan leather, walking-canes, looking glasses, swords, horn spoons, steel knives, even plain wooden trenchers and earthenware dishes, along with brass buckles and shabby pairs of shoes. One shelf is given over to candlesticks, another to clothing, not just fine suits and gowns but articles as humble as shifts and stockings, shawls and caps. A basket in one corner is piled with wigs, and another with items their owners must sorely miss, such as tinder boxes, cooking-pots, fire-irons and pocket knives.

The shop is snug and warm, thanks to well-fitting shutters and a glowing fire. As well as smelling of wood-smoke and old clothes the air is pungent from a grey powder Mr Sampson keeps in a jar on the counter, and which he sets about using to polish the item I brought him, resorting to a small brush to clean around the diamond.

'A lively stone,' he pronounces. 'We call this the rose cut, see? It was invented many years ago in Venice. I can give your mistress almost what she asks for—three pounds ten shillings. Tell her I wish it could have been more, but diamonds aren't worth what they were last year. Let me write out the deposit note, Mistress.'

My eyes continue to travel over the well-stocked shelves behind the counter. A small library of well-worn octavos and duodecimos fill the highest shelf. I eye them hungrily.

'Do many clients bring you books, Mr Sampson?'

'Ha! A scholar, eh?'

'I don't write so very well, Sir, but I love to read.'

'Then perhaps you would like to look at this?' He reaches down a chap-book and offers it to me. *Jack the Giant-Killer*.

I read *Jack the Giant-Killer* when I was at dame school, and used to tell the tale aloud to Tom by firelight before he went to bed. It is a pleasure to turn the pages again and remember the Giant with his voice like thunder, and his three heads, and Jack when Arthur made him a Knight as a reward for what he had done.

'There.' Mr Sampson has finished writing his note, and blots the ink with sand. 'Place your mark here, if you would be so kind, Mistress.'

As neatly as I am able, I write *A.C.* where he points. Then, returning *Jack the Giant-Killer* to the shelf, Mr Sampson lifts out a money-box and sorts through it, lining up coins on the counter until he has the quantity needed. He ties them in a brown linen purse, nodding approval as I tuck it out of sight.

A sound of coughing comes from the room behind the shop, and Mr Sampson pauses. 'Forgive me, Mistress.'

He disappears into the back-room. I hear murmurs, and the sound of a cup being filled, then Mr Sampson returns to see me out, and I cannot resist. 'Might I be permitted to say good day to Mr Espinosa, Sir? I know the gentleman a little.'

Mr Sampson looks surprised, but quickly recovers his manners. 'I suppose my young clerk might be heartened to have a visitor. Just for a minute or two, Mistress, he is still weak.'

He lifts a section of the counter and beckons me past a leather curtain to a snug parlour where the fire burns cheerfully and Mr Espinosa lies on a row of chairs, his hands, thinner than ever, resting on a blanket.

He winces as he turns his head, but manages to smile. 'Miss Amesbury. I am not so unwell, I assure you.' Yet his voice is feeble. 'Do you care to sit?'

Mr Sampson looks between us, nods, and raising a finger to remind me not to stay for long, returns to his shop.

I try not to stare at the wound on Mr Espinosa's forehead. His lower lip is split, and one wrist is thickly bandaged. 'I am grieved at what happened, Sir. Some people are worse than wolves yet call themselves Christians.'

'I have no reason to think religion was the motive for the attack, Miss Amesbury. My memory is incomplete, but I am certain only one man was involved.'

I had assumed Mr Espinosa was set on by a gang, the same that hurt the two papists on Gunpowder Plot Day. 'Did you see the man, Sir? Did he say anything to you?'

Mr Espinosa tries to make himself more comfortable on the hard oak chairs. 'Excuse me, Miss Amesbury. My ribs … He was quick on his feet, not big but powerful. His face was hooded. He carried a heavy piece of wood—a plank, perhaps.'

I flinch. 'And his voice?'

'I'd know if I heard him again. I don't remember what he said.' Mr Espinosa puts a fingertip to his scalp. The surgeon has shaved his hair; the scar is livid and looks slow to heal.

'Sir, if it would not distress you to re-live the assault, will you tell me what you do remember?' I add, 'There must be a chance the criminal could be brought to justice.'

'Very well.' Mr Espinosa shuts his eyes, remembering. 'I was invited to Mr Wharton's house. I left here later than intended, and I was walking through Jacob's-wells when somebody called out, and I turned, and before I knew anything I was knocked to the ground. He wore heavy boots such as drivers wear, I know because he kicked me. The surgeon tells me I have three broken ribs. The man kept saying something, "That'll do for you, damn you." Excuse me, Miss Amesbury, those were his words. He brought his weapon down on my head I suppose, for I don't recall any more until I came round.'

'Mr Wharton found you?'

'He set off to look for me, and by a miracle he saw something lying in the ditch, and though he did not know at once what it was, instinct told him to look closer. Two men helped him carry me here, and Mr Sampson fetched a surgeon who refused payment for stitching my head. So you see, not all Christian men in Bristol are viciously disposed to other races.' His thin, kind smile again. 'Nor all Christian women.'

'The tale makes me ashamed of my countrymen, whether or not the villain acted out of hatred for your religion.' You were alone and had no means of defending yourself, I almost say, but I do not want to imply that Mr Espinosa is unmanly.

Mr Sampson reappears. 'Sleep now, Sir.' I rise to my feet. 'The more you rest, the quicker you'll be well again.'

'Good-bye, Miss Amesbury. I am almost well, I assure you.' But his eyes are closing as he speaks.

'Whoever did this should be tried for attempted murder,' Mr Sampson says, when the leather curtain closes.

'It is fortunate Mr Wharton found Mr Espinosa when he did.'

'They are friends of long-standing. Though I also wonder if Mr Wharton was the reason for the attack.'

'Surely not? Why would he be?'

Mr Sampson spreads his hands as if lost for an explanation. 'Perhaps Mr Espinosa is loyal to his friend, and forgets his own interests as a consequence.'

'You mean he said something to Mr Wharton and put himself in danger?'

'Aaron knows better than to reveal anything about my clients here. Nevertheless, love of Mr Wharton could have prompted him to say more than was wise, given the lady in question. But I am guilty of indiscretion too, I fear.' Mr Sampson looks at me. 'I beseech you, be careful, Miss. You are young, kind-hearted; learn from Mr Espinosa's example. Never forget that fear engenders evil.'

'I suppose it may, Sir.'

'Most merchants' wives do not rely on the contents of their cabinets to satisfy their creditors. Remember that, I beseech you.'

Were it not for the thought of Mr Espinosa lying bruised and broken in the room behind I might smile at Mr Sampson's earnestness. Instead I walk back to Barbuda House trying not to look behind me at every turn.

***

Mrs Tuffnell is in her russet bed-gown when I return from Mr Sampson' shop. Her face is rosy, her hair gleaming tresses, and while I darn a pair of silk stockings she nibbles roasted almonds, and prattles about her husband and how they are to take the coach to Clifton Downs on Sunday so she can learn to drive.

'The best of it is, the coach is lined just as I would have chosen if James had asked my preference—midnight blue, red-and-white trim. More distinctive than common black, don't you think? The same blue the Duke of Marlborough has for his three carriages, the limner said.'

I hide a smile, for Mrs Tuffnell would believe anything the limner told her. However, I am sobered by how short a time it is since she prized those colours for chiming with Abraham's blue velvet suit and his red-and-white cockade.

'Deep blue, vermillion, white. They are the colours beloved of the aristocracy in general, not just the Duke, you know. I should like to paint this room by and by, Ames. These dull wood panels are so old-fashioned. Perhaps the same blue as my coach, though a lighter shade, of course. Remind me to speak to Mr Tuffnell about my scheme.'

Truthfully, I could be anyone willing to listen. Few of Mrs Tuffnell's own station in life visit her, and for all her talk of Mr Tuffnell, he dines out most nights, and often comes home late. She reads my thoughts.

'I shan't see him this evening, you see, nor tomorrow.'

'He has his engagements, don't he, Madam?'

'Exactly. Now the ship has set sail they will be restless until they have another project underway. Ah, well, it is the price I pay for marrying an ambitious man, so I do not complain.'

'What kind of project, Madam? Another expedition to Calabar or Guinea? When the first is still at sea? Is that wise? When so many ships go down?'

'Amesbury, you forget yourself. I will not strike you, for I was wrong to speak in a way that encouraged you to express an opinion. You cannot read, or write your name, or understand the least small thing about a venture such as Mr Tuffnell is engaged in. Pick up your work basket and take yourself away. And remember your place if you wish to keep it.'

'I'm sorry, Madam.' I make my voice humble, though I know she will be sorry when I have gone, and will find some ruse to call me back.

I would love to see Mrs Maria Tuffnell's face if she knew I could read as well as she, and write the Lord's prayer, and recite some Latin too. Her dear husband may not recall what Captain Stiles said of their confederate Mr Cheatley, but I certainly do, having read the captain's letter and grasped its meaning enough to frighten Mrs Tuffnell for the security of her lavish equipage if I was to tell her the losses Mr Tuffnell faces when his ship comes home.

***

Yet Mrs Tuffnell so regrets her temper-fit that rather than call down, she comes to find me, holding out a pair of new worsted stockings and saying she found them in her closet and would be glad if I would find a home for them. 'And there is a quantity of yarn you might be pleased with, Amesbury, if you will look and tell me you like it.'

'She's lonely,' Nell Grey says, when we are lying in our garret. 'It makes her cross.'

'She's fickle and vain, you mean to say. I don't forget I shall be homeless and penniless if Mrs Tuffnell carries out her threat to turn me off.'

'You'd find another place, Corrie. And if you leave I shall shed many a tear, for I could never love Suke Cross as I do you.'

'I should think not. But there are worse mistresses in Bristol than Mrs Tuffnell. Not every employer threatens dismissal in one breath, only to offer stockings with the next.' I stretch out my new-clad foot and prod Nell Grey across the gap between our beds.

'Provoke her again tomorrow, Corrie. I could use some new stockings. Only tell her I would rather grey than brown, if she would be so good as to oblige.'

'I'm glad of any colour. Is winter always as cold as this in Bristol?'

'No, it's worse. We've often been snowed in.'

'We were too, at Christmas.' Snug in bed, our memories of blocked roads and frozen fields warm us, and we begin to fall asleep.

We are such good friends, Nell Grey and I, that I would dearly like to question her again over what Jonty said after he carried in Abraham's body. But Nell Grey is fonder of Jonty than she is of me, and besides, I shy away from letting even Nell Grey know how curious I am about the child's death.

Chapter Twenty-Two

Monday, 19th November, 1703

The journey from Wiltshire already seems a year ago, so much has happened since I left Erlestoke. I had half-forgotten those I met on my way to Bristol, excepting Mr Espinosa, until one afternoon I am brushing the stairs when Nell Grey comes to say I have a visitor. 'A young woman with bad skin and ginger hair.'

'Is it my sister?'

We speak at the same time, so that Nell Grey blushes and laughs at her unflattering description.

'Don't worry, Liz has brown hair,' I say, and when I go to the yard there is Miss Bridget Lamborne, looking just as she did when she climbed off her father's cart at Chippenham, which is to say awkward and at the same time, mightily stuck-up.

'How d'you do, Miss Lamborne? How is Miss Jane?' I expect her to say she is risen to first housemaid at No. 3 Queen-square, with every perquisite rich guests provide, and next for her to say how much she pities me, as one who belongs to a household notorious for a murder, but I am ashamed of my suspicions when her eyes fill with tears.

'My sister is not at all well, Miss Amesbury. She is … very ill of a sudden. I confess she's been sent home to Chippenham just this afternoon.'

'Sent home ill? How can she travel?'

'She is not quite ill in that way.' Miss Lamborne's reddened eyes meet mine. 'For this past week and more she has been vomiting. In the mornings. Our aunt found her in the privy, unable to stand. Then all yesterday morning she could neither eat or drink without she purged. Aunt put her on the mail coach at two o'clock.' Miss Lamborne's face flames. 'Before then my aunt questioned and questioned her, and my foolish helpless sister admitted a gentleman had been free with her, the night we stayed in Bath. You remember? Mrs

Buckley and her gentlemen friends. So my sister is disgraced, and my aunt will have no more to do with her, and Father will beat her black-and-blue if he does not kill her when she gets home. The worst of it is, my aunt blames me. As eldest I should have taken better care of Jane. You saw how it was. The old bitch tricked us, didn't she?'

'Oh, Miss Lamborne, I am so sorry. Her abuser should be hanged for rape.' Miss Bridget makes a little sound and we share a bitter look, both of us knowing how unlikely that is. 'How old is your sister?'

'Thirteen. Her birthday is September. When Father remarried, our stepmother was severe with us. She made us work long hours. Jane was never strong; it wore her out and made her weaker.' She bites her lips and speaks in a rush. 'You must be pleased, Miss Amesbury. There we were a month ago, good positions given us before we arrived in Bristol, and you had nothing. Now your master is among the richest men in the city, and my aunt is pleased to say I shall keep in the scullery and outhouses another year until she's satisfied my character is better than my sister's.'

'I hope I would never gloat over anyone's ill fortune. I am sorry, truly, Miss Lamborne. If it's any comfort, my situation is less than perfect. My own sister is poor and unhappy. This household lies under a shadow. Some of the servants are afraid to go to bed at night since the body was found.'

'And yet the murderer's hardly likely to come here again.'

'He'd regret it if he did. My master sleeps with his sword by his bed, and the groom keeps a stave and a pair of long knives in easy reach. Nell Grey who you saw when you arrived—I share her garret and we've armed ourselves with a couple of heavy stones. There are extra locks on all the doors.'

'I heard the murderer undid the locks.' She shivers. 'Sometimes I wish I'd never come to Bristol. Do you?'

'I daresay there are wicked people everywhere. If you write to your sister, tell her I hope it will all come right.'

'I shan't be writing to her. I am forbid, and she can barely read in any case.' She gives a gasping sob. 'Oh, I miss Jane more than I ever thought I could.' Dignity deserts her, and she sobs as though her heart will break.

'Don't assume the worst,' I say, 'perhaps they'll find a decent man to marry her.'

'Aye, some old goat of fifty who wants a slave to wash his linen and cook for his farmhands twice a day. That's if she doesn't die in childbed. All that is sad enough, but the little fool has ruined my chances too. How will I ever marry on the wages of a skivvy?'

Now I see that Miss Lamborne has not really changed from the selfish, sniping creature I first met, and I am glad when she sniffs and says she had better hasten back before her aunt discovers another reason to box her ears and send her supper-less to bed. Even so, Miss Bridget's spirit is not entirely quenched, for Jonty comes whistling across the yard as she takes her leave, and I see her eyelashes flutter as if she does not fully give up hope of some man rescuing her from scouring slop buckets in Queen-square.

***

Suke Cross comes back from her half day puffed up with malice. She has been to an alehouse, for her breath stinks, and she cannot wait to share the gossip she has picked up.

'I'll help Cook, Suke Cross. You need to sober up.'

Suke Cross's eyes flash, and she sways, proving I am right to think she should not be sharpening knives in her condition. 'Tell Mrs Hucker who your sister is wed to, Corrie Amesbury. Ha! That's whipped the smile off your face. I'd be shy too if I was you. A villain like that.'

I would rather not tell Mrs Hucker that my brother-in-law is Bill Eardley, but better that than she imagine my sister is married to a rogue.

'Mr Eardley is a vermin-catcher, Mrs Hucker. It's an honest trade.'

'Honest?' Suke Cross says, scathing. 'He drinks down at the quays from midday every day. Don't be fooled by this one, Mrs

Hucker. She acts high and mighty, but if Mrs Tuffnell knew her brother sold conies and hares belonging to the farmers who pay him, she wouldn't be so keen to have Miss here for her maid. Perhaps somebody should let her know.'

I hold my breath. Suke puts her hands on her hips, waiting for Mrs Hucker to agree.

If Mrs Tuffnell throws me out without a character I am sunk. Mrs Hucker looks me over shrewdly.

'Well now, Corrie Amesbury is not responsible for her sister's husband's faults. Have you proof he steals, Suke Cross? I thought not. Slander is an offence, and I should be sorry if you was fined for spreading evil rumours. Say you're sorry to Corrie Amesbury for dragging down her name and her family's name. Go on, let's hear it.'

Suke Cross's crafty eyes flick back and forth between us.

'Sorry,' she mutters finally.

'Apology accepted.'

'There,' Mrs Hucker says. 'Let's hear no more about it. Suke Cross, you carry up the coals this morning. It is Corrie Amesbury's turn to put away the knives and spoons.'

Cook goes off to the storeroom to fetch the bread. The moment her back is turned Suke Cross grabs a knife and points it at me.

'Don't think you've bested me. If you had not seen your chance, and pushed your way in here after Mrs Tuffnell got rid of Hannah, then Nell Grey would have been her maid, and I would have taken Nell Grey's place. I owe you, Miss.'

Even though Mrs Hucker is just a few yards from us it takes all my will-power to ignore that trembling knife point and walk away.

***

Tuesday, 20ᵗʰ November, 1703

It is a fortnight now since George Goodfellow went home. He returns on the carrier's cart this afternoon, and comes running in while

I am hanging laundry to air before the kitchen fire. He throws his arms around me and declares he has missed me every day.

'Of course you did, when you had your mother and father and seven little brothers and sisters to talk to.'

'Don't tease, Corrie, I did miss you.' He hugs me again, and I slip a few raisins from the pantry jar into his pocket.

'I believe you have grown an inch since we last saw you, George. Look at these long legs.'

Even Mrs Hucker ruffles his hair and says she is glad he is back safe. 'I hope your mother was pleased when she saw your round cheeks. Did she notice your teeth were whiter since you came to live with us?'

'Mother sent you this.' He produces a small parcel from inside his waistcoat. Mrs Hucker unties it to reveal a neatly worked pin-cushion stuck with half-a-dozen pins.

'I must say this is kind of your mother, George. Such tiny stitches. It shall go on the dresser here. I always did like a pincushion. The one I had for Christmas a few years back is really in need of replac-ing. This is just the size and colour I would have chosen.' Tired of listening, George wanders away to stroke the cat who crouches be-neath the table, and next I see him throwing sticks around the yard. Mr Roach returns, and not long afterwards I overhear him ordering the stables to be raked out, a job I fancy has not been done thor-oughly since George went home.

***

Later Mrs Tuffnell returns from a tea-party out of sorts, saying other merchants' wives invite her only on account of her husband and not for her own sake. Meanwhile, she complains, Mr Tuffnell dines out without her, and she is tired of playing picquet and cribbage with fat matrons of fifty, and being told her coach is nothing to this lady's fine equipage, or that "Houses in Wine-street are sadly old-fash-ioned, don't you know?"

A Pair of Sharp Eyes

She frets and snaps and sends me away and calls me back, and at last orders Jonty to rearrange the movables in her parlour and her closet, 'which is beastly dark, and why I have the desk so far from the window I do not know.'

Jonty is there above an hour, and when I go to ask if Mrs Tuffnell wants her supper, I meet him on the staircase looking livelier than I expected from one who has just been made to shift a tester bed and a heavy desk. He cheerfully salutes me, takes the stairs two at a time, whistling, and when I knock and enter, Mrs Tuffnell's movables are exactly where they were before.

When I tell Nell Grey she giggles.

'What are you laughing at?' I say. 'She must have made him shift them, then move them back.'

'Corrie Amesbury, can't you guess? What's sauce for the goose. She likes a kiss and a tickle, same as Master.'

'With *Jonty*?'

'I ought to hate him, but he swears he only obliges her because she insists on it. They do no more than kiss, he says.'

'I'm sure they don't,' I say, not wishing to upset Nell Grey, but Jonty looked to me more content than a man teased with kisses, and more than once after that I run into him coming away from my mistress' closet with flushed cheeks.

Whatever their conversation, it leaves my mistress no less ill-tempered than usual, so I suppose Mrs Tuffnell pays the price for her dalliance by being uneasy in her conscience.

She is right to be so. Mr Tuffnell would not see his fumblings with his servant-girls as excuse for a lapse on her part. Mrs Hucker tells many a tale of cuckolds and wanton wives. I shiver to think what revenge Mr Tuffnell would wreak on Mistress Maria, if he knew what she and his footman were about.

***

Later that night George Goodfellow and I sit by the fire, and while the other servants doze, we share a few cobnuts he brought from

179

Keynsham, and he informs me earnestly that he would like to marry a 'lady' like me when he grows up.

'Saucy and impudent, you mean? You had better find you such as Nell Grey. She would make a steady wife.'

'Nell Grey is dull,' he whispers, and we smother giggles as I crack another nut and Mrs Hucker groans and twitches in her sleep. 'Nell Grey is kind and good,' I say, looking across fondly to my sleeping friend. Her cap has slipped over one eye, and the kitchen tabby cat is curled upon her knee. 'I'm sure you missed us all, George.'

'Not old Roach.' George eyes Mr Roach's sleeping form resentfully. 'When he took me to Keynsham he told Father I am lazy.'

'Shh. Speak lower. And did your father believe him?'

'At first, but afterwards my uncle spoke up for me. He worked in Bath one time, and he said he knew Mr Roach. He was plain Pete Roach then, and he used to fight with other men. He was turned away from the house where he was working. Uncle Frank reckons that's why he's come to Bristol, where none knows his bad name.'

I watch for any sign that Mr Roach may be listening, but the coachman's face is slack with sleep and his breaths are deep and steady.

'Was Uncle Frank certain it was the same man, George? I can't think Mr Tuffnell would trust his valuable horses to a rough fellow.'

'I don't think Mr Tuffnell likes old Roach very much. It is Mrs Tuffnell talks to him the most.'

'Only about her blessed coach.'

'No, Corrie, she always does. She comes out in the yard and they talk low so I can't hear them. Yet he killed her dog, and when I tried to tell her she struck me and told me to hold my tongue.'

My flesh shrivels as I remember Abraham's reference to Mrs Tuffnell's dog. 'Killed it?'

'Mr Roach wanted to teach Abraham a lesson. Abraham loved Philo. Abe was playing in the stables, we both were, throwing hay about. I got a whipping, but Mr Roach said he dursn't whip Mrs Tuffnell's page so the dog would have to take his punishment. He put Philo in the stall with Mr Tuffnell's bad-tempered horse, and

Philo nipped his hocks and Caesar trampled him until he died. Abe cried, and Mrs Tuffnell was angry because he wouldn't stop, and Mr Roach told her it was Abraham put Philo in the stall, for sport. So Abe got a whipping in the end from Mrs Tuffnell.'

'I am glad you have the measure of Mr Roach, George. You must be careful to keep on his right side.'

'I dursn't get on his wrong side. He says if I don't obey him he'll have me run over by the coach and horses and tell everyone it was my fault for getting in the way.'

'And we'll believe him? I hardly think so.' But George looks at me askance: how would a child's word trump a man's? 'Roach ought to consider that another death in the household might mean the finger of suspicion points at him,' I add.

'He knows he's not suspected of killing Abe. He was drinking with Mr Cheatley's groom the night my friend was murdered. I heard him say so, and then I heard Mr Tuffnell asking Mr Cheatley if it was true. "You're a rough lot, aren't you, Roach, but you're no cutthroat," Mr Tuffnell said. And Mr Cheatley said, "I can vouch for him, for the rascals stole a flagon of my good perry and drank the lot while we was having dinner." And they roared with laughter, which I was amazed at, since Mr Tuffnell pulled my ear when I took and ate a horse carrot when I thought he wasn't looking.' George touches his ear in memory of the injustice.

Just then the log slips in the grate, and the noise wakens Mrs Hucker. She starts to cough, and the other servants stir and rub their eyes.

'Oh, I am weary,' Cook says, as she does every night, 'time we went up,' and while Suke carries the pots through and Nell fetches our tapers, George lights the lantern ready to cross the yard. It is a wild night, full of the sound of wind beating the trees, and I am sorry he must go outside.

'Wait, I'll walk you over,' I say. Jonty has already gone out to escort home Mr Tuffnell, and Mr Roach has left George to make his own way across the yard.

'I don't need walking over,' he says, immediately putting his hand in mine.

'I know you don't.' I find a sack and drape it round him. 'Put this over you.' We step outside; the frost is sparkling on the flagstones. 'I hope you have a thick blanket in that loft of yours. Make sure you lock the door from the inside.'

'I always do.' I listen for the turning of the key and creaks as George climbs the ladder to the loft.

'Good night, Corrie.' George's piping voice comes from above my head.

'Good night little chap.' I say the last words very quietly, so George can't hear and object.

A Pair of Sharp Eyes

Chapter Twenty-Three

Wednesday, 21ˢᵗ November, 1703

We waken to one of those November days when the sky never lightens. The intervals between downpours are dark and fleeting, and wind rocks the house like a beast roaring to get in. By silent agreement we keep to our beds 'til after sunrise, and it is past nine when Mr Tuffnell and his wife call for bread and coffee.

The horses can be heard stamping in their stalls by then, and still no sign of George Goodfellow or Mr Roach.

'Run over, Corrie Amesbury,' says Mrs Hucker, 'hammer on the doors until the lazy devils waken.'

A minute is too long to stand hatless in the black rain, and my skirts are soaked in mud as I cross the yard.

The door hangs open, and my first thought is that groom and lad must be at the bottom of the garden taking barrows to the dung-hills. I step inside, puzzled. The barrow is propped inside the door. The pitch-forks are lined up on their hooks.

'George? Wake up!'

Something tells me the loft is empty as I climb the ladder. I wonder if George can have flit home to Keynsham, his holiday having unsettled him, or perhaps he woke hours ago when the rest of us were slug-a-beds, and went to beg a bite of breakfast from next door.

I poke my head through the hatch and come face to face with the soles of George's boots. No child could sleep with his legs twisted that way. I venture closer, and George's eyes are wide open and staring, Lord bless him; the life is gone from him. The straw beneath his head is dark with blood, and worse of all, the fingers of his small, pale hands are brutally cut about, as if he tried to fight off his attacker.

My legs turn to water, and I don't know how I get back down the ladder. I pelt into the house where Mr Roach is in the scullery taking off his boots, and almost fall over him.

'What is it, girl? You been jumped at by a rat? Never mind, I'll send my boy in there.' He means his spaniel.

'George is dead. Someone's stabbed him.'

The house is thrown into confusion. Mr Roach and Jonty rush to the stable, Nell Grey bursts into tears, and Mrs Hucker dashes upstairs to tell the master and his wife. Suke falls to screaming until I seize her and shake her hard. 'What use is that? Be quiet.'

She looks at me in terror. 'It's Red John, next he'll come for one of us.'

'What's that on your forehead?' Her hair tumbled to one side when I shook her, and I see a fresh red bruise.

She flushes. 'Walked into a door, didn't I? I shared a jar with Mr Roach last night, after you'd gone to bed.'

I would like to rat on her to Mrs Hucker, but this is not the time.

Mr Tuffnell, grim-faced, strides in. 'Nell Grey? Fetch the constable.'

'Nell Grey and Amesbury will go together, Sir.' Mrs Hucker tries to give Mr Tuffnell his cloak, for the rain is coming down in arrows, but he brushes her aside.

Mrs Tuffnell appears in the passage in her night things, her voice high with terror. 'Ames? Where are you?'

'I'll go, Mrs Hucker,' Nell Grey says hastily, and she leaves as quickly as our master, heedless of the rain.

'Come back upstairs, Madam.' My only thought is to keep her away in case they bring in the body. I put my arm around her waist, and in her distress she lets me guide her from the kitchen.

'It must be Red John,' she says. 'It has to be. Why does he prey on us? The house is cursed, we can't live here. We women will be next. Oh God, I shall never sleep again.'

Though Nell Grey has assured me Mrs Tuffnell is two-and-twenty she sounds like a child of three. I sit her down and wrap her coverlet round her, and with trembling hands do my best to stoke the fire. The room is dim and cold, and the rain runs down the window-panes, squeezing in around the frame and darkening the panelled walls.

A Pair of Sharp Eyes

I hear the men splash through the mud as they carry the body to the house, and I make a clatter with the poker to try and mask the sound. Mrs Tuffnell's fingers pluck at her coverlet, and her eyes shine with fear. 'My husband had new locks put on, did he not? The yard was shut as usual and the gates were bolted. Has the murderer unpicked the lock to the stable, Amesbury, do you suppose? Or did he put a ladder to the window?'

'The door was open, Madam. Someone had opened it before any of us was about.' I do not like Mr Roach, but his surprise at my alarm when I found the body was not feigned. I am certain he knew no more of the unlocked stable than I did.

Mr Tuffnell's tread is audible on the stairs. I cannot question his tender feelings for his wife when I see the searching look he gives her.

'Dearest.' He folds her in his arms. 'Amesbury? Stay with your mistress today. Bear her up, do your best to keep her cheerful.'

I stop myself before I suggest Mrs Tuffnell and I take turns reading one of her romances. A romance hardly seems suitable today; besides, I do not care to admit that I can read.

'Madam is almost finished her embroidery of the Garden of Eden, Sir. I will help her with the serpent's tail.'

'Embroidery, very suitable, Amesbury. Be sure not to strain your eyes, my love.' He kisses Mrs Tuffnell's neck.

Shortly afterwards George Goodfellow's body is put on the carrier's cart by Mr Roach, and driven home to Keynsham. Next a magistrate takes a room in a coffee-house on Broad-street, and sends for us to be interviewed one by one. Mr Tuffnell explains we will be asked what we may have seen and heard last night, and who we believe is responsible for the deed.

As the one who found the body, I am first to be called. Mr Tuffnell says I may be anxious speaking to so eminent a gentleman, and therefore he will go with me.

The coffee-house is a meeting-place for every kind of gentleman seeking to do business in the city, and the aroma of roast coffee surrounds it from dawn to dusk, but there is none of the usual hubbub today as we draw near, and the proprietor sets down his silver pot at the sight of Mr Tuffnell, and leads us to a back-room where the small tables have been moved to make room for a heavy chair and writing desk. The magistrate wears a long red gown and flowing wig, and is as fat as any miller, though his shoes are elegant and his hands so soft and white that Mrs Tuffnell would admire them. A long-faced clerk stands at the magistrate's elbow, his lips stained with ink from licking at his quill.

The magistrate rises and shakes Mr Tuffnell's hand. 'I'm sorely grieved, Sir, that such evil befalls your house a second time. Be assured we will sift to the bottom of this matter.' Then the magistrate adds, in a much more cheerful voice, 'I believe we are both invited to the Lord Mayor's banquet seven nights' hence, Mr Tuffnell. I look forward to seeing you there, Sir, under happier circumstances. I must ask after the health of your dear wife—I am sure all at the banquet will agree with me that so fair an adornment is rarely seen among us, though I would prefer my own lady didn't hear me say so.'

After one or two more compliments in the same vein he turns to me.

'Your name, young miss, if you please.'

'Miss Coronation Amesbury, Sir. Late of Erlestoke in Wiltshire.'

He lifts an eyebrow as if to say plain 'Amesbury' would have done. 'So it was you who found George Goodfellow this morning?'

'And the last to see him alive,' Mr Tuffnell puts in. 'My wife's maid walked the lad across the yard last night.'

'Oh? Why was that?' the magistrate asks.

'George was frightened of the dark, Sir,' I say. 'He was used to crossing to the stables with his master, Mr Roach, but Mr Roach had gone ahead last night.'

'I see. Well, tell me, when you were in the yard did you see signs of any person lurking there? Hear anything untoward?'

'No, Sir. It was cold and windy, as soon as George called down to me I hurried in.'

'I should think you did. Knowing one servant from the house had been the subject of a savage murder, you were brave to step out in the first place. Were you not afraid you might be the next victim of this notorious pedlar?'

I regard the magistrate, whose pudgy face and pale blue eyes remind me of a hedge-cutter my father used to know, and who was known as 'Quicksilver' owing to his unusually slow wits.

'My mistress's page-boy died within the house, Sir.'

Mr Tuffnell tuts. 'Don't mislead Sir William, Amesbury. Our slave was found dead in the yard, Sir, as I'm sure you will recall.'

'Indeed. And I also recall that his throat was cut, so it is inescapable that the same monstrous and inhumane creature who deprived you of your blackamoor, Mr Tuffnell, is responsible for this second heinous crime. To butcher children in their sleep. It is impossible to comprehend who would do such a thing. Pineshott, cease your infernal sniffing or I will have you horsewhipped, you rheumy, good-for-nothing scribbler.' With this he addresses the clerk, who responds with a melancholy nod of apology and a hasty hunt up his sleeve for a rag. 'The latest crime brings the total murdered in Bristol to nine children since last summer.' Sir William closes his eyes and draws a long pious breath. '*Media vita in morte sumus.*'

'Quite.' Mr Tuffnell reaches for his purse. 'These deaths are, as you say, egregious. I propose to offer a reward of five guineas to anyone who can furnish information leading to the discovery of the culprit, Sir.'

'You are all charity, Mr Tuffnell. I venture that if we advertise your generosity, other men of property in the city will contribute to augment the prize, and it shan't be long before our pedlar is under lock and key.' Sir William pauses, and I expect him to say that he will be the first of these other gentlemen to add to Mr Tuffnell's bounty, but instead he turns to Pineshott. 'I trust you have that minuted, you lazy dog.'

'They must needs be strong locks, Sir William,' I say. 'George Goodfellow was secure in the stable, for I locked the door myself, and yet whoever killed him got past the locks as well as if they had the key.'

Mr Tuffnell huffs impatiently. 'A stable is not a strong-room, Amesbury. Any determined person could scale the walls and enter via the loft.' He turns to the magistrate. 'Forgive my servant, Sir William. She forgets the building's modest size.'

Sir William lifts a finger. 'And yet the girl makes a good point, Mr Tuffnell. It may be that this pedlar has powers of witchcraft, indeed it seems likely that he does. If not, someone in the household would surely have heard him going about his diabolical work.'

It does not surprise me that the likes of Suke Cross talk with wild eyes of pedlars who can walk through walls and open doors with spells, but I had thought a wealthy gentleman might scoff at superstition and wonder how a roofless pedlar could escape the efforts of an entire city to track him down. I suppose I should be grateful he views me as a mere girl. A shrewder gentleman would have wondered if I had killed poor George.

'Mr Tuffnell,' the magistrate continues, 'your house does seem to labour under a curse, and it may be as well to ask the parson to say prayers with your family in the coming days. Meanwhile it is my solemn duty to look into the matter so far as it concerns the law, so I must ask you to bring your servants to speak to me in turn that I may question them as scrupulously and rigorously as I have done this young person. Good day, Sir. Miss.'

Sir William may be less shrewd than I hoped for, but he is right in one regard, for by nightfall Mr Tuffnell returns from the city to report that his prize money has been multiplied by the generosity of his fellow merchants, and the reward now stands at twenty guineas.

By then Jonty tells us that upward of a dozen people have presented themselves claiming to have seen Red John, including an old woman, an oyster-seller, who was certain she passed a man with ginger whiskers at first light on College-green, a basket on his back and his shirt-front stained with blood. Two choristers say they saw a redheaded pedlar lurking beyond the cathedral, and that when they walked towards him the apparition seemed to melt away like fog. A gentlewoman, respectably dressed and well-spoken, said a vagrant with reddish hair and forked beard brushed past her near the Corn-exchange, but shortly after her testimony her brother arrived to offer his apologies, explaining the young lady is prone to delusions and possessed of crafty ways to draw attention to herself. Jonty assures us that if Red John is guilty, he will not wait to be taken up now the city is on watch. Though there is no proof he is the murderer, there seems little will to consider any other might be guilty of the deed.

Somehow the day is got through by washing and starching quan-tities of clothes, a task that fills the time though it also fills the rooms with damp linen since the rain keeps falling and we cannot dry out-side. Suke Cross steers the talk to ghoulish stories of Red John when she can, and I never knew a longer afternoon than the one spent in the scullery boiling shifts and underclothes and listening to Suke droning about sorcerers and headless boys. We eat supper early and in silence, tender-hearted Nell Grey dripping tears as she chews her mutton. Afterwards Jonty and Mr Roach bank the fires and check the doors and windows, making no remark of the weather though ordinarily we would be exclaiming at the rising wind and the fact the yard is under water.

After a short span of time Nell Grey says quietly that we are going to bed, and Mrs Hucker nods. 'I will come up too, girls. And you, Suke Cross, enough talk of evil pedlars or none of us will sleep a wink.' Tapers in hand, we troop to the garrets, Mrs Hucker jabbing Suke in the ribs when the sound of Mrs Tuffnell weeping in her chamber proves contagious.

'I don't know what her game is,' Nell Grey says, after we have shut our door. 'Suke was never but half-decent to George Goodfel-low.'

'Had she been fond of him she wouldn't have had the stomach to carry on all day. Notice how she dodged the heavy work, and left us to do the scrubbing? Lazy heifer.'

Nell Grey unpins her hair. 'I know how hard it has been for you, Corrie. I don't want you leaving Mrs Tuffnell's service, but I shan't blame you if you do.'

At her kind words, grief swells up in me like flood water. I comb out my hair fiercely to save looking at her. 'Two children have died in this house, Nell Grey, yet there's no will to blame any but some old pedlar nobody's ever seen. I'm not about to jump ship. I'm staying put 'til we find out what's happened.'

'Oh, Corrie Amesbury. What makes you think you can discover more than the constable, or magistrates, or Mr Tuffnell? If you did name the murderer who would listen to a servant-girl?'

'Am I a negro slave, bound in chains, forbid to speak? I am free-born.' I take hold of Nell Grey by the arms. 'I saw injustice once upon a time, more than once. My brother killed, my virtue put in danger.' I stop before I tell Nell Grey too much about the lecherous old squire. 'I vowed I'd never stand by again and leave wicked folk unpunished. I don't believe this Red John is the guilty man. Or if he is, I want the proof of it.'

'God bless and save you, but don't ask me to stand with you, Corrie Amesbury. Mrs Tuffnell will beat you if she thinks you bring her house into disrepute. And what if you do find out the killer? He'll stop at nothing.'

'I promise to be careful. But I don't think I am in as much danger as you fear, Nell Grey. All the victims were boys, remember.'

Nell Grey is undressed, and she climbs into bed in her shift, shivering as her flesh touches the sheets. 'Well, I only hope you're right.' She blows out her taper. 'Lord, but it is dark. I wish it would cease blustering. Jonty said the old plum tree is half out of the ground. It was planted by Mr Tuffnell's grandfather in the reign of the first King Charles. Worst winter weather for seventy years.' She yawns, and her words are slurred. 'It'll rain forty days and nights, and Bristol will be washed away.'

'You're dreaming, my lover,' I say softly, as I used to say when Tom muttered of giant-slayers in his sleep. Exhausted by the events of the day just gone, Nell Grey makes no reply save a snore, and that is the last thing I hear before I too fall asleep.

A Pair of Sharp Eyes

Chapter Twenty-Four

My master stops me in the hall this morning as I am carrying coals upstairs.

'I want you to deliver a letter, Ames. To Mr Wharton, if you please.'

The wind blows round the street door, and rain is drumming on the windows.

'You won't melt,' he says, seeing my face. 'Jonathan attends me in the Tolzey Walk, and I won't trust Scrub with a letter of business. I'll ask my wife to give you a half day next time she can spare you. There's my good girl.' And the Devil take Mr Roving-Hands, he has his hands in my skirts before I can dodge him, and nearly reaches to where he should not.

Unawares, Mrs Hucker steps into the passage with a tray of chocolate, and smiling to Master says in the same breath, 'Idle girl. This chocolate's getting cold. Take it up to Mistress this moment or I'll have you whipped.' She bustles off, and Mr Tuffnell murmurs, 'Whipped, eh? I should like that.'

He is a wicked man, and yet there is something I cannot dislike about him, whether it be his crinkling eyes or his habit of straightening his face comically when Mrs Hucker grumbles. Some merchants dress in fustian and look more like parsons than men of business, whereas Mr Tuffnell sports lace at his cuffs, wears kidskin gloves, and a white lace collar that sets off his handsome eyes and fine complexion, and I do not always resent his attentions as much as I ought to.

In town the rain beats across the quays like great black wings, and the ships thump the harbour walls, tormented by the wind. I am blinkered by my bonnet, and do not see Mr Wharton standing beneath the eaves of Mr Tuffnell's warehouse until he whistles to catch my attention.

'Good day, Sir.' I pull the letter from my shawl, careful not to get it wet. 'Shall I wait for a reply?'

He scans the letter, grim-faced. 'Tell Mr Tuffnell I'll ship the rest of his sugar to Barbuda House as soon as I can find a carrier.'

'Doesn't Mr Tuffnell trust his warehouse to withstand the storms?'

He looks at me sarcastically. 'Are you his steward?'

'I was only asking, Sir.'

'Like many merchants Mr Tuffnell prefers his property to lie under his own roof in winter. Off you go, girl.'

'May I first ask how Mrs Wharton does, Sir? She was kind to me when I took your letter. You have two fine children, Sir.'

As the sternest fellow will, he softens at mention of his family. 'They do well enough. Mrs Wharton is in good health. Though she is somewhat upset by the latest news. It is difficult for those of her caste and religion. Being so few of them in Bristol, of course they know one another.'

'Beg pardon, Sir?'

'A body was found last night, a Jewish man. Forgive me, the corpse had been badly mistreated, and was much decayed. My wife believes the man was killed from ignorant superstition. He was red-haired, his name was Jacob—Jacob Stein, but "Red Jack" or "Red John" to those who know no better.' He sees my shocked expression. 'What? The unfortunate man's innocence is proven. He was dead long before the recent murders. Now perhaps the good citizens of Bristol will see we cannot blame Jews for every evil that befalls us.'

'Please tell Mrs Wharton I am sorry, Sir.' And I am. The name 'Coronation', which commemorates a king who saved England from popery and wooden shoes, is shaming when I remember that those who chiefly hate Jews are Protestants.

'Time you ran back to Wine-street, young miss,' he says, 'the sky is clearing. Tell Mr Tuffnell the matter will be arranged by midday tomorrow.'

I find no patch of blue above us and need no reminding to run. The rain is so cold I think only of getting home as fast as my legs will carry me. Only as I cross High-street does it occur to me to call on Liz and tell her what I have been told. If Red John truly is John Hench, she and Bill should know.

***

I find Liz crouched over a pan of boiling suds, and the whole place reeks of lye.

'However will you dry it all? Lord, Liz, don't you hate this weather?'

'Good day to you too, Sister. I shall have to give it back wrung out instead of dry. Meaning half the pay.'

'It never rained like this in Wiltshire.'

'We had a better roof. At least the cold keeps Bill away. He goes supping with his mates.'

'Has he spoken of John Hench lately?'

'Why?'

'Some say our stable boy was murdered by a red-haired Jew, but the Jew's dead. I'm told he died months ago, judging by the state the body's in.'

'Well, don't let Bill hear you pestering me about John Hench.'

'I won't.' Her tone is so snappish I forbear to say it was Liz who mentioned John Hench last time I visited.

'Hench is a rogue and a thief, but that's not the same as a murderer. Fetch me a pail of water, would you, Corrie? I'm ready for rinsing.'

The pump runs slowly, so I am gone a while. Liz's mood has altered when I return. She takes the pail but sets it to one side, and closing the door firmly, indicates for me to sit.

'I have something to say, and you mustn't tell anyone.'

As children we used to solemnize our promises to each other by linking fingers. I hold up my little finger but she does not smile. 'It is a serious matter, Corrie. Life and death, perhaps. I know what you suspect. You're wrong. John Hench is mixed up in something bad, and so is Bill because of him, but it's nothing to do with murdered boys.'

I can't quite bring myself to assure her I had no such thought in my head. I sit quietly as she goes on, and try not to notice her twisting fingers. 'John Hench shot a deer the other day,' she says.

'A deer? Whose deer?'

'Never mind whose deer. Some lord with a great park outside Bristol. Hench made Bill sell it to a butcher friend of his. He's done it half-a-dozen times. Bill poaches hares and rabbits here and there, which is folly enough, but a deer is different.' She looks at the floor, biting her lips. We both remember men in Wiltshire hanged for poaching deer.

'Where'd Bill put a deer, for pity's sake? How does he move it without being seen?'

'He hangs them out the back, and takes them to the butcher in two goes. He has an old wheelbarrow we use for carrying firewood.'

'He's mad.'

'I know.'

'They'll hang him.'

'Stop it. I'm only telling you so you'll quit badgering me about John Hench.'

I contemplate her for a moment, lost for words. She's poor, and will be poorer still if Bill goes to the gallows for being too weak to stand up to his friend.

Liz seems to brush aside my pity. 'Don't look like that. I'm not the one risking their neck.' She gets to her feet. 'I must rinse these shirts and see if I can't dry them somehow. Help me empty the dirty water outside, then you'd best be getting back.'

Her manner is so sharp that I am glad to leave, though my spirits are low as I make my way to Wine-street. One worry is laid to rest, only for another to take its place. I am glad John Hench is not the murderer. But if 'Red John' is a bogeyman dreamt up from fear and foolish superstition, and John Hench a common poacher, who did kill Abraham and the other boys?

I promised Liz I would stop asking questions about John Hench. I never promised to stop asking questions altogether.

A Pair of Sharp Eyes

***

The wind blows me back down Wine-street to Barbuda House, and after I hang up my cloak in the scullery a puddle spreads across the flagstones.

'Is Mr Tuffnell still at home, Nell Grey? I've brought a message.'

'Don't go near him, Corrie Amesbury. A skipper came into port this morning and the Tolzey's in uproar. There are storms at sea worse by far than we've seen in Bristol. Mr Tuffnell came back saying his vessel is likely at the bottom of the ocean, and half his worldly wealth with it. He's been shouting this past hour, and Mistress is in tears. And Mrs Hucker is in a foul temper too. The weather has made the hams go mouldy, and she snapped at Mr Roach for bringing in damp wood.'

'Is Cook brave, or stupid?'

'Stupid, I'd say. Mrs Tuffnell always takes Roach's side. I heard her telling him not to grieve for George Goodfellow. Roach wouldn't grieve if it was his own old mother died, never mind a lad he cared for as a handy object to shine his fists on. Mrs Hucker is the one I pity. She loved George in her way. Roach locked him in the cellar once. Mrs Hucker let him out, and told Roach if he tried that trick again she would tell on him to Mr Tuffnell. Roach stole the cellar key when Master's back was turned.'

'But surely Master noticed when he came to lock up?'

'Oh, Roach gave it back. But only after he took a print of it, in a clod of garden clay. If Mr Tuffnell ever misses anything from his cellar I shall tell him to search the bothy before he accuses us women-servants. I wager a pound to a penny Roach took that mould and had some blacksmith make a copy from it.'

'Why did you never tell me this before, Nell Grey?'

'What does it signify? It is only another reason not to like Mr Roach. You never liked him anyway. Most servants steal their master's rum now and then, especially men.'

'Do they? Does Jonty?'

'Keep your voice down! He's borrowed the key once or twice, aye, and helped himself to a dram or two. I wouldn't be so bold myself, but I don't care for rum, and I'd be scared of being caught. I don't judge Jonty for it.'

I watch her as she saunters off. Nell Grey is as honest as the day is long, and yet her fondness for Jonty makes her forget right and wrong. I hope it does not lead her to risk her place one day—Jonty is handsome, but I doubt he is worth the loss.

A Pair of Sharp Eyes

Chapter Twenty-Five

Monday, 26th November, 1703

A day or two later we are sitting round the fire complaining at the draughts and agreeing the wind has blown hard these fourteen days when Master strides in.

'Pack up the house. At once—a storm is coming. I want the household on high ground safe from floods.'

As we scurry to obey Nell Grey explains we are to go to Clifton, where Mr Tuffnell owns a country villa.

Everything is upside-down. Mrs Hucker stands in the hall and shrieks orders while Nell Grey and I roll up the feather beds and Suke Cross packs iron pots in straw. Mrs Tuffnell has me lay her petticoats and mantuas in chests, then the chests are wrapped in tarpaulin and Jonty carries them to the carts.

Nell Grey and I are allowed a moment to fetch our boxes before Nell Grey is ordered to climb into one cart along with Suke Cross, while Jonty and Mrs Hucker take the other. I am bid travel with Mrs Tuffnell in the coach; Mr Roach will drive us while Master follows on horseback when he has secured the house.

The winds are rising, the rain is beating down, and the streets run with filthy water. Our horses slip and struggle, and the coach rocks alarmingly as we begin the ascent up Park-street. Mrs Tuffnell grips my hand with clammy fingers. 'What if the horses lose their footing and we slide back down?'

'Mr Roach won't let that happen, Madam.' *He will whip the horses until their flanks are bloody, don't doubt it.* 'The master is right to send us out of the city, Madam. The river has been high all week.' As I finish this speech a jet of water lashes the side of the coach, and Mrs Tuffnell cries out. 'The spray must be coming from the harbour. Oh God, Amesbury.'

'The storm will pass through soon and we'll go home,' I say desperately. 'Tell me about Mr Tuffnell's villa, Madam. Are the gardens pretty?'

'He sealed the cellars, did he? The water could not get through oak and pitch?'

'Of course not, Madam.'

'He pays to a company of underwriters, you know. He assured me it was prudent to pay the premium to insure the house and the stock we keep there, and now he is proved right. I was sorry to leave behind my still-room, but I have the comfort of knowing the contents are covered. And of course there is the *Prudence*—thank God it left before the storm arrived. We are guaranteed riches in twelve months' time.'

She has evidently forgotten the letter I brought from Captain Stiles, and the captain's plan to under-man the *Prudence* and risk a slave rebellion, but in our present plight I am not very interested in the details of Mr Tuffnell's business affairs, unless talking of them makes his lady easier to distract. 'I'm sure whatever he does is for the best,' I say, wincing as a wooden sign hurtles past, torn from a nearby chandler's shop. Although we have travelled barely quarter of a mile, at that moment the coach door is snatched open and Mr Tuffnell thrusts in his head.

'Get out. The horses cannot manage in this wind. Wait for the carts.' The house on our left gives way to the storm and crashes to the ground. Mere weeks ago I sat to eat my bit of dinner and spoke to one of the bricklayers who built that house. Now it might as well be made of straw as bricks. And next the roof collapses at the house next door, to heart-wrenching cries from the people huddled inside, exposed to cold, rain and battering wind.

Suddenly I think of Liz in her flimsy hovel. 'I can't leave my sister, Madam,' I say. 'Please let me out to look for her.' In her terror Mrs Tuffnell pays no attention to me but scans the road behind for the carts.

So many trees are falling that the carts may never reach us, and roof tiles fly through the air like sycamore keys. Somewhere close by a church spire gives way, and the ships' masts on the river are torn to splinters. All the while the rain pelts down, as if an ocean voids itself on Bristol, intent on drowning every living thing.

At last Nell Grey's cart draws level.

'Come, Mrs Tuffnell, get in with us,' she cried. 'Help her, Corrie.'

Mrs Tuffnell is wild-eyed. 'I want to wait for Jonty. He's the better driver.'

'Jonty's cart is stuck, Ma'am. He's lost a wheel. Come with us.'

My mistress looks more distraught than ever, but at last Nell Grey coaxes her aboard, and as soon as I have helped the lady up, puts out a hand for me.

'I must find my sister, Nell Grey, I will come to Clifton soon as I can,' I call, and good Nell Grey makes no argument, but orders the carrier to move the horses on.

In moments my clothes are soaked through. I can barely make out the way, and with every breath I seem to swallow water. Scenes of destruction lie on every side, more unfolding as I pass. A gilded weather-vane lies across a pile of fallen masonry; a piece of lead guttering comes close to knocking my head from my shoulders as it flies past. Yet I am determined to reach Liz, and with the tower of All-Saints' church as my guide, at last I reach the entrance to the yard. Bill Eardley can't begrudge me calling, I tell myself between weeping and laughing; he will let me creep under his roof until the Almighty reins in the horses of the apocalypse.

Part of me knows Liz's house cannot be standing when so many others have given way. When I reach it I find a heap of sodden cobs, spoiled thatch scattered in the middle, and broken timbers from the neighbouring house lying every which way. My only comfort is that there is no sign of Liz, but now, quite alone, I do not know where I should go. I cannot walk to Clifton now.

Certain every step will be my last, I turn and retrace my route to Wine-street, hoping that a few walls may be standing at Barbuda House, and that I can open the cellar and find safety there.

Kat Armstrong

The Lord is my shepherd, I shall not want. Barbuda, larger and better-built than its neighbours, remains much as we left it, though a portion of the roof is off, and many window-panes are shattered. Round at the back of the house the door hangs off its hinges, and thieves have broken the cellar padlocks, though they were surprised in the act for I see no sign of them when I peer in.

A crash, and a chimney stack smashes through the roof above the garret. To creep down into the cellar in the pitch dark is a dreadful prospect, but to stay above ground worse. I arm myself with the yard broom, though it seems impossible anyone could think of assault when the streets are under water and every hay-rick in the neighbourhood is destroyed.

The steps are wet, uneven; I see little and hear nothing save the churning water and the furious thrashing of the wind. There must be a chance that part of the cellar lies above flood level. I cling to the rough stone as I creep down, testing each step in case I reach the lapping water sooner than expected. My prayers are answered: half-way down I find a small chamber, higher than the main cellar, into which I grope my way, catching my foot painfully on the raised stone threshold, grateful beyond speech to reach safety.

Best of all, barrels are stored here and I clamber onto them, since the wood, however damp, is warmer than the wet stone floor.

And here I sit, imploring Him to spare me, terrified the water will rise and drive me out again.

By good fortune this part of the cellar has been used for storing odds and ends, such as flasks, jars, empty sacks and disused baskets. I pull a meal sack round me, and little by little my shivering abates. The barrel has already become home, and I press my fingers against the rough wood, thankful to find it real and solid, and that I have not died and woken in purgatory or a worse place. These cellars must have been made in ancient times, and I wonder who hacked at the rock to make this place, how long it took him, and whether his master paid him fair and square. There are grooves in the facings of the wall, and I picture the mason toiling with his chisel day upon day. Was he treated fairly by his master? I must be a little delirious, I think, for my mind wanders. Did the fellow go home to his wife and children and sit by the fire to sup on broth and barley bread? Or was he made to work for nothing like a slave, and found himself turned off when he grew old and frail?

It strikes me the mason might have left his mark upon the stone. Shutting my ears to the tempest, I search the wall for a letter, or what the Romans used as numbers, M, D, C, and so on, in the system I was shown once, and have seen in the fronts of the novels Mrs Tuffnell leaves half-finished on her table.

There is no carving, but I find something unexpected when I slide my hand behind the barrel to my right. A hollow in the rock, smaller than the several cubby-holes used for holding candles, and with something so tightly lodged within I cannot pull it out. I work away until at last I have it loose. Another moment and it is in my hand. A leather purse or money-bag, well-made and tightly tied with stout waxed cord. From its weight it holds a number of gold coins—fifteen or even twenty guineas.

Can this be why Mr Tuffnell was so careful of his cellar? But why would he hide his gold instead of putting it with his banker?

An idea flies into my mind before I can prevent it. With a handful of gold I could buy a cook-shop near the Corn-exchange. The city half-destroyed, Mr Tuffnell has more to worry him than the loss of a few coins. With this small sum I could set up in business and never fear hardship again.

And yet the money is not mine. I am about to return the bag to its rightful place when the door at the top of the steps swings open, letting in the weakest shaft of light.

I go towards the steps, ready to fight hand-to-hand with a common thief if I must. Then I cry out. It is Mrs Tuffnell, her clothes torn and sodden, her headdress ripped from her by the wind and her hair hanging over her face. The same moonlight reveals my face to her, and she lifts her fist.

'So this is why you ran away!' She scrambles down the rough steps. '"To help my poor sister"? To help yourself, you should have said.' She strikes my head with such force I see stars. Then I regain my balance, and catch her hand before she lands another blow.

'Madam, I found the money by chance. See, the bag is closed, I was about to put it back. I am honest, Madam, you know I am.'

A roaring sound, as the stable behind the house wrenches from its stone foundations and bricks and timber fly across the yard. The house itself shakes at a stronger gust that strikes the roof and strips off a shower of tiles. Mrs Tuffnell screams. 'The Day of Judgment is come. Lord have mercy on my soul.' She breaks into sobs, her rage forgotten.

'Here.' I grasp her hand and drag her into the narrow space where I was sheltering, and where rock is behind and above us, so thorough were those ancient masons when they carved out this place. 'Sit tight, put your arms around your knees, so. We are safe from the tempest if we keep still.'

Another dreadful crash, and plaster dust fills the air. Mrs Tuffnell whimpers. 'We shall surely die, Amesbury. They do say we are all equal in the eyes of God. St Peter may say you are better than I, because I have blood on my hands.' She falls into a fit of weeping.

'Madam, I hope we are not bound to die. Under here we shall not be crushed, I think. Please, Madam, if we should be spared, know I was not about to take my master's money.'

'I believe you. You would confess, would you not? Being in mortal danger? Oh God, let me confess to you, Amesbury. I must tell someone before I die.'

She struggles past me and to my amazement, returns to the steps and stands there, mere feet from the treacherous floodwater.

'Hear me, Lord. Have mercy on your poor sinner. I am to blame for the death of my black boy. Though I did not wield the knife I shall suffer for eternity.'

'Madam, the storm frightens you from your wits. Come here before you're injured.'

'I am in my wits, Amesbury, don't doubt it. The purse you found, it belonged to Mr Roach. One day Pug was mischievous, and Mr Roach locked him in here to teach him a lesson. Pug found the purse, and the innocent brought it to me, saying Mr Tuffnell should be told his gold was not so safe as he believed.'

'But how could Mr Roach possibly own such a sum?'

She weeps. 'He extracted it from me. He threatened me.'

I am bewildered. 'Madam, how could he? A servant, and you a lady?'

'He is more cunning than you could know, Amesbury. He has a cruel streak, a nature that will stop at nothing. I should know—I used it for my own ends.'

My heart thumps. Mrs Tuffnell goes on, between sobs. 'Roach, angry at Pug for causing trouble, whipped him, and Pug was so badly hurt he ... died, Amesbury. He died. I shall be hanged for murder.'

'You shan't, Madam. Roach shall.'

'The money was rightfully mine, extorted from me though it was, and so I will be blamed. Oh God, Amesbury, what shall I do? God will punish me, He sees everything.' She puts her face into her hands and cries as if her heart will break.

'Don't despair, Mrs Tuffnell. You may repent your sins. We are not bound to die tonight, at least I hope not. The storm will pass, we'll venture above ground. I shan't tell on you, Madam, I promise.'

She laughs, and her laughter turns my blood cold, for I see what I did not truly believe until this moment. She is not in her right mind.

'I fooled my husband and the rest, but I cannot fool you, Amesbury. You're a clever girl, but I must be cleverer after all. I won't let you go, now you know my secret. If I should die, you would blacken my name, would you not?' Something gleams in the near-darkness, and I scream. She holds a knife.

'Don't risk your soul a second time, Madam.' I try to speak calmly but the sweat breaks out on my face. 'God may forgive you for the boy's death, it was not you injured him. But God will not forgive you killing me in cold blood.'

'God cannot send me to hell twice over. I shan't have you telling on me when I am dead, and in any case I may not die.'

She raises the knife and I close my eyes and pray to my Maker. Then a roar comes as if the jaws of hell themselves have opened, and I look up to see the vaulted ceiling above Mrs Tuffnell collapse. The weight of the house bears her down into the water; there is no possibility she lives.

Shielded in my alcove I am unscathed, and yet the dust and soot are enough to make me choke. I cough and spit and scrape the filth that clogs my eyes and clamber from the ruins as the rain hurls down and the air around me fills with straw, tiles and even pieces of iron and stone.

'Mrs Tuffnell!'

Where the yard-gate used to be stands Mr Roach in a tattered, soaking coachman's cape. His face twists with contempt as he sees me. 'Where is she? What have you done with her, you bitch? Where's the money?'

I gamble his fury will wane if he has it in his grasp. 'You're welcome to it. Mrs Tuffnell is dead, poor creature. Crushed beneath her own house.' I take the bag of coins and hurl it at him.

'Liar.' But he snatches up the money, and in the rain and darkness he is out of sight in moments.

Terror overtakes me and I fall to my knees, unable to support my weight until I have endured a fit of trembling which loses its hold when the wind drops suddenly, releasing a squall of rain that brings me to my senses. I begin to hear the cries from suffering souls in nearby houses, pleading for help and screaming with terror each time a dismal crash signals the destruction of another tree or steeple. Horses scream too, trapped beneath the ruins of their stables, maddened by the flashes of lightning and dreadful thunder claps that rend the air.

If I stay I am in danger at every moment from flying rubbish, tile-shards, bricks, and yet to reach Clifton is impossible when the roads are deep in water and every path blocked with fallen trees and rubble. All I can do is pray, and I kneel again and implore the Lord to have mercy on me.

'Is that Miss Amesbury? Can you hear me, Mistress?'

I raise my head, amazed. Since the tempest reached its height the streets have been deserted, yet coming towards me, climbing over the obstacles in his way, is Mr Espinosa.

He is out of breath; I quail to recollect his recent injuries.

'Sir!'

'I volunteered to take a message from Mr Wharton to Mr Tuffnell. The warehouse is under water. The servants told me you'd left the party. I thought I might find you if I came to Wine-street. God, this storm. We are lucky to be alive, are we not?'

'God has sent you, Sir. I had a refuge, but Barbuda is destroyed. And worse, Mr Espinosa, my mistress with it.' I point, but in the blackness there is little to see.

'God help her husband.'

'God help all Bristol. If such a house has fallen, what chance the rest?'

'Mr Sampson's house was sound when I left it. We should go there, Miss Amesbury.'

'Thank you, Sir. If you can bear with me, I can't walk fast. I lost my shoes in the confusion.'

'Your feet will be cut to pieces.'

'I can manage.' But it is just as well Jewry-lane is close to Wine-street. Were it not so dark he would see me limping. 'And you, Sir. Still recovering. I am shocked to find you out.'

'I hoped to find Mr Tuffnell, but in the event I gave up the search. The road to Clifton is impassable. Here, let me.' I daresay Mr Espinosa would carry me the remaining yards to Mr Sampson's were he not still weak from the assault. A shower of rain drives towards us, but we are on the threshold now, and as Mr Espinosa beats on his master's door it opens and we fall into the arms of Mr Sampson.

Chapter Twenty-Six

Tuesday, 27ᵗʰ November, 1703

For the rest of the night the tempest blows, the city quakes under its onslaught, and we lie beneath the oak table in Mr Sampson's parlour, unable to keep a candle alight, dozing whenever the noise lessens, fearful the chimney stack will fall through the roof or the windows pierce us with glass shards.

The hours seem endless, but at last sunrise comes creeping through the shutters, and the gales that caused such havoc die away. Immediately we long to see the aftermath; our clothes are dripping wet, but Mr Sampson has a large quantity of unredeemed stock, and he lends me a petticoat and a pair of shoes, and gives Mr Espinosa a pair of breeches and an old frock-coat. We set off for Barbuda House, determined to raise a party to recover Mrs Tuffnell's body from the ruins.

Nothing prepares me for the sight of Bristol, once so fine, reduced to sodden rubble. Whole streets lie under water, rows of houses are flattened, windows buckled, doors torn off, roofs collapsed, walls reduced to heaps. Everywhere, dazed people pick through the wreckage of their homes. A church has lost the top portion of its tower, which lies slantwise on the chantry, itself a pile of stones and broken slates. We pass an aged woman weeping on her doorstep; the rest of her house has blown away like straw. A younger woman stands dumbly, surrounded by fallen lath and plaster. In her arms she holds her only belongings: a single shoe, a wooden dish, sodden bedding. Yet elsewhere a line of cheerful labourers passes tiles hand-to-hand, already intent on rebuilding a workshop whose only remaining traces are a set of wooden posts. At the end of Wine-street a pair of sawyers are hard at work cutting up a fallen tree that blocks the way.

Barbuda House appears undamaged, but when we clamber over the flattened gate to the yard the kitchen and the offices are a jumble of timbers and spoiled thatch. The yard is choked with thick black mud. No one could survive in what remains of Mr Tuffnell's cellar; the rubbish lies in feet of dirty floodwater.

His wife lies somewhere here, dead or as close to death as makes no difference. 'Poor lady.' I did not love my mistress, but I would not wish such a fate on anyone. Her body wracked, her fear beyond imagining. 'Her end was quick, at least I pray it was.'

'My God!' Mr Tuffnell clambers, tripping and cursing, over the debris, his face ghastly as he takes in the damage to his property.

I clutch Mr Espinosa's arm. 'You tell him. I can't.' Picking my way out to the street as quickly as I can, I leave the clerk to tell the truth to Mrs Tuffnell's widower.

An awful moment, and the gentlemen appear, pale-faced but purposeful, and in no time Mr Tuffnell is shouting orders and mustering men to help him search. Mr Espinosa shakes his head when I suggest the task is hopeless, and it is clear Mr Tuffnell will not give up until every part of the ruined cellar has been dug out. Every few moments he orders the men to pause, cup their hands to their ears, and listen for sounds of life beneath the rubble.

At one point a dog belonging to one of the labourers darts forward, cocks an ear, and worries at a heap of pantiles. Immediately the men form a chain, passing the tiles down the line with speed. However, after a minute or two the dog loses interest, and when the entire mound has been shifted and no one is discovered, hope ebbs and the work goes on steadily as before.

One man, older than the rest, has been set to sifting through the rubbish for items that may be salvaged, and after I explain I am a member of the household he hands me a trowel I can use to scrape earth and dust away from objects as I find them. In the next hour I find a candle snuffer, a set of andirons (bent and twisted, but good enough a smith could repair them), a drinking cup with only one small chip from its lip, and a heap of linen sheets stained and wet but un-torn. These I set aside for the villa in Clifton since that is now our home.

One discovery upsets me greatly, which is the collar Abraham was once forced to wear. It used to lie in Mrs Tuffnell's closet, and I suppose that in her haste to escape the storm she overlooked it. She might have pawned it to Mr Sampson, were the device not so distinctive her husband surely would have missed it.

The ivory is highly polished, the silver finely worked, yet I would have hated to see such an object on the boy, it being more suitable for a dog than a child, and I am glad Mrs Tuffnell did not make Abraham wear it in the short time that I knew him.

'Silence!' Mr Tuffnell speaks with such authority he is instantly obeyed. We wait, ears straining, until from the heap of bricks and shattered tiles and splintered beams comes a faint and desperate cry. Every man leaves off where he was working, and immediately digs away with bare hands at the place the sound came from. Mr Tuffnell is most eager of all, and Mr Espinosa and I join the effort, until Master shouts again: 'Easy does it. Slow and careful.' A piece of russet cloth, crumpled, white with dust; a torn bit of lace I last saw when Mrs Tuffnell made her confession; finally, an inch of human flesh, not pallid as a corpse would be, but pink and stirring as if the person we have found struggles to break free. Another minute, the removal of a pair of timbers, and my mistress is lifted out, coughing and crying until exhaustion and shock overtake her and she falls into a swoon.

Mr Tuffnell calls out. 'Fetch water, Amesbury.'

I seize the cup I have just recovered, and run to fill it. A conduit-pipe on the corner of Wine-street survived the night, and a line of dazed and thirsty citizens queue there with pails and pitchers.

Mr Tuffnell dips his own shirt-sleeve in the water, and moistens his wife's lips. He wipes the dirt from her brow, speaking softly.

No answer comes. He bends his face, hoping to detect a breath, seems to believe there is none, and casts about for help.

'Let me try, Sir.' I kneel at Mrs Tuffnell's side and loosen her stays. I dampen my finger and hold it to her nostrils; she breathes, but barely.

A Pair of Sharp Eyes

I lift the cup and let a drop of water trickle through the blue-tinged lips. She moans. I touch her cheek, whisper in her ear that she is safe. Her eyelids flutter; she lets out a groan and a cheer goes up.

I call to the men. 'Bring that board. That house will give us shelter, Sir, they are good neighbours.'

Lying on the makeshift stretcher his wife looks small, and she flinches as the men begin to lift her. Mr Tuffnell strokes her fingers. 'She's ice-cold,' he says.

'Put this round her,' I say, untying my neckerchief, and when the gentleman answers his door I bid the men bring her in and place her by the parlour fire.

While Mr Tuffnell is poured a glass of brandy, the neighbour's wife makes Mrs Tuffnell comfortable with a feather bed, and even fetches a straw pallet so I may stop tonight to nurse my lady. Mr Espinosa brings the surgeon, who dresses Mrs Tuffnell's wounds and binds her left arm, which he fears may be broken, then prescribes a draught, saying she has a concussion and needs to sleep.

I am busy washing my mistress's hands and face, changing her linen, combing the dust from her hair and coaxing her to take the sleeping-draught, when Mr Espinosa comes to take his leave.

'She looks very ill, doesn't she?' I whisper.

'She may surprise you.' I suppose he reflects on his own recovery these last few weeks. 'In a day or two she may be well enough to be moved to Clifton. The country air ...'

'I wonder if I might ask you a favour, Mr Espinosa. Would you make enquiries about my sister as you go about today? She worked at Elliott's Market Garden, as I'm sure you remember.'

'Of course. Though already people are returning to the city, and patching up their houses. I expect your sister will get word to you soon.'

While Mrs Tuffnell lives, I cannot bring myself to tell anyone, even Mr Espinosa, what my mistress claimed in her confession, but I cannot resist mentioning Mr Roach.

'Sir, the attack on your person from which you have so well recovered. Would it surprise you if I said Mr Tuffnell's coachman was the man who assaulted you?'

'It would surprise me very much.' He flushes. 'It may be unsavoury, Miss Amesbury, but these sorts of attacks are the result of prejudice of a general sort. Mr Tuffnell's coachman could have no particular quarrel with me.'

'Mrs Tuffnell was afraid of Roach on her own behalf last night, and I believe he was her creature when he set on you, Mr Espinosa.'

'What did she say last night?' He lowers his voice. 'We were all out of our wits while the storm was raging, and Mrs Tuffnell is highly-strung.'

'She's terrified her husband will discover her dealings with your master. It's my suspicion that before you could say anything to Mr Wharton, she had you silenced.'

He gazes at my mistress's pale face, the bluish circles beneath her eyes. 'Forget anything she told you when she was hysterical, Miss Amesbury. You are both sorely in need of rest. Try to set aside wild assertions made when Mrs Tuffnell feared for her life.'

I have done my best. If Mr Espinosa does not choose to probe into the Tuffnells' affairs I cannot force him.

Mrs Tuffnell lies quietly once the clerk has gone, and I sit by her and begin to doze. The clocks are mostly silent, damaged by the storm, and church bells are nowhere to be heard, but time passes, and when I open my eyes the light in the room is fading.

'Amesbury? Are you there?' Mrs Tuffnell's voice is strangely wistful, as if she is further from me than the few feet between her bed and my chair.

'Yes, Madam.'

'Where's my husband?'

'He'll be here soon, Madam. Can you manage a dish of gruel, if I ask the Cook to make some? Or a little bread-and-milk?'

'Let me be.' She shifts painfully on the mattress, and pulls the sheet up to her chin. 'Has Mr Tuffnell mentioned Jonathan Berwick, Amesbury?' Her voice is as weak as an old woman's.

'No, Madam. Let me tell what I see from the window here. One or two elm trees are down, but your neighbours' garden has not suffered as it might have done. The sundial still stands, and it is very pretty, Madam. Perhaps Mr Tuffnell would buy you a sundial when you recover.'

'You must tell my husband to find Jonathan Berwick, I insist. I sought him last night, only he must have lost his way amid the storm.'

'Madam, put your troubles out of mind. Mr Tuffnell wants you to bring your will to bear on getting well.'

'Hold my hand.' I take it, and she squeezes it harder than expected. 'I am dying, and I shall tell the truth, so help me God.'

'You told the truth last night, Madam. God heard your confession, I know He did.'

'Then I am damned. I told you Mr Roach killed my black boy. Did you believe me, Amesbury? What did you tell your friend the Jew?' Her fingernails dig into my wrist.

'Try to sleep, Madam. Master will be here soon. Shall I send for another draught? The doctor ordered me to keep you calm.'

The words are useless. Her face and hands burn and she does not know me. A sheen breaks out on her forehead, and she shivers violently. Then for a moment her breathing seems to stop. I snatch up her hand and find no pulse.

Desperate, I shout for help, and the lady of the house comes running. She sends for the surgeon, and we rub Mrs Tuffnell's face with brandy and try to help her sip.

She rallies, sinks, rallies; then draws an agonising breath, the last she takes upon this earth. May God have mercy on her soul. Before the surgeon reaches her, just as her husband comes running in, my lady breathes out with a sound I hope is her soul departing to a better place, and she dies.

Chapter Twenty-Seven

Monday, 10ᵗʰ December, 1703

A week or two after we move to Clifton, Nell Grey and I are turning beds and sweeping half a year's worth of cobwebs from the bedroom ceilings when Mrs Hucker shouts for me.

I look at Nell Grey. 'That's it. There's no lady for me to wait upon so Mr Tuffnell wants rid of me.'

Nell Grey swats me with a feather duster. 'You'd better be mistaken. I need you here to deal with these spiders.'

I am more hopeful when I find Mrs Hucker up to her elbows in flour. If she intended to dismiss me she would surely take her apron off. 'A visitor for you,' she says. 'Don't be long.' She jerks her head in the direction of the yard.

There, by the back door, is my sister Liz. She wears a new brown jacket and a smart pair of leather shoes, and her hat is freshly trimmed with bright blue ribbon. Far from looking worn and gaunt she has roses in her cheeks, and is decidedly plumper than when I saw her last.

'Liz! I was frightened you were injured or worse. How did you know to find me here?'

'I went to Wine-street and the neighbours told me where you'd gone.'

I kiss her, and she must be more pleased to see me than she lets on, for she gives my shoulder an awkward pat.

'I tried to find you, Liz, when the storm struck. I saw what happened to your house.'

'When the back wall blew down I ran to Mr Elliott's. Bill had gone already—he'd heard bad weather was on the way. And I've not seen him since,' she adds contemptuously.

'He's abandoned you?'

She juts out her chin. 'Mr Elliott has been kind to me. He says he'll keep a roof over my head.'

'But where's Bill?'

'I don't care, unless news comes he's dead and I am free to marry.' She blushes. 'Mr Elliott's not that old. He says he's been sweet on me since the day I started in his garden. He has no heirs, and when he dies he intends to leave me his business. We'd wed if we knew for certain Bill was dead.'

'Oh, Liz. I'm happy for you. Come here.' I plant another kiss on her cheek. 'Why did Bill go, though, Liz?'

She closes her eyes in impatience. 'You know why. I didn't fool you the day you asked about John Hench. Come here.' She moves a few yards from the house, so we cannot be overheard; her voice is low and rapid. 'Hench did kill those boys, three of them.' She sees my face, and hurries on. 'The other three were accidents. Bill swears two drowned in a quarry, one in the Frome. The bodies were bruised and cut about, but none was knifed whatever some folk say.'

'How would Bill know? Why believe him?'

'The mortuary men drink down at the harbour along with him and John Hench. They examined the bodies of the boys who drowned. And Bill admitted to me what happened to the other three.' She shuts her eyes. 'He and John Hench got greedy. They stole a cow from someone's byre first. They contrived to scare off the boy who was sleeping in the loft. Next time they weren't so lucky. Bill never meant to hurt anyone. He's stupid, but he isn't wicked.'

I let the statement pass.

'They were after taking a cow and her calf. A farm-lad startled them. He tried to raise the alarm, and John Hench went to silence him. Put his hand over his mouth. Next thing Bill knew John Hench was all over blood and the boy was dead.'

I cannot swallow.

'It changed John Hench. After that he said he didn't care, he'd hang anyway. A month later he killed a gamekeeper's lad, and shot a deer. Then he planned another robbery, and made Bill help him. I didn't know what they were up to, or I'd never have told Bill the whereabouts of Mr Elliott's bothy. Bill got it out of me.'

'John Hench killed Davy Roxall? How much did Hench expect to sell a few old shovels for? The price of someone's son? Don't tell me he murdered Abraham and George Goodfellow for what he hoped to thieve from Mr Tuffnell.' My face is hot with anger. 'What did he think we keep in our stable yard? Was he after robbing horse-shit and hawking it round the city gardens?'

I spit the words in my contempt. Liz wipes her cheek.

'He didn't kill either of them.' Her voice is low. 'He ran up country after Davy Roxall died. He was scared they'd trace him through me and Bill. Bill took his chance when the storm struck, and ran away. He'll be hoping people think he's dead. Bill's a liar and a coward but he didn't kill those other three boys, and I don't know who killed the two belonging to your master.'

The yard is silent, and the garden beyond is silent too, except for a gull crying, and the wind in the birch trees between Mr Tuffnell's land and his neighbour's. The house and garden overlook the Avon Gorge, and beyond the Gorge, the harbour and the river.

The rocks and the hanging woods have stood for centuries. I wonder what they make of men who think a cow reward enough for murdering a child. I let the wind carry away my tears, and Liz does not notice them.

'I'm glad you've the chance of a fresh start,' I say at last.

Her voice is defiant. 'Bill led me a miserable life. I should have told somebody what he and Hench were up to. Mr Elliott and I, we're making a payment to Thomas Roxall, to compensate him for his loss.'

I remember Mother crying when the inn-keeper said I could ride to Bristol in his brother's coach as recompense for Tommy being killed. 'That's kind, Liz,' I say. 'Mr Roxall will be grateful.'

Failing to notice the bitterness in my voice, she looks around. 'You've a good berth here. It's even grander than the other house. Do you think they'll keep you on past New Year's Day?'

'I hope so.' I may as well tell her the truth. 'The master likes me.'

'Oh,' she says meaningfully. 'Well, mind yourself, there's no wife now to catch him trying to stick a hand in your petticoats. He's hardly likely to make an honest woman of you.' Unlike her doting Mr Elliott, she means.

'I know that. I don't want him to.'

'What?' Liz casts her eyes over the back of the villa, the high brick chimneys and painted wooden gables. 'You can't fool me, Corrie Amesbury. You missed the chance to marry one fine gentleman, you won't refuse another.'

I am thankful Liz was spared in the tempest, but her voice is like a dog that will not give up yapping.

'Liz, Robert's father wouldn't let us marry. The squire sent him to the West Indies to get the two of us apart.' I swore never to tell the rest, but the words spill out. 'I was on Back-lane one day, sorrowing for Robert, when his father rode up and laid into me, calling me a whore who'd ruined his son's life. He raised his whip, I thought he'd kill me. All of a sudden he was grabbing hold of me, kissing my neck, putting his filthy fingers in my bodice.'

Liz's hand covers her mouth. Her eyes are shocked, but she is laughing. 'Then what?'

'I broke free and ran into the Rough. He couldn't find me. In the end he rode away.'

'So that's why you came to Bristol.'

I won't have her pity me, or think I would flee from anyone.

'No, Liz. I came to Bristol for a better life. As you did.'

She pinches her lips, about to retort, when Mrs Hucker appears at the back door, coughing sharply.

'You've work to do, Amesbury. Good day, young woman.' Abashed, Liz makes a bob, and before I can offer her a kiss, she hurries off.

***

So badly did his home suffer in the storm that Mr Wharton remains at the Hot-wells to supervise repairs. Mr Espinosa is acting as Mr Tuffnell's agent in his friend's absence, and tonight he comes to Clifton to discuss Mr Tuffnell's losses from the floods.

Afterwards Nell Grey comes to say that Mr Espinosa is waiting for me in the yard. 'Don't tell me he's courting you, Corrie Amesbury. A Jew!'

I would rather Nell Grey believed Mr Espinosa and I were lovers than she suspected we were in league to find the truth about Abraham's death. She already considers me an oddity; if she thought I was looking into the past of our late mistress she would think me odder still.

I find Mr Espinosa standing with his back to the villa, surveying Mr Tuffnell's flower plot.

'Good day, Sir.'

He lifts his hat. Without it his face is younger, and I am surprised as always by the kindness and shrewdness of his eyes. 'You may be interested to hear what I've discovered, Miss Amesbury. Your brother-in-law proved impossible to trace, but I was asked to make additional enquiries on behalf of Mr Tuffnell.'

'Not about Bill Eardley?'

'No, no. Mr Tuffnell's menservants who vanished in the storm. No one could tell me the whereabouts of Mr Roach, but it seems that Jonathan Berwick was arrested the day after. Mr Tuffnell suspected he'd seized advantage of the crisis to abscond with several articles of clothing.'

I do not voice what I suspect: that Jonty knew of Mr Roach's money, having found it on his forays to our master's casks of rum. He surely hoped to take the purse that night, only to find Barbuda lay in ruins. And Mrs Tuffnell followed Jonty there, hoping to elope with him.

'He was sheltering in a deserted barn near Temple-Meads. A falling branch had lamed him and he was too badly injured to go on. The villagers examined him and found a suit of clothes hidden on his person. He broke down under questioning, and admitted stealing the suit from his master. He's bound to be transported. Or worse.'

'Where is he? Bristol Newgate?' The city's gaol is only yards from Wine-street. 'Poor man, the place is notorious. We must take him food and blankets.'

'Miss Amesbury, you mustn't think of visiting him. A common prisoner isn't housed in goal as debtors are.' He hurries on. 'His cell will be crowded, rat-ridden, full of dangerous miasmas; the inmates suffer from scrofula and worse. Were I your brother I would forbid you to go.'

'Mr Espinosa, I thank you for your concern, but you are not my brother.'

He purses his lips unhappily. 'Jonathan Berwick deserves neither your interest nor your kindness.'

'He may not. Yet he has both. I cannot help it.'

Mr Espinosa rubs his face. 'Then will you let me come with you?'

I can think of no objection, and secretly I will feel safer in Mr Espinosa's company, so it is fixed that our visit to Bristol Newgate will take place after my trip to market tomorrow, it being easy to pass this off as taking longer than usual, since many of the roads and footpaths are blocked with trees and fallen buildings.

**

Tuesday, 11ᵗʰ December, 1703

Jonty was the handsomest fellow I ever saw when I took up my post with Mrs Tuffnell. As manservant he wore a smart grey suit, fine linen, and each day before he helped Mr Tuffnell to dress, he shaved his own face with pumice, powdered his wig and pared his finger-nails. Added to this he had the natural looks of any man of five-and-twenty who is tall, well-formed, with clear eyes, a good complexion and a ready smile. They denied it, but I used to think Jonty and Nell Grey might wed one day, if they succeeded in courting without our mistress finding out.

The gaoler leads us along a freezing, ill-lit passage to an evil-smelling cell lined with straw so soiled it would disgrace a stable, and here are crammed a dozen wretches chained to the walls, dressed in rags that cannot keep out the cold, it being as draughty here as in the street.

Mr Espinosa approaches a man I did not notice at first, and who lies with his face covered by his arm. 'Jonathan Berwick?'

Jonty startles and sits upright. His face takes on a hunted expression. 'What are you doing here?'

'To ask the same question of you, Mr Berwick. Will you speak to us?'

Jonty shrugs as if he would rather not, but after all, he can hardly walk away.

'I brought you a pie.' Mr Espinosa produces a parcel from his pocket. Jonty must be as hungry as he looks, for he swallows at the sight of it and devours it in moments, tearing at the pastry and snatching every crumb.

'So what happened to make you run away?'

'You know what happened, I'm sure.'

'You don't indict yourself by speaking to Miss Amesbury and me. We are your friends. If you tell us the truth we may be able to coax Mr Tuffnell to help you.'

Jonty makes a mirthless sound. 'Him help me? Hardly.'

'Why did you rob him?'

Jonty's eyes are raw-rimmed. 'I told you, I shan't answer.'

Mr Espinosa clears his throat. 'Mr Berwick, have you spoken to the Prison Ordinary? And made confession?'

'Confession?' Jonty's voice is rough. 'What good would that do?'

'It might save your soul, when you go before the Almighty. Admit to us, it was you killed the black boy, was it not? I must tell you, Mr Berwick, with my own eyes I saw you strike him not long before he died.'

'I struck him for his own good. To teach him to keep his mouth shut. Miss Amesbury will tell you how the child milked any argument to make himself seem blameless, just as children will do. He needed saving from himself, given who he lived with. You should speak to other servants belonging to Mr Tuffnell, not I.'

'Mr Berwick, are you accusing Mr Tuffnell's coachman? Be careful what you say.'

'I do accuse him.'

'His motive?'

'The lad found a stash of money Roach had hidden in the cellar at Barbuda. God bless him, Pug thought it belonged to Mr Tuffnell, and that Mr Tuffnell should know his gold was not so well concealed as it ought to be. Roach caught him carrying the purse to Master, and in rage at having his ill-gotten hoard discovered, he beat the lad.'

Mr Espinosa looks at me and lifts an eyebrow. 'We can vouch for the viciousness of Mr Roach.'

Yet something troubles me. 'Why would Mr Tuffnell conceal his coachman's violent behaviour?'

Jonty shrugs. 'Mr Tuffnell didn't know of it. His wife begged me not to tell him, after I found Abraham half-dead, lying in the yard. His head was broken when Roach knocked him down. I carried the boy indoors, cleaned his wounds, wrapped him in a blanket, and took him to my own bed by the kitchen fire. When I woke next morning I found him cold. Dead of his injuries, poor innocent. He died in dead of night, and the only comfort is he weren't alone.'

I am puzzled why Mrs Hucker did not find the pair when she went to light the kitchen range. 'You must have woken very early. Did you not go straight to Mrs Tuffnell?'

'Instead of accusing Roach, she said I would be blamed for the death. It looked bad for me, that I had taken the boy into my bed. I would be called unnatural. She said my only hope was to throw the blame on Red John.' Jonty begins to cry. 'She told me to cut the boy's throat, so his body would look like the other victims.'

'But why?' Mr Espinosa's astonished tone conveys his doubt that what we are hearing can be true.

'I think I know the answer,' I say slowly. 'She sought to throw suspicion away from Mr Roach. Whatever the reason, she was determined to protect him.'

'Why should she care about a fellow like that?'

'I reckon he knew things to her discredit. He was a well-known bully, he used to live in Bath. Perhaps Mrs Tuffnell lived there too before her marriage. It all hints to me that she had things to hide.'

'Please, leave off your questions,' Jonty says, anguished. 'If you drag up more, they are bound to hang me. Even if you found proof of Roach's guilt they won't believe you. A maidservant and a Jew. Go. You torment me.'

'Jonty, don't despair. We will prove your innocence, shan't we, Sir?'

Mr Espinosa puts his hand on Jonty's shoulder. 'Mr Berwick, I am Mr Tuffnell's deputy while his agent's indisposed. I will ask him this favour, that Miss Amesbury and I may travel to Bath to confirm or disprove the explanation you give us. If we discover intelligence concerning Mr Roach that suggests his guilt, be sure Mr Tuffnell will listen to me, or if not to me, to my friend Mr Wharton. If James Tuffnell is convinced, he may be relied on to present evidence of your innocence to the justices at the assizes. Do not lose all hope yet, my friend.'

I wait for Jonathan to nod and thank Mr Espinosa for his kind offer. But he must be as far from hope as he claims, for his eyes are dull, and even before we leave his cell he slumps down again, his face turned to the wall.

'One final question, Berwick. Will you swear you had nothing to do with George Goodfellow's death?'

Jonty scrambles up so fast, and his expression is so fierce, I cannot help but take a step back, though his shackles prevent him laying hands on me.

'How can you ask such a thing? I was George Goodfellow's friend. I worked alongside him since he came to Mr Tuffnell's house aged seven. Leave me alone, will you? I can't bear to be accused any longer.' Pulling his dirty coat over his head, he turns away once more, and it is plain we will get no more out of him today.

Mr Espinosa calls for the turnkey, and we make our way back up from the dismal pit. A thought strikes me.

'Sir, before we leave let me speak to Mr Ambrose Ayres. He may not know of Mrs Tuffnell's death.'

Mr Espinosa nods, and the gaoler who waited while we spoke to Jonty makes an ironic bow before leading us to the debtors' gaol.

A Pair of Sharp Eyes

After the prison pit the faded courtyard is almost a haven, and Mr Ayres is gracious as ever when the turnkey delivers us to his cell. He poses on a hard wooden chair draped in a length of dirty reddish velvet, and addresses the turnkey with all the civil condescension of a lord who amazes a crossing-sweeper by presenting him with a shilling rather than a penny.

Except in this case there is no shilling.

'Leave us, there's a good fellow.' A wave of the hand. 'How may I help you young people? Miss Amesbury, good afternoon. Good God, a Jew. I knew a Jew once. Chief Rabbi of a synagogue near Tower Bridge. Perhaps you know him too, Sir?'

This sort of whimsy does not help us with our quest.

'Mr Ayres, we bring sad news. The lady who used to send me to you is dead, Sir, a victim of the storm.'

Mr Ayres's smile disappears, though he quickly recovers. 'Shocking, to be sure.' He holds up his palm. 'Withhold the details, please. They would haunt me in here in my simple hermitage. Dear, dear. I'd thought to propose a bowl of punch for two most welcome guests. Punch is hardly apt after so dismal an announcement.' He subsides into a fluttering performance with a worn scrap of silk that serves him for a pocket handkerchief.

Mr Espinosa waits until the handkerchief is folded into Mr Ayres's frayed sleeve.

'Sir, we would be greatly indebted if you could confirm for us the nature of your connection with Mrs Tuffnell. Miss Amesbury here suggests you were a relative.'

'You were her father, weren't you, Sir?'

'Father? I am a bachelor, a respectable bachelor. If Mrs Tuffnell chose to sprinkle a little benison upon me now and then, I did not choose to offend her by sending back her charitable gifts. But there was never any question of obligation of kinship.' He smiles. 'I was an object of benevolence, pure and simple.' His face falls. 'It pains me to admit I shall miss her kindnesses, trifling as they were. My current circumstances are quite comfortable, of course.' He fingers the balding velvet of his seat. 'Nonetheless, I'm unlikely to die from a surfeit or any other excess.' He gives a barking laugh.

I wait for Mr Espinosa to express his sympathy and promise Mr Ayres assistance, but instead the clerk draws the interview smartly to a close, and as we take our leave his face wears a look of disapproval tending to dislike.

'Mr Ayres has charm, don't he, Sir?' I venture. 'He must have been a handsome man in his youth. Perhaps Mrs Tuffnell is to be forgiven if her heart was captured by him to a small degree.'

'He's a charlatan. Mrs Tuffnell was less worldly than she liked to think if she could be taken in by such an egregious rogue.'

'He must have been someone once upon a time, Sir. He knew the Chief Rabbi, don't forget.' But as I say it I blush, for it is hardly likely a West Country bankrupt could be close friends with such a person.

'There's no synagogue near Tower Bridge. I suppose Mr Ayres told you he was best friends with the Lord Lieutenant of Wiltshire?'

I pick my way over the cobbles without answering.

'Reserve your sympathy for Mrs Tuffnell, Miss Amesbury. How many more people will come forward to admit they duped her?'

Suddenly I tire of his scathing tone. 'I don't know, Mr Espinosa, but I was the one who thought of speaking to Jonathan Berwick, so I don't think I'm such a gull, do you?'

He is startled, and softens. 'You are right, of course. Mr Ayres isn't worth quarrelling over. Let us focus our minds on what we may find in Bath.'

Chapter Twenty-Eight

Bath
Wednesday, 12th December, 1703

Mr Espinosa is as good as his word. That afternoon, with what amazing words of diplomacy I do not know, he speaks to Mr Tuffnell and obtains permission to go to Bath the following day, taking me with him as his servant. Any reluctance from Mr Tuffnell is overcome when Mr Espinosa hints his fear that Mrs Tuffnell was made to suffer in the months before her death, and that he hopes to find proof with which to prosecute her abuser.

'Luckily for us,' Mr Espinosa tells me, 'Mr Tuffnell was so distressed by this suggestion he begged me to spare him any details until the case is proven.'

'Perhaps you should never reveal to Master quite what his wife was led to do, Sir.' I speak in a roundabout way, since we are in the carrier's cart, and the other passengers can hear me.

Mr Espinosa winces. 'No indeed.' He drops his voice further. 'To think she proposed the mutilation of the boy's body. It is incredible.'

'She stopped at nothing to protect herself as mistress of Barbuda House. Yet she did love Abraham in her way, and I know she loved her husband.' Out of respect for Mr Espinosa's feelings I forbear to add that Mrs Tuffnell may have loved her husband more than he deserved.

'Poor fellow. He should have chosen better. An honourable man.'

'Shall we take our dinner at the West-gate Inn, Sir?'

'Must we? They were most reluctant to serve me last time, if you recall.'

'I'd be grateful if you was willing to put up with their ignorance one more time, Sir. I have a score to settle.' My hope is that Mrs Buckley will be treating another group of guests to dinner, and cannot dodge me in a public dining-room without a scene that causes her more embarrassment than it does me.

Mr Espinosa's lips twitch. 'Never let it be said you shirk a fight, Miss Amesbury. Very well. I shall hope I am served beef and not ham on this occasion.'

We begin to notice the curious looks we attract, and given the general waste, from blown-down trees to flooded fields, visible from the carrier's cart, we join with our fellow passengers in swapping stories of the storm. A miller from Twyning in Gloucestershire tells of eleven barns blown down in that village; a fellow chips in to say he heard of one who fell from a ladder trying to save his hovel, and who landed on his plough and never spoke a word before he died. And this as far off as Northamptonshire, while in London it is said a dozen people lost their lives that awful night.

A shipwright from Bristol retorts that eighty people died in the marshes and the river there, whole families perishing together. He claims to know of 15,000 sheep drowned in the Somerset Levels, and the country lying under water for twenty miles either side of the River Severn.

Finally, we run out of words to express our horror at this calamity, which speaks of the Almighty's anger with his godless people, and turn our attention to the view of Bath as the cart begins its descent towards the city.

***

Entering the dining-room at the West-gate I fear I may have been foolish in expecting to encounter Mrs Buckley. The inn is crammed with dinner guests, as well as those who sleep here overnight and for whom gout, gallstones, breathlessness and corpulence are no hindrance to a dinner of four courses with a plentiful array of meats and sweet dishes at each, as well as ale, beer, claret, cider, brandy, rum and sherry wine. The hubbub is such I wonder if I may fail to find Mrs Buckley even if she is here. Then an outburst of ribald laughter from a side-room prompts me to glance round, and there she is, presiding over a table laden with expensive dishes, holding forth to a throng that includes several extravagantly dressed gentlemen and a greater number of young ladies attired in simple straw bonnets and petticoats of calico and cambric.

Supper is well advanced, judging by the guests' red faces and the number of empty platters carried off by the serving-woman. As I watch, a maiden is swept from her chair by the gentleman next to her. Holding her on his knee and proceeding to plant several kisses on her blushing cheeks, he hands her to his friend, who does the same, though this second fellow is bold enough to kiss her lips. Smiling yet indignant, she struggles and protests, but it seems the game is to hand her round the table, each gentleman helping himself by fondling her bosom or pressing his lips to hers. It cannot be long before the parties leave for some less reputable establishment, and I see that my best, nay my only, chance lies in confronting Mrs Buckley at this very moment.

'Miss Amesbury!' Mr Espinosa calls to hinder me, but too late; I have crossed the room.

'Mrs Buckley? My name is Miss Coronation Amesbury. You have forgotten me, I dare say. Will you oblige me, Madam, by speaking to me privately?'

Mrs Buckley's mouth drops open, and she turns to her nearest companion, a naval officer, and pulls a droll face as if to say: What impertinence is this?

'I believe you would rather hear what I have to say in confidence, Madam. Of course, I could address you and your friends, the choice is yours.'

Spots of colour mount her cheeks, and she scrapes back her chair. 'Very well, I can spare a moment. We were about to leave, you know.'

'Of course, you have a great friend lives nearby, have you not? Mrs Charlton.'

We have reached the doorway between the private dining-room and the public one, and her eyes narrow. 'Who did you say you were, Miss?'

'Just as I thought, you forgot me the day I left Bath. And I'm sure you've forgotten my friend, Miss Jane Lamborne of Chippenham.

Miss Jane was sorely abused the night you gave us hospitality, Mrs Buckley. She has lost her good place in Bristol, and her good name. I am minded to let those maids in there know what befell my friend, lest they make the same mistake she did. Perhaps you will let me through to speak to them?'

This is a gamble on my part, for the company grows raucous, and the young women might not hearken to me however loudly I addressed them. However, the threat is enough to alarm Mrs Buckley.

'How dare you, Miss! I am twice your age, and well known in Bath and held in high esteem. You are a country miss without even the usual charms of youth, and I do not wonder at you for mentioning your friend. I expect she was highly admired when she was here, and let me guess, you was overlooked.'

'Mrs Buckley, I am an honest maid. I worked for Mrs Maria Tuffnell until her untimely death. On the evening I spent in Bath I had more sense than to be tricked by you, Madam.' I am about to test whether a reference to Mr Roach will light a spark of recognition in Mrs Buckley's eyes, but her expression alters to horror at the mention of Mrs Tuffnell.

'Dead?' she gasps. 'It isn't true.'

'Before she died, she revealed to me she had been cruelly mistreated by a certain Mr Roach.'

'But I can't believe she's dead. Not Mary.' Her face crumples, and if it were not for Miss Jane Lamborne I would sincerely pity her. 'What happened?' she asks, as a tear slips down her cheek.

'A beam collapsed, and crushed her in the storm. She seemed to rally, but she died the day after. When the surgeon opened her, he found a great loss of blood internally.'

Mrs Buckley grasps the wainscot. 'Then she suffered grievously.'

'She died in agony, Madam. And some of her pain was mental as well as physical. Her servant, Mr Roach, had been tricking her. And an elderly gentleman living nearby claimed to be her bankrupt father, and dunned her for money, yet when I took the sad news to him he said he was no relation to the lady. He would miss her charity but was otherwise indifferent to her.' I cannot but sound contemptuous as I relate this brief account of my last meeting with Mr Ayres.

'God forgive me.' In her awe Mrs Buckley's mask seems to slip and I glimpse the hollow creature within. 'My darling, dead,' she says. She grabs the arm of a passing pot-boy. 'Show us to a private room.'

The boy gestures to the throng as if to say the place is full, but Mrs Buckley thrusts her face at him. 'A room,' she says hoarsely.

I am aware of Mr Espinosa shadowing us as the boy shrugs and leads us to the back of the inn and into a small windowless chamber where the grate is cold and the few furnishings are stacked against the wall.

Taking one look at Mrs Buckley's pallor, I fetch a chair and she sinks onto it.

'I can't comprehend what you said. She was so young.' She covers her face with her plump, jewel-clad fingers. I stand over her as she sobs, and when eventually she looks up, I see she will tell me all I need to know.

'You were her mother.'

Mrs Buckley's ringlets quiver. 'I gave her a good start. She might have married a baronet or a viscount if she had let me take charge of her. But she was wilful.'

'You mean you hoped to sell her to the highest bidder?'

She ignores the question. 'She fell in love with a West Indian planter. She was only supposed to make him happy for a night, but no, the very next day she declared she was in love. Fifteen years old, and she ran away from home. Then he went back to Jamaica, didn't he? Leaving her with child.'

'She had no child. What happened to it?'

'It died at three days old. At least she had the sense to make the planter promise to support his infant—and to forget to tell him when it died.'

'You mean she continued to receive monies though the child was dead? How, when the planter was so far away?'

'Ignorant girl. Bills of exchange—any money-lender will honour them. She bore the child, and mourned for it. The man was rich enough. He ought to have supported her.'

'No doubt you sought to take her back, once she had a steady income?'

'What? No. She wanted nothing more to do with me. Next thing I knew she was in Bristol, passing herself off as the widow of a rich Creole.' Mrs Buckley gives a mirthless laugh. 'Not plain Mary Buckley any more. She was "Mrs Maria Buckingham." Good luck to you, I said.' Her voice breaks. 'Much good it did her in the end.'

I allow the old vixen a moment to weep, but I am determined to extract all the intelligence she can provide.

'Tell me why she was giving money to Mr Ayres. Was he her father?'

Another sob, designed to draw out my pity though it falls far short of the mark. 'She may have believed so. He was fond of me once—perhaps Mary remembered him. He was gentlemanly, I expect she wanted to credit his claims. Or perhaps he threatened to expose her past unless she helped him. He probably put it this way: her old friends helped to make her what she was.' She sniffs, her confidence returning. I see she defies me to contest her own part in Mrs Tuffnell's 'success'.

I step closer until Mrs Buckley cringes. 'Would another of her good friends be Mr Roach, by any chance?' I hiss. 'Or plain Pete, as he used to call himself?'

It crosses Mrs Buckley's mind to lie but, 'We knew Pete, yes,' she admits.

'He brawled and bullied when he lived in Bath, by all accounts. Then he moved to Bristol, where he terrified your daughter into stealing her husband's property, and went on to beat her page-boy 'til he died. He will hang when they find him, be in no doubt. You are a cold cruel woman who sought to sell your own child, and if it was up to me, you'd hang too.'

To my amazement Mrs Buckley laughs. 'Pete, stealing property from one of Bristol's merchant venturers? Pete, who eked out a living as a bully? 'Til he went to Bristol the most he earned was a shilling here and there for press-ganging fathead country boys to go to sea. If Pete was rich, why would he risk his neck by murdering a slave-child? You thought yourself quicker-witted than your friends the night you stopped in Bath, Miss. You flattered yourself.'

'And you may mock me all you like, but when Mr Tuffnell learns how you treated his beloved wife you will be sorry.'

Mrs Buckley leaps to her feet, but Mr Espinosa has been skulking outside the chamber throughout our conference, and he bursts through the door as she lifts a hand to strike me.

'You again!' she cries. He has her arm tightly gripped. 'Sneaking Israelite! I remember you.'

His eyes flash. 'And my sister, Miss Hannah Espinosa, do you remember her? Whom you almost destroyed when she came to Bath last summer? Forcing strong spirits on her, and dragging her to a bawdy-house?'

I stare, astonished. Mr Espinosa has never been frank with me about his sister. Mrs Buckley sneers. 'Ugly Jewess, she could never have found work in a respectable household. She should have thrown in her lot with me.'

Mr Espinosa is white with anger. He speaks through clenched teeth. 'My sister is a virtuous woman, but no one, virtuous or otherwise, deserves to fall into the hands of such as you, Madam. We will ensure Mr Tuffnell and his friends among the magistrates learn who you are and what you did. Be assured you will not escape justice. You have 'til tomorrow morning to hand yourself to the constable.'

Before Mrs Buckley can form a reply, Mr Espinosa takes my hand and leads me through the dining-room and out into the street. 'We'll take rooms elsewhere and catch the mail coach back to Bristol in the morning. Let Mrs Buckley think we are already on our way to see the magistrate.'

'Do you truly believe Mr Tuffnell will listen to us, Sir?'

'I think he will be grateful to learn that his wife was guilty of no more than seeking to cover up her past. She cannot be blamed unduly for that.'

'Except she also sought to cover up the brutal murder of her page-boy.'

'That is true.' We are silent. Mr Espinosa hesitates. 'As you point out, she was far from perfect, though I forgive Mr Tuffnell if he chooses not to dwell on the worst in her character now she is gone.'

'Perhaps the worst in his was his blindness when it came to her.'

'Indeed. I hope we can convince him to campaign for Jonathan Berwick's release, and exert his power to have Mr Roach brought to justice.'

'Mrs Buckley could say nothing to convince us Roach is innocent. We know him too well.' Mr Espinosa's hand goes to his scar, healed now but noticeable where the hair has not grown back.

'Mr Espinosa? There is one more thing that troubles me about Mr Tuffnell. I believe it troubles Mr Wharton too.' I choose my words carefully, for these men are close friends. 'Mr Tuffnell trusted his business partner, Mr Cheatley. I carried a letter which warned my master that Mr Cheatley had altered the terms of their business contract before the *Prudence* set sail for Calabar. His wife read the letter and destroyed it, Sir, because it went on to hint at difficulties in her own affairs.'

'Be direct, Miss Amesbury. No one overhears us.'

'Mr Wharton would have told Mr Tuffnell in person that Cheatley was insisting on higher prices than were originally agreed. What neither men knew was that the *Prudence* set sail with fewer hands than were needed to supervise the negroes they would buy in Calabar. The captain planned to make up the shortfall caused by Mr Cheatley by tight-packing. I take it he meant he would carry more negroes than he had room for. If the slaves should mutiny, Sir, the crew themselves may rebel, forced to oversee so many negroes and perhaps in small expectation of fair payment.'

'What do you suggest? There is little to be gained in warning Mr Tuffnell. He can do nothing to avert disaster from such a distance.'

'I thought it worth mentioning to you and Mr Sampson, and perhaps to Mr Wharton, Sir. I should be sorry if men who are honest suffer for the follies of those who aren't.'

'Miss Amesbury, I don't discount your kindness in warning us, but I'm disappointed you think so little of your master. We agreed it wasn't his fault his wife bewitched him.'

'As it was not entirely her fault she set out to marry him. I'd have more respect for Mr Tuffnell if I thought he cared a jot about those whose labour he depends on.'

'You can hardly blame him for employing others. Do you wish yourself out of work and starving?'

I am suddenly weary of explaining myself to someone who is obstinately wedded to his own views of the world, notwithstanding the cruel blows that world delivers to his own door.

'Of course not, Sir. I meant something quite different. It is late, Mr Espinosa, will we go in and ask for rooms? When we have slept a good night's sleep we may continue our conversation on our journey home tomorrow.'

His face clears. He is relieved to drop the subject. 'That is a good idea. Well, to tomorrow. Ha! Here is the inn-keeper. May we have two chambers, Sir? My maidservant here will be happy to share with another female. I would be glad of a room of my own.'

I expect the whistling host who leads us upstairs imagines I am Mr Espinosa's mistress rather than his servant, and is surprised we do not ask to share a room. But I intend never to bed or wed any man, and if I do it must be one who looks with clear eyes at the world around him.

Were I to search from here to the West Indies, I doubt if there is more than one who does.

Chapter Twenty-Nine

Clifton
Thursday, 13th December, 1703

The mail coach brings us to Bristol just after noon, and the roads being strewn with rubbish from the storm, we agree it will be quicker to go on foot to Mr Tuffnell's villa.

Who should we meet as we pass College-green but Mrs Wharton and little Harry, baskets in hands, heading to market?

'Aaron.' She curtseys to him, giving me a kindly smile.

'Esther. Good day to you. How do the repairs progress at home?'

She pulls a face. 'Noisily. The men have been hammering on the roof since eight o'clock, so Harry and I left Baby Emma in the care of a village girl. We hope to buy some dinner that won't need a fire, the chimney being unfit to use. How is Mr Tuffnell, Sir?'

'Still desolate.'

'Poor gentleman. To think Henry and I saw Mrs Tuffnell at the Merchant Venturers' feast just weeks ago.'

A thought strikes me and makes me bold. 'Did Mrs Tuffnell seem herself that night, Madam?' She frowns. 'Yes.' Then she catches Mr Espinosa's eye. 'As you can vouch, Sir, she was given to avoiding me. We met in the ladies' cloakroom at the end of the evening. She nodded as we were putting on our cloaks, that was all.'

'Mrs Tuffnell was a hardened anti-Semite, make no mistake.' Mr Espinosa turns to me. 'She did not wish to be seen in public on friendly terms with one of our tribe.'

'Because she was uncertain of her standing here in Bristol, Sir.' I am loath to speak uncharitably a second time; all three of us depend on Mr Tuffnell for our livelihoods.

'Perhaps. You are right, of course. That is, I hope so.'

Mrs Wharton, understandably, has limited interest in a woman, now dead, who slighted her and betrayed her friend. Her young son has been jumping on and off a pile of bricks during the conversation.

A Pair of Sharp Eyes

'Come on, Harry. You will spoil your shoes. Say good-bye.'

***

Mr Tuffnell is seated by the fire in his shirt-sleeves when we arrive.

'Espinosa. I have been waiting these two hours. I have been think-ing while you were gone. It must be Roach who abused my wife. When you were in Bath did you uncover any information to suggest he had been taking money from her?'

'May we sit, Sir?' Mr Espinosa asks. He indicates for me to take a stool by the window, and draws his own chair close to Mr Tuff-nell's. I glance into the garden where Suke Cross is plucking laun-dry off the bushes and bundling it in her apron as furtively as if she plans to run away and sell her master's linen.

'We found the person in Bath we hoped would help us understand the matter,' Mr Espinosa says. Seemingly, he does not feel a need to acknowledge my role in Mrs Buckley's discovery. 'She knew your wife well. She knows Mr Roach too, and cast doubt on the notion Mr Roach blackmailed Mrs Tuffnell. She claimed he might have been a petty thief but was incapable of greater cunning.'

'Then who did extort money from my wife?'

'It remains a mystery. I am convinced Mr Roach was the man who attacked me in November. Jonathan Berwick confirmed Roach's brutishness when we visited him in prison.'

'Roach must be found at once if that is true.'

'Thank you, Sir, though I imagine he is far away by now.'

Both gentlemen seem to have forgotten me. I catch my master's eye. 'Sir, can I recall for you the annual feast given by the Merchant Venturers on All Hallows Eve?'

Mr Tuffnell looks startled, then puzzled by my question. 'I beg your pardon?'

'You attended the feast that night, and your wife went with you. Who sat at your right hand, Sir?'

'My agent's wife. She and her husband always sit with me on such occasions. One day, I like to tell Mr Wharton, he too will be a member of the Merchant Venturers' Society.'

'And who sat on your left?'

Mr Tuffnell's expression saddens. 'My late wife. She wore her flowered silk. You yourself helped her dress that night, Ames.'

'Sir, will you tell us how you travelled home? Did Mr Roach fetch you in the coach?'

Irritated, Mr Tuffnell shakes his head. 'The banqueting hall is less than a furlong from Barbuda House, and the way too narrow for the coach, in any case. We walked.'

'With Jonathan Berwick carrying the lantern for you?'

'Naturally.'

'Before you left, as the feast came to an end, did Mr Wharton say anything to you, Sir? While your wife was busy putting on her cloak and gloves? We met Mrs Wharton on our way today, and she chanced to mention that Mrs Tuffnell would not acknowledge her at the feast, but what interested me was that the ladies retired to the cloakroom before the evening ended, meaning the gentlemen could speak to each other without their wives overhearing.'

'I had nothing to say that night that Mrs Tuffnell could not be privy to.'

'You might not, Sir, but Mr Wharton did.'

'He may have said a few words to me on a business matter. The *Prudence* was rumoured to be struggling in bad weather. I recall Mr Wharton mentioned it, having received a letter sent by schooner from the skipper of the *Prudence*, Captain Stiles.'

'That's as may be, Sir, but Mr Wharton raised another concern, didn't he? One he had mentioned by letter, though the letter never reached you. That night he told you he suspected your wife had no business connections with the West Indies that could profit you. Quite the contrary, though Mr Wharton didn't know the half of it. As I found out in Bath, the husband she claimed to have lost is alive and well and living in Jamaica.'

A Pair of Sharp Eyes

Mr Tuffnell blinks, speechless. Mr Espinosa looks most uncomfortable, and breaks in. 'Miss Amesbury, this is no way to speak about your late mistress.'

I understand his qualms, but am determined to have the matter in the open.

'It was you yourself, Mr Espinosa, who alerted Mr Wharton to her correspondence with a gentleman in the West Indies. That gentleman, a planter much older than Mrs Tuffnell, made regular payments to her through bills of exchange he sent to Mr Sampson. You paid a high price—almost the highest. She set Roach on you, to silence you.'

Mr Espinosa sends Mr Tuffnell an anguished look. 'This is only an allegation Miss Amesbury makes, she has no proof.'

His spinelessness is vexing, but he hates to see my master suffer so I forgive him.

'It was very hard, Mr Espinosa, to be beaten and robbed and left for dead when you simply wanted to help your friend. You feared that once Mr Tuffnell discovered his wife's deceit, he might blame Mr Wharton for failing to alert him sooner.'

Mr Tuffnell, unaware of the way the discussion is tending, regards Mr Espinosa with a kind, if weary smile. 'No need to deny it, Aaron. You acted from honourable motives. Though I must assure you that however falsely my wife played me, I should never want to save forty pounds *per annum* by dismissing Henry Wharton.'

Mr Espinosa bites his lip, then speaks in a rush.

'I had a second motive to alert others to Mrs Tuffnell's—weaknesses. Pardon me, Sir, forgive my candour, but Mrs Tuffnell did not treat my sister Hannah justly. She befriended her, and showered her with affection. She led Hannah to believe she would offer her a position as her paid companion. Then, for no other reason than that some of her female acquaintance objected to Hannah on the grounds she was a Jewess, she beat and cast my sister out without a character.'

I can scarcely bear to look at Mr Tuffnell. His expression is so hurt I almost wish that we had let the matter lie. Then I think back to the day I saw the body of a child, dead and bleeding in the yard at Barbuda House. Mr Tuffnell hardly spared the boy a glance. His only thoughts were for his wife and for himself.

'May I go on, Sir?' I ask. 'When Mr Wharton confided his fears to you after the feast, Sir, Jonathan Berwick was listening. He was a well-trained servant, his face gave away nothing. But next day he told your wife you knew something that was bound to compromise her in your eyes. Instantly Mrs Tuffnell guessed that Mr Wharton knew she was no wealthy widow. That same night, locked in the cellar by Mr Roach, Abraham happened on a stash of money, far more than could be accounted for by Mrs Tuffnell's beautifying business. It was money Mrs Tuffnell had given to Jonty, to thank him for his ... attentions to her person. Forgive me, Sir.'

I cannot look at my master, but I sense his shock. He barely breathes as I deliver my speech with as much solemn certainty as I can muster.

'Abraham thought the money yours, Sir, and he was about to show it to you and advise you to find a safer hiding-place. He might have done, but Mrs Tuffnell and Jonathan had come home early from the feast. Jonathan sought to help himself to rum from your cellar, Sir. He and Mr Roach shared a secret key that Mr Roach had made for the purpose. There was an altercation between Jonathan and Abraham, and in his anger Jonathan struck the boy so hard he fell and died. That night Mrs Tuffnell couldn't admit to you what Jonty had done because he would have named her part in it. Each of them lied and covered for the other.'

Mr Tuffnell is pale. He is careful to control himself, though the emotion in his voice is unmistakable. 'But Maria was innocent of murder, at least.'

'Yes, Sir. Though I believe it was her idea to cut the boy's throat after death, to throw suspicion on Red John. Did you not notice the bloodstains on the cellar stairs, Sir? Or wonder why so little blood was on the body when you saw how much was shed when George Goodfellow was murdered?' My voice rises despite myself. Abraham might have kept the money to buy his freedom; instead he died trying to protect his master's interests. 'Or think to ask yourself how a pedlar no one ever saw could break in and no one hear him?'

For a moment Mr Tuffnell is lost for a reply. Then he rallies, indignant.

'This is nonsense. It must have been Red John or some other stranger who killed Pug. You forget the other boy, George Goodfellow. Red John killed him for certain, or if not he, then Roach did. And if one of them killed George, the same killed Pug.'

'I beg pardon, Sir, I do not forget George Goodfellow. He was my friend. There's no reason to think the same cruel individual killed George as killed Abraham. The cases are quite different.'

A commotion within the villa causes all of us to fall silent as Mrs Hucker scolds Suke Cross, and Suke Cross bangs pots in the sink and slams the scullery door. Mr Tuffnell turns apologetically to Mr Espinosa. 'How these women love to quarrel.'

Mr Espinosa nods gravely, evidently sharing Mr Tuffnell's low opinion of females.

'Nell Grey rarely disagrees with anyone,' I put in. 'Even Mrs Hucker is a good soul, and far from bad-tempered as Cooks are often said to be.'

It is kind of me to say this, given how Mrs Hucker is generally inclined to take Suke Cross's side against me, and it does not help my case that Mrs Hucker marches into the parlour as I finish, and stands in the middle of the room, red-faced and out of breath.

'Excuse me, Sir, but that trollop Suke Cross has tried to give in her notice. I locked her in the pantry to cool her heels, Sir. We'd be in a sorry pickle, Sir, with only Nell Grey and I and Corrie Amesbury here, and the villa not properly aired and cleaned. Unless we have a Scrub, Sir, I shall be forced to give notice too.'

Mr Tuffnell looks dismayed, and Mr Espinosa raises a finger to forestall another outburst from the cook. 'Mr Tuffnell, may I suggest you ask Mrs Wharton to help you find persons likely to replace the servants you are missing? She will be efficient and quick. Neither will she cheat you as the hiring-man is sure to do.' He opens the door and gestures politely for Mrs Hucker to leave the room.

Still flushed she does so, though she sends a look of resentment in Mr Espinosa's direction that I am glad he does not see.

'God, if I only had my wife to help me,' Mr Tuffnell says. 'Yet she was weak and venal,' he adds dejectedly.

The flash of inspiration that strikes me is hard to account for, though the thought of Suke Cross itching to leave the villa may explain it. 'Mr Tuffnell, I believe I know who killed George Goodfellow. Your wife played no part in it, nor Jonty. George wrongly suspected Mr Roach of murdering Abraham. He told me so in the kitchen one night. We thought the other servants were fast asleep, but I hazard Suke was only pretending so she could eavesdrop. I reckon Suke Cross stabbed George lest he accuse Mr Roach publicly.'

Mr Tuffnell is dumbfounded. 'Have you lost your reason, girl? Why would Scrub care for Roach?'

'He's an ugly fellow, if you'll excuse me saying so, but she does love him. Abraham caught them kissing the day I joined the household. Mr Espinosa, we should tell the constable.'

Mr Espinosa taps his fingers, considering, then nods. 'Men kill from revenge, Mr Tuffnell. Women from love.'

I pass over this doubtful statement given that it serves my cause.

'Think it over carefully, Mr Tuffnell. Suke Cross cleans the household knives. She slept closer to the stable loft than anyone but Mr Roach. And I know myself Roach did not kill George. He was astonished the morning the boy was found. After Abraham was murdered Suke Cross wept and wailed. But when it came to George Goodfellow her eyes were dry.'

A long pause, while both men reflect on this damning proof of Suke Cross's guilt. Then Mr Tuffnell nods wearily. 'Forgive me, there has been so much to comprehend ... I believe I scarcely knew my wife. To think she struggled with such enemies. She hoped to shield me from the truth, did she not, Aaron?'

Mr Espinosa rests a hand on Mr Tuffnell's shoulder. For a moment he looks the older of the two. 'Sir, in all her difficulties her feelings for you never faltered.'

Mr Tuffnell gives a wondering laugh. 'Let no man say that Jews lack human kindness. You are as good a fellow, Aaron, as any Christian.'

This compliment strikes me as none too generous, but Mr Espinosa seems content with it. 'I'll fetch the constable. Meanwhile, Miss Amesbury, go and tell Mr Tuffnell's cook she is to be commended for putting the suspect under lock and key. By tonight let us be sure to have the murderess joining Jonathan Berwick in Newgate Prison.'

It occurs to me to tell Mr Tuffnell one last thing: that Mr Roach took his wife's money in the storm. On reflection I have burdened him with enough for one day. And it will interest me to see whether he succeeds in discovering for himself the reason for the coachman's disappearance.

**

An hour has passed by the time the constable arrives. We are gathered in the kitchen, where Mrs Hucker fairly bursts with pride. 'I bested her, Mr Tuffnell. The wildcat nearly had my eye out, but I landed her such a slap I'll wager she saw stars.' She waits for his praise.

Mr Tuffnell strides to the pantry and raps the door. 'Listen to me, Susan Cross. While you were at loggerheads with Cook, proof arrived that it was you who killed George Goodfellow. Do you hear? The constable is sent for. You are charged with murder.'

As the significance of this strikes home, Mrs Hucker's mouth falls open. Her eyes meet mine and I put my finger to my lips. There is no reply from the pantry. With the pommel of his sword Mr Tuffnell thumps the door. 'Murder,' he repeats.

Suke Cross, kicking and shouting moments ago, is silent in her makeshift prison. Mr Espinosa shakes his head. 'This is cast-iron proof of her guilt, Sir. She'd protest determinedly if she were innocent.'

Mr Tuffnell's face is grim. 'When she stands up in court she will be made to speak. Hear that, Susan Cross? The day you go before the judge at the assizes you shall tell the truth.' Mr Tuffnell rattles the latch. 'And then you will pay the price for your most horrid crime.'

I am ashamed to admit it, but I am afraid of laughing. 'Sir, shall I go outside and station myself at the pantry window? It is barred, but you never know, Sir.'

'Go on then, Amesbury.'

As I suspected, Suke Cross is pressed up against the unglazed window. She thrusts her face between the bars when she hears me coming, and I keep a distance despite myself. Her eyes glitter with tears and her voice is hoarse.

'Corrie Amesbury, don't let them take me, I beg you. They will hang me. Help me.'

'How can I? You had better pray to your Maker, not to me, Suke Cross.' For the first time I picture how it will be when day breaks after sentencing and they lead her to the gibbet.

'The r-r-rope will hurt so much, I can't bear it.' She gives a hic-cupping sob. 'I'm too young to die, Corrie. I thought I would be reunited with Mr Roach by now. And what has become of me?'

'You're too young? Then why did you risk it? Murdering a child.' At the thought of George Goodfellow my temper flares. 'An inno-cent boy not ten years old.'

There is a pause, and her voice sinks to a whisper. 'I'm not a mur-derer, Corrie. I swear to you.'

For a moment I waver, then I harden my heart, for I know she lies. 'It will go worse with you if you deny it, Suke Cross.' From the side of my eye I see the constable climb from a cart and open the garden gate.

'In there, is she?' he asks, a set of fetters swinging from his hand as he strides up the path. I think of the negroes I saw at the quays, and the chains that chafed their necks until they bled. 'She's only a slip of a thing, Sir,' I say, about to ask him to content himself with tying her wrists; but he mistakes my meaning.

'Don't worry, Mistress. She won't give me the slip. Come on, then. Lead the way.'

Eager and fearful, I take him to the house.

In the kitchen Mrs Hucker watches all that passes, her glee ill-concealed. 'It was I cornered her, Constable,' she begins.

He gestures at her to be quiet. 'Got her pinned, have you, Master Tuffnell? Well done, Sir. We'll soon have her in Bristol Newgate.'

Mr Tuffnell flourishes the pantry key. 'Have your cudgel ready, Constable. She may fly at you.' He raises his voice. 'Stand back, Susan Cross.'

I have never seen such a hopeless, abject creature as the one discovered when the pantry door is opened. Master and the constable peer in and Suke Cross mewls with terror. As they go to drag her out her legs give way. The constable is forced to lift her up.

She stammers. 'I never meant to harm George, I swear I didn't.' A squeal of pain as the constable grips her wrists. 'You're hurting me.'

'Then don't struggle. It does no good.'

'I wanted to frighten him, I admit it.' She is gabbling. 'I wanted to stop him telling tales about his elders and betters. Please Sir, don't chain me, please.' The constable, implacable, ignores her, busying himself with fastening the fetters round her wrists. 'George started crying and he grabbed at me. He used my weapon of defence against me. Cut my hand open—see the scar? I wanted to scratch him a little likewise, so he'd know I was in earnest, but he moved and somehow the knife went right through him. I never meant it to, I swear. You believe me, don't you, Corrie Amesbury? You know I wouldn't kill a child.'

'Be quiet, girl,' the constable says. 'You did kill him, by your own admission.'

'But they can't hang me for an accident. He hurt me first, he had a huge great rock and he hurled it at me. He bruised my forehead, see?' Her hands being held she tries to toss back her lanky hair to show us.

I am fearful she may rouse her listeners to pity. 'Don't twist the truth, Suke Cross. I found the corpse, remember? You butchered him.' My voice breaks as I remember George's abraded hands. 'You stabbed him a dozen times. Then you lied about how you got that bruise.'

The constable, grimly binding Suke Cross's arms, pulls harder on the cords until she cries out. 'Mercy, Sir. I only hoped to make it look like Red John did it. The boy died with the first strike. I never could have cut him alive, you cannot think it. My petticoat was splashed with blood.' She shudders.

Her cowardice riles me even further. 'There for hours, were you, rinsing out your clothes?' As I say it, I remember the day we spent after George was found, and Suke's idea to pass the time with laundering. She had Nell Grey and I do the work, too—her hand must have been sore. 'Don't ask pity or forgiveness, Suke Cross. You killed George Goodfellow and you will hang for it.'

Mr Tuffnell takes my arm. 'We know you loved the lad, Amesbury. Let the constable have her.'

I obey, though before the constable takes her outside Suke Cross thrusts out her stomach and declaims. 'I shall plead my belly. It is Mr Roach's child, and Bristol will hear how you kept a bawdy-house Mr Tuffnell, for all your wealth and fame. Your own wife turned a blind eye to our goings-on, and why did she? Because she was at it like the rest of us.'

Mr Tuffnell is sickly pale, and the constable has had enough. He drags a sack over Suke Cross's head. Her protests are muffled, and when the constable delivers a cut to her jaw she cries out in pain. Unmoved, he manhandles her towards the waiting cart.

***

Once we are alone Nell Grey demands I tell her all I know.

When I explain it was Roach who injured Mr Espinosa she is not surprised. 'He would have done anything Mrs Tuffnell ordered him to do,' she says. 'He was stupid, and a bully.'

'Suke picked that fight with Mrs Hucker, you know. I believe she wanted to be dismissed, thinking Roach was out there waiting for her somewhere. Silly wench, Roach never loved her. To think she murdered in cold blood for his sake.'

A grim pause, as we both remember George Goodfellow.

'Listen, Nell, this will be hard to hear. Suke killed George but Roach didn't murder Abraham. That was the work of Jonty Berwick.'

The poor girl turns green. 'Jonty could never harm a child.'

'He was weak, Nell Grey. He was in thrall to Mrs Tuffnell.' I tell her about the hidden gold, and, haltingly, explain how Jonty behaved with Mrs Tuffnell and how she made him lie for her.

Nell Grey cries when I have finished. 'Even Suke Cross acted out of love,' she sobs. 'Jonty only cared for his own skin. Poor Pug. How could he?'

'Because he didn't think he mattered, being a negro. You said yourself that Mrs Tuffnell treated Abraham like a lap-dog. Tricking him up in plush suits, forcing him to pose with her coffee pot, making him sit on her knee, a great fellow of eight. I never saw such an unhappy child.' I feel a great ache, remembering how lonely the boy avowed himself to be. 'I wonder what his real name was.'

'What?'

'Abraham's a strange name for an African. Most are called Sambo, aren't they? Still … shall we make a wooden cross and write *Abraham* on it, and see if the verger can be coaxed to put it on his grave? Next time we go to Bristol?'

Nell Grey agrees it would be fitting, and with our hearts consoled a little by our kindness, we go in search of supper.

***

Later I find Mr Tuffnell hunched by his parlour fire, head bowed low. I am used to my master striding about the house, shouting orders, pulling on his boots or writing at furious speed, splashing his sleeves with ink and calling for someone to run and fetch more paper from the stationer's. Now he is stricken.

'Shall I stoke the fire, Sir?' He usually prefers to have the charge of it himself, but tonight he has let it burn away to ash.

He reaches out his hand. 'Thank you for what you did to uncover the truth, Amesbury. Though I ought not to thank you, for I would rather remember Maria otherwise. I suppose you proved her innocence in most respects.'

Although I would like to pull my hand away it is awkward to do so when he is so forlorn.

'She deserved none of it, Sir. Her mother used her very ill, and she tried to make a better life for herself. She lived in terror she would be found out.'

He reaches for my other hand, and idly kissing it, watches the yellow flames begin to leap. 'You are a wise, good creature, Amesbury. In a week or two rebuilding will be underway in Bristol. I shan't return to Wine-street. When my mutual society pays out I intend to build a new house further from the quays. I shall want good servants.' He laughs shakily. 'I want them now.'

'Will you excuse me, Sir?' I carefully extract my hand. 'I haven't washed or changed since coming back from Bath, and Mrs Hucker needs me in the kitchen.'

'What? Oh, very well. Back to work, eh? I like to see you work, I must say. When you are done in the kitchen come back in here, and I can watch you tidy the supper things and, er, so forth.' He has so little notion of what I do he trails off.

'Yes, Sir.'

To Mr Tuffnell I am a helpmeet, good to bank up his fires and listen to his troubles, or to kiss and cuddle when he misses his Maria. It is vexing, but no more than I expect, and you could say that in a certain light it serves me well. Mr Tuffnell never guessed—no one ever did, not even Mr Espinosa—that I was watching them.

And in no time at all they will forget I ever did.

Chapter Thirty

Clifton
Thursday, January 31ˢᵗ 1704

Christmas comes and goes, with little to mark the day, our household being quiet and sombre. January is almost over when Mr Cheatley invites himself to dinner. Mr Tuffnell cannot make an enemy of his business partner while the *Prudence* remains at sea, though I am sure he would rather not play host to one who reneged on the terms of their agreement. I make sure to carry in the refreshments and linger as long as possible, removing one or two dead blossoms from the vase on the sideboard, tutting quietly as if the room is not as neat as it ought to be. After all, Mr Tuffnell did say he likes to see me work.

'So, you are going to London next week, Mr Cheatley?' my master says.

Mr Cheatley smiles thinly. 'The Worshipful Company of Iron-mongers hosts a banquet in their great hall on Fenchurch-street, and my great friend Master Ralph Fowler invites me to attend. He is a considerable person in the Navy-Office, by the way, as well as owning a substantial manufactory in Bishop's-gate.'

'Indeed. Then I wonder if I might ask a favour?' My master sounds hesitant, and I think to myself that indeed he ought to feel able to ask for help from Mr Cheatley since that gentleman will owe him handsomely when the *Prudence* returns to Bristol, supposing it does. 'I am loath to mention it,' Mr Tuffnell continues, 'but I seek intelligence about my coachman. He was mixed up in the unfortunate business ...' Mr Tuffnell stops to clear his throat, and Mr Cheatley gives a dry 'hmph' as if no explanation is required. 'Mr Roach is his name, Mr Cheatley. At least I think it is.' Mr Tuffnell runs out of words, having as much as admitted he does not know who he entrusted with his employ, and after an awkward silence Mr Cheatley turns the conversation to the fascinating subject of his iron manufactory and its importance to the trade in general. I gather the empty coffee cups and retreat to the kitchen, glad I do not have to stay and listen.

***

Friday, March 14th, 1704

Some weeks later, however, and two days before the assizes, Mr Cheatley rides back to Mr Tuffnell's villa, and this time I have no need to feign dissatisfaction with the flower arrangements in the parlour. The gentlemen are dining, Mrs Hucker has been asked to provide three good courses, and Nell Grey being confined to bed with a toothache, I am to serve and able to hear the conversation from start to finish.

Mr Tuffnell endures a blow-by-blow account of Mr Cheatley's worshipful dinner, and another of a dull-sounding evening he passed somewhere called St James, which is not a church as I first thought but some grand square where rich folk go to stroll. I wonder what the lords and ladies of Westminster made of drab Mr Cheatley with his never-ending sneezes and his rusty-smelling woollen suit.

Finally, the gentlemen settled at the fireside, Mr Tuffnell plucks up courage to mention Mr Roach, whereupon Mr Cheatley purses his mouth fastidiously. 'I did make some enquiries, Sir, explaining I did so on your behalf. A man from Bristol applied to the skipper of the *Henry* last month, giving his name as Peter Smith and his occupation as coachman. It is possible this was an alias for your Mr Roach. Am I to understand Roach stole from you before he vanished?'

Mr Tuffnell catches my eye. I give the smallest nod. He bites his lip. 'He may have done. That is, I very much suspect it.'

'Well, you had better assume the loss is permanent. The *Henry* is halfway to St Kitts by now.' Mr Cheatley sighs comfortably, and takes a pinch of snuff. 'We Bristolians must look to our laurels if London is not to overtake our port. These men know where better wages can be had. Two other Bristol men joined the *Henry*. Their names—' He sneezes, hunts for his handkerchief, and I cannot resist. 'Were William Eardley and John Hench, were they not, Sir?'

Mr Cheatley recoils and Mr Tuffnell feigns a frown at my impertinence. I know he does not really resent anyone who stands up to Mr Cheatley, me least of all. I go on.

'Pardon me, Sirs. I've heard of all those fellows, and not to their credit, and it don't surprise me they ran away and sought to leave their ill deeds behind them. Mr Roach is a bully and a thief, William Eardley a wife-deserter, and John Hench is as savage a rogue as you could have the ill luck to run across. I believe he committed many of the murders credited to Red John, though I cannot prove it. Pity the ship that takes those three aboard.'

From Mr Cheatley's face I wonder if he has a business interest in the *Henry*. He glares at me. 'Many sailors are rough-and-ready. There is no reason to suppose these three better or worse than any other.'

'They might be worse, Sir, trust me, they won't be better. Will they, Mr Tuffnell?'

Mr Tuffnell winces. 'My servant may be right, Mr Cheatley. Roach was mixed up in the attack on Aaron Espinosa. I had hoped to see him brought to justice.'

A newspaper is resting in the grate, ready to serve as kindling when tomorrow's fire is set. Mr Cheatley nudges it idly with his foot. 'Then your hopes could not be more dashed if the *Henry* were reported in next Tuesday's *Post Boy* as driven ashore by storms and all the crew drowned. It left Deptford on Monday last. It will not return before the end of next year, Mr Tuffnell. Be comforted. What are the chances any of the common seamen will be seen again in England? Scant, I should say. What shall it be, do you suppose? Pirates? Flux? Let us hope they fall overboard, and make a dinner for the sharks. Now then, where is this game of cards you promised?' Mr Tuffnell immediately busies himself setting up the table and sends me to fetch some brandy.

It is left to me to shed a silent tear for Jonty and Mrs Tuffnell and above all Abraham and the other little boys, all of whom died for less than these gentlemen spend on a single night of cards.

***

Clifton
Monday, March 17th, 1704

Mr Espinosa has been to Bristol Newgate and spoken to the chaplain, the Ordinary as they call him, and Jonathan Berwick avers he will plead Guilty, hoping, I daresay, to have his sentence softened to transportation, in which hope he shall be disappointed. The case is open and shut, and besides Mr Espinosa says that both Justices at the Quarter Sessions are associates of Mr Tuffnell, one being Mayor of Bristol, the other an alderman, and sure to be severe on any who wrong their business friend. I remember Jonathan Berwick as merry and impudent but he has grown thin and does not smile, and begs the Ordinary to pray with and for him whenever that gentleman visits the prison pit.

As for Suke Cross, the midwives who examined her found no sign of a child, so she cannot plead her belly, and if she did it would go hard with her, to deliver the babe and be hanged after, and know the child would be sent to the parish and given to a nurse who might overlay it or starve it or let it tumble in the fire. Suke Cross's mother is on the parish too from what I know, there being no more stolen meats from Mr Tuffnell's kitchen to find their way to Gammer Cross's pot.

The day of the trial Nell Grey and I strip the beds and boil and rinse the sheets, spreading them in the garden to dry as best they can in the chilly winter sun. We turn and beat the feather beds and shake the blankets, toiling as hard if it were the start of spring. The chambers are cold and empty, and we make up the beds with clean linen, and hang lavender from the ceilings, and Suke Cross's bed bears the impress of her bones no more, nor smells of the crusts of cheese she used to hide before she bundled them off to her mother.

Nell Grey finds a rabbit's foot charm beneath the pillow. 'Her neck, Corrie.' Her mild eyes shine with tears. 'I wonder why she never wore it, the day they came for her.'

'Throw it in the kitchen fireplace, Nell Grey. It was just like her to tie such a nasty thing about her throat.' I shudder to see the grey bit of string that showed whenever Suke Cross's neckerchief slipped down.

We peep into the hall when Mr Tuffnell comes home, and he looks older, and seems not to want the usual care taken of him when we run out to fold his cloak and tell him there is roast beef for supper and a good fire in the parlour.

'You're tired, Sir,' I say, as he pulls off his riding-boots. 'It threatens snow, don't it? The sky so white and dreary this afternoon.'

He does not answer, and after Nell Grey has brought his dinner out again, his slice of beef barely touched, I go in and find my master sitting at his fireside, eyes shut, as if the day in court has wrung the life from him.

'Here's a fresh candle, Sir.'

He does not look up.

'Mr Tuffnell, may I ask if you got the verdicts you was looking for?'

'Yes, Amesbury, I did.'

I wish he did not sound solemn when he should be glad.

'Not that there was any doubt of it,' I say.

'Yet the scullery maid protested her innocence as they took her down.' He grimaces. 'To think my house harboured that creature. I thought her harmless. Indeed, I took her for a simpleton.'

'Susan Cross is a great deal cleverer than she looks, Sir.' I kneel to pick up the fire-irons Mr Tuffnell has left lying in the hearth. 'Among us servants she harped on Red John this and Red John that, and all the while she knew her favourite was mixed up in something wrong.'

Mr Tuffnell shakes his head. 'Thank Heaven not all my servants wish me ill. Hucker is a good soul and Grey is faithful. And you of course, Amesbury, you are a loyal servant in every way. You must go, the three of you.' He sees my surprise and hastens to make his meaning clear. 'To the place of execution, St Michael's Hill. You shall have Friday as a holiday.'

In the kitchen we had taken this for granted, but I curtsey. 'Will you be there to see the executions yourself, Sir?'

Mr Tuffnell drops his gaze to the glowing embers. 'I have little heart for such grisly proceedings since the loss of my dear wife.'

I keep my distance lest his tenderness seeks an outlet and he tries to coax me to perch upon his lap. 'None of us wishes to look on Death, Sir. Excepting Jonathan Berwick and our friend Scrub, of course. They had no qualms.'

'God! What monsters they were. Pour me a glass of sherry, would you, Amesbury? However close to the fire I sit tonight, I cannot get warm.'

***

Friday, March 28th 1704

In the coming days it is as if we wait for the plague to strike our household, or the constable to return for one of us. A cold, hard stone is lodged in me when I wake on Friday morning. I see the prisoners pinched and shivering, hear the gaoler saying it is time.

At Mr Tuffnell's villa no one speaks as we pretend to eat our porridge. Nell Grey's eyes slide to the window that overlooks the yard, and I know she watches the sun creep up and wishes noon might never come. I did not know how bleak a kitchen could be when the fire is out. The water in the scullery pails has turned to ice.

'Wrap up warm, girls,' says Mrs Hucker, as she comes in from the outhouse. She drops onto a stool and rolls a pair of white stockings over her grey workaday ones. 'We'll take bread with us in case we're late home. Fetch a loaf from the pantry, Corrie Amesbury.'

A Pair of Sharp Eyes

I shrink from seeing the place where Suke Cross cowered from Mr Tuffnell, and wish Mrs Hucker would send Nell Grey to find the bread. But she does not notice. She wraps our bit of dinner in a rag, and puts it in a basket with three hard-boiled eggs.

'Here, let me,' says Cook, tying our cloak-strings to save us taking off our mittens. Nell Grey's hat is the one she wears for church, and mine is trimmed with jay's feathers and a scarlet ribbon. Anyone would take us for mother and daughters, except that none would choose a January morning for a pleasure outing.

Yet we step into the lane to find that every man, woman and child in Clifton makes for St Michael's Hill, a few on horseback, most on foot. On the Downs we fall into place behind a family of seven who walk steadily, quietly, as if a spell draws them to Bewell's-Cross— Gallow's-Cross, as many call it. The father and his eldest son wear snowdrops in their buttonholes, the wife a fine lace veil. The little girls and boys plod in silence, and their elders only speak when needed: an offer to hold hands across a patch of ice, a word of greeting to a neighbour.

Few chimneys smoke in the still air; even the hens huddle beneath the hedges. Reaching the end of the half-frozen muddy footpath we take the road to Bristol, and before long the tapering church tower of St Michael's comes into sight. A hundred or more villagers stand round the cross. Most avert their eyes as we approach, perhaps considering us friends of the accused. The well-to-do sit on a platform close to the gallow-tree, while tethered to a post beyond the church their horses stamp and snort.

Mrs Hucker leads us to a patch of rising ground somewhat closer to the gallows than I would like. Several people are there already, and I catch a hint of sweat and wood-smoke from the man next to me. Some seated on the platform wear black ribbons or black silk flowers in their caps. Tokens of respect for the dead boys, I trust, not for their murderers.

We shuffle to warm our feet. The ground is iron-hard, and the cold air catches in our throats and makes us cough. Now and then a gust of wind brings with it flakes of snow.

Some close their eyes in prayer, while those of the better sort glance at their pocket watches or stand on tiptoe to peer down the hill. The prison cart is due at any moment.

At last the sun is at its height, a silver smudge in a grey dull sky, and across the city the church bells toll for noon.

Moments later a disorderly noise rises from the city. A faint tremble, a far-off murmur, rising by degrees to a steady hum, and finally a roar. I picture the crammed streets as the death-cart leaves the prison, officers holding back the onlookers to let the driver clear the gates, the mob surging forward to surround the vehicle, lifting their fists and jeering. The noise grows louder until those either side of us stir and mutter and begin to growl. Finally, the cart heaves into sight, the horses straining at the steepness of the hill, a swarm of people following behind, some outstripping the procession in their eagerness.

The prisoners, dressed in Holland shifts and tightly bound, stand at the tail of the cart, facing their audience. They are jolted by the roughness of the road, and now and then the chaplain is forced to put out a hand to steady them.

Their faces are so drawn and pale, their eyes so raw, that at first I hardly know them. Jonathan Berwick's head is shaved, his feet scarred and grained with dirt, and when he grimaces I see his top front teeth are missing. Stripped of her heavy woollen gown and knitted shawl Suke Cross is no bigger than a child. The officers have cropped her hair above the nape, and she perishes in the cruel wind; her hands are blue.

As the cart, having gained the summit, draws up at the gallows the villagers of Clifton forget the solemn mood that reigned over us this last hour. They begin to mumble, then to call out and finally to shout. The crowds merge and within moments we might be at a fair; the place erupts with yells and cries. A group of chimney sweeps bear their brushes aloft like halberds. Children bounce on their fathers' shoulders, waving their fists and cheering. A schoolmaster has brought his class of scholars to the event, and each brandishes a fluttering paper flag. Weaving through the throng, a hawker hands out broadsides so rapidly I wonder he has time to check the coins his customers press upon him.

One group of young apprentice butchers comes from Bristol carrying the effigy of a black boy. The body is fashioned from a sack stuffed with straw or something like it, and the shirt-front stained with quantities of beetroot juice. I shudder when two of the apprentices hold up the figure to taunt the prisoners. A leather ball has been painted to resemble the crudest notion of a negro's face, jet black, with frizzy tufts of wool, wide eyes and pouting scarlet lips.

The gaoler will have given both prisoners a quart of ale before their journey, but I see no evidence their senses are dulled. When one of the apprentice butchers hops onto a wall with the effigy and proceeds to mime a bestial act upon it, Jonathan turns a sickly grey.

Someone calls out 'Berwick! Shake hands with the Devil when you reach the other side.' The crowd laughs good-naturedly, and an object, a sharp stone or a shard of glass, strikes Jonathan above the eye, inflicting a wound from which blood begins to trickle.

Feigning deafness to the slow hand-claps of the onlookers, the constables undo and remove the prisoners' halters. Next, they unscrew their ankle-chains, and in a strange display of tenderness, one officer wipes the blood from Jonathan's temple with his own pocket handkerchief, and the other stoops and examines Suke Cross's foot, seeming to ask her if she is hurt.

Satisfied their captives are fit to face what is to come, the constables retire and the chaplain steps forward. He looks at Jonathan questioningly, and when Jonathan nods, he gestures for the crowd to let the condemned man speak.

Slowly, reluctantly, the uproar fades. Jonathan's voice quavers as he begins.

'To all here today, I beseech you pray for my soul and to the Almighty to pardon my offence. I am guilty of the crime for which I am to hang, and repent my sins, especially this most gravest one of which I am accused. May I beg forgiveness from my dear mother and father, for bringing shame on our family and on all those I love. I never set out to do what I did, I scarcely know how I did it except

I know I did do it, how it happened is a mystery to me almost as much as to any.'

As he rambles the crowd begins to shout and drown him out, and he stops, defeated; the chaplain pats his arm and leads him back to where he stood before.

Suke Cross does not learn from this example. She shakes off the constable who holds her arm, and steps forward, lifting her chin to face the crowd.

'Lord, don't argue with your sentence,' Mrs Hucker murmurs. 'They will have you dance an hour.'

Suke's blood is up too much for caution. And perhaps the people hope to see her endure the cruellest fate in the hangman's power to give her, or perhaps they want to hear the confession of a female child-killer, but whatever the reason they are silent as she utters:

'May God forgive me and have mercy on my soul.' It is a promising enough beginning. Then she adds in a rush: 'But all we the rest, though baptized and born again in Christ, yet offend in many things, and if we say we have no sin, we deceive ourselves, and the truth is not in us.'

A pause as her effrontery sinks in, and order gives way to riot, the crowd howling and pelting the cart and its occupants with whatever they can find. The constable drags Suke Cross back while her audience stamps with fury and several women spit at her.

My eye is caught by a small, round-shouldered woman moving through the masses towards the gallows. She must be fifty-odd years old, and as she reaches the cart she makes herself heard to an officer, who nods and indicates for her to use the mounting block to climb aboard. Once there she falls on Suke Cross, tears rolling down her face, clasping her daughter's bony hands, then running her fingers over the shorn head and shaking her own in seeming disbelief.

She clings to her daughter until at last the constable parts them and helps Gammer Cross from the cart. Suke still cranes for glimpses of her mother when another officer takes out a linen hood from a crate and pulls it over her head, while a second does the same to Jonathan Berwick.

A Pair of Sharp Eyes

Muffled weeping can be heard from the prisoners as the chaplain prays. 'Almighty God, Father of our Lord Jesus Christ, maker of all things, judge of all men; We acknowledge and bewail our manifold sins and wickedness, which we from time to time most grievously have committed, by thought, word, and deed, against thy divine majesty, provoking most justly thy wrath and indignation against us. We do earnestly repent.' Considering these general words too scant, he improvises a prayer of his own devising: 'For the souls of this wicked man and woman, whose crimes are the most detestable that may be imagined, and for the innocent children deprived by them of life, and for all Christians who see by their example that the wages of sin are death.'

Then, nodding genially to some of the children in the crowd, he offers a homely prayer: 'For this great city and its brave sea-faring men, for our friends in the West Indies and the East Indies and Guinea and around the world,' and God forgive my impatience but I wish he would give over his canting and let the hangman do his business. Jonathan's hood bears a spreading stain where the half-brick gashed his forehead, and Suke Cross sways on her feet.

At last the chaplain claps shut his book.

'Mother! Father!' Jonathan calls, his voice faint; but no one answers.

The hangman clambers up, a little brown-skinned man with a peppering of moles; I had not noticed him perched on the cart-box next to the driver.

'Ah! Make them wait!' someone jests, and others laugh and cry 'Aye!' but with no sign he hears these rude suggestions the hangman reaches for a noose, loops it over Suke Cross's head, and tightens the knot.

The same for the other. Over the head slides the rope, and carefully the hangman checks the knot. A pause, a satisfied nod at his handiwork, then, turning, he slowly scans the crowd until his eye alights on the effigy of the black boy. Delighted, the apprentices thrust the manikin above their heads again, handling it so roughly that it sprays the crowd with sawdust.

A whisper turns into a chant, and soon the place echoes to gleeful cries of 'Beast! Beast!'

The chaplain is obliged to stand before the crowd for many minutes, patiently half-smiling now and then, before the noise abates, but at last, save for a stray catcall, the crowd is quiet. From the hood over Suke Cross's face comes a stifled cry; her knees sag, but the nearest constable has her elbows gripped.

Suddenly, without a sign, he lets her go. The driver lifts his whip and strikes the horse. The cart is off, dragging the prisoners a yard or two before they drop. All is creaking, juddering timber as the gallows take the strain.

A lurch, weak spasms, and Suke Cross's body spins like a sack of flour. Jonathan Berwick is very much alive. He writhes and gurgles. A man steps up to shorten his suffering, but the hangman puts out a hand to bar his way. The body struggles, lets out a set of rasping cries, seems to smother, then twists and shudders and emits a sound like boiling glue.

Not a soul in the crowd speaks. The feet flex, curl inward, flutter and quiver until at last they dangle lifeless. No more sounds come from the hood. A dead weight turning in the wind; a bundle of logs in a loose white sack.

The chaplain clambers up once more. Opening his book, he resumes droning. 'I am the resurrection and the life, saith the Lord: he that believeth in me, though he were dead, yet shall he live.'

On the ground a constable mops his face.

'Don't cry, Corrie,' breathes Nell Grey.

'I won't,' I say, indignant. I was there when Suke Cross prated about the 'evil pedlar'. I saw the look of horror Jonathan put on to mask his guilt. I swabbed the floor of blood when Abraham was killed, and I wept for my little fellow George, as good as these two wicked souls are damned.

Mrs Hucker turns to us, eyes bright with righteousness. 'So help me God, I wish the crowd had torn them both in pieces.'

Only then do I turn so no one sees my tears.

A Pair of Sharp Eyes

Chapter Thirty-One

Wednesday, April 2nd 1704

A day or two later Nell Grey, Mrs Hucker and I are at our chores when Mr Tuffnell calls me to the parlour.

Mr Wharton and Mr Espinosa are there, and I expect to be told to fetch three glasses and a bottle of sherry wine. Instead he bids me stand before him.

Mr Espinosa brings across a chair and smiles. 'You had better sit, Miss Amesbury, I think.'

My heart patters. 'Is it my sister, Sir? Is there bad news?'

Mr Tuffnell beams. 'By no means. I have good news for you, Amesbury—extraordinarily good news.'

I look from face to face. Mr Wharton, usually so stern and solemn, has unbent enough that he is grinning. Mr Espinosa takes a sealed packet from his frock-coat. If I am not mistaken his eyes twinkle.

'You'd better spit it out, Sir,' I say.

Mr Tuffnell draws breath. 'Remember the prize that I and several other merchants put up for anyone discovering the murderer of my stable boy? Twenty guineas were lodged with Mr Sampson, and Mr Espinosa has them here. Aaron?' Mr Espinosa hands the packet to Mr Tuffnell. 'With the grateful thanks of the Merchant Venturers' Society of Bristol, I hereby present Mistress Coronation Amesbury with twenty guineas, a reward for her brave, determined and shrewd pursuit of the person hanged for the murder of a servant belonging to my household. Here.'

He presses it in my hand. I think it would be ungracious if I were to ask why the packet feels so light, but fortunately Mr Espinosa guesses my train of thought. 'It's a bill of exchange, Miss Amesbury. If you go to my master's shop, he'll give you the sum in gold.'

'Of course. Thank you, thank you kindly, Sirs. Though I only sought the truth, Mr Tuffnell.'

'Of course you did, Amesbury. Virtue is its own reward. But a little gilding don't come amiss, eh?'

The gentlemen chuckle, and so do I, too surprised to make a pretty speech of thanks to the Merchant Venturers for their generosity, or to wonder why they are willing to reward me though the other murders remain a mystery. My eyes are moist. 'I always dreamt of owning my own shop, Sir. I never thought I should.'

It may be my fancy, but Mr Tuffnell looks a touch put out. 'Well now, shop-keeping can be profitable, to be sure. But it requires an outlay, and the hours are long and returns exceeding variable.'

'I have my capital now, Sir. I can work hard. I expect I will turn a profit by and by.'

'I for one don't doubt it,' Mr Espinosa says. 'I wish you the best of luck, Miss Amesbury. You deserve a chance to be independent.' He catches sight of Mr Tuffnell's face. 'Though you are most fortunate in your current situation, of course.'

'And you may wish to continue here for now, Amesbury. In which case I recommend that you allow Mr Espinosa to retain the bill of exchange for safe-keeping. He can ask Mr Sampson to look after it for you.'

'Thank you, Sir, but I will keep it if you don't mind. I may take it to Mr Sampson to be exchanged on my next half-holiday. Or I may not.'

'Oh.' My master speaks a trifle stiffly. 'Well, it is yours to do with as you wish, of course.'

'Meanwhile I thank you and had better return to carrying in the coal pails, if you don't mind, Sirs?'

Off I go to share my good news with Nell Grey and promise her two new pairs of stockings when my ship comes in, and I smile, remembering the looks on the faces of those gentlemen, when they hardly knew how to speak to me, a servant and a woman of property at one and the same time.

***

A Pair of Sharp Eyes

That evening Mr Tuffnell calls me to the parlour again, and this time I find two glasses of sherry wine on the table.

'I'm sure you agree we should celebrate, Amesbury,' he says, waving me to sit in the Turkey-work chair that his wife preferred when they shared the parlour. Not that they shared it as often as they might have done. 'I must work tonight, but a glass of sherry don't go amiss.'

'Sir?'

'To toast your new-won wealth, and my new house. Mr Wharton has been busy these past two weeks, when I was occupied with the assizes. He's bought a plot of land on my behalf and hired an architect. In little more than a year I will be removing back to Bristol, to a fine new mansion.'

The sherry wine is sweet and spicy, and I am happy to clink glasses with Mr Tuffnell. 'I'm pleased to hear it, Sir.'

'Queen-square,' he says. 'My dear late father would have been astonished. But I've worked hard for my success, as he did for his.'

'Was he a merchant too, Sir? Did he sell Africans in the Indies?'

'On a small scale.' A pause, as Mr Tuffnell muses on his humble roots. He returns to the present. 'Of course, I shall need a helpmeet when I am master of so substantial a household.'

My heart flips. 'Will you, Sir?'

He eyes me playfully. 'Come, Amesbury, what's your answer?'

'To what, Mr Tuffnell? You haven't asked me anything.'

He fidgets. 'Now then, Amesbury. No call to make this difficult. You are a young woman with many attributes, but your portion is small.' He smiles to himself. 'You must be wondering why you were awarded twenty guineas though certain of the murders continue unexplained. Let us just say, I took it upon myself to ensure you were remunerated—never let it be said I am niggardly to my servants. Quite the opposite. Hang it all, Amesbury, you cannot need persuading—no over-sentimental declarations of undying love and so forth—to accept my proposal.'

'Proposal as to what, Sir?'

'Great God! Are my needs not obvious? Nor my feelings plain? When my wife was alive of course I stifled those feelings—dismissed them as animal urges. But my wife, may it please God to rest her soul in peace, is dead, and although in the ordinary course of things I might have chosen to wait before remarrying, I am very happy to embark on a fresh chapter of my life without delay.'

'You are asking me to be your wife, Sir?'

'What else? To be sure, it is a vast leap from your station to wife of a man of my wealth and standing, but you will adapt, I think. You are,' he beams, 'a young woman of resourcefulness and intelligence. I beguile myself with the prospect you may in time be of assistance to me in my business.' He drops to his knees and reaches for my hand. 'Think of it, Amesbury—Coronation. Member of the powerful Society of Merchant Venturers in all but name. Helping to send vessels round the world. Judging what to sell and what to buy. Involved in all I do, and adding your wisdom and common sense to every one of my business decisions. I've one to make tonight.' He nods to the pile of papers waiting on his desk. 'A proposal from Mr Osmund, who wishes to be my equal partner in a voyage to Guinea in the spring.' Mr Tuffnell taps my hand flirtatiously. 'What do you advise, Coronation? He's a novice investor in the slave trade, but a man of influence in Jamaica. Shall I take the risk?'

He means to be humorous, and I respond accordingly. I am not really expected to give an opinion on the matter. I smile. 'You ask me to marry you but I'd rather you asked me to be your housekeeper, Sir.'

His expression is amazed and crestfallen. 'Housekeeper? You'd rather remain a servant than become my wife?'

'A nest egg such as mine in combination with an upper servants' salary is a good foundation for a young person, Mr Tuffnell. A few years' service will set me up very well for establishing my own business. I should like my own business, as I believe I told you earlier, Sir.'

'Miss Amesbury, I can scarcely believe what I hear.' His expression is comically disappointed. 'Well, this is a salutary correction to my pretensions as a suitor. I had not thought myself quite so undesirable.'

'A housekeeper is head of the household, saving yourself, Sir. With responsibility for all the indoor servants and keeping the accounts for the kitchen and other expenses, such as lighting and fuel. She plans menus, and sends items for repair. Hires tradesmen, and keeps a tally of such of your stock as is kept at home, Sir, and not in your warehouse. She ensures your house is clean and in good repair. She acts as moral instructress to her fellow servants, and is trusted to inform of any indiscretions committed by them.'

My master begins to look anxious at this recital. 'You might be capable, in time, Amesbury—you are a little young for some of the duties you mention.'

'I am quick to learn. As you said so yourself, I am resourceful.' I pause. 'It would be an honour to serve you in such a capacity. After all, the role of housekeeper is hardly as exacting as a wife's. You offered me the greater, Sir.'

Mr Tuffnell's palms must be damp, for he wipes them surreptitiously on his coat-skirts. 'Well, I suppose you make a good point, Amesbury. Indeed you do. That's settled then. Housekeeper.' He coughs hastily. 'At least, when my new house is ready. Until then perhaps you will consider yourself housekeeper-in-waiting. Who knows, you may change your mind given time,' he adds, murmuring to himself rather than to me.

'Housekeeper-in-waiting. That will do very well. Thank you, Sir. Now then, shall I clear these glasses and leave you to your papers? You did say you have a great many papers to read and sign tonight. I have kept you over-long.'

I collect the tray and the flask of sherry, and my hand is on the door knob when a thought strikes me. 'If you are sincerely interested in my view of Mr Osmund's offer, Sir, I advise you to decline it.'

He blinks.

'Mr Osmund is not an honourable man. You can take it as certain, for I have met him and found him boorish and ungentlemanly, and his own friends hold him in low esteem. Don't trust him, Sir. Good night.'

Mrs Hucker and Nell Grey are seated by the kitchen fire. Cook looks at me concerned. 'Corrie, if Master makes a nuisance of himself, don't endure his attentions in silence. When he asks to see you of an evening, Nell Grey or I will come too, or I'll go in your stead. His fancy will wander elsewhere in time, I'm sure. He misses his wife, poor fellow.'

Making no reply, I set down my tray and refill the glasses to the brim with Mr Tuffnell's best sherry. Then I place the glasses on the tray and offer it to my companions. Nell Grey looks shocked, and hesitates to help herself, but Mrs Hucker draws a breath and taking hold of the glass nearest to her, bursts out laughing.

Nell Grey stares at her in puzzlement as the cook exclaims. 'I knew it. I knew he couldn't hold out any longer. When's it to be?' She swipes Nell Grey's knee. 'He's asked her to marry him. I'm right, aren't I? I'm delighted for you, girl. I venture to say he's a lucky man. Congratulations. I hope you'll be happy and all your troubles will be little ones. Mrs Coronation Tuffnell, eh? Well, you have the right Christian name for a lady, that's for sure.'

Though she makes me laugh I can't let her run on any longer. 'You've leapt to conclusions, Mrs Hucker. Mr Tuffnell made me a proposal which I have gladly accepted, but it is to be his housekeeper when he removes to Queen-square.'

The good old soul sinks back into her chair. 'Oh, bless me, is that it, after all? I beg you forget what I just said, both of you. I was dozing before you came in, I daresay I was half-asleep. You must think I'm daft.' She titters, and falls silent.

'Housekeeper?' Nell Grey repeats, frowning. 'Are you sure, Corrie? You're a clever girl, and capable, but you're not yet fifteen years old.' Then she tilts her head and looks at me kindly. 'Do you think it possible he may change his mind? He's all at sea at present. It must be hard to keep a cool head so soon after a loss like the one he's suffered. You mustn't be disappointed if he bethinks himself, Corrie, dear. He does have a high regard for you, and I'm sure he'll want you to stay on in his new house. Let's say a toast to all of us. May our wages be raised in the next twelve months.'

'Hear hear,' says Cook, and the two of them sip solemnly and Nell Grey offers me her glass that I may share it.

But by and by the sherry takes the edge away from Mrs Hucker's awkwardness, and chases off Nell Grey's doubts about my advancement, and they begin to speculate about my life as housekeeper, the pleasant small room I shall call my own, how it will have a mantelshelf and a feather bed, and a chair and table and a sideboard with plates and cups for my own use, and they agree that if they butter me up I will be sure to invite them in to share a dish of tea and a baked apple now and then.

'She'll be good to us, Cook,' says Nell Grey, taking a sip of her sherry wine. 'She'll remember who her best friends were when she first came into Mr Tuffnell's service.'

They run on until I decide it is time to rein them in. 'I confess that whatever Mr Tuffnell believes, I may not remain in his employ long enough to be his housekeeper. But I enjoin you two to keep that to yourselves.'

Mrs Hucker shakes her head. 'Not another surprise. I doubt my old heart can stand any more shocks tonight. Don't say you're about to run away to sea. Or is Mr Tuffnell sending you to Africa to barter for some slaves? Or maybe you're going back to Wiltshire to marry your childhood sweetheart?'

Nell Grey watches me closely. 'Come on, Corrie. Tell us.'

I shan't tell them everything, of course. But they are my nearest thing to friends in Bristol.

'When I have enough saved, I intend to buy my passage to the West Indies. I may stay there or I may come back. But there's someone in Jamaica I must find again before I die.'

Mrs Hucker is at a loss for once, and looks at me round-eyed. The kitchen is quiet save for the puttering of the fire. Then Nell Grey speaks.

'Go, Corrie. Follow your heart.'

Another silence, more solemn than the first, then Nell Grey grins. 'Promise you'll remember us, when you're mistress of a hundred acres. Send us a letter now and then, a parcel of sugar at Christmas-time, and a cask of rum.'

She is unfathomably generous to speak in this merry way when her own lover is cold and dead. I could retort that I would never wish to be mistress of a plantation were I to live a thousand years, but instead I rise and kiss her.

Then, when the fire is banked, we retire to our garret, leaving Mr Tuffnell in his parlour to weigh Mr Osmund's offer and reflect more generally on partners and their usefulness.

Time enough to reveal who it is I seek. That is a story for another night.

***

Thursday, April 3rd 1704

One morning Mr Tuffnell is working at his writing table and I am dusting the ledgers when a sound of hooves draws both of us to the window that overlooks the drive. Mr Wharton and Mr Espinosa are come from Bristol on a pair of hired horses.

Having had a proposal of marriage from my master I find I cannot linger unnoticed as I used to do when visitors arrive. Mr Tuffnell dismisses me when Nell Grey shows the gentlemen in so I take care to leave the door open a crack, and station myself directly outside, broom in hand lest anyone suspect me of that well-worn servant's trick of eavesdropping.

'The news is grave, James,' Mr Wharton begins. 'The sailor with the information is one of Captain Stiles's most trusted able seamen. Wilks provided a detailed account, plausible in all respects. The *Prudence* ran aground just past the 38th degree, precisely where it should have been when the storm struck on December 6th. There were two survivors, the other man died a few days later. Wilks stayed in Lisbon until a Bristol skipper took him on.'

'Sunk without trace? The crew lost, including William Stiles? I apologise, gentlemen.' There is a pause; Mr Tuffnell's voice is strained, and I hear a chink as Mr Wharton pours his employer a glass of sherry.

'James,' says the agent after a moment, 'matters could be worse. You recollect the letter I sent Captain Stiles before the ship set sail? His answer never reached you, but I alluded to the original document when we spoke at the All Hallows feast.'

Mr Tuffnell clears his throat. 'Spare me the memory, please.'

A moment's silence; I picture Mr Wharton gripping Mr Tuffnell's arm in sympathy. 'Mrs Tuffnell, God rest her soul, never set out to deceive you about the *Prudence*. She was only concerned you might discover that her claims of owning property in Jamaica were—shall we say—exaggerated.' A further tactful pause, and Mr Wharton continues. 'The point is this. When Captain Stiles set sail without replying to my letter regarding Cheatley's altered terms I took it in my own hands to ensure your share in the expedition was adequately underwritten.'

A rustle of papers, and Mr Espinosa, who has been silent until now, presents Mr Tuffnell with a sheaf of papers.

He riffles through them, bewildered. 'But how did you pay for this additional insurance?'

Mr Wharton's voice betrays a certain wry amusement. 'Since you ask, I borrowed from Mr Josiah Cheatley. We shall have to reimburse Cheatley, and pay his terms of interest, but the policy has paid out, so we have the capital. In fact, I've paid off Cheatley already, just this morning. I thought it wise to pre-empt any situation where Cheatley might seek to revise his terms, given his record in such matters.'

Through the chink between the door and the jamb I glimpse Mr Tuffnell's baffled face. 'Let me get this straight. You come to tell me that the ship on which my security depends has sunk with virtually no survivors. Then you tell me that thanks to your offices I am better off than I would have been if the ship was now in Guinea

265

bartering for slaves with iron bought at prices which rendered success at best unlikely?'

'That is the sum of it,' Mr Wharton admits. 'Aaron has a draft for you, signed and sealed by Mr Sampson. When you subtract the value of the ship and its cargo, the notional value of the slaves it would have carried, and the value of the sugar and tobacco you would have imported when the *Prudence* docked in Bristol, you have made a profit clear of eleven hundred pounds.'

A sound of racing footsteps, astonished laughter, and I peep in to see Mr Tuffnell seize Mr Wharton by the waist and spin him round and round in giddy delight. All three gentlemen are grinning, even Mr Espinosa, who surely feels some pity for poor Mr Sampson.

'Christ's blood, gentlemen, this calls for more than a thimbleful of sherry. Let me find Cook, and order us a celebratory dinner.'

Mr Tuffnell strides across the parlour, and I am just in time to whisk behind the door before he discovers me and subjects me to a grope and a fumble in his joy.

Chapter Thirty-Two

Thursday, May 1ˢᵗ 1704

After the flurry of Mr Wharton's announcement about the *Prudence*, life in Clifton returns to the dull quiet that followed the hangings. I am given extra duties, less to prepare me for my future role than because we are short of hands. For Cook and Nell Grey and me the days are a round of chores, preparing meals, tending fires and managing the household in the absence of a scullery maid. So when, this morning, Mr Tuffnell needs a letter taking to his foreman in Queen-square, I jump at the chance of a walk to Bristol. The day is bright and fresh, and I am glad to escape the house and take the air.

With instructions from Mrs Hucker to visit the butcher in Corne-street on my way home, I walk briskly down the hill to the Hot-well, past Jacob's-wells and over College-green, light of heart to be in the busy streets again and thinking over the day I first set foot in Bristol.

At Queen-square I deliver my letter to a foreman who stands ankle-deep in mud as he and Mr Wharton puzzle over a set of plans. I am told there will be no reply for me to wait on, and it being not yet noon I cannot resist a glimpse of the quays before my journey back to Clifton.

***

As usual, the noise of a dozen ships loading and unloading deafens me, what with the groaning of winches, cries of workmen, and the thunder of wheels on the cobbles as cart after cart arrives, delivers or collects its load, and rattles off towards the city. Wooden crates and hogsheads are stacked along each wharf, and seabirds perch on every ledge and roof, splitting the air with shrieks as they take flight. There are tobacco-chewing sailors, wiry turbaned lascars, ship's dogs of every mongrel breed, shipwrights wielding hammers and carriers smoking pipes, greasy-faced dockers and frowning clerks

and black-suited agents, and draymen in smocks, and sweating far-
riers. I see precious few women besides a fruit-seller in a striped
Welsh dress stationed with her basket on a wall below the bridge,
and a couple of fancy-dressed girls who loll, legs apart and winking,
outside the Sign of the Hope and Anchor. Holding my head high at
the catcalls from a pair of grimy-handed colliers, I pick my way to
Mr Tuffnell's warehouse, where I stop and gaze across the river towards the Bristol Channel.

Behind me lies the city, its church towers, spires and chimneys
rising through the brown smoke haze; ahead the mist is pierced by
masts and cranes. Nearby a skipper with a dinghy laden with water
casks sets off towards a Guineaman just visible through the fog, sails
furled as it waits in the harbour mouth for the east wind.

'Miss Amesbury, I hope you don't plan to act the part of stowa-
way?'

A slight, dark figure with a familiar dog-eared notebook tucked
under his arm appears from Mr Tuffnell's warehouse. When he
doffs his hat, his long black locks fall down, and I smile as he tucks
them back under his brim.

'Good day, Mr Espinosa. If you're wanting Mr Wharton he's at
Queen-square, speaking with the architect.'

'I've just come from Queen-square. Henry said he'd seen you.'

An awkward pause, while I consider the possibility Mr Espinosa
has come to the quays to look for me. 'I was sorry to learn of your
master's losses from the *Prudence*, Mr Espinosa. Please give Mr
Sampson my regards.'

The clerk smiles wryly. 'I suspected you'd find out the news one
way or another, Miss Amesbury. Where were you hid at our meeting
up in Clifton? Behind the panelling in Mr Tuffnell's study?'

I give him what Liz would call my pert face. 'I'm heartily sorry
Mr Sampson had to pay out such a sum. Is he ruined?'

Mr Espinosa laughs. It is an unusual sound with him, and I like
the way his face brightens and loses its usual watchfulness. 'Dismiss
your concerns, Miss Amesbury. Mr Sampson is only a small broker.
He sold the risk on before the *Prudence* left the English Channel.'

'Sold the risk on?'

'To a bigger insurance company that can ably afford to compensate Mr Tuffnell and his partners. Henry Wharton, for one, is a hundred pounds richer than if the ship had come home full of rum and sugar.'

I am at a loss for words.

'The Merchant Venturers and their friends can be depended upon to win out, one way or another,' Mr Espinosa observes. As if to prove him right a porter staggers past us carrying a sumptuous Turkish carpet, herded by a footman towards a sledge already laden with plump bales of silk.

'You must be bitter, Mr Espinosa. As the only one who hasn't come out of it with something.' I furrow my brow, for even I have my prize money.

'Mr Sampson is an honourable man and a generous employer. There was no slave rebellion on the Middle Passage such as Henry feared, because the ship never got that far, but Mr Sampson is thankful I alerted him to the possibility.' Mr Espinosa coughs modestly. 'He awarded me a small token of his gratitude. Not so small if I compare it with my regular salary. I hope presently to move to better lodgings. There is,' he hesitates, 'a good chance I shall be made partner before long.'

'Sampson and Espinosa. It has a ring to it.'

He cocks an eyebrow, blushing a little.

I turn from Mr Espinosa to gaze at the crowded river. 'I wonder which of these vessels will make their passage safely home. A ship is lost at sea, and all concerned have profited. The poor mariners on the *Prudence* paid the highest price.'

'True, but it is the way of things, Miss Amesbury. At least some three hundred Africans were spared the Middle Passage. Bristol sailors know what they're in for when they go to sea.'

'Unless they're simple country lads pressed by the likes of Mr Roach.' My eyes follow the plodding steps of a dray-horse as it hauls a sledge towards the back, and I think for a moment of my father, who worked with horses all his life and barely travelled beyond his parish.

'You miss your home and your family, Miss Amesbury.' Mr Espinosa never fails to surprise me with his understanding. 'Bristol must seem harsh to someone who spent her childhood in a Wiltshire village.'

'Not at all, Sir. Life is as hard and unjust in the country as it is in the city, let me assure you.'

'Of course.' Those dark and sympathetic eyes of his. 'I don't forget your infant brother, Mistress.'

His kindness softens me. 'Nor I your sister, Sir. Perhaps your bonus will pay for a trip to London in the spring, so you can visit Miss Hannah Espinosa.'

'I hope it shall. By the by, you may smile when you hear that among the underwriters forced to pay out to Mr Tuffnell was a certain planter from Spanish Town who owns shares in an insurance company here in Bristol.'

'Mr Osmund!'

'Indeed. So you see, Miss Amesbury, Bristol is not entirely inimical to justice, despite appearances.' He sees me grimace at the long words, and adds, 'Bluntly, some do indeed get what they deserve.'

'Yet why not all? Why do those with the most get most? And what of the murderer of those other lads, who got away scot-free?' I feel an urge to tell the clerk how Davy Roxall died, but dare not implicate my sister. In any case the rumble of a passing waggon makes further speech impossible, and Mr Espinosa, startled by a church clock ringing out the hour, lifts his hat. 'I'm sure Mr Sampson would understand if I took an hour to accompany you back to Clifton, Miss Amesbury. I don't like to leave you here alone.' He looks frowningly at a group of bricklayers, who roll from the alehouse and begin a raucous song for the benefit of the gaudy women waiting at the entry.

'I like to be alone, Sir. Thank you, but I will stay a little longer. The comings and goings down here interest me.' The wind is rising, and I turn back to the river, where the pilots in their twin tug-boats slowly spin the Guineaman round to face the Channel. A cry goes up as the boatswain weighs the anchor and the mariners high in the rigging let out the shrouds.

Mr Espinosa begins to protest, but I shake my head. 'I am a servant, Sir. I can watch, and listen, and think, and no one notices.' I can tell it crosses his mind to say that he notices me and always has, but after another moment he bows, and straightening his notebook beneath his arm, takes the footpath to the back, leaving me to watch the Guineaman as the wind fills the sails and it begins its journey out to sea.

Acknowledgments

My first thanks are to writer and artist S.E. Crowder, whose marvelous editing and all-round brilliance make a world of difference to my writing life.

The debt I owe to David and Lucy Armstrong is immeasurable.

Deep thanks are due to Clare Brant, who first led me into the eighteenth century, and whose love, encouragement and passion for words have been an inspiration ever since.

Thank you to the members of the Brereton Novel Group: Claire Connolly, Joanna Crowley, Jess Davies, Katie Pierce, Barbara Smith and Kate Taylor. Your dedication was awesome.

To the students who joined my writing class in Sandbach, Cheshire, thank you for ten years' commitment and creativity. Special thanks to Niki Dalton, Jo Davies, Barbara Jelf, Heather and Paul Savvides, and Val West. Thank you, Lisa Oliver and Liz Middleton, for talking shop, swapping work, and drinking tea.

The writers who welcomed me to their group when I moved to Essex were especially generous with their time in the autumn of 2017. Thank you, Bev Morris, Judi Sissons, Louise Taylor, and Sarah Wragg.

I owe a huge debt to the tutors on the courses I attended, in particular Stephen Booth, Joanna Courtney, Livi Michael, and my supervisor at the Centre for New Writing at the University of Manchester, Ian McGuire. Thanks to Roz Watkins and Sophie Draper for timely advice as I took my first steps into crime.

My friends have been indispensable on the path to publication. The love and support of Marg Bolton, Catherine Anderson, Heather Gage, Sheila Dillon, Joan Bartholomew, Di Sutton, Nicola Swinnerton, Ruth Price and especially Susan Watkins kept me going when publishing a novel seemed an unlikely dream. All writers need friends and readers like Diana Dunn, Jo Pryke and Pauline Rollins, who gave up their time to read my work and offer feedback.

Wendy Graham shared her expertise in publishing and sales, and I am most grateful to her.

To my fabulous editor Yvonne Barlow I owe everything. Thank you, Yvonne, and Claire Bell, my copy-editor, for your sharp eyes.

To Bill, Eleanor and Tom Armstrong-Mortlock, thank you for reminding me (frequently!) that people matter more than writing books.

Lastly, and most of all, I thank Andrew Mortlock.

Kat Armstrong grew up in Bristol, and became an English lecturer after writing a doctoral thesis on eighteenth-century fiction at the University of Oxford. She has an MA in Creative Writing from the University of Manchester, and has written articles for *The Guardian* as well as a scholarly study of Daniel Defoe.

Lightning Source UK Ltd.
Milton Keynes UK
UKHW011012161120
373487UK00002B/543

9 781916 410336